Runaway Heart

Also by Stephen J. Cannell
in Large Print:

Hollywood Tough

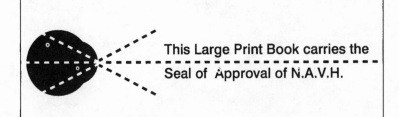

Runaway Heart

Stephen J. Cannell

WHEELER
PUBLISHING

Published in 2003 by arrangement with St. Martin's Press, LLC.

Wheeler Large Print Hardcover.

The text of this Large Print edition is unabridged.
Other aspects of the book may vary from the original edition.

Set in 16 pt. Plantin.

Printed in the United States on permanent paper.

Library of Congress Cataloging-in-Publication Data

Cannell, Stephen J.
    Runaway heart / Stephen J. Cannell.
        p. cm.
      ISBN 1-58724-515-9 (lg. print : hc : alk. paper)
      1. Fathers and daughters — Fiction.   2. Genetic
engineering — Fiction.   3. Ex-police officers — Fiction.
4. Soldiers — Fiction.   5. Large type books.   I. Title.
PS3553.A4995R865 2003b
    813'.54—dc22   2003058057

To Mike Post . . .
My Music Man, partner, and great friend.
You have enriched my life.

As the Founder/CEO of NAVH, the only national health agency solely devoted to those who, although not totally blind, have an eye disease which could lead to serious visual impairment, I am pleased to recognize Thorndike Press★ as one of the leading publishers in the large print field.

Founded in 1954 in San Francisco to prepare large print textbooks for partially seeing children, NAVH became the pioneer and standard setting agency in the preparation of large type.

Today, those publishers who meet our standards carry the prestigious "Seal of Approval" indicating high quality large print. We are delighted that Thorndike Press is one of the publishers whose titles meet these standards. We are also pleased to recognize the significant contribution Thorndike Press is making in this important and growing field.

Lorraine H. Marchi, L.H.D.
Founder/CEO
NAVH

★ Thorndike Press encompasses the following imprints: Thorndike, Wheeler, Walker and Large Print Press.

Acknowledgments

I would like to thank all my usual suspects: Grace Curcio, Kathy Ezso, and Christine Trepczyk for their tireless help in fielding the manuscript each day, Stan Green for his usual clever help on computers, and Dr. Roger Fouts for his insights on primate behavior. Dr. Wayne Grody explained the complex field of genetic engineering and Sandy Toye helped me on animal-rights law. Wayne Williams and Jo Swerling proved their worth as always, while my agents, Eric Simonoff and Mort Janklow, helped me chart the right course.

I am blessed with a wonderful group at St. Martin's Press: Sally Richardson, our publisher and guiding light, Charlie Spicer, my editor and workmate, Matt Baldacci, Joe Cleemann, Gregg Sullivan, and Mathew Shear all do a remarkable job to bring these books to you.

Finally, thanks to my three children: Tawnia, Chelsea, and Cody. You keep the smiles coming. And to my wonderful wife, Marcia; next year makes forty. I'd be lost without you.

Advances in genetic engineering, which one day could transform animals into subhuman slaves, are developing much faster than expected, and Congress must monitor the field. Our legal and ethical structures are unprepared for the question that will be forced upon us by human genetic engineering.

— ALBERT GORE, JR. (D-TENN.), 1982

The development of subhuman slaves by genetic transfer is a possibility and must be guarded against. There is no evidence that any government is now using the idea, but we must remember that Nazi Germany once experimented with eugenic theory against the Jews, slaves, and mentally retarded people.

— TESTIMONY BEFORE THE SUBCOMMITTEE ON INVESTIGATIONS AND OVERSIGHT OF THE HOUSE COMMITTEE ON SCIENCE AND TECHNOLOGY; FROM THE PRESIDENTIAL COMMISSION REPORT *SPLICING LIFE* (1982)

Chapter One

Herman Strockmire Jr., attorney at law, got his fourth severe ventricular arrhythmia at 7:45 Tuesday morning while riding up to his borrowed office on the thirtieth floor of the Century City high-rise. It was the day before he was scheduled to appear in federal court to argue his case to protect the monarch butterfly. He was in the plush-pile elevator, rocketing upwards at blast-off speeds, his ears popping every ten floors, his short, bulging body feeling as if it were pulling at least two Gs. His heart arrhythmias always started with the same curious sensation: first a mild loss of energy, followed by a sinking feeling as if a hundred extra pounds had just been strapped onto his five-foot-eight-inch, lunchbox-shaped frame. This heavy sluggishness was immediately accompanied by a sensation of light-headedness that quickly left him short of breath, dizzy, and slightly woozy. Fifty-five-year-old Herman didn't have to take his pulse to know that the old ticker had just gone into severe arterial flutter. He didn't have to, but he did anyway — force of habit.

He set his faded briefcase down, grabbed his fat, furry left wrist, and wrapped his stubby fingers around it, finding his pulse.

"Jesus," he muttered into the elevator Muzak. "It's doing a damn fandango." He didn't want to count beats; didn't have to, really. He knew from past episodes that it was up over 150, maybe as high as 185.

I don't need this now, he thought.

On the thirtieth floor the elevator doors hissed open revealing the art deco foyer of Lipman, Castle & Stein, Entertainment Law. They had thoughtfully placed a marbleized mirror on the opposing wall (actors love mirrors) and Herman Strockmire Jr. was forced to take a depressing personal inventory as he stepped off the elevator into his own sagging, bulging reflection. He looked like shit.

In the last ten years his Bavarian gene map had veered. The decade had turned him into a stocky carbon copy of his dead father.

Herman Strockmire Sr. had been a foundry worker — a metal press operator — banging out steel sheets in the humid heat of a Pittsburgh mill, each thudding, hammering stroke of the metal press pounding the poor, elder Herman shorter and lower, until the old German immigrant seemed like a fun-house distortion of a human being.

Now, as Herman Jr. studied himself in the law firm's marbleized mirror, he saw his dead father: short, Teutonic, absurd. The hand of gravity was reaching out with gnarled fingers and pulling him down toward the grave, while his runaway heart spun wildly out of control.

Herman's borrowed office at Lipman, Castle & Stein was an accommodation that his dear friend, Barbra Streisand, had arranged for him. These power brokers were her show business lawyers and they constantly reminded him of their huge respect for her star power. $tar was spelled with a dollar sign at Lipman, Castle & Stein. The partners, two Jerrys and a Marty, had acceded to Barbra's "request" and loaned him a small, one-window office that overlooked Century City and the Fox movie studios across the street. For some reason that defied natural selection, Herman had learned that most agents and entertainment lawyers were named Jerry or Marty, with a liberal sprinkling of Sids. Herman had spent the last two weeks in this slick retreat, doing pretrial deps and federal court writs.

Because the trial started tomorrow, Herman had driven in from Barbra and Jim's beach house early that morning, via Malibu Canyon Drive, just before sun-up.

Dear, sweet, politically conscious Barbra had not only prevailed upon her show biz attorneys to loan Herman the office while he was in L.A., but she had lent him the use of the oceanfront pool house at her Malibu estate while she and her husband James Brolin were on vacation in Corsica.

Herman and his thirty-year-old daughter, Susan, had been residing there, using the cars and eating the food, and had permission to do so until Herman's current federal case was adjudicated — which, he figured, would be in about two weeks — if he didn't die of a coronary first.

He shuffled down the hall to the men's room thinking it looked more like a sultan's harem than a shitter. Black marble floors, brown Doric columns, and decorator washbasins with arched dolphin faucets profiled under directional pin lights. The little, gilded, flippered critters spit water delicately into hammered artificial gold sinks. Herman hefted his briefcase full of writs, pretrial motions, and law books onto the marble counter and popped the latch. It wheezed open like a broken accordion. He rummaged around inside for his pill bottles and, finding the Warfarin first, shook two of the little capsules into his palm. They were blood thinners to prevent strokes during an arrhythmia. He dug out the bottle of Digoxin that was supposed to control his heart rate, then grabbed a paper cup from the built-in dispenser. He had never before been in a corporate men's room that supplied Dixie cups. Herman tossed the pills into his mouth and washed them down. That was when he got a second look at himself in the well-lit bathroom mirror. He was used up and tired. He'd seen raccoons with subtler eye markings.

But he had no choice; he had to go on. He was on a mission, maybe the most important of his life. An entire species of butterfly was about to be wiped out by biologically enhanced foods. It wasn't just any butterfly he was fighting for, but the heart-stoppingly-beautiful monarch, the majestic creature that had introduced Herman to the wonders of nature as a child. He had studied the beautiful orange-and-black-winged treasures for hours as a boy, lying on his stomach in the grass behind his parents' tiny row house, marveling at their delicate markings, seeing in them God's divine artistry.

The monarch butterfly, once the most common in North America, was now in danger of going onto the endangered species list. Unless Herman blocked the FDA, EPA, USDA, and all the other federal letter agencies that controlled bio-enhanced foods, these priceless treasures of nature might disappear forever, unintended victims of the new gene-spliced Frankenfoods. Specifically corn.

His federal lawsuit was for injunctive relief and damages on behalf of two organizations chartered to protect the monarch. It had been filed and fast-tracked to beat the spring planting season. If successful, it would stop this year's trans-genetic corn crop from going into the ground in May and would pay out damages to his two client organizations. However, the real reason for the suit was to force the government to reexamine the long-term, down-stream effects of bio-enhanced food.

Herman felt a surge of anger as he had these thoughts, and with it adrenaline coursed through his tired, sluggish body, doing god-knows-what to his already jackhammering heart. He fumed about his lawsuit and the arrogant disinterest of the government watchdog agencies and private labs he was suing. The biologically enhanced corn was engineered to kill off mites and pests that ate the cornstalks, but because of inadequate or sloppy testing, it was killing the monarch butterfly as well, and no one else seemed to give a damn.

Herman stood in front of the men's room mirror and glowered at his sagging jowls and shaggy, curly hair that always seemed un-kempt. It was then, he noted with mild con-sternation, that he had "mixed his numbers" again. Herman was colorblind and used a number scheme to stay in one color zone or another. He had the clothing taste of a mill worker, which, like his poor dead father, he'd once been. He never paid attention to trends, always bought cheap, and wore it until the stitches broke. After all, he reasoned, it was hard to dress for success when you were built like a steamer trunk.

His lovely daughter, Susan, light of his life, friend, colleague, and paralegal, carefully chose his court attire, sewing little numbers on the labels of matching outfits. Unfortunately, he had dressed in the dark this morning, not wanting to wake her. She'd been up all night, typing pretrial motions. He had decided this would be a number-3 day, but standing in the dark closet, squinting at the numbers, he had mixed some 8s in with the 3s. He now realized he had on his gray-and-black-checked jacket, a blue-and-green-striped shirt, and a bright yellow tie. He thought he must look like the host of a Saturday-morning cartoon show.

Herman turned away from the mirror, unable to stomach any further self-examination, grabbed his heavy briefcase, then lugged it down the hall to the borrowed office, turned on the lights, and sat behind his desk. Across the Avenue of the Stars the sound stages of Twentieth Century Fox movie studio were already teeming with activity. The productions started very early, almost at the crack of dawn. At 8 a.m. trucks, cars, and actors were already bustling between sound stages, well into their morning labors. Lipman, Castle & Stein took a more gentlemanly approach to the morning. He'd learned that agents and lawyers in show business started at around nine-thirty with a leisurely power breakfast, usually at the Polo Lounge in Beverly Hills, or Jerry's Deli in the Valley. Most of the hip Lipman crowd came sharking in at 10:30 or

11:00 toting their expensive wafer cases — young, lean, sculpted men and women with tanning-salon complexions and improbably perfect teeth. Herman was a rolling, lumbering walrus in this sleek, fast-moving school of piranhas.

He decided not to tell Susan about the tachycardia when she got in. She would just insist he go back to the hospital. The doctors at Cedars-Sinai had "converted" him once already last week, using medication. It had taken four hours on an IV bag.

His condition was called ventricular arrhythmia, which was more dangerous than the supraventricular kind. The first episode had hit him six months ago without warning. His second arrhythmia occurred four months later, and now this one made two in ten days. Not a good sign. The cardio docs at Cedars were urging that a "procedure" be performed. Procedure was their PR-friendly way of saying operation. But Herman couldn't take two weeks off now. He had just dragged three federal agencies and four private research labs kicking and screaming into court. This case finally had a hearing date set for tomorrow, and if he missed it he'd never get back in front of a judge before this year's planting season. Once the new crop of genetically engineered corn went into the ground, it guaranteed that millions more monarch butterflies would die. Herman was determined to prevent this from happening. He felt as if he was the only one left protecting one of God's great treasures. In the meantime he was popping more and more pills, which seemed to be doing him less and less good.

The morning dragged by like mud oozing downhill. It was eleven o'clock when Susan finally came through the door and dropped her briefcase on the chair opposite his desk. Every time he saw her he was overcome by her style and beauty. She had inherited all of her mother's physical perfection and mental activity but none of her shallowness. Okay, maybe that was harsh, but, damn it, that's the way he felt. His ex had a keen mind but no interest in using it.

Lillian was a wealthy country club brat who had rebelled against her waspish upbringing by choosing Herman Strockmire Jr. over a field of more acceptable, attractive suitors. He had always been puzzled by her choice, until he finally realized it was just her spoiled way of giving her domineering father the finger. *Take that, Daddy, you controlling, overbearing shitheel!*

Lillian had said she loved Herman's idealism, that she had never met anyone with thoughts as deep as his . . . thoughts about the environment, or civil rights, or governmental abuse. She once complained that all her country club friends ever worried about was their golf scores.

17

She fascinated him like a delicate crystal treasure. He used to marvel at her classic, fine-boned beauty as she flitted around in their small, rundown Boston apartment, fluffing pillows and promising to do the dishes that were piling up in the sink.

Her allowance, given to her by her father each month, was more than Strockmire Sr. took home from his mill job, and it helped Herman through the last year of Harvard Law School. So, although he resented taking the money, it allowed him to quit his side jobs and concentrate on his studies full time. He had kept his mouth shut to get his diploma.

However, Lillian soon found out that a steady diet of idealism and heavy thoughts, like her membership in the Vegan Society, was boring. Bottom line: Herman was pretty much of a drag. "You're no fun," she'd pout. "No fun and always brooding. Would it kill you to smile, for Chrissake?"

But Herman, fresh out of law school, was already overwhelmed with the injustices he saw all around him. Injustices that nobody else seemed to care about because there was no money to be made in fixing them. He passed on an offer from an old-line Philadelphia law firm in order to pursue his passion for important legal redress, filing a rash of lawsuits: *Miller v. USDA* — a drug-testing case; *Billingsley v. CIA* — domestic espionage; *Clark v. FBI* — Fourth Amendment search and seizure. More and more, Herman found he had powerful federal agencies on the other side of the "v." His IRS tax audits became annual and punitive.

He loved Lillian, but it was hard not to brood when he was constantly fighting city hall, overmatched, and behind the eight ball. Like most members of spirited-but-pampered species, Lillian soon flitted away from him, as beautiful and carefree as the monarch butterfly he now defended, leaving behind one lasting treasure — his daughter, Susan.

Lillian had bestowed her physical genes on Susan as surely as the old mill worker had cursed Herman Jr. with his. But Susan also had Herman's single-mindedness and sense of social outrage. Unlike her mother, she never became bored with Herman's struggle. She often seemed more dismayed at the injustices they fought against than he did.

Sometimes Herman Strockmire Jr. wondered how he and Lillian had made such a remarkable creature. Both of them were so flawed: Herman — plodding, overinvolved, and physically unremarkable; Lillian — beautiful, pampered, and quick-tempered. In Susan, they had filtered out their worst traits without losing any of their best. Talk about miracles.

"You heard from Roland yet?" Susan asked, carrying a stack of pretrial motions across the office. She set them on the side table, kicked off her shoes, then sat and put her nyloned feet up on his desk.

"Nope. Guess he's still up in San Francisco looking for the lab where those pricks are hiding their research. Once I get the right data bank I'll spring a discovery motion on them, and hopefully they won't have time to digitally erase the evidence before I get ahold of it. Roland will find it for me; he can't stand to lose."

Roland Minton was a twenty-two-year-old computer hacker with dyed purple hair who worked for Herman as an electronic detective. He was one of four full-time employees of Herman's law firm, The Institute for Planetary Justice. Okay — smile if you must, but that's what it was, damn it.

"Dad, are you okay? You look terrible." Susan leaned forward and studied him carefully.

Herman went for an airy grin and a casual wave of his meaty right hand, then turned toward the window to avoid closer scrutiny. "Just stressed, baby. Did you call to see which federal judge we got after Miller was reassigned?" They had received the notification just yesterday. The chief district court judge had reassigned the jurist on their case after jury selection and only two days before the injunction hearing. They were waiting to be notified of the new judge so they could look him up in the "Federal Reporter" and read about his past decisions. Herman was

20

also trying to steer Susan onto another subject to get her off his appearance, which he damn well knew was worrisome.

"You have the number for the federal district court?" she asked. "I'll call over there now. They said they'd have the name by ten o'clock."

Herman flipped through a legal pad, found the number of the federal building in L.A., and slid it across the desk toward her. She crossed to the guest phone and dialed.

"Hello, I'd like the clerk's office, please," she said as she searched for a pencil. "This is Herman Strockmire's office. We're seeking injunctive relief and damages on behalf of the *Food Policy Research Center and the Union of Concerned Scientists v. USDA, EPA, FDA, et al.* Case number CO3769M. We were notified that the Chief Judge made a last-minute change in the judicial roster, that Judge Miller is not going to be able to hear the case, and that a new judge is being assigned." She dug into her purse. "Yes . . . yes, I have a pencil. Go." She scowled and started to write, broke the lead, stopped, and tossed the pencil onto the table. "Thanks." She slammed down the receiver and muttered, "For nothing."

"What's wrong? Who is it?"

"You're not going to believe it. We got her again."

"Awww, no. Come on . . . I thought she

21

was taking a pregnancy leave."

"She is, but I guess she made time in her prenatal schedule to hammer us into the ground."

"Judge King? You sure?"

"How many Melissa Kings could there be on the Ninth Circuit Federal bench?"

"One is plenty," Herman said, realizing this reassignment was just one more anti-Strockmire missile from the federal government. With that realization came an additional weight that descended on his shoulders and chest, pulling him lower, squashing him, making him even more like his dead father.

"Dad, we can't go in front of her."

"We have no grounds to request that she recuse herself. What am I gonna say? She hates me and the way I practice law? That's not grounds for recusal."

"But Dad . . ."

"Honey, we'll just have to try this thing on its merits, okay? We'll note every one of her prejudicial rulings or statements, and if we have to go to Circuit Court and get her reversed, then that's where we'll go. But if I don't take this in now we'll miss the planting season next month."

Then the buzzer sounded. "Mr. Strockmire?" The voice of a Lipman, Castle & Stein secretary came over the intercom. They were ice queens who always managed to convey their extreme distaste at having a slob like Herman in their sleek environs. He wasn't show biz; he didn't have a personal trainer; he was soiling their palatial offices, like axle grease on their white decorator carpet. "Your clients have arrived." The words pronounced like a death sentence.

"Send them in," Susan said, checking her father to make sure he was presentable. It was the habit of a lifetime. She had started trying to fix his look way back when she was six or seven and realized that her beloved daddy often resembled a five-foot stack of laundry.

"Dad, why didn't you use the numbers?"

"It was dark. I thought I was getting all threes. I must have missed. I was trying not to wake you up."

She scurried around the desk and helped him out of the jacket, took a look, then shook her head and put it back on. "Jeez, you look like Pee Wee Herman on acid."

"That good?" He smiled ruefully.

The door opened and three glum people walked in. From their expressions Herman could tell that his day had not yet hit bottom.

Chapter Two

Jim Litke, M.D., Ph.D., and Valerie Taylor, M.S., Ph.D., were copresidents of the Union of Concerned Scientists. True to their organization, they looked concerned. Their brows were furrowed and pulled close together like caterpillars in a mating dance as they came through the door ahead of J. Thomas Stinson, managing director of the Food Policy Research Center. All three of them looked like they were about to bury their best friend. They found seats in Herman's small, one-window office.

Herman was feeling worse by the minute. His arrhythmia was escalating and he was becoming dizzy and light-headed, but he didn't want to reach into his briefcase for his pills for fear that he would appear weak. Nobody wanted to have a sick, weak lawyer. Clients wanted their lawyer to be a meat eater. A carnivore. A killer. So Herman tried to fix a killer look on his tired, sagging *ponim,* projecting confidence on the eve of trial. Herman of Bavaria, sword raised, ready to lead his troops into the Valley of Death and come out driving a Cadillac.

"Things are looking very good . . . surpris-

ingly good," he started to say. But a frog unexpectedly jumped up into his throat — so
he more or less gargled this fantasy at them.
He cleared his pipes and went on. "We
should have the information we need to file
our last discovery motions against the defense
first thing tomorrow. My senior investigator,
Roland Minton, is in San Francisco right
now getting that data. He tells me it's going
to prove devastating." A lie, but a necessary
one. Never let a client sense concern. Client
doubt is the wood rot of legal architecture.

"Oh . . ." Jim Litke of the Union of Concerned Scientists said. That one little word a
packed suitcase of concern.

"Yes?" Herman smelled trouble. A lawyer
had to know how to gauge his clients, how to
sense the winds of discontent. Herman
thought he had a gale blowing here. "You
look troubled," he said, stating the obvious.

"Yes," Valerie Taylor, M.S., Ph.D., intoned
gravely, glancing over at J. Thomas Stinson
of the Food Policy Research Center. It was
sort of a "Take it away, Tom," look. He was
the designated talker.

"Yes . . . yes," Thomas said. "*Troubled*
would pretty much capture it."

"How can I help?" Herman asked softly,
trying to sound like a friendly priest in a
confessional.

"You didn't tell us you were about to be
disbarred in California." Thomas was injecting

25

some attitude now — anger and frustration — mixing them into that ugly little declarative sentence.

"Lawyers with difficult cases often have review hearings before the Bar Association. To put it into a medical context, it's like a hospital review where a doctor is being asked to describe a complicated procedure. It's . . . it's . . . well, it's very common in the law."

"We also understand that several of your old clients are currently suing you for malpractice," Thomas continued. "There's even stuff about it on the Internet."

"Uh . . . frequently, when you get an unfavorable result in court, an emotional client will question tactics. Again, the jury, as we like to say, is out. The Bar Review hasn't ruled on any of this yet."

"Tell him about the other," Valerie Taylor said, prompting the tall, thin Stinson.

Herman thought that for a guy who ran a food research center, J. Tom wasn't getting enough to eat. But like a shadow across a picket fence, that unnecessary rumination flitted on his dizzy thoughts without much effect. Herman suddenly reached inside his briefcase and took out the Warafin and Digoxin. He shook several pills randomly into his palm, threw them down his throat and dry swallowed, trying to appear lusty as he did it — Thor tossing back a pint of ale. Then he rubbed his eyes to clear his blurred vision.

"Dad?" Susan was looking at him with concern.

"It's okay, baby," he said, and smiled at his clients with about the same degree of humor found in a coroner's report.

"We also understand that you have some controversial cases already filed against various agencies of the federal government — far-fetched, conspiracy-type lawsuits," J. Thomas Stinson cross-examined.

"The Institute for Planetary Justice seeks to expose government malfeasance wherever it exists," Herman countered. "It's our specialty. However, I certainly wouldn't call the cases far-fetched." Jesus, he was feeling horrible. Herman wanted to let his head fall into his big, meaty hands. Catcher's mitts, they'd been called by his tormenters in high school. The fact that he was recalling forty-year-old teenage insults during this meeting was in it-self mildly noteworthy. In high school Herman had been teased constantly and was the brunt of constant practical jokes. His locker had hosted more strange concoctions than a skid row garbage can. He could feel himself slipping into one of his old inferiority complexes. During times of stress he always ended up back in that mindset. Underneath it all he was still just "Herman the German," a slow, fat, unpopular kid.

"We understand," J. Thomas continued, "that you have sued the Department of the

27

Air Force over alien research supposedly taking place at Area Fifty-one in central Nevada."

"Yes . . . yes . . . that's the truth," Herman said. "We are in appellate review on that important piece of business. Why? Is there something about it that's troubling you?" Herman could feel his heart now. It was beating so fast it was tickling the walls of his throat. He was going back into arterial fibrillation. *Shit!* He wished he could just lie down on the leather sofa in the office.

Susan was watching him like a hen with one chick, her beautiful features arranged into an expression of alarm. "Dad," she said softly. "Dad, I think we need to . . ."

"I'm fine, Susie, just fine." He looked at his clients and tried to salvage his case. He could sense a dismissal coming, but he needed these clients in order to go into court tomorrow. He couldn't litigate a suit for damages without a client who had been irreparably damaged. He needed a plaintiff.

"Research on aliens?" J. Thomas said, pouring more than his fair share of disdain into those three words.

"Let me ask you a question . . ." Herman was having trouble focusing on J. Thomas Stinson because the room had just started spinning. The first signs of acid reflux were burning his esophagus, then acute nausea arrived like the last guest at a hanging. "Let me ask you how you would feel if, in fact, experiments on aliens *were* being done in the desert. Let's say, for instance, that in nineteen forty-five an alien spacecraft *did* crash in New Mexico. Let's say our government captured some dead alien life-forms and transported them to Area Fifty-one, where for over fifty years they have spent billions, maybe even a trillion dollars in taxpayer money, conducting illegal experiments — building a huge, electronically secure science pod around the crashed spaceship, freezing the dead life forms, studying them. And, while this is happening — while our tax dollars are being used for this ill-conceived experiment, Social Security is going broke, many Americans are without health care, and high school reading scores are going to hell. Money that should have been spent on these important social functions was and is, instead, being diverted to do research on dead extra-terrestrials! You're damn right, I'm suing them!" All of this came out without much thought or effort. Herman had made this speech a hundred times at university fundraisers. It was one of his prepackaged sound bites.

"Aliens?" This was the first word of the meeting James Litke, M.D., Ph.D., said, but he hissed it at Herman like a curse. "So you don't even deny any of this?"

"Not only do I not deny it, I'm proud to be trying to expose this colossally wasteful research. I'm attempting to divert the staggering

29

sums thrown away on that project into necessary and worthwhile social programs."

"Tell him about the other thing," Valerie
prodded again. "The Rockefeller thing, for
the love of God."

"We understand you've filed a RICO suit
against the Rockefeller family, charging them
with conspiracy in creating the Trilateral
Commission."

"I'm afraid my father doesn't want to be
grilled about his other cases," Susan said
jumping in, trying to fend them off, concerned that her father was in an arrhythmic
crisis, wanting to get these three assholes out
of the office so she could take his pulse and
find out.

"What is it you came here to tell me?"
Herman asked, his voice sagging like a sack
full of broken dreams.

"That you're fired. We no longer want you
to represent us. We intend to find another attorney," J. Thomas Stinson replied.

"You can't fire me, sonny," Herman said,
looking at the fifty-five-year-old man who was
approximately his same age but looked ten
years younger. "I came to *you*, remember? I
told you about the butterflies. *I* solicited *you*.
You didn't hire me, ergo, you can't fire me."
He couldn't help it now; he was so dizzy, he
had to put his elbows up on the desk and
grab his shaggy head in both hands. He felt
like he was about to vomit, and swallowed

twice to keep the bile down.

"You're going to lose the case. From what we found out yesterday, you're a less than brilliant lawyer, and that's being kind," J. Thomas said. "We all agree this is an important case, but if you lose it you'll have established an important legal precedent that will be difficult to overcome later."

"Precedent? There's no precedent here! Stick to science, Jimmy boy, *I'll* do the legal stuff," Herman growled, suddenly seeing his high school locker, remembering the hateful gray metal rectangle and the fear he felt each time he opened it. Remembering the turd somebody had once put inside.

"Then there's the whole problem of your standing in the legal community," Valerie was saying. "What if the California Bar decertifies you? If we're in the middle of this trial or on appeal, and you lose your license . . . what do we do then?" Valerie Taylor had snatched the ball, or maybe it was a planned hand off. Either way, she had the old pigskin wrapped up tight and was charging at him, knees high, going for extra yardage.

"To begin with, Dr. Taylor, my hearing is a year away, and I'm going to prevail. . . . It's a no-brainer. But even if I don't, some kind of writ of goddamnus on appeal would tie up the State Bar for two more years, and by then our butterfly case will be history." He held her gaze, then got up. "Excuse me for a

31

minute." He lumbered out of the office hoping he could make it to the men's room, but he had to detour at Marty Castle's secretary.

"Excuse me, could I borrow your wastebasket for a moment, please?" he asked.

She glanced up, wrinkled her Barbie-like features, and handed Herman the round plastic container.

Herman, still teetering from dizziness, promptly vomited into her wastebasket. "Thank you." With as much dignity as he could manage he set it down. "Got a bad Egg McMuffin, I think." He turned, and weaving dangerously, made his way back to his office. As he neared his closed door, he heard Susan inside, reading their ex-clients the riot act.

"You people don't know what you're throwing away," she said hotly. "Where else will you find an advocate who is so damned committed to his cases that he works most of them pro-bono, even spends his own money? The damages he's suing for were incurred by *him*, not you. If you can look at him and not see how great — how *beautiful* he is, then you don't deserve him!"

Herman heard chairs scraping inside.

"And one other thing," Susan said. "My father is right. This is not your case, it's ours. It's being filed by the Institute for Planetary Justice. It doesn't belong to you. It doesn't belong to any of us. It belongs to the people of the United States of America, and it is in the very capable hands of Herman Strockmire Jr."

The door opened and, while Herman slumped pitifully against the doorjamb, they filed out, not acknowledging him, their eyes down, sparking anger. Susan followed, but stopped in the threshold and looked at her father.

"Y'know, baby, I think maybe I do need to go to the hospital," Herman the German admitted sadly.

Chapter Three

Roland Minton parked his white, piece-of-shit rental Camry across from the shiny, blue-tiled, windowless buildings that looked like five huge blocks of ice scattered randomly across three or four acres of manicured lawn. The property was fenced and had more digitized security than the Midwestern Federal Reserve.

A monument sign out front announced:

GEN-A-TEC
A BIO-SCIENCE CORPORATION

Roland stuffed his new purple hair into his white phone company hard hat, glancing at himself in his rearview mirror as he tucked the last strands up under the hatband. God, he loved this new shade. It was Technicolor-tight. The gay hairdresser at the San Francisco beauty salon had mixed some awesome red-and-blue streaks in with the purple, and Roland thought the do rocked majorly. He pulled the bill down on the hard hat and grabbed his computer cracking kit out of the backseat: a tool belt with screwdrivers, pliers, wire cutters, lines, and alligator clips. He

34

checked his phony ID badge made with his new CD-ROM computer package. His picture, geeky and proud, grinned back at him; PACIFIC BELL was in block sans-serif letters underneath. Roland clipped it on, grabbed his computer packed in its expensive Cordura case, and again turned his attention to the shimmering, blue, fortress-like science lab. "Bet you assholes got a load'a pixel-dust security," he muttered, "but I is de Dustbuster."

Roland Minton looked up the street at the rest of the block. The science lab was in Sausalito, across the bay from San Francisco. From where he stood he could just barely see the top of the Golden Gate Bridge fading away into the late afternoon mist, the orange-red suspension cables arching like the top of an amusement park devil ride.

Gen-A-Tec was in a commercial neighborhood a mile from Sausalito's shopping district. Several small, low-roofed factories and warehouses lined the remainder of the street. Gen-A-Tec was the only secure layout on the block, but he knew from previous research that they had enough security to make up for everyone else. Roland could hardly wait to try his skill against the Gen-A-Tec systems administrator. The guy was probably money. Roland was ready to put his game in play. He loved going up against cream because he knew he was boss dawg. The ultimate big guy — master of the game.

He backed the rental car out of sight of the blue tile buildings, then got out dragging his cracking equipment with him. He buckled his utility belt around his bony hips and started up the street, looking for the telephone company junction box. Usually it was located somewhere around the middle of the block and pretty easy to spot. Halfway down the street he found it in the ivy: a four-foot high, one-foot deep, green metal rectangle that served the telephonic needs of the entire neighborhood. It was camouflaged behind a scraggly hedge near a warehouse park, under the shade of an old pepper tree.

Roland stepped carefully through the ivy and kneeled down next to it. "We be strollin' with Roland," he whispered as he opened the box. He wanted to do his hacking from a number that seemed like it originated inside the Gen-A-Tec building. To do that, he had decided to work from here because the junction box had the easiest terminal access. He had elected to do this hack in the late afternoon in broad daylight for two reasons: First, most electronic security shifts turned over at 5:30 p.m., and during the first half hour after the changing of the guard the new crowd would not be up to speed. They'd be getting coffee and checking attendance logs. Second, phone company techs normally work around junction boxes only during daylight hours. To attempt the crack at night would automatically arouse suspicion.

Roland studied the box and its myriad of terminals. Using his lineman's handset to connect to each phone jack, he phreaked the terminals breaking into them in sequence to find out which lines belonged to whom. After five minutes he had the Gen-A-Tec phones isolated. Their lines were in a block of numbers beginning with 555-6000 — the main switchboard line, and going to 555-6999. Roland unzipped the Cordura case, lovingly took out his laptop computer, and hooked it up to one of the science lab's phone lines.

Earlier that afternoon he had visited Gen-A-Tec's website and downloaded the company prospectus. He now pulled it out of his pocket and laid it on top of the junction box where it would be handy. He had memorized most of the important corporate officers, the cheese who would have unlimited access to the computer system and had written down their e-mail addresses — that were also thoughtfully supplied by the same prospectus.

Before driving out here, Roland had logged on to Gen-A-Tec's e-mail host and asked it what version it was. When the host answered he quickly logged off. Now, as he crouched behind the hedge, he began looking for several notorious security holes in that particular software version; holes that sometimes went unpatched by lazy dick-smack systems administrators. But he didn't really expect to find any, because Gen-A-Tec seemed so security-conscious. He was sure this systems boss had probably patched them all over, but he was wrong. Roland was surprised and delighted to find several unpatched holes in the software.

"Bust on, Super Daddy," he murmured to himself as he picked one, wondering at the stupidity of having full-boat security and leaving such easy access through systems defects. He accessed the Gen-A-Tec home page, but instead of signing on with them he went through one of the security holes. It let him slip past all of their warning alarms and access the company e-mail system. "Kickin' ass," Roland smiled as he crouched in the bushes and worked. But he was also slightly let down. This systems administrator was whack. Their security was a joke. He liked to ply his trade against the best, but this SA wasn't going to present him any challenge. Bummage.

Roland quickly went through his next few cracker steps. He needed to access his ISP — where he had already set up a phony account using a stolen credit card number. "Man, what don't I do for the Strockmeister?" He smiled as he thought of the overweight attorney. When he first met Herman he thought the dude was a complete drudge, but Herman had slowly won him over with his passion for causes and his fairness. Roland's mother, Madge, had found Strock while

Roland was fielding grounders in the federal joint, convicted of computer crimes. Strock took his case on appeal and got it overturned. In exchange Roland had volunteered his hacking services. The two became an unlikely pair, as different emotionally as they were physically, but they shared a blistering intelligence, and now there was very little that Roland wouldn't do for Strock. He thought Strock was the bomb — finer than frog hair.

Roland dialed into his ISP using one of the phone numbers from inside the Gen-A-Tec phone block, then logged on to his new phony Internet account. He had already composed a special e-mail message. The Gen-A-Tec e-mail host was only supposed to pass e-mails on to the recipient it was addressed to, but the hole Roland was using allowed him to add a few commands that the host would automatically execute. He sent an e-mail request to send a complete list of Gen-A-Tec's password files to the bogus account. All he had to do now was settle back and wait.

The late afternoon sun was hot on his skinny shoulders, but Roland didn't mind. He was thinking about pussy now, wondering how he was going to open some clam after work. He was thinking about cruising the bars, looking for cream, maybe making a trip out to Berkeley to flash his new sash out there, let his awesome purple headdress vacuum up the skank, throw those college girls a sausage party.

While he was pursuing those fantasies his computer beeped and he looked at the screen that flashed: YOU'VE GOT MAIL. He opened the e-mail and, sure as shit, there was the Gen-A-Tec password file. Among other things, it had pairs of user names and encrypted passwords for the 3,500 Gen-A-Tec employees:

Rhyde	OROTHu
Pzimmer	2Bfib7
Bnorton	SEoblp#w81
Flieter	COM725M
Jsasson	13Jen45
Klezso	1415ube

It went on for pages. Roland knew it was mathematically impossible for him to decipher these encryptions, but he also knew that most corporate executives were pretty sloppy about what passwords they used. Usually a wife's name or a child's was a good candidate. Roland picked a program out of his CD case. The one he chose first had the two hundred most common adult names already encrypted. He quickly ran that program against the list the e-mail host had just supplied him. Nothing. Then he picked out a second CD and did the same for the two hundred most common baby names.

Bingo! Two matches popped up. One was a

secretary and not worth working on. She wouldn't have top-shelf security. But the other match was JSASSON. He already knew from studying the corporate prospectus that this was probably the user name for Jack Sasson. Sasson's encrypted password was "2Bfib7," which matched the encryption in Roland's baby-name file for "Brandon."

"Go no further, my man," Roland told himself. Jack Sasson was major corporate cheese, Gen-A-Tec's chief financial officer.

Now Roland could go right through the front door, right past their bullshit security system directly into the company e-mail. He logged in with the user name JSASSON, then typed the password BRANDON. The e-mail host immediately displayed a Gen-A-Tec welcome screen. One of the choices listed was SYSTEMS PROMPT.

"Fuckin' A," Roland giggled. This system has more holes than a military rectal exam, he thought. Roland quickly clicked on SYSTEMS PROMPT and was immediately into their Local Area Network inside the Gen-A-Tec building. Roland was losing respect for this systems administrator at warp speed. The fool hadn't patched the known security holes in his software. He hadn't even guarded against frequently used passwords. The guy was a complete pant-load. Butt toast.

The Gen-A-Tec nighttime systems administrator's computer beeped a warning and Lincoln Fellows, a skinny, twenty-three-year-old African American, master geek and computer nerd, whose net handle was *Darkstar,* ambled over and pushed his ebony features down into the blue-lit screen.

"What have we got here, my man?" he said softly as a window popped up on his screen with the warning:

CRACKER IN THE SHADOWS. MONITOR?

Lincoln clicked on OK and the alert window went away.

Linc got one or two of these a day. Kids mostly, trying their skill against an organized security system, trying to see if they could break in. Everything here, the holes in the version software, the easy-to-crack password files, everything was put there intentionally by Lincoln Fellows. Just hard enough to seem real, just easy enough to let them in. Once the kiddy crackers thought they were in, they would bounce around inside his BS shadow system thinking they had found the real deal, but it was just an elaborate stage set designed and orchestrated by Lincoln Fellows, master of the game. The crackers would screw with worthless data, download dummy files, do their best to steal or change shit, and leave their mark on the system. But as soon as they logged off the shadow system went back to the way it was before they came in, waiting for the next moron to try. The cracker always left without ever getting past Lincoln's little funhouse to the real computer and data systems beyond. Brilliant. Unorthodox. Devastating. "I am de man. I rule." Lincoln smiled to himself as he watched the intruder move around in his shadow system.

Outside in the bushes Roland decided to try to find out how employees might be organized into work groups at Gen-A-Tec. He tried looking at the *letc/group* file and the systems administrator let him do it. Roland's contempt for this SA was becoming enormous. The guy was a beast, a Barney, an e-jerkoff.

Roland could see that Jack Sasson's systems access rights were pretty high. In fact, he was on all the key user groups, including the one called RESHCORN, that probably stood for Research Corn. "There we go, my man. We is strollin' with Roland . . . hittin' wid Minton." Roland grinned as he downloaded the entire corn file, but as it came in on his screen it seemed pretty damned ordinary. The kind of stuff you'd find in the newspaper: descriptions of bio-enhanced corn, stories about its new insect-repellent qualities and increased vitamin content — nothing that the Strockmeister could use in court. Roland shrugged. At least he got the goods as promised. Before logging off he downloaded a few of the company's "Mahogany Row" e-mail boxes for perusal later.

He disconnected his laptop, closed the phone junction box, packed up his equipment, then calmly walked back to his rental, got in, and pulled away.

"Adios, dickhead. You've just been kavorked," Roland said to the five giant blocks of blue tile as he drove off.

Lincoln Fellows watched as the cracker in the shadows logged off. The hacker had downloaded some newspaper articles and dummy e-mails. "Good crack, butt-munch," he said softly to the empty screen. "Come back any time."

Chapter four

"He's not converting as fast as I'd like," the solemn-faced Dr. Lance Shiller said, slapping nervously the metal clipboard in his right hand against his thigh. He was looking at Susan Strockmire and she, not her father, was the one causing his nervousness. The woman was exquisite. He was determined to impress her with some medical wire-walking, maybe take her downstairs for a cup of mud and a little case consultation, get her away from the manic frenzy of the Cardiac Care Unit at Cedars.

It was hard to get any romantic traction with code blues going off all over the place, while crash carts whizzed by and cardiovascular post-ops rolled through on bloodstained sheets.

"If you want, we could explore some options," Shiller said. "Tell you what, I'm off in twenty minutes and I haven't eaten since this morning." He looked at his gold watch. "Holy Moley, that's almost eight-and-a-half hours ago. No wonder I'm starved. How 'bout we jump downstairs now and get a bite. I think we need to discuss getting your father a more permanent result. The drug therapy doesn't seem to be doing it."

"Okay," she said nervously. "Okay . . . sure . . . whatever you think is best, Dr. Shiller."

"Right. Well, that's what I think is best . . . and I prefer Lance."

The windowless cafeteria was overlit and bustling with medical people of all shapes and specialties, as well as a few civilians from the four o'clock visitors crowd. Most were carrying trays or hunched over processed meals at institutional tables, looking uncomfortable in straight-back metal chairs. Susan and Lance were in one of the few leather booths along the wall. Susan only ordered coffee and Lance was poking at something called "The California Plate" that was just an avocado and chicken salad with honey-mustard dressing. He really wasn't hungry because, truth be told, he had eaten only an hour ago.

"What other kinds of things are you suggesting?" Susan asked, leaning forward, her beautiful, delicate features porcelain and perfect even under the harsh neon glare. But her pale blue eyes, the color of reef water, were clouded with concern.

God . . . I am falling in love, Lance thought, as he nibbled and considered. "To begin with, you have to understand how the heart works." He took a gold pen out of his hospital white coat, clicked it open, and started to draw on the paper place mat. "Your heart is shaped like this." He drew a rough oval and divided it into four quadrants. "The atria and the ventricles work together, alternately contracting and relaxing to pump blood. The neuro-electrical system of our body is the power source that makes this pumping action possible." He looked up and smiled. He thought he had a killer smile — and he did. Susan smiled back. "This electrical pulse is triggered in the sinus node, up here in your nasal passage." He drew a small circle somewhere above the heart then traced a line down to the oval as he talked. "The impulse travels a special pathway like this, down and through your heart, where it then triggers the heartbeat. In your father's case, something — age, maybe diet or alcohol, or even stress — has interfered with this delicate process, and when that happens the heart fails to respond to the impulse and goes out of rhythm. It can then start to beat erratically. It speeds up or goes way too slow, even sometimes threatening to shut down, and this is the general condition we call arrhythmia." He clicked his ballpoint closed for emphasis. "Lecture over." He returned the pen to his pocket and smiled again.

"Doctor, I don't mean to be rude, but I know all of this. He's had four arrhythmias now. I've had the condition explained to me three times. I'm not looking for a description of his problem. I'm looking for a cure. Would you mind if we get to the bottom line? I want facts. I want an actuarial prognosis. I want survival percentages." A legal mind used to finding solutions jumped out from behind that angelic mask and surprised him.

Okay, Lance thought. *Go for it. Give her what she wants.* "Your father has severe ventricular tachycardia fibrillation, which is one of the life-threatening arrhythmias. It requires urgent treatment or death can occur. Generally, we start with drug therapy and, often, as you know, this can correct the problem for long periods of time. In your father's case we have seen that option come and go. Failing that, we still have a range of other options available to us. One is electrical shock cardioversion. It's basically paddles and juice to the chest walls. The idea is to shock the heart back into a normal rhythm."

"Will that last, if you do it?"

"It might. It's a case-by-case situation. Sometimes, yes. Sometimes, no."

"What else?"

"We can install a pacemaker under the skin on the chest. It's a battery unit that monitors the heart rhythm, and when it senses an arrhythmia it gives the heart a little electric boost that gets it back in rhythm."

"How long does that take?"

"About two days. It's normally an outpatient procedure, but speaking quite bluntly, your father is in pretty bad physical shape. I would want him here for at least two days."

"He's got a trial that begins tomorrow morning. He'll never go for that."

"Convince him."

"Yeah, right," she said. "You don't know him. What else?"

"Surgery. We induce an arrhythmia, get his heart in fibrillation, and then, using cameras and probes, we go in through the groin, snake our way up a vein to the heart, and look for the offending spot — usually, it's a fatty growth of some kind. We probe for it, watching his heart rate on the monitors and on the TV. When we hit the problem spot his heart will stop fibrillating, and then we give that place a little zap of radio frequency and burn it off. In ninety-five percent of the patients it fixes the problem forever."

"What are the risks?" Susan asked, prompting Lance to lean back and lay down his fork.

"With yours truly on the drums, almost none. I've done forty or fifty of these radio frequency ablations — never one mishap."

"How long will he be in here?"

"One day of preop, a day of postop, and a week of bed rest."

"Too long," she said. "He won't go for it."

"Make him."

"Listen — you think I haven't tried? He's a warrior. He fights for causes he views as more important than himself. He won't do it, and he's in charge of his life, not me. If it's

49

going to take that long he's not going to sign a consent for surgery."

"Then we should try and convert him with the paddles. That's the next best option. If it works, he should be able to leave first thing in the morning. But he's nuts if he tries a case in his condition. He's very sick. The man needs rest. Christ, he must feel like hell."

She sat absolutely still, and for a moment Lance Shiller didn't think she was going to respond. Then she looked up at him and in her eyes he now saw something else. It was resolve. No, not quite resolve — it was more like fierce pride.

"He told me once that most of the important work being done in the world is being done by people who don't feel very well," she said.

"How much of it is being done by dead people?" Dr. Shiller said angrily. He saw her eyes go cold and knew instantly he had blown it with her, but, damn it, even though he wanted to connect with Susan Strockmire he was still a doctor, a brilliant chest-cutter, and a fine fucking surgeon. He hated it when his patients chose the wrong option.

Susan left Dr. Lance Shiller in the cafeteria still picking at his California plate. She wandered out onto the patio where the sun was just going down. She couldn't believe that L.A. was this hot in April. She thought of her apartment in Washington, D.C., and of her father's cramped little house where she grew up after her mother split, leaving them to take care of each other. Now that little bungalow located two blocks off the beltway housed Herman and the Institute for Planetary Justice.

It was still cold in D.C. at this time of year — blustery. L.A. had it all: beaches, mountains, deserts, and bright sunshine twelve months a year. And yet there seemed something prefab and superficial about it. A town designed for tourists. The fringe celebrity commerce of Tinseltown seemed absurd to her: maps to the stars' homes, a tour of famous actors' gravesites in a twenty-year-old black Cadillac hearse, plus the tacky Hollywood sign. In L.A. fame towered over accomplishment. That was a concept that didn't fit the heroic proportions of Herman Strockmire Jr., a man she fought daily to protect and whom she adored.

Susan had grown up watching her beloved father run headlong into legal and political brick walls, often badly damaging himself. "No, Daddy, don't!" she would yell, feeling helpless to stop him, even as an adult. Then she'd watch in awe as her battered father would pick himself up, shake it off, back up, and do it all over again. Always in pursuit of an idea, a principle, an underdog. He became her hero early in life and had never once disappointed her. She never saw him do one thing she couldn't respect.

Not that he didn't have his shortcomings. Hell, he wore them like plates of tarnished armor — and he had plenty. He didn't seem to know that sometimes discretion *was* the better part of valor. He couldn't distinguish between causes, taking on an important lawsuit against the Pentagon for illegally developing bio-weapons at Fort Detrick with the same fervor that he chased after the silly Area 51 alien thing. But, to Herman they were equally important, because to him it was always about morality, honor, and integrity.

Herman was the last defender of justice in a world that no longer cared, because life in America now seemed to be only about celebrity, money, and success. The core values her father stood for had been left in the vapor trail of a seesawing Dow Jones Average.

Sometimes she cried for her father as she watched him standing alone against huge corporate bullies and government tyrants, sick and bloodied, but unbowed. A squat little warrior with a runaway heart who wouldn't back down no matter what; not when he was protecting the weak, not when the cause was just. And yet somehow, despite all of his courage, she knew that to most people who bothered to look, he came off as old-fashioned, silly, and more than a little bit corny.

Susan sat on the stone bench in the courtyard and watched the windows of Cedars-Sinai Hospital turn orange with the reflected sunset. She couldn't let her father die. She couldn't let him risk his life, but she didn't know how to stop him. When he was committed there was no turning him back. She had tried everything in the past: tears, begging, prayers, but he would just hold her hand and smile sadly, because he wanted her, above all others, to understand. He wanted her to get it.

"Honey," he would say. "Some people are unlucky, and you know why?"

"Why, Daddy?" But she knew.

"Because they have second sight. Or maybe it's just that they have a better view. They can really see what's going on, while the rest of society is out buying a new, hip wardrobe. But if you've been given this gift of sight you must use it. It's bigger than any one life, certainly bigger than mine." That was what he would tell her. If she went up there now and pleaded with him to ask the court for a continuance so he could get the radio frequency ablation, he would just smile sadly — mildly disappointed that she didn't understand. Then he would tell her all over again.

Herman Strockmire Jr. is the last great knight, she thought proudly.

She turned and trudged to the elevator for the ride back up to the cardio unit, thinking that if she lost her father she would just as soon die herself.

Chapter five

Roland Minton had taken a room in the new Fairview Hotel, on the thirty-second floor, with a spectacular vista of the San Francisco Bay. He always stayed at the new Fairview, because he thought the place looked like a huge rectal thermometer jutting up into the San Francisco sky, round and silver-tipped, its lone, mirrored spire flipping off the whole town.

He was planning to hit the bricks later in search of some prime female tatta, but first he decided to pursue the downloads he had cracked from Gen-A-Tec. Trouble was, the more he studied the stuff, the lamer it looked to him. The bio-corn file seemed like it was just low-grade PR, not the kind of sophisticated technical material you'd put in a secure computer.

So what gives? he wondered. He had just clicked over to the e-mails and was fast-scanning the messages when something got his hackles up. He couldn't pin it down at first, but something was definitely skeevy here.

What was it? He slowed his scan and began to page the e-mails one sheet at a time.

Hold it! Stop!

The e-mail he was looking at was a communique from the head of personnel. He'd seen that e-mail before, somewhere else. He selected a different e-mail box and searched through it.

There it was again. The same request to submit credit forms for reevaluation.

What is going on here? Roland wondered. He tried a few more boxes, and each one of them had the same e-mail loaded in with a bunch of other worthless clutter. Come to think of it, none of these e-mails looked legit. There were no letters containing specific project names, and that same, damned e-mail from personnel was in half-dozen inboxes. *Okay,* he thought. *So maybe the company sent this same request to a bunch of employees.* Roland switched to the outbox files and started scanning.

There it was again!

The same e-mail requesting credit forms. *What is going on?* He could see how a group of employees could all have *received* the same e-mail, but how in the hell did ten or twelve people all *send out* the same e-mail, each message worded exactly the same?

What the fuck is this? Am I getting chewed here?

Was this whole system he'd accessed just an elaborate shadowbox of some kind? Had he been tricked? He sat back and scratched his purple hair, all thoughts of poontang gone. His credentials as "master of the game" had been severely called into question. Maybe the systems administrator at Gen-A-Tec wasn't such a Barney after all.

As Roland scanned through his stolen material he became more convinced that he'd been scammed. The lousy security, the holes in the version software, the easy password file — the whole thing was dogwash. Roland Minton, Cyber Hood of the Internet, had gone down in front of this scam like a broken deck chair.

The systems administrator was smart, but in the end he'd gotten lazy and started to fill up his dummy mailboxes with the same memos — and Roland caught him.

The shadowbox is a nice little piece of security, Roland thought. *But what are they protecting? Whatever it is, they sure don't want anybody outside the company A-list to see it.* Roland decided he would find a way in, even if it meant forgoing the belly ride in Berkeley.

As he continued to scan the e-mails, another line popped out at him:

We should put in a request for additional funding before darpa closes its budget in the fall.

Roland had heard of DARPA. It was a black-ops U.S. government defense agency that developed advanced weaponry. The ac-

56

ronym stood for Defense Advanced Research Projects Agency.

In composing his phony e-mails, Gen-A-Tec's SA had obviously cut up some real ones and scattered them around in the boxes as filler. This reference to DARPA was ominous and interesting. *Why does DARPA, a weapons research agency, fund genetically enhanced foods? Damn strange . . .*

Roland sat back, glared at his screen, and tried to devise another way to gain access to the mainframe of the Gen-A-Tec computer. He needed to get around the shadowbox that protected it. He sat on the edge of his bed and ran through his options for almost fifteen minutes.

In the end, he decided it would be best to go in the way someone at Gen-A-Tec would go in if they were working from home. *Would they go in via the Net?* He decided the security system looked way too slick for that. Gen-A-Tec would have layers and layers of safeguards to protect them from the millions of nosey Net users.

So, how then?

After a half hour of more brain-drain he decided to use the company's own phone lines again. Most big companies have lines with some sort of remote phone access, usually for the bigwigs who want to work at home.

Roland knew that, no matter how state-of-the-art a Local Area Network was, Murphy's

Law assures that if something can go wrong it will. Roland hooked up his laptop to the modem jack in his hotel room and brought up a piece of software called a Tone-Loc. It was also known as a War Dialer, or Demon Dialer.

Roland then told the Tone-Loc to dial every number, beginning at 555-6000, through 555-6999, and to log the results on his laptop. When his dialer called each of those lines, one of six things would happen: If it got a live person, the dialer would immediately hang up, it might also get a no-answer, a fax, an answering machine, voice mail, or a busy. Roland was looking for busy signals, and he particularly wanted one on a line that belonged to a high ranking officer at Gen-A-Tec — someone with A-level systems access.

He knew this process would take a few hours, but he had gone into killer mode. He viewed his defeat earlier that day as a personal challenge. Roland Minton was about to kick some cyber-ass.

Two hours later, he printed out the results of his demon dialer:

```
5556000........ANSWERING MACHINE      1734 HRS
5556001........DISCONNECT             1734 HRS
- - - - -
- - - - -
5556191 ........VOICE                 1840 HRS
5556198........VOICE MAIL             1842 HRS
```

```
5556195........BUSY                        1842 HRS
- - - - -
- - - - -
5556309........BUSY                        1915 HRS
5556419........V. 39 FAX                   1915 HRS
```

It went on like that for twenty pages. Now
Roland concentrated on the busy lines. He
noted who was talking, or if they were talking
at all. Often a busy meant somebody was
working from home on a computer. Roland
needed to phreak the phone system and eaves-
drop on each of these busy connections.

Feeding a specific sequence of paired tones
much like touch tones down the phone line,
Roland was able to get a behind-the-scenes
look at the local system. A little more
phreaking and his computer was acting as a
terminal to the phone company System-7
switch-operating software. In essence, he now
had the same access and capabilities as a 611
Repair Operator. Next, he brought up the
Gen-A-Tec numbers that were busy and sam-
pled them one at a time. Several were conversations, but then he got one with the
distinctive sound of a modem hiss, indicating
that the person was hooked to the mainframe
computer inside Gen-A-Tec from his home
computer. One by one, Roland went down
his list of busies, accessing each, checking
against his management list, looking for the
right password, searching for a Mahogany

Row guy with total access.

After an hour of sampling lines, Roland finally hit upon exactly what he was hoping for. It was his old bud, Jack Sasson. He was working on-line from home.

Roland set a monitor on Sasson's phone line to steal any data that crossed that port, then kicked Mr. Sasson off the system.

Roland smiled. He could imagine the CFO at home, cursing the computer system that had just fed him a line error and unceremoniously logged him off. Now Sasson would have to go through the complicated relog-on process with all the damned security checks just to get back in, and Roland Minton, master of the game, would vacuum up the entire security code.

Roland waited patiently in his hotel room for Sasson to log back in. Within seconds, the CFO was coming back on-line. Now, Roland's little sniffer captured all of Sasson's secure data, line by line. The access and security code would give Roland a red-carpet ride right past the shadow system, straight into the main data bank at Gen-A-Tec.

Once he had the code, Roland turned off his computer and looked at his watch. It was 7:40 in the evening. He picked up the hotel phone and requested a wakeup call for 2:30 a.m. He figured by then Mr. Sasson would long be off the system and Roland could jump on and take his place.

He lay back and laced his bony fingers behind his neck. He couldn't help but smile, because he knew he had assed-out the systems administrator, big time. The Robin Hood of cyberspace was back in charge, about to jack some serious shit.

Chapter Six

Susan watched through the window in the cardio unit as her father was placed on the bed next to the defib machine. The nurses removed his shirt and had him lie back on the table, then smeared gel on his furry chest. Herman looked up and saw her worried expression through the glass. He stuck his tongue out at her. She couldn't help herself — she laughed. Then she put her thumbs in her ears and wiggled her fingers back at him. She was scared out of her mind, but as she'd predicted when she suggested the more intrusive operations to him twenty minutes ago, he had just listened with a sad expression and shook his head no.

Now Dr. Lance Shiller and two nurses manned an electro-shock machine. They hooked Herman to a negative ground and placed a rubber plug between his teeth to prevent him from biting his tongue. Dr. Shiller picked up the defib paddles, put them against Herman's chest, and let him have it.

Susan jumped; she actually cried out when her father arched his back under the current. Then she leaned forward, trying desperately to read the faces of the people in the room.

Did it work? She couldn't tell.

They did it three more times and Susan thought she was going to faint. Tears of relief came to her eyes when Dr. Shiller turned and gave her the thumbs up. A few minutes later he left the room, joining her outside where she was still glued with her nose to the window.

"Okay. He's converted," Dr. Shiller said.

Susan nodded and smiled, but she couldn't speak. Her eyes were still on her father, who was being disconnected from the negative ground and getting the goop cleaned off his hairy chest.

"We'll keep him here overnight on an EKG monitor to make sure he's all settled down. Then you two can go roll the bones with his life, if that's still your plan. Go fight your damn lawsuit, Miss Strockmire, but this is, in my opinion, an extremely high-risk idea. So you keep your eye on him. Here's my pager number. If he goes into an arrhythmia I want to know immediately."

She took his card. "Thank you, Doctor," she said, finally looking away from her dad and fixing her reef-water blues on Dr. Shiller, seeing anger flash in his dark browns. "Don't be mad at him; he's only trying to do what he thinks is right."

"So am I," the young heart surgeon said.

Susan brought Herman a tuna sandwich on a

tray from the cafeteria. The cardio unit food was bland, vitamin-enhanced pabulum. While she went over the pretrial briefs and motions Herman revised his opening statement, eating and scribbling notes on a yellow legal pad. He had a nine o'clock appointment to prep the last of his three butterfly experts.

Dr. Deborah DeVere was a world-renowned entomologist Herman had flown in from the University of Texas. He was going to put her on the stand first, to explain the monarch butterfly's eating and migration pattern. He had another doctor and a university professor on retainer to describe the deadly effects of bio-corn on the monarch's genetic structure and reproduction. Dr. DeVere, whom he hadn't actually met but had briefed over the phone, was scheduled to arrive in about twenty minutes.

Herman continued scribbling on his yellow pad, scratching out phrases, reconstructing ideas and arguments, while Susan worked on her laptop retyping the new version and printing it out on her portable printer. She glanced at the heart monitor beeping ominously from his bedside table.

"Stop looking at that thing, it's not going to go off. It is in my control," Herman said, switching to his spooky *Outer Limits* voice: "We control the horizontal. We control the vertical."

She reached out and took the hand that was

still finger-clipped with several electrical feeds. She squeezed it carefully. "I still don't see why you won't just ask for a continuance."

"Honey," he said, "you know we don't have a choice here. You know we have to go now. This is really important. If I ask for a continuance with the federal docket so congested we'll never get back in front of a judge before the monarch migration."

"I know, Daddy. It's just . . ." She wanted to say how frustrated he made her sometimes, how her own heart was aching right along with his, and how desperately she needed him to be alive and there for her. "It's just — I don't want to lose you." He turned, pulled his half glasses off his nose, and looked at her.

"Understandable. Why would anybody want to lose something as beautiful as this?" he spread his hands out to include his fat, hairy body. "I'm just too big and sexy to lose."

"You know what I mean, dummy." She smiled at him.

"Honey, I'll make you a promise, okay?"

"Yeah, sure," she said, knowing what was coming because he'd made this "I'll take care of myself" promise a hundred times before, and it was always just to shut her up.

"I'll tell you what . . . if I start to feel even slightly wrong I'll get the continuance and I'll check back in here quick as a bunny."

"You mean, like you did this morning, when you had a pulse rate of a hundred and eighty while you were trying to hold onto our three wussy clients instead of getting your big, sexy ass over here?"

"Well, maybe this morning was bad judgment on my part . . . pretty foolish, okay? I'm admitting that. I'll cop to it, but from now on I'm gonna be a good patient, okay? Gonna win the Patient-of-the-Year Award."

"Okay." She squeezed his hand again and sighed. There was a light knock on the door, and a surprisingly attractive forty-eight-year-old woman with salt-and-pepper hair stuck her head in.

"Hi," she said. "I'm Doctor Deborah DeVere." Her anxious eyes immediately taking in all of the bedside equipment beeping and flashing like a NASA launch computer.

"Come in, Doctor. Pull up a chair. Can we get you a bypass, a heart transplant, or a manicure?" Herman said, smiling at her. She smiled back and Herman liked her on sight. Over the phone she had sounded knowledge-able and angry at the government's callous disregard for the monarch. Now, looking at her, he was sure she was his kind of witness: a doctor who worked hard to save threatened life-forms, did cutting-edge research science, and had a pretty fine ass on her to boot.

She strode into the room displaying runner's legs. Susan rose to shake her hand. "I'm Susan Strockmire, Herman's daughter. We spoke."

"I assumed," she smiled. "Nice to meet you." Dr. DeVere pulled up a chair and sat, but a frown crept across her handsome face, spreading like a dark shadow. "Are you really okay? This looks serious."

"I always do this before court," Herman grinned and put down his legal pad. "You'd be surprised how a little electro-cardioversion and an EKG can calm you before a trial."

"Seriously, Mr. Strockmire, are you okay to go into court?"

"I have my doctor's approval. Right, baby?" He looked over at Susan, who smiled and nodded, then turned her gaze back to the window so she wouldn't give away her true feelings.

They spent the next half hour prepping Dr. Deborah DeVere, although she was already up to speed on the issues. She was going to be a dynamite witness. She even suggested some good secondary questions to ask that would allow her to interject some overpowering scientific facts, including how genetically engineered bio-foods that produce their own pesticides not only affect the butterfly, but also damage the caterpillar before its metamorphosis.

At 10:30 the nurses cleared the hospital room and Dr. DeVere, who had become

Dedee, got up to leave. She shook Herman's hand and smiled at him.

"See you in court, Dedee," Herman said. "I'll be the one wearing the backless nightgown and the EKG clips."

"I can hardly wait for that one, Herm," she said with a wink, then left.

There could definitely be something going on here, Herman thought as he watched her go.

Susan gathered up her laptop and printer and started packing her stuff away. "Dad, what are you going to do about getting another client?" she asked. "You said, don't worry about it, but I can't help but worry. Judge King is going to demand we represent someone. In order to get a jury trial we had to add a suit for damages to the injunctive relief. We need a plaintiff who's been damaged."

"We're in luck. We've just been hired by the Danaus Plexippus Foundation," he said.

"And what on earth is the Danaus Plexippus Foundation?" She was smiling at him now. That was just like him to have something up his sleeve.

"It happens to be Latin for 'butterfly.' It's a DBA operating in Michigan, and they've gone all over the country spending money on saving the monarch. I had it on standby, just in case. By the way, you're the secretary-treasurer, and you are looking at the president and founding partner."

"A sham foundation?" she said, arching her brow at him.

"Honey, it's the best we've got. It's going to pass muster. We'll just amend the plaintiff list with this motion before court tomorrow." He ripped a page from his yellow pad and handed it to her. She scanned it. It was in his curlycue, hard-to-decipher script. Only Susan and Leona Mae Johnson, his secretary back in D.C., had ever successfully translated an entire page. She folded it and put it into her purse.

"Dad, if Judge King finds out . . ."

"How is Judge King gonna find out? Three people know about it. You, me, and Leona Mae, and unless you guys blow me in, we're cool."

She nodded, then turned off his bed lamp. "I love you, Daddy."

"I love you, too, sweetheart. I count on you more than you know."

Then she leaned down and kissed him, holding her father close to her, almost afraid to let go. His heart was beating with hers as she pressed against his chest, strangely in rhythm, his was electronically beeping from the bedside monitor while hers was frightened about the future.

She closed her eyes as she hugged him.

Beep . . . beep . . . beep. Thump . . . thump . . . thump.

His was the heart of a lion.

Chapter Seven

The phone rang, pulling Roland up with a start.

Where was he? His one-bedroom apartment in D.C.? His cot at the Institute for Planetary Justice? Then he landed back in time and place. He was in San Fran, asleep in the rectal monstrosity. It was the middle of the night and he was ready to do battle with the Gen-A-Tec cyber-shit who kavorked him that afternoon. He fumbled the phone off the hook. "Your wakeup call," the operator said.

"Bitchin'." Roland hung up, got out of bed, and went into the bathroom where he splashed cold water on his face, then returned to his computer and turned it on. He looked down at his weapon of choice while it booted up. With this little twenty-four-ounce spaceship he could fly anywhere in the universe, visit secure sites, soar above it all — a bird of prey searching for rabbits in the system.

Once his laptop was up he grabbed a Coke out of the minibar and went to work. He logged into the Gen-A-Tec mainframe using the stolen security codes that his line-sniffer had lifted from Jack Sasson's log-on. In seconds he was accepted and welcomed into the real Gen-A-Tec computer system.

"Eat my shorts," Roland said to his screen as he got in.

The rest was cake.

He found the real RESHCORN file and downloaded it, scanning as it copied to the zip disk. Everything Herman wanted was in there: the almost total lack of testing Gen-A-Tec had done; the callous disregard for collateral damage that the genetically enhanced corn might wreak with its self-generated pesticides. He pulled up the EPA and FDA reports. Those agencies had really done a piss-poor job of vetting this Frankenfood. The whole program had been fast-tracked by the Department of Agriculture, probably because of Gen-A-Tec's strong-arm lobbying tactics.

Roland downloaded the file on human testing, which consisted of not one single test, but just a bunch of scientific opinion. Then he went on a search to find out what the fuck DARPA had to do with this private-sector lab. He started back in e-mail and screened the executive boxes. Several e-mails cropped up with DARPA in them. He read them all and finally saw the same fragment of the message he had seen in the shadow system:

We should put in a request for additional funding before darpa

71

closes its budget in the fall.

Below the message were listed the Gen-A-Tec projects that DARPA was interested in. There were two.

One was [DNA ENHANCED GENE SPLICING]. *That could include the Frankenfood,* Roland thought, *the corn, soybeans, all the other stuff.* The second program was something called the [TEN-EYCK CHIMERA PROJECT].

This was the first mention of the Ten-Eyck Chimera Project he had seen in all of the browsing he had done in the Gen-A-Tec system, so he went all the way to the root directory and gerped for the text string on TEN-EYCK CHIMERA. This took him a while, but the search came back:

NO RESULTS

The only mention was in the e-mails he already had. He looked for the table of file systems and found it. There were two related files:

/dev/hda8/chimera
/dev/hda9/chimera

So there was a Chimera *file.* He had no idea what the hell it was, but Roland was getting jazzed. He was on the case. He issued a mount-a-command to load up every related file in the system. Then he asked for a complete list of file directories. What he got back looked like gibberish. "What the fuck is this?" he wondered aloud.

Inside the Gen-A-Tec building an alarm went off and Lincoln Fellows walked over to his computer and saw that a window had popped up, warning:

TEN-EYCK CHIMERA ACCESSED BY SASSON. MONITOR?

Linc was about to allow it when he decided, just to be safe, to check the sign-in logbook. It was after 2 a.m. and, although some Gen-A-Tec employees worked screwy hours, this seemed worth investigating. The Chimera file was restricted to A-list in-building use. For Sasson to legally access the file he would have to be in his office down the hall, and it was a little strange for the CFO to be working here at this hour.

Linc checked the logbook. Dr. Sasson had gone home at five and had not signed back into the building. Link resented it when corporate cheese thought they could just walk in at strange hours and ignore his security system. He was the one who would get reamed if there was a breach. So Lincoln Fellows left the control room and walked down the hall to the corporate offices on Mahogany Row.

Sasson's office was empty and dark.

The guy was downloading secure files from his home computer . . . a complete breach of security!

Link stormed back to his control room and snatched up the phone.

While Lincoln was waking up Jack Sasson, Roland was downloading the corn file. He went back to the systems directory to prowl around, and found another strange encryption: >@☐Ā•p&AE01. This one was shorter, so Roland thought he could break it with the encryption programs in his toolkit. He downloaded it for later.

Then, as the RESHCORN files completed downloading, Roland went back to the problem of penetrating the Ten-Eyck Chimera file.

"Yes?" Jack Sasson's voice was thick with sleep.

"Dr. Sasson," Lincoln said, trying to keep the anger out of his voice.

"Who is this? It's two in the goddamn morning."

"This is Lincoln Fellows, the night systems administrator at Gen-A-Tec. I need to advise you, Doctor, that you are in violation of our security mandates right now."

"What the fuck are you talking about?" More awake now, and really pissed.

"We, Doctor — you, that is, have clearance

to work from home, sir, but you cannot copy secure files off-site to your home computer."

"I'm not working. I'm sleeping. I've got to be on the damn six a.m. flight to L.A. today for that silly butterfly trial, so leave me alone, you idiot!"

"You're not at your computer right now?"

"No, dammit. Stop bothering me!" And Jack Sasson hung up.

In his hotel room Roland now had the Ten-Eyck Chimera file up on the screen. The entire fifty-two-page program was completely encrypted.

Roland knew that if the Gen-A-Tec systems administrator was on his toes he'd certainly be aware of the security breach by now and would be trying to run a back-finger search program to trace Roland to this computer site. He had to get out of the system pretty soon. He downloaded the fifty-two-page encrypted file, wondering what could be so important that the file would be in code inside an already secure system . . . secure that is, to anybody but Roland Minton.

Once the file was downloaded Roland logged off the Gen-A-Tec system. He knew he hadn't been back-fingered, because the alarm in his hard drive, set to detect such nastiness, hadn't gone off. He shut down his laptop and lay back again, lacing his fingers behind his head. "Chew me, dickhead," he said to his opposite number in the control room back at Gen-A-Tec. But he *had* developed some respect for the guy. Whoever it was, he was pretty good. He just wasn't the best. He wasn't the "master of the game."

Lincoln Fellows knew he had been breached and knew he was about to get toasted for it. He launched a back-finger program to try and trace the cracker, but, as he feared, the guy was already a ghost.

Lincoln knew he couldn't call Vincent Valdez at DARPA with a bag full of apologies. His only chance of saving his job was to come up with some counterintelligence to give to Mr. Valdez, some critical piece of the puzzle. He turned to the Gen-A-Tec exterior security cameras and accessed the video tape decks, starting with the late-afternoon shift change. He ran the four camera platforms high-speed, fast-forward, scanning all four screens. There were three cameras on each platform: one regular, one light-enhanced, one infrared. There were also two front gate camera positions. Lincoln figured that in order to phreak the system so effectively the cracker must have, at some time, been working from the telephone company junction box up the street. He watched as cars and trucks zipped past the gate in fast-forward. After twenty minutes he saw him — a figure moving past the front gate, a telephone repairman with a white hat and tool belt. Lincoln froze the tape with the man in midstride.

"Is that you, Clarence?" he said to the dark image of the man whom he had frozen, his left heel down, right toe pointed up.

In the shot the sun had just disappeared behind the hills, throwing the street into shadow. The picture was too dark to get a good look. He switched to the infrared camera. It didn't improve the shot much, so he went for the light-enhanced. Instantly, the shadowy shot lightened. Lincoln could now see what the guy looked like — rail-thin, with wisps of hair escaping from under the brim of the white hard hat. *A geek-a-thon.* Lincoln released the tape and fast-forwarded. He saw the guy driving away in a white Camry, hat off, purple hair blazing. Lincoln froze the shot with the car still in frame. He looked hard at the rear license plate, couldn't quite read it, but he figured this was all he was going to get. His security command sheet said any breach on DARPA projects had to be communicated first to the DARPA A.D. in Washington.

With a shaking hand he called the emergency number. It was 2:45 a.m. here, which meant 5:45 a.m. in Washington, D.C., but he had been told that Mr. Valdez always got in before sunup.

"Agency," a voice said after two rings.

"I need to speak with the assistant director. This is Lincoln Fellows," he said.

"Is this an emergency?" the secure operator replied. Linc could hear a beeping sound indicating that his call was being taped.

"I'm afraid so. Tell him it's the Night SA at Gen-A-Tec in San Francisco and that the secure computer has been breached. We have downloads."

While he waited for Valdez, Linc made a digital transfer of the cracker's image and drive-away, copying from the security tape to a backup, then loaded it on the sat-link to send to DARPA in D.C. He knew it was the first thing Mr. Valdez would ask for.

The assistant director came on the line. Linc had only met him once, a swarthy, dark-haired spook with black eyes and the cold disposition of a desert reptile.

"This is Valdez."

"Sir, our secure computer has been compromised. A cracker penetrated our shadow system and completed some downloads."

"What did he get?" Valdez's voice was calm. That was the thing about Mr. Valdez, he never seemed to be alarmed, as if he always had a tight rein on himself and the situation. It was his one overriding personality trait; that, and a reputation for utter ruthlessness.

"He got the program on engineered food. Corn mostly, some test results, some e-mail . . ." Lincoln's heart was beating

78

harder against his chest, "and the entire encryption for the Ten-Eyck Chimera project."

There was a long silence on the other end of the line.

"You're joking," was all Valdez said.

"I think I have him on a security camera," the trembling SA inserted quickly. "A shot of him and his car pulling past the gate. I'm going to sat-link it to you right now."

"While I'm dealing with that, I want you to look through the entire hack and see if he left any electronic clutter behind."

"I will, but I don't think so, sir. He was pretty damned sharp."

"Right. Of course he was. But I thought *you* were sharp. That's what you said when we hired you. Obviously, we were both wrong."

Before Linc could present his alibi, Valdez hung up.

Linc hurried across the room and hit the satellite SEND button. A secure channel on a scrambled frequency shot the digital image into space, where it bounced off a platform a mile up, then streaked down to the windowless DARPA headquarters inside the beltway in Washington, D.C. Elapsed time: fifteen seconds.

Vincent Valdez quickly scanned the tape when it arrived, then sent it down to Video Enhancement with instructions to digitally enhance the license plate.

Fifteen minutes later he had a hard copy

printout in his hand. It was a blowup of the back bumper on a white Camry, with California plate IGI 378.

"And?" Valdez said softly to his assistant, Paul Talbot, who had just handed him the photo.

"The car came from the concierge at the new Fairview Hotel in San Francisco," Talbot said. "It was rented to a guest there. A Mr. Roland Minton, Room 3015." Talbot survived in close proximity to Valdez because, like the male black widow spider, he had learned to interact with his poisonous mate by appearing innocuous, moving fast, and staying out of range. Talbot's bland personality masked a shrewd mind that was always scheming.

Vincent Valdez stared at the photo. He hated screwups. But, he reasoned, at least the ball was still in play. He looked at his watch. It was currently 3:07 a.m. in San Francisco.

"How fast can we put a response-retrieval team in play?" he asked Talbot.

"We can scramble a team from Ten-Eyck and have them ready in less than an hour."

"That puts 'em there before five a.m. Daylight Savings out there gives us an extra hour of dark. So do it." Victor leaned back. A second thought crossed his mind . . . dangerous, ironic, but maybe exactly right. They were ready for a field test on one of the D-units, so why not now? He spun

80

around and stopped Paul Talbot before he left the office. "Tell Captain Silver to send a DU along with the team."

"You sure you want to do that?" his assistant asked, turning and wrinkling his pale brow.

"Let's see if what we've been building is really worth all this trouble," Victor Valdez said, thinking that at least this would add some excitement to a monumental cluster-fuck. "Tell Silver to put a chip vest on the unit with full abort-destroy capabilities. I don't want to leave any DNA behind if it goes bad."

Talbot nodded and left the room.

Twenty minutes later, a helicopter was touching down in the desert north of Palm Springs. Its landing lights illuminated the sagebrush and sand that blew under the chopper, tattooing the side of an old weathered barn. The pilot was from a DOD scramble flight group in L.A., but he'd never been out in this part of the desert before. The area was restricted by a Code 61, which prohibited flyovers without special DOD clearance. When he landed, the chopper captain was puzzled because the place looked deserted — just barren miles of fenced, open desert. He watched as four men ran out of the old barn dressed in black government assault gear, flak-jacketed with body armor, and packing fully automatic MP-5s with thirty-round clips. Two of them were wheeling a metal cage. They slid the heavy box into the bay of the helicopter and piled in after it. The pilot looked back. There was Something alive in the box. For a second he saw unearthly fingers come out and grasp the metal bars, but then they disappeared inside the cage. *What the hell?* Then he heard heavy breathing and a very strange noise, unlike anything he'd ever heard before, high-pitched and angry. Suddenly, a dank, fetid odor clogged his nostrils.

"Shhh, Pan," one of the soldiers said.

"Let's go. Get it up," Ranger Captain Dave Silver ordered as he jumped into the helicopter.

The pilot pulled back the collective and the Bell Jet Ranger lifted off the desert floor, heading toward the landing pad on top of the Federal Building in San Francisco.

Roland was still hunched over his computer working off-line an hour after he had finished the download from Gen-A-Tec.

He was in the zone.

It happened like that sometimes — you just lost track of everything. He couldn't get Herman on the cell phone, and the overweight attorney wasn't at Streisand's house, so Roland finished composing an e-mail to Strockmire and sent it off to Herman's computer.

TO: strockmeister@earthlink.net
FROM: cyberhood@thirdwave.net
SUBJECT: no subject
CC:

DEAR STROCK . . .
I want a raise . . . I'm too fucking good
. . . I have again saved your dumpy
white ass & am expecting some big
bucks in return. No more of your empty
promises. Send $$$!!! (heh-heh-heh)

I am e-mailing some downloads I got
from the Gen-A-Tec computer. I was
magnificent, by the way. I wrecked the
SA they had on night duty out there.
Stole all this shit right out from under
his bony ass.

Enc. include the RESH file on corn, e-m,
& some skeevy looking encryptions that
were filed under DARPA (Defense Ad-
vanced Research Projects Agency).
DARPA is a secret gov't weapons re-
search org I've heard some evil shit
about . . . I think we found some boda-
cious bogosity. Why would gov't spooks
be investing in food research? What evil
lurks? Gen-A-Tec had this program coded
in a secure data bank so this is
DEFINITELY something they don't want
seen.

If you or Susie get a chance, run this out to Zimmy, my bud I told you about. He's a cryptology freak who plays with this kinda shit when no one's looking after-hours. He ties ten sun solar mega-workstations together & does complicated decoding problems for fun. He'll jump at this challenge, but keep it to yourself, Strock, 'cause if they catch him he'll get booted for misuse of computer time. Zimmy should be able to break this in a few nights of gut-tickling fun (heh-heh-heh).

PS: There was something else in the Gen-A-Tec computer that was encrypted — a short line that I'm doing myself. (I need my workout, too.) I'll let you know if it turns into anything juicy. In the meantime . . .

I remain the one and only. MASTER OF THE GAME

ATTACH

After he sent the e-mail, Roland went back to work decoding the short line of code he had found in the Gen-A-Tec database. Like his buddy Zimmy, Roland thought that breaking code was a wonderful mind game. He had been working for a half hour and already had three letters. He wrote them on a paper cocktail napkin on his bedside table, then looked down at the letters once again, wondering what they might stand for:

OCT

He was just starting the cracking sequence on the fourth.

OCT. October, maybe? But why would Gen-A-Tec go to all the trouble of decoding the name of a month? Probably because it wasn't a month. It was something else. Then his program beeped and he quickly had the next letter, O.

OCTO

October: the tenth month. Ten maybe? He wrote it down. October? Octogeneric? Octopod? Keep going, he thought. He was already over halfway through deciphering it and started running sequences on the next two symbols.

The windowless van had been parked outside the new Fairview Hotel for almost ten minutes when Ranger Captain Dave "Hi-Ho" Silver returned. He was dressed in a black business suit, and he immediately began stripping off his tie as soon as he got back inside the vehicle that was loaded with video and sound monitors.

"I think Valdez must be psychic," Captain Silver said. "They have security cameras on all the floors . . . in boxes. We could disable the one on his floor, or maybe throw the hotel video system into temporary phase jitter, but it's not gonna be covert and will take too much time, so I'm gonna put a DU down."

The entire response-retrieval team looked at the heavy metal cage on the floor of the van. They couldn't see the DU but they could smell it and hear it breathing.

"Pan," Captain Silver said. "It's time."

Chapter Eight

Pan is sitting in the box, his Geega thoughts coming slowly at first. Most times Pan uses only his strange language of the dark place. His memories of a shadowed past are verdant, humid, and atmospheric. Murderous urges are at times just below the surface, more powerful than even the Geega's commands. He has to fight to keep these urges under control, to do what the alpha Geega wants. The murderous impulse is natural to him, like tasting blood, or eating meat, or the savage instinct of the kill. Hunting and killing are deep inside Pan, although shadowed and obscured. The other things the Geegas want him to do are much harder. Geegas feed him and tell him things. They make him run, and kill, and work with their fire-sticks. Geegas are alpha and Pan knows he has to obey them. Sometimes he presents himself to the main Geega, turning around, raising his privates, offering himself to be fucked. But the alpha Geega never accepts Pan's presentation. Pan then lowers his head to the alpha Geega's feet, placing his soft pink lips in the sand, humbling himself. But the alpha Geega just says his strange speaking words that Pan has to struggle to understand. Then Pan turns back and sits, waiting to be told what he must do. *They are the leaders. He is nothing. He is alive only at their pleasure. On his arm is the machine to make the Geega talk. He looks down at it and finds the symbols on the keyboard. He punches in two syllables and waits. An electronic voice emits from his vest:*

"Pan go?" *It says with metallic Geega precision.*

"Thirty stories up," *the alpha Geega answers.*

Pan cocks his head and tries to listen, tries to do the Geega talk . . . so hard for him, but he can do it. Pan looks down at the thing on his arm with all the buttons and little symbols that he has practiced on for hours. It does the Geega talk for him, but he has to concentrate for a minute to decide how to make the right talk. Pan pushes several buttons and waits while the strange Geega voice comes out of the heavy vest that he wears, with its lightbox screen and cold metal straps.

"Thirty what?" *the mechanical voice on his vest asks, while Pan jumps up and down in pleasure. This is good talk. This is the right Geega talk.*

The alpha Geega, Dave, looks into the cage, opens the door and lets Pan out. He leads Pan to the front seat of the van. It is dark outside.

Night . . . the word coming to Pan in Geega talk, which sometimes happens now.

"Up there, Pan," *Dave points.* "Thirty floors up," *he says, pointing at a high place on the huge building across the street. Then Dave takes* out a picture of a strange-looking Geega and shows it to Pan.

"This is our enemy," Dave says.

Pan takes the picture in his gray-white fingers. The Geega enemy looks skinny and small. "I'll direct you from here," Dave says. "Pan, you must fetch the lightbox! You must kill this Geega!" Dave points to the headset around Pan's neck: "Dave will talk over the radio and get Pan to the right spot," he says. "It's on this corner." The alpha Geega points at a spot on the side of the building. Dave looks right at Pan. Pan immediately drops his head, turns around, and presents. It is forbidden to look into the alpha's eyes, so Pan offers his privates in a show of respect.

"Not now, Pan. Do you understand where to go?" Dave says as he opens the door of the van.

Pan pushes a button on his talk machine. The mechanical voice responds. "Yes."

Dave puts the leather gloves with the suction pads on Pan's four hands and buckles them on tight.

"I'll be watching from here, so keep the camera on," the alpha Geega instructs as he taps the little glass eye on the front of Pan's metal vest. "Now go. Fetch. Kill."

Pan is out of the vehicle, moving fast, his speed and strength on full display now. He reaches the glass building then starts up the side, going faster and faster. He climbs up the rounded glass, all four hands gripping the walls with the suction pads the Geegas designed for wall walking. Pan glimpses the inside of rooms as he scales the glass tower.

"Further right," Dave's voice is loud in Pan's ear. Pan has to stop to remember . . . right . . . right is the machine side, so he reaches over, secures his suctioned tentacle on the window, then walks sideways across the glass to the next set of windows on the tower. Again he hears the alpha Geega speaking through the earpiece:

"Okay, stop. That's far enough. Now, up, Pan, up." So Pan climbs higher, walking right up the side of the glass structure, pausing once to look down, hanging in that moment by only one extender . . . dangerous but secure. He looks down and sees the lights of the city. Again he has a shadow memory. He is somewhere else for that instant, lost in darkness, a lifetime away, his primal thoughts suddenly of warmth and sharing — shadows that sometimes hit him at moments like this. Suddenly, he wants to ride through space and time on the long, green, fertile arcs against dark shadows. He doesn't really know what any of this is, or why he cares, or where he came from; he just knows these are shadow feelings from some other lifetime, and they haunt him.

"Up, Pan, up." Dave, the alpha Geega commands, so Pan keeps climbing until, finally, Dave says, "Stop!"

Pan obeys. He looks in at the room where he is hanging. He sees nothing but Geega things and a light coming from a second room.

"*Go, Pan. Fetch the lightbox. Kill!*"

And now Pan finds the edge of the window. With his strong, bony, gloved fingers, he hooks his hands under the frame and pulls. Pan is powerful, with more strength than ten Geegas. He once pulled many Geegas across a field. Although he is smaller than a Geega, he has very special muscles.

He hears the metal window frame pop as he bends it open. Finally, using all his strength, the opening is wide enough for him to crawl through.

Pan slips his hairy body and its bulky vest of metal lights through the window and lands on his front extenders, walking that way for a moment before slowly bringing his other extenders down until he is on all fours. His pink nose sniffs for danger. His Geega-like ears listen for sound. He hears a clicking noise in the next room . . . someone working on a lightbox? Pan moves softly across the floor, no longer worried about understanding the Geega talk. Now he can just be Pan. He is born to be a warrior, a soldier, and a relentless predator. He is from far, far away, but the vicious urges are still in him, programmed there by millions of years of combat. He knows he is expendable, existing only to protect the group. A distant shadow of that instinct now controls his thoughts. Pan hurries to the second door and looks in. Sitting on a Geega sleeping mat, working at a lightbox, is the one in the picture. He is a very small, skinny Geega, with funny colored hair. Pan thinks he will be easy to destroy. Just then, the little Geega finishes working, picks the paper up and studies it. He glances over, and sees Pan standing in the doorway.

"Holy shit," the Geega says. Fear is in his eyes. Pan attacks! As he charges, the Geega does a stupid thing: Instead of running or trying to fight, he jams the paper into his mouth and swallows it.

Pan grabs the long strands of the Geega's colored hair. He yanks the Geega to him, holds him, then using all of his extenders, he pulls and rips.

The Geega screams in pain, but that only makes Pan stronger. He rips one Geega arm loose and waves it over his head triumphantly before he throws it across the room. He grabs the Geega's head and, using all four extenders, twists and pulls until it comes off with a horrible snap. He throws it hard against the wall. It bounces loudly and lands on the bed. Pan shreds the Geega's other arm and both legs, throwing oozing Geega parts everywhere. The gushing blood excites Pan.

He was taught by the Geegas to be silent, but he is so happy he cannot stop himself. He makes the victory yell. He jumps up and down on the shredded parts. He runs from one piece of Geega to another, licking up blood, tasting it, chewing Geega meat. Then he lifts up his privates and urinates on the dead Geega — a message to *others that this is Pan's kill.*

He hears a noise outside — a knocking on the door. Pan is frightened. He doesn't know what he is supposed to do.

"Get the lightbox," the alpha Geega commands in his earpiece. Dave can see what Pan is doing through the glass eye in his vest. "It's next to the bed. Go!"

Pan runs to the lightbox on the table, grabs it, runs to the other room, then leaps out the mangled open window. Catching the ledge with one hand, he swings effortlessly. The street looms thirty floors below, but Pan is not afraid. He loves height, loves danger. He slowly lowers himself down the side of the building. Pan can see the sun coming up on the horizon and reflecting in his eyes from the mirrored glass.

Moments later he is back in the van handing the lightbox to Dave.

"Good, Pan. I saw it all. We'll watch it on the tape later," Dave says as he points to the picture boxes that are set up in the van to tape what Pan is doing.

Pan tries to figure his answer. He wants to please alpha Dave. He looks down at his keyboard then pushes two symbols and waits.

"Pan win," the mechanical voice says.

Chapter Nine

The federal courthouse was tucked neatly between two old-fashioned turn-of-the-century buildings in downtown L.A.

Herman was dressed in his best pinstripe, decked out all in 4s: the black-and-white ensemble. He had brushed his unruly hair to one side, plastering it over with water. But as it dried the curls began rising like gray smoke, until, now, his do was in a sort of modified Bozo.

He sat in the attorney's room with Susan and Dr. Deborah DeVere. Dedee was nervous but ready. Herman thought she looked good in her tailored blue dress.

"You were supposed to be wearing the backless hospital gown," she said. "I've been looking forward to that all morning."

"Visual orgies of that nature have to be enjoyed episodically," he deadpanned.

She laughed, deep throated and lusty and Herman liked her laugh.

"Seriously, are you feeling better?" She pulled her smile down like a poster after a show, leaning in and studying him.

"Ready to kick butt." He looked at Susan, who was searching through their pretrial motions, putting them in order. "Susie, did you file the application for the amended complaint?"

She nodded, "The court clerk got it this morning. Judge King should have it by now."

"Good." Herman felt strong, his heart was in battle rhythm, his head clear. So why, he wondered, was Deborah DeVere looking at him with one eyebrow raised?

"An amended complaint?" she asked.

"It's nothing. We just made a change on the plaintiff's list. No big deal. Now, Dedee, it's important that we get across to the jury the devastation that this bio-corn is going to cause the monarch population. Everybody can remember their first butterfly hunt, looking at it up close, seeing its feelers waving gracefully in the air, its tiny little head and big, beautiful eyes . . . the orange-and-black perfection. Everyone can remember thinking how delicate and tiny it was. We've got to make them remember; we've got to make them wonder what the world will be like without this wonderful species sharing the planet with us."

There was a knock on the mahogany door and a young man from Elite Messenger Service entered carrying a glass terrarium with three beautiful monarchs fluttering inside. Herman had actually netted the butterflies in the field next to Barbra and Jim's house over the weekend. Herman and Susan had spent last night at the hospital, so Herman had sent the messenger to pick them up from the housekeeper in Malibu. He peeled off some bills and handed them to the man, then signed the delivery slip and waited in silence until the messenger left. Dedee looked closely at the terrarium while Herman tapped on the side. The butterflies landed and were now sitting on twigs, apparently unaware that their entire subgroup was facing biological extinction.

"Okay," Herman said. "Let's go barbecue some USDA Prime."

The courtroom was an ornate, old-fashioned job with Doric columns and spindled balconies. The U.S. and State of California flags flanked the bench against a curtained wall where the government seal was affixed. The room was large and overpowering; the building material mostly dark, polished mahogany.

Herman watched as the jury he had voir dired two days ago was led in. He thought it was a pretty good bunch. Herman never used jury specialists. The gaggle of defense attorneys opposite him had employed a virtual choir of experts during the three days of jury selection. Throughout that entire process they'd been huddled in a semicircle poring over demographic spreadsheets, graphs, and background checks. Herman used a much more primitive method. All he would do is look at each potential juror and try to decide whether he would like to go out to dinner with them. Would this person be fun to spend a few hours with? Herman looked only for a sense of warmth and humanity. Race, color, creed, sex, or financial condition meant nothing to him.

The jurors filed past and sat in their up-holstered swivel chairs. Herman stole a look at his opposing counsels — all ten of them. Some were government lawyers, others were hired by the three private research labs. The lead counsel was legendary Joseph Amato — the Count Dracula of the legal community. He was dressed in hit-man black and seemed oblivious to his cocounsels, who were eagerly gathered around the defense table like or-phans at a picnic, all of them scrunched to-gether, their legal books piled around them, briefcases open, miniature tape recorders ready for last-minute whispered reminders.

The Institute for Planetary Justice had only Herman and Susan . . . and, of course, the butterflies. The glass terrarium sat covered with a hospital towel, awaiting the appro-priate moment in his opening statement to be introduced to the jury.

"Oyez, oyez, oyez. Federal District Court Fifteen is now in session. The Honorable Judge Melissa King, presiding. All rise," the bailiff called out.

The courtroom rose in unison as the back door opened and Melissa King strode into court.

Jesus! The woman is ready to give birth any minute, Herman thought as she waddled through the door and around the mahogany platform, then labored up the three steps to the bench. Her narrow shoulders were thrown back for counterbalance. She had gained thirty pounds since she had thrown his last case out. A dishwater blond with a pinched expression and narrow eyes, she looked uncomfortable and angry in her last month of pregnancy. She eased herself into the big, high-backed judicial swivel, looked down at the court, opened a folder, and then while everybody waited began reading documents.

Aside from the jury and the attorneys, there was the usual array of courtroom groupies: old men and women who preferred daily legal jousts in air-conditioned comfort to the eighty-degree L.A. heat in the park across the street. They sat like a row of vultures in their baggy street clothes, cutting up apples with penknives and drinking tap water out of recycled Evian bottles.

"So, this is the butterfly thing . . . CO3769M," Judge King said, looking at her folder. "Is everyone present? Can we get moving?" No bullshit from Melissa this morning.

"Yes, Your Honor," Herman said. "The Institute for Planetary Justice is ready to try its case."

"Good morning, Herman. New suit?"

"Yes, Your Honor. I wanted to look nice for you."

She smiled down at him, but it was a grim, humorless little number that could peel the paint off a grain silo. Then she snapped her gaze over to the crowded defense table. "Are there enough of you over there, Mr. Amato?" she quipped.

Joseph Amato smiled and stood. "Your Honor, we represent the FDA, the EPA, the Department of Agriculture, the Pierpoint Laboratories, Gen-A-Tec, and Malorite Labs, et al. I've been selected as lead counsel. I think you've been supplied with a list of my cocounsels."

Judge King held it up. "I have my score card all ready, Counselor. Let's play ball."

Herman thought she was in fine form — smart-assing her way along. He had absolutely no traction with the woman.

She turned to him. "An amended complaint form was delivered to me this morning by messenger. What's the deal?"

"Yes, Your Honor, we have dismissed on behalf of two plaintiffs and substituted a new one."

"I see you removed the Concerned Scientists. Did they become 'concerned' with your legal tactics?"

"Your Honor . . . uh . . . is it really necessary to . . ."

"Yes, Herman? What?" A clear challenge.

Herman paused. *Shit.* It pissed him off that she had just insulted him in front of the jury, but he also didn't want to start the case in a mud fight with the judge.

"Nothing, Your Honor," he said softly.

"And this new plaintiff, the Danaus Plexippus Foundation. What is that?" She went on reading from the amended complaint before her.

"It is the foremost foundation researching the world migration and breeding habits of the monarch butterfly."

"The *foremost* foundation?" she said, milking it for laughs. "In the whole *world?*"

"Yes, Your Honor . . . the whole *wide* world." Herman smiled, trying to keep it light.

"In the whole wide world. Well, fancy that." She heaved a sigh, tired of him already. "Okay, I'm going to take that under submission pending demonstration by testimony that the Danaus Plexippus Foundation does, in fact, have fiscal damages as well as a history of protecting the monarch butterfly and the public's interest in it." Melissa King shifted uncomfortably, as did Herman, who didn't like the sound of that. "Let's get this show-stopper rolling," she continued. "What's in the box, Herman?"

"Uh, Your Honor, if I might get to that in due course."

"You have some butterflies in there?"

"Your Honor, I really appreciate your help, but perhaps you might let me put on my opening statement by myself?"

"Sure. Let's do it then. You're up."

Herman looked at Susan, who reached over and squeezed his hand.

He stood and straightened his tie, then moved around in front of the plaintiff's table. Herman looked at the jury while the street people swigged their Evian bottles and leaned forward in expectation.

"Ladies and gentlemen of the jury," Herman began. "I come before you today to tell you about an issue that may very well affect your lives.

"Most of you have seen butterflies; perhaps some of you, or all of you, even enjoy them. They are beautiful creatures. They decorate our lives, and enhance the God-given wonder of our planet." He let that sink in, pausing for dramatic effect, letting the moment hang there while he put a look of concern on his flushed face.

"Do you have anything else, or is that it?" Judge King interrupted, rudely stepping on his heartfelt moment.

"I have more, Your Honor," Herman said, getting pissed.

"Well, let's go then. Get to it."

Herman nodded, composed himself, and went on: "Perhaps you think about the beauty of the butterfly, or perhaps many of you might not think of butterflies at all. But in the next few days I am going to ask you to think about them. I'm going to ask you to pause in your busy day and look at them, study them. Think about the millions of years of evolution that it took to beautify them and bring them to this place in the history of our planet. I'm going to ask you to wonder about the awesome process of their metamorphosis, from lowly caterpillar to graceful winged beauty. I'll ask you to notice how effortlessly they take flight, how magnificently they flutter, soft as a feather, traveling with powerful determination to distant locations. As a matter of fact, did you know that a butterfly can travel thousands of miles over the span of their short lifetimes? Incredible, isn't it?"

Judge Melissa King now stifled a yawn and shifted uncomfortably in her swivel chair. The jury shifted their gaze toward her. She had broken his rhythm again.

Herman needed some drama to get them back. So he strode over and, like David Copperfield, snapped the towel off his case with a flourish, revealing the three beautiful monarchs, which were flying around inside the terrarium as if on cue. The eyes of the jury were riveted as Herman stood aside to

102

afford them a better view. "Behold the plaintiff," he said with a touch too much drama. "In this state alone monarch butterflies travel a distance of two thousand miles each year, down the coast of California to the middle of South America, where they build their homes and raise their families. Amazing isn't it? Amazing and inspiring."

Herman had planned another *Wild Kingdom* pause here to allow the jury to study the beautiful species of butterfly, but he didn't want Melissa King to jump in again, so he kept going.

"Amazing that their little brainstems know exactly where to go, guiding them year after year to the same breeding ground thousands of miles from where they came from. I'm asking you to keep this fact in mind the next time you see one of these breathtaking organisms.

"Over the course of the next few days I'll be inviting some brilliant doctors and professors from around the country to explain these butterflies to you. Dr. DeVere is going to explain their eating patterns and how they breed, reproduce, and migrate. Dr. Masuka is going to explain, and even demonstrate to you, why they are dying in such vast numbers. Professor Viotti is going to explain the evolution of these magnificent creatures — take you on a voyage of natural selection and show you the evolutionary steps, millions of years in the making, that created this unbelievable species of butterfly that is now being threatened with destruction by one generation of careless science.

"In the end you will know more about butterflies than you can imagine, but that is just part of what you will have discovered. Although these magnificent creatures are enchanting, their existence, and, yes, even their ultimate fate, is merely a symptom of a much greater problem. Ladies and gentlemen, I implore you to help me with this problem. The problem lies with a new, dangerous kind of science. *Biologically Enhanced Foods*." He pronounced the words like a death sentence. "In this case, a strain of corn that produces its own insecticide. In an attempt to quickly make this new, bio-enhanced Frankencorn and rush it, untested, into the market, the defendants have completely overlooked their responsibility to this three-million-year-old species, and in a larger sense, to us, as well."

"Objection, Your Honor. He's arguing the case. This is supposed to be an opening statement," Joseph Amato said from his seat.

Judge King smiled. "Objection sustained, Mr. Amato." Then she swiveled in her chair. "Herman, maybe you should control yourself."

"Yes, I'm afraid I'm very passionate about this. I'm sorry, Your Honor." Herman was once again dismayed. She had called his opponent *Mr.* Amato, and him Herman, like he was just some sort of courtroom joke. Worse still, he had let the defense break up his opening statement with an objection. Shitty tactics, and he knew better.

Herman went on. "Dr. Masuka is going to explain to you how this biologically enhanced corn is producing a chemical that gets into the corn pollen that blows with the wind. This pollen from the transgenetic corn, or TG corn, then lands in the milkweed that surrounds most cornfields. Milkweed, it turns out, is a staple of the monarch butterfly's diet, so the butterflies are eating this pollen and are dying off by the millions.

"Dr. Masuka will tell you about GMO crops — Genetically Modified Organisms. Right now, GMOs make up over half the U.S. soybean crop and over one third of the U.S. corn crop. Thousands of crops in the U.S. today are transgenetic crops, and that calls into question the safeguards that are being taken not only for butterflies, but also for human beings who ingest these same untested products. Are we safe, or will we follow the path of the tragically beautiful monarch butterfly?

"Over the course of this trial you will see that the defendants are blatantly disregarding these earth-sharing organisms. You will be asked to remember the cross-breeding of African honeybees, a well-intentioned experiment aimed at producing hives with more honey, but, instead, produced swarms of disastrous killer bees that have overtaken half the American continent. In their rush to try to improve upon God's work, science all too often makes tragic mistakes. We don't seem to be able to learn this lesson. So, while commercial science plays genetic roulette the rest of the life-forms on this planet suffer. Over the course of this trial you will discover that the defendants are failing to do an adequate job of testing these genetically enhanced crops prior to their worldwide distribution. How long will it be before other species suffer and die? How long before we find *ourselves* in the crosshairs of this new, careless science?

"Frightening, isn't it?" Herman paused for maximum effect. He had one eye on Judge King, watching her body language, hoping she wouldn't cut him off. She shifted, so he resumed immediately. "Because, like Agent Orange and Gulf War Disease, we have come to learn that the government agencies sworn to protect us are often more interested in protecting themselves — or the balance sheets of huge corporations and laboratories that contribute to politics and buy influence in Washington."

"Objection."

"Sustained."

"I'm done," Herman said. "Ladies and gentlemen, it is in your hands."

After a lot of shuffling, and whispering,

and passing of notes between attorneys at the defense table, Joseph Amato got to his feet and moved front and center.

"Ladies and gentlemen of the jury," he began. "I'm Joseph Amato, and I represent the government. So, in essence, I represent you. I'm here to explain to you about the great care and diligence that must take place before any new food product, no matter how insignificant, can enter your lives. The monarch butterfly is dying off at alarming rates and we do not contest this fact. But my clients are also not responsible for it. Oh, yes, I suspect a few butterflies have died from eating milkweed with TG corn pollen on it. This is far from the disaster the plaintiff makes it out to be. We will show that many more butterflies are being killed off by insecticide spraying than by GMO food, but the plaintiff will ignore that fact. The plaintiff will give you no figures about butterfly deaths from insecticide spraying, because, of course, that wouldn't help his case. However, I am here to keep him honest, so you will hear from me about the devastation insecticides cause to monarch butterflies.

"You will also learn about the horrible downstream effect this frivolous lawsuit will have on starving Third World children who, if the plaintiff prevails, will die at an even more alarming rate than the monarch butterfly. Poor children who now directly benefit from these enhanced foods. What does the plaintiff hope to accomplish with his legal action? Well, I'll tell you. He is attempting to shut down this entire new and exciting field of genetic food research.

"We will show that tomatoes can be designed to contain enhanced vitamin A. Think of it. Super vegetables can be grown and fed to children in Africa, or in the Sudan where babies die by the thousands from vitamin A deficiency. We'll show how, in the future, because of this science it will be possible to make soybeans and vegetables with larger mass and added nutrients and grow more produce per acre — and that product will be vitamin-enriched and healthier. One day this science may well save the people of our over-populated planet from starvation.

"You will learn that the impact of GMO foods on the monarch, is in fact very small, perhaps even infinitesimal, because this corn pollen that Mr. Strockmire is so concerned about is only produced for a very short time during the growing season — less than two weeks. It does not easily blow in the wind, and the monarchs' host plant, the milkweed, is vigorously controlled around cornfields.

"We will show you that most of the concerns about this new food technology are overblown and misunderstood; that this science is based on the laws of natural selection. We will show you how many plants over time have even developed their own natural resistance to pests. What is being done here, simply put, is to scientifically speed up this natural process of evolution. As the population of the planet grows exponentially and hunger becomes our major world problem, the labs and federal agencies Mr. Strockmire finds so dastardly are in fact attempting to beat the clock and feed the planet. However, you won't hear about any of this from the plaintiff.

"You will see that the men and women of science, who I will bring before you during this trial, are not monsters. They are not Frankensteins who are cooking up genetic nightmares. Instead, you will see that they are people not unlike yourselves who are concerned with the problems facing our society, concerned with world hunger. In fact, far from heartless monsters, you will see that they are the real heroes in this war against starvation.

"I beg you, don't listen to fanatics. Don't side with alarmists like Mr. Strockmire and his radical plaintiffs, but be messengers for the future. Be careful, and sure, and apply common sense to your judgment. The children of the world may live or starve by the outcome of your deliberations. Thank you."

Joseph Amato walked back and sat, elegant, assured, tugging at his French cuffs, diamond studs glittering.

Herman had left his jewelry case in Washington, so he had been forced to use paper brads from some scripts he'd found at Lipman, Castle & Stein to hold his frayed cuffs together. The little metal tacks glittered dully.

"Okay, first witness, Herman," Judge King ordered.

"The plaintiffs call Dr. Deborah DeVere."

The door opened and Deborah moved into the courtroom. She looked smart and confident as she took the stand and was sworn in.

"Dr. DeVere," Herman began. "Would you please cite your qualifications for testimony here today?"

"I graduated from UCLA with honors in undergraduate studies, then completed my master's at the School of Entomology at the University of Virginia. I graduated in the top ten percent of my class, then went on to take my doctorate there and, again, graduated in the top ten percent. I've won several awards in research from Tulane University, where I did some postdoctoral work on arachnid reproduction and earned several grants, among them a Fulbright and a Holenbeck. I am currently the head of the Entomology Department at the University of Texas."

"So, you would be considered an expert in the field of butterflies, with a wide-ranging knowledge of their breeding and feeding habits?"

"Objection. Calls for speculation."

"I'll withdraw it. On that basis, Dr. DeVere, would you consider yourself an expert on the feeding and reproduction habits of the monarch butterfly?"

"I've done extensive work on the disappearance of the monarch butterfly due to its ingestion of TG corn."

"Excuse me, Dr. DeVere," Judge King asked sweetly from the bench. "Since you are a leading expert in the plight of the monarch butterfly, I have one question."

"Of course. Go ahead, Your Honor," Herman demurred.

"Have you ever heard of the Danaus Plexippus Foundation?"

"I beg your pardon?" Dr. DeVere shot a worried look at Herman, who just barely managed to keep his growing panic under control.

Judge King said, "I've just been assured by counsel in a sworn affidavit this morning that the Danaus Plexippus Foundation, his new client, is a world-leading organization, devoted to the preservation of the monarch butterfly. As a renowned academic expert on the monarch, I was wondering if you'd ever heard of this world-famous foundation?"

"Uh . . . of the ahh . . . Danaus Plexippus Foundation?"

"That's the one," Melissa said from the bench, a smile now tickling the edge of her

111

mouth. "Counsel said that it's the 'foremost foundation.' I said, 'In the *world?*' And he said, 'In the whole *wide* world.' I figure a leading doctor on monarch butterfly feeding and reproduction would certainly know about the leading foundation chartered with the protection of same. How about it? Ever heard of these guys?"

"No, Your Honor."

"*No?*" Melissa shifted, her pregnancy signaling more discomfort, but a smile twitched happily at the corners of her mean, ruler-straight little mouth. "This is very strange. How could this be? The leading doctor on monarchs has never heard of the leading preservation society. Herman, are you as shocked as I am?"

Herman didn't answer, didn't know what to say. He'd been busted.

Judge King went on. "I'd hate to think that an attorney trying a case before me would stretch the truth — would *lie!* Please tell me that's not what's going on here, Herman?"

"Well, Your Honor, technically, what I said was . . ."

"Herman, I want a straight answer. *Who* and *what* is the Danaus Plexippus Foundation? And I don't need a snow job. Your motion to amend calls them a research group. Yes or no?"

"*Danaus plexippus* is Latin for 'butterfly,' Your Honor."

"*Literae scriptae manet* is Latin for 'never put b.s. in writing.'" She held up his motion as proof.

"Your Honor . . ."

"Yesssss, Herrrrmannn?" drawing it out dangerously.

Herman couldn't finish. His mind was a blank. Suddenly he felt another arrhythmia coming on — the same sluggishness and lightheadedness.

"Are you on the board of this thing, Herman? Is this a sham foundation?"

Herman stood before her, head down, face reddening, heart racing.

"I can go to the Corporations Commissioner in Michigan and get the filing with a list of its officers. Don't put me through that."

"Your Honor, I have the right, as a U.S. citizen with access to the federal court system, to file a suit on behalf of a corporation I happen to control," he protested.

"That's a fact. But you don't have the right to file a false affidavit in my court and lie to me about it. I'm holding you in contempt and I'm throwing this whole mess out. I won't hear a case where one of the principal attorneys before me is filing bogus paper. Furthermore, Herman, I think you and I have come to the end of the road. I can't tell you how angry your courtroom behavior makes me. I have been wracking my brain, trying to think of a way to demonstrate my displeasure to you."

"Your Honor . . ."

"Shut up!" she ordered, and now he feared the worst.

"I'm going to apply Rule Eleven of the U.S. Code of Civil Procedure." Rule Eleven gave a sitting judge the right to discipline lawyers for filing frivolous, groundless, or harassing lawsuits.

"Your Honor, this isn't a Rule Eleven situation. This lawsuit has legal merit. I would like to meet with you in chambers to discuss this," Herman said.

"I'm sure you would, but that isn't going to happen Herman, at least not today. So you'll get the point, the fine I'm going to attach to this incident is in the amount of one million dollars."

Herman heard a sharp intake of breath from Susan and even from a few of the defense attorneys seated behind him.

"What?" Now Herman's heart was beating so fast it was tickling the inside of his throat. He could feel his arteries expanding and contracting with each rapid heartbeat.

"A million dollars, Your Honor? I've never heard of a Rule Eleven penalty exceeding ten or twelve thousand dollars. You can't be . . ."

"You're damn right I'm serious!" she interrupted.

He glanced back at Susan, who had a

defeated look on her face. She found his eyes, but shook her head sadly. They didn't have anything *close* to a million dollars.

"I'm going to arrange for a meeting in my chambers tomorrow with an order to show cause why such a sanction should not be imposed. My clerk will get in touch to set the time. Do not be late, Mr. Strockmire." It was the first time she had used his surname. Then she cleared her throat and started to rise, but hesitated. "One more thing," she said, looking down at him like Moses from the mountaintop. "I've been made aware of your spat with the California Bar. I'm going to write them a letter detailing this incident, to be included in that file. Case dismissed. Witness is excused."

Melissa King banged her gavel, got up, and waddled off the platform. All eyes followed her as she made her way through the back door to her chambers, slamming it shut as she exited.

Herman was left in the center of the courtroom, his tired body sagging. He began to feel woozy. The opposing attorneys had stopped slapping each other on the back and were now packing up their briefcases. The old men and women in Vulture's Row shook their heads and muttered. They'd been cheated out of the full day's entertainment. "What a gyp," one of them said.

Herman felt Susan's hand on his arm.

"Come on, Dad," she said. "Let's go."

He moved with her, feeling shame and anger at himself. He picked up the glass box containing the three monarchs and carried it out of the courtroom. Susan and Dr. DeVere followed in his wake. They watched him from the steps of the courthouse as he took the glass terrarium across the street into the park and set the three monarchs free.

"What happened?" Dr. DeVere asked Susan.

"Dad took a chance and he lost."

"You mean we can't get this back into court?"

"Probably not. She was gonna kill us anyway, but Dad never sees that. Never thinks it will happen. All he sees is what he's trying to do."

Herman flushed the last orange and black monarch out of the terrarium. The three beautiful butterflies fluttered around his head for a moment as he watched, then two of them flew away. But the third one landed on Herman's shoulder. It posed there, delicate wings pulsing just inches from his nose, almost as if it were saying, "Thanks, anyway, we know you tried." Then it, too, flew away, leaving Herman standing by himself in the park.

A squat little man with a runaway heart.

Chapter Ten

Herman was back in the cardio unit hooked up to flashing, beeping monitors. He had once again been electronically converted, while Susan endured another stern lecture from Dr. Shiller, who scolded her that Herman could easily have a heart attack next time, or even a stroke, and that they couldn't continue to cheat the odds.

"I'll talk to him about it, I promise," she said, as Shiller was being called into an emergency. He walked off at a brisk gait to fix the heart of a more reasonable patient.

Susan went back into the C.C.U. and sat with her father. He seemed crushed by the events of the day, his chin down on his furry chest. The hospital gown, printed with strange little red balloon drawings, looked comical and inappropriate, but at least the balloons matched Herman's bloodshot eyes.

"Dad, you need to get the operation," she said creeping up on the subject carefully.

"And miss out on all this heart-unit fun?" he said, trying to elicit a smile but getting nothing from her.

"Dad, they say if you don't you're gonna die."

"At least that'll cheat Melissa King out of her damn million-dollar fine," he said.

"Daddy, I can't lose you." She put her head on his chest and hugged him. "You're all I've ever had. You're the person I most want to be like. I need you with me. I need you to teach me."

"Don't bullshit your daddy," he said, smiling down at the top of her head.

She looked up at him as he stroked her long blond hair, running his fat, sausage-like fingers through it.

"Daddy, promise me you'll get this operation."

"Okay," he said softly. "If the food in here was better, I probably wouldn't. But, I don't think I can eat another cardboard sandwich." She hugged him with gratitude. "But I can't do it till I get this thing squared away with Melissa on the fine." He added, "I gotta get that cut down somehow. She misapplied Rule Eleven. The suit wasn't groundless. I'll work something out with her tomorrow, but we'll probably have to sell some stuff in D.C. — the antique cabinets, or some computers, maybe my car. I'll probably have to set up another university speaking tour to get some cash. Once I make those arrangements I'll do the radio ablation thing."

"Thank you, God," she said softly.

"I admit there's a strong resemblance, but I'm just his mouthpiece," he teased her.

There was a knock at the door. The Korean floor nurse appeared with two men wearing Sears and Roebuck suits, brown shoes, and athletic socks. Everything about them screamed "Cop."

"Yes," Herman said.

"These gentlemen were asking to see you," the nurse said.

The men entered the room clawing at their back pockets like bubbas about to pay for the last round of beers, but coming out instead with faded brown badge carriers, flopping them open, flashing gold shields.

"I'm Sergeant Lester Cole and this is Detective Investigator Dusty Halverchek," the heavier and shorter of the two said. Sergeant Cole was about Herman Strockmire's height, but with a muscular, weightlifter's body and eyes so tired they seemed to hold disgust for everything they saw. Dusty Halverchek was younger. Blond, in a tan suit. He was average in all respects: height, weight, and coloring. Beige. Nondescript. Dusty.

"We're with the San Francisco PD."

Oh, shit, Herman thought. *Roland got himself busted.*

"I wouldn't normally bother you under these circumstances, but this can't wait," Sergeant Cole said, his eyes flickering across the beeping, flashing table full of monitors.

Halverchek was checking out Susan, staring at her, undressing her with his eyes as if he'd

119

never seen a pretty woman before.

"This is my daughter, Susan," Herman said, trying to interrupt Halverchek's ten-second fantasy.

The beige cop shook her hand eagerly. "We're with Homicide," trying to impress.

Herman's spirits plunged. Roland. *Homicide?*

"Did you have someone named Roland Minton working for you?" Cole pulled Roland's California driver's license out of his pocket and showed it to Herman. The d-l picture of Roland was thin, geeky, with punk hair.

"Yes," Herman nodded. "Please don't tell me he's dead." The sentence wheezed out of him, like air through a broken pipe.

"Dead barely covers what happened to him," Halverchek said with an easy, almost friendly calm. "He was ripped apart. Pieces of him spread all over his damn hotel room."

Susan put her hands up to her mouth and started sobbing.

"Jesus," Sergeant Cole said, looking at his young partner. "Why don't ya just lob a grenade at 'em?" He turned back to Herman. "I'm sorry. He's only been on this detail a month."

"How? You say he was . . ." Herman took a breath. "He was . . ."

"Mutilated." Cole finished the sentence. "We're still trying to get a handle on exactly

120

what happened. It's a little strange. We're not exactly sure how the room was accessed. There were video cameras on every hotel floor, but according to the hallway security tape nobody went in or out of his room at that time in the morning. There is no way down from the roof, no balconies — real whodunit."

"Roland is dead?" Herman tried to make it stick in his spinning brain, thinking this was easily the worst day of his life. He felt responsible. He had sent Roland up there.

"Sir, I'm sorry to have to do this while you're in here with heart problems, but in a homicide investigation time is everything and we have to move quickly. I need to know in what capacity Mr. Minton was working for you."

"He was an electronic forensic investigator," Herman said evasively. "Sometimes, when we're in a trial and aren't able to get data from a defendant that we've subpoenaed information from, I would employ Roland to help me locate it."

"You mean steal it, don't you? You hack it off someone's computer," Sergeant Cole said.

"No," Herman fudged. "He would access Web pages, read corporate reports, try and make an informed guess as to which computer or company might have the stuff we're looking for. Then I would file a new discovery motion and try to get my hands on the electronic data."

"And he had to go to San Francisco to do this? The Internet is everywhere."

Herman didn't answer. He just shrugged.

"Have it your way, but I wasn't born yesterday, Mr. Strockmire. My take is, he went up there to steal some corporate documents, then sent them down to you, so you could decide if they were worth going after — then you'd write your discovery motions. If that's what happened, I want whatever he sent you, and I want it *now*. It's evidence. It might contain a motive."

"I received nothing," Herman said. "And I resent the implication that I would cheat to win a case." A lie, but what choice did he have?

"And I resent the way this guy was murdered," Cole shot back. "Mr. Minton is in a morgue refrigerator in six separate rubber bags. I'm looking for evidence in a murder. Computer crime is way down on my list, so relax. Whoever did this is a vicious son of a bitch. We're still trying to figure out how the body was ripped apart like that."

"You're sure it was him? That it was Roland?" Herman asked. "If the body was . . . was mutilated, maybe his license was planted on someone else's body."

"We have his head," Halverchek said. "It's a match."

"I beg your pardon?"

"He was decapitated." Dusty Halverchek seemed to be enjoying this. It was as if they

122

were discussing ball scores. "His head was ripped off and thrown on the bed."

Susan turned and ran out of the room in tears.

"Shit, Dusty," Cole said.

Herman was wondering how he would get through the next few minutes. Miraculously, his heart stayed on rhythm, although the bedside monitor beeped ominously.

"What kind of information was he after?" Cole asked.

"He was looking for information regarding a case we had in court. We were suing three labs and a handful of federal agencies over careless testing of bio-enhanced corn."

"I see," Cole said, looking over at Halverchek, who shrugged. "And you say he sent you nothing?"

Herman nodded. "He hadn't contacted me in two or three days, which is unlike him. I was expecting to hear yesterday, because we started trial this morning. When he didn't call I got worried. I didn't know what could have happened to him."

"He died sometime around five this morning," Cole said. "You're absolutely sure he gave you nothing? Sent you nothing? No material — or anything that might suggest who could have killed him?"

"How many times do I have to tell you? We were expecting him to call. He didn't. I was getting worried."

"I see." Cole looked at Halverchek again and they had some kind of silent cop moment. Then Cole turned back to Herman. "Anything else you can think of that might be important?"

"He has a mother. Have you notified her?" Herman asked.

"Not yet. We didn't have any next of kin. If you have her number, we'll do it."

"I'd like to be the one to call her. He was her only child."

"Sorry," Cole said. "We have to do the notification of death, *then* you can contact her. Where does she live?"

"Washington, D.C."

"You can call her sometime tomorrow after lunch."

Herman wrote the number down and handed it to Sergeant Cole.

"We'll need a list of names of the corporations and agencies you were suing."

"It's in my briefcase . . . on the top. They're listed on a motion I filed yesterday. It's a copy, so you can have it."

Halverchek opened the briefcase, found the motion, and held it up for Herman to see. He nodded. Then the nondescript cop folded it and put it in his side pocket.

"Okay, then you have no further knowledge of who or what might have killed him?" Cole asked.

"Did you say *what* might have killed him?"

Herman furrowed his brow.

"The body was ripped apart. Shredded," Cole said. "There was no surgical intervention. He wasn't cut apart, is what I'm trying to say. We know of nothing that would have enough strength to disjoint a man physically like that . . . pull him limb from limb. Our ME is telling us it would take more than a thousand pounds per square inch to accomplish that. Also, the window frame was bent open. We can't imagine the killer got in that way, because there was no balcony to stand on, but the window *was* pried. No human would be strong enough to do it. There was urine mixed in with all the blood. It doesn't match the urine left in the deceased's bladder, so whoever or whatever did this urinated on the body parts."

Herman's mind was wrestling with what Sergeant Cole had just said.

"Okay, Mr. Strockmire. I'm going to end this now because your doctor says it's a terrible time for this interview, and he wanted us to keep it short. But I'm going to have to ask some follow-up questions later. I may require you to come up to San Francisco. Would that be possible?"

"Yes."

"Here are my numbers," Sergeant Cole said, handing him an embossed card that was a lot nicer than the flat, cheap Institute for Planetary Justice cards that Herman gave to his clients.

After Sergeant Cole and Detective Halverchek left Herman lay quietly in the hospital bed listening as his heart beeped hypnotically from the bedside monitor. He was horrified about Roland, feeling responsible and full of remorse. But his mind kept coming back to Sergeant Cole's statement:

We know of nothing that could have enough strength to disjoint a man physically.

With all that he knew about the abuses of the federal government, Herman had a few ideas of his own. But he dared not even contemplate their ramifications.

Chapter Eleven

At 9:45 the next morning Herman was still in the hospital. He had changed into his regular clothes, waiting to be released, and was sitting on the side of the bed talking to Roland's mother on the phone.

"I'm so sorry, Madge." His voice cracked. Tears stung his eyes. "I feel like . . . I don't know. I feel like . . . like I sent him to his death."

There was a long silence on the phone while Roland's devastated mother evaluated that admission. "No," she finally said. "It wasn't you."

But he knew it was. He would never forgive himself. He had really come to like Roland. More than like, even — Roland had been a treasured friend.

He remembered his first meeting with the geeky hacker. They'd been in the attorney's room at the D.C. federal lockup. Roland Minton had been convicted of federal computer crimes. He'd penetrated the White House Budget Office mainframe for some harebrained reason that was never fully explained. *God only knew what he had been up to.* What the feds were doing with the national budget was bad enough without having Roland in their damn computer, screwing around with the data. Herman had agreed to represent the skinny little hacker whose mother was a motel maid.

Herman wondered why Roland didn't get a job, didn't do something to help Madge and his two sisters, instead of doing show-off criminal hacks — but that was beside the point. Herman had been hired to get Roland's conviction overturned on appeal. If he didn't get it reversed, this skinny, vulnerable kid was going to end up at Raiford, and Herman didn't wish that on some computer geek with purple hair.

That was four years ago. Herman had found a loophole in the search and seizure of Roland's computer, which the original trial judge had wrongfully admitted as evidence. Then Herman did a standard "fruit of the poisonous tree" defense, which dictated that all evidence or testimony resulting from an illegal search and seizure was inadmissible. After that, the government's case came apart like antique stitching and Herman had Roland back on the streets.

During the appeal he discovered the skinny hacker was much more intriguing than he would have guessed. Roland had a sly sense of humor and a world-class IQ. As a high school student Roland also had no friends, so he and Herman compared locker stories. Roland was so smart that he became bored easily and withdrew into his computer world. His criminal hacks began a year later. He and Herman began matching wits. Herman usually won on theory and abstract thought, Roland on anal logic and X-over-Y deductive reasoning.

Herman often tried out his legal arguments on Roland and found, to his surprise, that the young hacker could almost always find embellishments and improvements. His mind was so logically bulletproof that Herman was often put to shame.

They soon learned that they shared the same latent anger and sense of disenfranchisement. They began to bond with each other for support . . . or for protection? Or both?

Now his friend was gone.

He could hear Madge sniffling on the other end of the phone, in her little walk-up apartment in Washington, D.C. He could picture her chapped, dishwater hands, her soft-but-wrinkled complexion, her tired gray eyes.

"Madge, I'm going to find out who killed him," Herman promised, not using the pronoun *what*, as Sergeant Cole had. Not wanting to add the specter of some savage, unearthly beast ripping and shredding her only son.

"Herman, it's not your fault," she repeated, sniffling. But Herman shook his head, vigorously denying that, even though she couldn't see him.

"He was killed trying to get information that I asked him to get. How can it *not* be my fault?"

"The police said I couldn't have his body yet . . . that they . . . they . . ."

"I know," he said, interrupting, trying not to put her through that sentence. "Madge, I'll get his body back for you. It'll be the first thing I do, okay?"

"Would you?" she said softly. "Please — it would mean a lot. I feel . . . it's like . . . it's not finished until he's home with me."

"I promise. They can't hold it for long. Once the medical examiner is through I'll make them release it. I'll go up there myself if I have to."

"Thank you, Herm."

They were both silent, listening to each other's sad breathing on the phone. Madge finally spoke: "You know, he loved you, Herman. It was strange, the effect you had on him. He told me once that you were the most special person he had ever known. I guess that even included me."

"No, Madge, not you. You were his mother. I was . . . I was just somebody he could try stuff out on. I was like his intellectual godfather, or something."

"I've got to go now," she said. He could tell by her voice that she didn't want to talk about this anymore.

"I'll be in touch," he promised and, after

the good-byes, hung up the phone.

It was almost 10:00 a.m. and he was still waiting for his release form to be signed, when Susan came through the door with Dr. Shiller.

"I'd like to just move you upstairs right now and get you prepped for tomorrow," Dr. Shiller said.

"I know. I . . . it's just. It's just that I have to meet with a federal court judge this morning. Her office left a message that I should be in her chambers in an hour, at eleven. 'Don't be late,' she told me. If you ever got a chance to examine this judge, you'd discover a cardiopulmonary first: no heart and an extra lung. So I'd better do what she says and not be late."

"We'll see you back here no later than two or three, then?" Dr. Shiller said sternly.

"He promises to be here," Susan said.

Dr. Shiller signed Herman's release and handed it to him. "I'll get the floor nurse to bring a wheelchair and we'll get you on your way."

After the doctor left and Susan was alone with her father, she put an angry scowl on her beautiful face.

"What?" he asked.

"If you try and get out of this operation . . . I'll . . . I'll kill you myself. You *promised*, Dad."

"I know, I know . . . right, I promised, and

we both know what a lawyer's promise is worth."

"*Dad.*" It was a threat, the way she said it.

"Okay," he grinned. "But I gotta go see Melissa first, and, while I do that, I have a job for you."

"What?" she said, still suspicious.

"I want you to find us a new private detective — not a computer guy like Roland, but a real gumshoe, somebody with good resources in San Francisco. Resources means friends on the San Francisco Police Department. We need a look at the ME's report, the crime scene evidence. An ex-cop who's now a P.I. might be a good place to start."

"An ex–San Francisco cop?" she said.

"Maybe, but I think it's better if the guy lives down here and has worked cases up there, 'cause we're gonna be in L.A., and I don't wanna have to be flying him around, paying per diem, and stuff like that. So, call around. Start with the L.A. Police Department and get a list of ex-L.A. cops who are now in the P.I. business and who worked cases up north. If that doesn't work, try finding one in San Francisco."

"Dad, we can't investigate Roland's death, the police will do that. And you're going to be out of action until your condition is fixed."

"We can't *not* investigate it."

She looked at him for a long, painful moment.

"What?" he said, putting a little push on it. But it was just acting, because he couldn't help noticing how concerned she was standing at the foot of the bed, her fists on her hips, trying to figure a way to steer him, to get him to do what she wanted.

"Dad, if you don't do this, I'm gonna brain you."

"Can't hurt me if you hit me on the head . . . nothing much up there."

A nurse came in and unhooked Herman from the monitors. A few minutes later he was being rolled down the corridor on chrome and plastic wheels and pushed into the elevator like a two-hundred-pound holiday turkey. Susan followed. He was slumped, yet full of stubborn pride, heroic but clumsy, brave but ill-prepared. He was a million dollars in debt, yet headed downstairs to drive away in a movie star's expensive sports car.

Chapter Twelve

Whatta dump, Jack Wirta thought, staring at his newly rented office with open hostility. The three-story building was on Santa Monica Boulevard, near Fairfax. He was getting a rate on the rental because the building was owned by the estate of his ex-police-partner's son. His old partner, Shane Scully, had found out two years ago that he had fathered a child with a wealthy woman who had died and left their son the building. Shane agreed to give Jack Wirta, L.A.'s newest private eye and cosmic joke, a deal on the one-room office: twelve hundred a month, no furniture, and utilities included.

The place was poorly situated, especially for an ex-cop. Everywhere he looked, up and down the dingy third-floor corridor, he saw crime . . . vice, mostly. A gay male "dating service" that called itself Reflections occupied several adjoining offices down the hall. Why it was called Reflections, Jack Wirta didn't even want to guess. He'd already had a run-in with its proprietor, a willowy Hispanic ex-chorus boy named Casimiro Roca.

"I hope you aren't intending to put chairs

out in the hall," Roca said, arching a plucked eyebrow at Jack.

"Why the fuck would I put furniture out in the hall?" Jack snapped.

"One doesn't need to use foul language to make one's point."

"Sorry." Jack didn't really want to start up with this guy.

"The last people, the ones who had that office before you, they always had ten folding chairs out here with people sitting in them all day, smoking, talking, laughing. One could barely get one's work done."

"Well, I think that was a casting agency, but I'm not going to be having any casting calls, so I think we can forget about that problem. I'm Jack Wirta," he said, putting out his hand, trying to be nice.

"Casimiro Roca," the man shook it hesitantly. "But I go by Miro. You look like a cop," he added suspiciously.

"Used t'be. Not anymore."

"Well, just try and be quiet. Miro could use a little peace."

"You're not speaking euphemistically, I hope," Jack said, smiling.

"Don't be a child," Miro replied, then turned and actually *sashayed* down the hall — more hip action than the cast of *Cats*.

Jack Wirta watched Miro until he pirouetted at his door and paused theatrically. "Something else Miro can do for you?" he said. Not exactly an invitation, but not exactly a statement either.

"I was just thinking . . . that's some walk you got there."

"I used to dance professionally," he said.

That was Reflections.

At the other end of the hall was some kind of phone-bank boiler room called Herbal World Health Products. They had fifteen or twenty employees, and to Jack's cop eye all of them looked pretty badly tweaked. They scurried like junkies, heads down, carefully watching the ground. Strung-out little cowboys and cowgirls with twitchy movements and criminal eyes who spent the day on phones selling unlicensed health products. If he called Hollywood Vice they would come up here and take down the whole floor. But Jack was into "live and let live" these days. It was his new motto.

So much for his third-floor neighbors.

The office was located down the street from the West Hollywood Health Club, situated on the edge of five gay blocks along Santa Monica Boulevard that most Angelinos referred to as "Boy's Town."

Overbuilt guys in tank tops and muscle shirts strolled the sidewalks in too-tight jeans, swinging their shoulders and looking like they'd kick the shit out of anybody who even muttered the word "faggot." On the job Jack had never had a problem with the gay community. He'd always figured to each his own, but he was beginning to wonder if having his office here was such a good idea. He was ruggedly handsome and he'd been hit on twice already this morning within the half block he'd walked from his parking space to the front entrance.

By ten o'clock he had set up his desk and moved one club chair in. His old, ink-stained blotter was ready and waiting for that first big career-defining, high-profile case. Bring on a Robert Blake operetta. His new file cabinet was alphabetized but empty, anxious to be crammed full of important revenue-producing, adrenaline-pumping material.

As he worked, he tried to ignore the pain in his lower lumbar region — throbbing at first, then building, as always, until, by late morning his back was on fire. The pain came the same way as it had for almost six and a half years.

Each morning he had to unroll himself from the fetal position he seemed to be arranged in when he woke up. After half an hour of agonizing stretching, with one eye on his bottle of painkillers, he would finally leverage upright and limp into the tiny kitchen of his duplex, telling himself he wasn't going to pop one more Percocet — ever. The little bastards were addictive, and he knew he was badly hooked. But by eleven o'clock he was always in such agony he could hold out no longer. It was pain unlike anything he had ever experienced before he'd injured his back. He would inevitably find himself circling the pills until, finally, he would angrily grab the plastic bottle, shake one of the damn things into his hand, and wash it down, promising himself that this was absolutely the last one he would take.

End result: He would struggle back to a pain threshold of plus five — which was barely manageable. He would then wander through his day, feeling the pain building ominously until it hit a nerve-jangling nine about four hours later. Unable to find a position or an alcoholic state that enabled him to endure it for even another minute, he would break the solemn promise to himself, grab the bottle, take another, make one more empty promise, and so on. It had been like that ever since he'd stopped the armor-piercing nine-millimeter Parabellum fired by that shithead, Emil Matasareanu, or his buddy, Larry Eugene Phillips Jr., at the North Hollywood bank shootout in February of '97.

Four surgeries and two bone grafts later, he could finally stand up, but it wasn't easy. A grueling two-and-a-half-year rehab followed before he could reapply for duty. He'd been forced to retake the Police Academy physical, which of course included the dreaded obstacle course. He had eventually crashed and burned doing the wall climb, and they carried him off on a stretcher. One lawsuit and another two and a half years later, he was off the force on a 75-percent disability that paid him $2,800 a month, after taxes. But he was also completely addicted to Percocets. Since it was a triple-hit painkiller, three copies of each prescription were filed with various state agencies to guarantee you couldn't get more without a doctor's approval.

A year ago, when his most forgiving M.D. would no longer write him a prescription, Jack Wirta became an illegal drug user. He was now buying black market "Cets" from an African American drug dealer with a speech impediment, named "Carbon Paper" — a moniker derived not from the color of his skin, but from the fact that he was great at forging prescriptions under a variety of phony names.

It was past eleven and Jack had just started hanging pictures and plaques in his new office, trying to hide the wall scars, pounding in nails with a hammer, when, suddenly, the door swung open and Miro Roca was standing there again, hands defiantly on his slender hips.

"Is that supposed to be funny?" he said, lisping slightly. "You're knocking the wall down."

"Relax," Jack said, trying to talk with a nail between his teeth and lisping slightly himself.

"Gimme ten minutes and I'll be done. I don't have that many certificates anyway. My career in law enforcement was undistinguished."

Uninvited, Miro sashayed into his office — the hip motion really was something to watch. Then he dropped theatrically into the one worn leather chair: the spin, the drop, and the smile all executed in one fluid motion. Drum riff. Cymbals. Applause. Like that.

Miro started chewing at a cuticle, nibbling thoughtfully, picking up one of the four plaques on the desk with his free hand. It was a Certificate of Merit for the North Hollywood bank thing.

"Help yourself, there," Jack said as he finished pounding the nail in the wall and hung his police academy graduation picture. He was in the third row at the end, ramrod straight, his game face on.

Casimiro was still looking at the North Hollywood certificate, reading the citation. "This was some pretty serious shit," he said. "Miro saw this crazy bastard on the TV, walking around shooting people."

"One doesn't have to use foul language to make one's point," Jack smiled.

"I was being bitchy when I said that. Sorry," Miro conceded.

"Apology accepted." Jack climbed down from the stepladder, then appraised the pictures and plaques on the wall. "Straight?" he asked Miro, who was now also studying them.

"Funny thing to ask an obviously gay man," Miro said, and when Jack turned Miro smiled. "Just foolin' with ya, honey. Yes . . . yes . . . I think they're straight." And then he wrinkled his nose at the pictures, and for some unknown reason Jack found himself smiling, too. At least this guy didn't take himself too seriously, which Jack noticed was a growing problem among people who hung out west of La Brea.

"I was thinking . . ." Miro began, "since you used to be police, and since I have a few old issues there, I was wondering if maybe there would be some way we could help each other."

"You mean, I talk to somebody for you and get your file erased, and then you give me ten million dollars? Something like that?"

"Ten million seems a tad high," he replied with mock seriousness. "I was thinking more like I could get one of our boys to answer your phone or something. I have this new one, Jackson Mississippi — he doesn't have a place yet. He just sits around waiting for outcalls. Be nice to give him something useful."

"He's from Jackson, Mississippi?" Jack asked.

"No, that's his name. Don't tell him I told you, but I think he made it up. Least it's nicer than this other boy I had, named

Bangor Maine. So how 'bout it? Wanna trade favors?"

"No can do." Jack was beginning to wish Miro would just leave so he could take a few more Percocets.

Suddenly, like in a Bogart movie, the door opened and one of the most beautiful women he had seen in six months was standing in his doorway, briefcase in hand.

"Is this the Jack Wirta Detective Agency?" she asked hesitantly.

"Yes, ma'am," he said smiling, giving her his whole grill . . . the entire sixteen.

"Well, I guess Miro should go back and feed his ducks." Roca got to his feet and really worked it, heading toward the door.

The beautiful woman watched him walk away, and as soon as he was gone she smiled. "Graceful."

"He used to dance professionally," Jack said, and started to clear a space in the office. "Sorry about the clutter. I'm just moving in here."

She moved over to the cracked leather chair where Miro had been sitting and settled in. "I'm Susan Strockmire," she said, putting her knees together and laying her briefcase across her lap. "I called the LAPD. They gave me your name when I asked for recommendations on an agency."

"The police department recommended me?" He was puzzled.

"Yes. I talked to a Lieutenant Matthews. He said you had the qualifications necessary for a job I need done."

Lieutenant Steve Matthews had been Jack's CO back when he worked the Homicide table at Rampart. Jack had been in the Valley interviewing a witness on a triple drive-by gang killing when the bank shooting went down, heard the call on the scanner, and had rolled on it. He was the second blue on the scene. Not knowing the bandits were already out of the bank with assault weapons and full body armor, he'd walked right into a barrage of gunfire with only his puny little police-issue Beretta. That's how he ended up stopping the Parabellum. It had gone through his oblique and shattered two vertebrae — miraculously missing his spinal cord, or he would have finished out his life whizzing around in a motorized wheelchair. When Jack finally retired on a medical, Matthews put him up for the Medal of Valor, but it hadn't been approved. Cops who went down and didn't die or manage to neutralize the target rarely won the MOV. Instead he'd gotten the Certificate of Merit. All these years later it looked as if the lieutenant was still trying to even the score and throw some work his way. "What qualifications are we talking about?" Jack asked, fully prepared to lie like a street junkie to get his first job.

"I understand you worked a lot of cases up in San Francisco."

"More than my share," he said, wondering what on earth she was talking about. L.A. cops hardly ever worked up north. A few extradites, or the occasional nomadic criminal who started here and ended up there, or vice versa. But those were mostly phone jobs. The department rarely sprang to send you anywhere.

"Could you be slightly more specific?" he asked, his back pain now so bad he couldn't bear to go on for another moment. He reached into his pocket while she was fiddling in her briefcase for something, planning to use this moment to sneak a few more pills. He retrieved the bottle, quickly shook two into his hand then swallowed them dry, but she looked up and caught him. "Allergies," he smiled. "Santa Ana winds really get to me."

"Oh," she said, and handed him a newspaper article from the *San Francisco Chronicle*, headlined:

COMPUTER HACKER FOUND DEAD IN
HOTEL ROOM

While he read it he could see her out of the corner of his eye surveying the chipped walls, eyeing the faded furniture, taking inventory. It was a loser's hangout. Jim Rockford only lived in a trailer, but at least he had a nice view of the ocean. Rockford

144

would spit on this place.

He finished scanning the rest of the article. It was boilerplate reportage, no real info. It told how somebody named Roland Minton, who had a history of computer crime, was killed at the New Fairview Hotel in San Francisco. No details. Typical police b.s. *Foul play suspected. . . . No suspects . . . no leads.* That sort of thing.

"Okay," he said quickly, trying to get her to look back at him and stop surveying this sinkhole where he'd set up shop.

"The lieutenant said you had good contacts on the San Francisco Police Department," she said.

"Excellent. Among the best." He wondered what the hell Matthews was talking about. He knew no one up there.

"Roland Minton was working for our legal institute when he was killed. My father, Herman Strockmire, is the director and founder, and he wants to make sure the investigation is adequately pursued."

Jack liked that word, *institute.* Institutes were commercially secure, abundantly funded organizations, so Jack tacked another five hundred a day onto his price.

Then it hit him who he knew in San Francisco. He had told the lieutenant about it almost three years ago. It was one of his old love affairs that hadn't ended well. He'd dated a sergeant who worked the juvie detail

145

up there. He'd picked her up in a cop bar while she was in L.A. visiting her family. It ended like all of Jack's important female relationships — with recriminations and threats. Her name was Sergeant Eleanor — *If I ever see you again, you better run, you prick* — Drake.

"I think the lieutenant was referring to my extremely close working relationship with a Sergeant Drake of the SFPD."

"Do you think Sergeant Drake might be able to help us view some of the official case material related to Roland's death?"

"If I'm the one to ask her, I think I can say, without hesitation, no problemo." Another lie. But he reasoned now that he was in business that a lie was really just a sales promise.

The pills were beginning to take his pain threshold down below nine. At least that gave him hope for the next ten minutes.

"How much do you charge?" she asked.

"Tell you what, I need some coffee. There's a nice outdoor restaurant right downstairs. Whatta you say?" Jack needed to get out of his depressing office before he broke into tears.

She looked at her watch as if this was already taking too much of her time, but then she smiled — a hesitant little smile, so adorable that Jack had to stifle the urge to grab her hand and stroke it.

"Why not?" she finally said.

They sat in a patio restaurant called The All-American Boy, surrounded by gay trophy exhibits — musclemen in workout tanks and short shorts with plucked eyebrows and shaved bodies. Jack, with his rugged blonde attractiveness, was getting all the sidelong glances while Susan Strockmire was being ignored. She might as well have been wearing a Janet Reno mask. This neighborhood was going to take some getting used to.

"What exactly is your fee structure?" she inquired again.

He had called around after he got his license and found out that a good working rate for P.I.s in L.A. was a thousand a day. Long-range employment contracted out at between thirty-five hundred and four thousand on a weekly guarantee. But, for an institute he was compelled to charge a little more. Fifteen hundred is what he told her.

"It seems awfully high," she said, wrinkling her adorable nose, scowling slightly, bringing her laugh lines into play.

"You might think it's high, until you break it down," he said, launching into his pitch. "To begin with, I'm a trained police officer fifteen years on the force, both in squad cars and at the detective division. You can't buy that kind of on-the-job experience at any price. If you were hiring a psychiatrist, some guy in Armani with a Vandyke who got his doctorate through the mail, you wouldn't think twice about paying him a hundred and fifty dollars an hour. There are personal trainers in this town who get twice that."

"It's not that I'm questioning your fee structure . . ."

"I should hope not," he said, trying to look indignant.

"It's just that the Institute for Planetary Justice is a nonprofit institute and we have to watch expenses carefully."

If institute was a good word, nonprofit was a bad one. When they were in the same sentence it was disastrous. "Nonprofit institute" was a phrase as depressing as "fatal collision" or "aggressive malignancy."

"I see," he finally said. "Well, I guess because I'm sort of open at the moment I could take a small cut on my normal rate — say, down to a thousand dollars a day. But that's really the base number."

"Deal," she said, and reached out and shook his hand. Her grip was warm, her grasp firm. "I'll give you our local phone numbers." She dug into her purse and handed him a business card. He looked down at it: cheesy — the kind you get printed at Kinko's. She had crossed out the Washington, D.C., phone number and written a local one in pencil. Of course, he didn't even have a business card. It was on his list of things to

148

do, right after setting up some metal chairs in the hall to piss off Miro.

"Lemme write my number down," he said, grabbing a paper napkin, even though he wasn't dead sure of the number. The phone had only been installed yesterday. He thought for a minute, then wrote it down, *323-555-7890*. "Either that or 7809," he told her with a wave of his hand, as if it really didn't matter. "New office, new number." *But the same old bullshit,* he thought.

"You know, I guess I can tell you this now," she ventured hesitantly. "When I first looked into your office, it was so small, and well . . ."

"Dingy?" he offered, and she smiled an acknowledgment.

"Yes. So I wasn't even going to go in or even talk to you. You know what changed my mind?"

Jack didn't have a clue, so he just fixed an interested expression on his face and waited.

"It was your gay friend."

"Miro?" He was truly confused. "How so?"

"Our institute has advocated for gay rights. Most cops have this kind of overly macho thing going on. Y'know, like gay people aren't even worth spitting on, just because they have a different lifestyle. But I looked in and you're both sitting there chatting. He's your friend. That tells me something really important about you."

"Yes . . . yes," Jack said, hard-pressed to deal with that, but determined to try. "I find that people are just people, and that once you cut through all the surface stuff — the lifestyle choices, the color lines, the sexual whatevers — what really counts is who they are underneath." He smiled at a few of the overly developed men nearby to make his point. They smiled back. One of them waved.

"Exactly," she said earnestly, taking his heart and his breath away at the same time.

He gazed into her blue-green eyes swimming in their luminous beauty, thinking. *Maybe this neighborhood isn't gonna be so bad after all.*

Chapter Thirteen

When Herman walked in, Melissa King was sitting behind the huge oak desk in her office at the Federal Courthouse like a turret gunner about to flame some enemy aircraft. Volumes of the *U.S. Court Reporter* with mustard-yellow leather and gold bindings decorated three of the four office walls, giving the room just the right sense of awesome power. In those books was the gift of legal wisdom.

Judge King had decided not to dress up for the meeting, wearing no makeup and a blue-and-white muumuu printed with white Hawaiian flowers. She looked like Hilo Hattie in rehab. Her stringy blonde hair was pulled into a ponytail and held back with a rubber band. Her complexion was mottled with the heat rash of a third-trimester pregnancy. Her eyes were what scared him. They were as cold and deadly as two gun barrels — and they were sighting in on Herman over half-glasses perched on her nose.

He was back in his 'Number 4' court ensemble, his heart about as sound as the Canadian dollar — looking tired, but oh so presentable. Not that it mattered.

"Let's not waste a bunch a time on this,

Herman," Melissa King started without pre-amble. "I know you don't have a million dollars."

"That's correct, Your Honor. Very perceptive."

"So how we gonna get this done?"

"Well, Your Honor, I was hoping to prevail on your sense of fair play, given our long legal relationship."

"Relationship? Let's review that. Two years ago you appeared before me on that silly MK Ultra mind control case against the CIA. Accused them of trying to brainwash people using broadcast television to create photosensitive epilepsy in viewers. Wasn't that the drill? Remember that one?"

"Judge, I'm not here to argue that case again. Obviously, you failed to see the merits there."

"Merits? *Merits*, Herman? What merits?" She shifted on her flat, bony ass to get more comfortable, then ripped her glasses off like she was getting ready for a fistfight. "You drag the CIA, CBS, NBC, Fox, and two animation companies into court and accuse them of conspiring to devise ways to hypnotize the American population with subliminal flashes during TV programs. Some case! Like the public is gonna go brain-dead from watching *The A-Team*. Not that I don't think that might do it, but did you have a shred of evidence?"

"Yes."

"No."

"Because you limited the scope. Cut me down. Kept most of it out."

"Dammit, Herman, the system is crowded. We've got scheduling calendars that look like rainy-day traffic reports. People wait years to get to trial, and you're wasting court time on all this hopeless bullshit!" She was glowering at him. "Okay. So you have anything to say before I impose this monetary sanction?"

"Your Honor, if I might, I'd like to please try and convince you that a fine of a million dollars is excessive, and I really think this problem with the amended complaint doesn't deserve a Rule Eleven penalty. It's not about the validity of the lawsuit." She was scowling angrily and he was beginning to sweat. His forehead felt damp, so he took out his handkerchief and wiped his face, folding it afterwards, then putting it carefully away, trying to look like Spencer Tracy in *Inherit the Wind*, instead of a fat, sweating mouthpiece about to get reamed.

"Your Honor . . ." he cautiously went on. "Using Dannus Plexipus really didn't cause substantial harm, because anyone can pursue the public interest in preserving monarch butterflies. I could have used anyone as a plaintiff, so it's of no real merit that the plaintiff foundation wasn't precisely as advertised."

"That's not the point, Herman, and you know it," she growled. "I bifurcated the injunction and the case for damages, then let you put them on together. Now it turns out that in order to finagle yourself a jury trial at public expense you ginned up a phony foundation with bogus damages and lied about it in court. You've done that for the last time. The fine stands at a million dollars."

"I don't have anything close to a million dollars," he said.

"Then you'll have to raise it. Sell something."

"Judge, nothing I have even comes close to that. I hate to reveal this to Your Honor, but my practice does not make much money. We do a lot of very important work, but much of it is pro bono."

"Herman, let's cut to the chase. I'm not reducing the amount, okay? So, you'll appeal and I'll prevail. In the meantime, I want to set up a payment schedule."

"Your Honor, I need time. You're going to throw me into bankruptcy."

"We certainly don't want that now, do we?" She looked at her calendar, picked up a pencil, did some long division, than looked up. "Let's say, ten thousand dollars a month for the next eight years. How's that sound? I'll give you a break on the cost of money — we won't compound the interest."

"Even if I spend half my time doing paid speaking engagements I couldn't raise that."

"Who do you speak to, *Star Trek* conventions?" She was smiling now.

"I know you're enjoying yourself, Melissa, but this isn't funny to me. Just because you don't see the value in my legal actions doesn't mean they don't have value."

"Yeah, right. Okay, then. That's the deal. It's settled. I'll give you until the end of the month. That's four days to get the first payment in. The money will be distributed amongst the defense counsels to cover their legal fees for this joke of a case you filed against them. Once their expenses are met, the remainder will go to the circuit court."

"I'll have to sell all my office equipment."

"If that's what it takes, so be it."

He looked at her realizing that he had hit a wall. He was afraid if he didn't get out of there his heart was going to take off on him again, so he nodded his head. "All right, I'll do my best."

"Always nice to see you, Herman," she said sarcastically, then pushed a button on her phone. The bailiff opened the door and stood waiting.

"Make sure Mr. Strockmire gets his parking validation. He's gonna need to save every cent he has."

Herman turned and walked to the door, but he paused there and looked back at her. "Some time in the future, you're going to see that I was right," he said.

"Four days," she reminded him.

Then he was out of her chambers standing

in the cold marble hallway under a vaulted ceiling.

"Are you okay, Mr. Strockmire?" the bailiff asked. Herman had gotten to know him during jury selection. He was a nice, gray-haired old man in a federal marshal's uniform assigned to the courthouse until next year, when he would get his forty in and retire.

"Yep, I'm just great," Herman said, taking a deep breath. "Wonderful — tip-top, yes siree."

He walked down the hallway to the phone bank. His cell phone was out of service and all four pay phones were in use, so he sat on the bench across the hall to wait and consider what had just happened. She was right. He could appeal, and of course he would; but he would probably lose. The circuit court judges who heard his appeal would all have their own "Herman the German" stories. He didn't have many friends on the federal bench. Certainly it was wrong of Melissa to have thrown out his case, but he had fudged on the amended complaint and lied in front of her in court, trying to slide it past her. So, there it was — he was screwed.

He sat there and thought about his life: how his dreams had all been lost, how the things that he really cared about were just jokes to other people. Since she brought it up, he thought about his MK Ultra suit that Melissa had thrown out of court four years earlier. Yet, two years after she pitched it, a group of schoolchildren in Tokyo watching the Japanese cartoon program *Pikachu* had suddenly gone into convulsions. Some were hospitalized with a condition doctors diagnosed as very close to epilepsy. The Japanese government stated that it looked as if some sort of experiment in mind control had occurred in which children had been used as guinea pigs. When they examined the cartoon at slow speeds they discovered that the eyes of the animated character, Pikachu, flashed at high frequencies. Everybody finally admitted that this had caused a form of low-grade epilepsy. It was odd, they said. Odd to everybody but Herman, who found out that the cartoon had been designed in the United States, not Japan. He had traced its animators back to the CIA headquarters at Langley, Virginia.

Okay, to be perfectly honest, there was some hearsay there, so he couldn't use it in court yet, but he was still working on the case, getting ready to refile. No less a magazine than *U.S. News and World Report* had stated after the Japanese incident that: "U.S. information warfare experts conclude that there are no longer any technological hurdles to developing a mind control weapon that could be delivered by computer, television, or film." Such a weapon, they said, "would produce effects similar to the recent Pikachu-induced spasms."

There it was — almost an admission of what Herman had accused the CIA of doing, but Melissa had thrown it out. Even now, if he showed her this new research, including the facts of the Pikachu incident, she would just snort at him and tell him it was all bullshit. Some people just didn't have an inspired view of what was really going on in the world, and Herman had been dragging that fact behind him like a cross that he'd soon be hung on.

When one of the phones finally cleared, he got up, shuffled over, and dug into his pocket. He pulled out Sergeant Lester Cole's card and dialed the number in San Francisco, rubbing his thumb across the fancy embossed gold police shield on the lower-left-hand corner while he waited for the call to go through.

"San Francisco Police Department," a woman's voice said.

"I'd like to talk to Lester Cole in Homicide." He was transferred, then heard the steady beep alerting him that the call was being recorded.

"Sergeant Cole, Homicide Desk," a familiar voice answered. Herman pictured the short sergeant with the weightlifter's body and tired eyes.

"Sergeant, this is Herman Strockmire Jr. We talked last evening at the hospital in L.A."

"Yeah. How you feeling?"

"Oh, much better . . . very well, thank you."

"You remember something else?"

"Well, no. No — that isn't why I'm calling."

"Okay," Cole was disinterested now.

"Uh, Sergeant, I was wondering . . . when is your medical examiner planning on releasing Roland's body for burial?"

"Why?"

"Well, I talked to Roland's mother, Madge Minton, and she is very upset. She's trying to plan a service, and they wouldn't give her a date. She needs closure, and of course she wants the body flown back to Washington where she lives. I told her that I would get Roland released."

"Y'did, huh?"

"Yes, sir. Is that gonna be a problem?"

"Well, could be . . . the way it all ended up."

"Really?" Herman took a deep breath. "What way is that, Sergeant?"

"It ain't our case anymore. So you're talking to the wrong Indian."

"Whose case is it?"

"Federal government. They swooped in here first thing this morning, just after I got back from L.A. Took over the entire investigation — body, crime scene, ME reports, the works."

"No kidding? Isn't that a little strange?"

"They're feds. You ask me, everything they do seems strange."

"Well, I mean . . . how's it a federal crime? Roland was not on federal property. He wasn't a federal employee, so why would the federal government take it over? What's their legal authority? It's a local homicide, pure and simple."

"Only one reason," Sergeant Cole said.

Herman could hear coldness in his voice that matched the disgust he'd seen in Cole's eyes when the sergeant was standing at the foot of his bed. "What's that?" Herman asked.

"Somebody in the big bureaucracy don't agree. The case must have major federal implications, otherwise they wouldn't be here."

"Yeah — I see what you mean," Herman said and hung up the phone. He stood in the hallway feeling something close to vindication. He realized his theory, the one he dared not express to anyone, could in fact be true.

One thing he knew for sure, he couldn't go back to the hospital and be out of commission for two weeks. Not now, not with this going on. Herman had to move fast. He had to figure out what Roland had found in the Gen-A-Tec computer that was so important that it had gotten him ripped apart.

There was no doubt in Herman Strockmire's mind that whoever was investigating Roland Minton's murder also knew who killed him.

Chapter Fourteen

Susan found out that Herman hadn't returned to the hospital, because there was a message on her beeper from Dr. Shiller. She called the doctor on her cell phone after leaving Jack Wirta's office.

"He didn't show up," Shiller said angrily.

"Damn!" She made a U-turn, heading back to Fairfax and the Santa Monica Freeway.

"I feel like I'm always chasing an ambulance with this guy," Shiller said. "If he doesn't come back here, fine. That's it for me, Ms. Strockmire. I'm through. I can't help him."

"I understand," she said. "But, Doctor, at least let me find out why. I mean, maybe there's a good reason he didn't show up."

"I'm through trying to convince him. As far as I'm concerned, he should get another doctor."

"I'll get him there," she said. "I promise."

"Whatever."

It took her over forty minutes to get out to Malibu, because she took the Coast Highway and had forgotten how congested it could get in the late afternoon. She pulled the borrowed station wagon into the driveway of the huge French Provincial beach house and parked next to the Mercedes her father had been driving. That meant he was there.

She let herself in through the side gate, punching the security code numbers and using her key, then walked past the Olympic-size pool to the large one-story guesthouse.

It was empty, but as she passed through the billiards room she saw her father through the window, sitting out on the sandy beach about thirty yards away, his back to her, staring at the ocean. He had his arms wrapped around his knees, looking very small and alone.

She slid open the glass doors and walked across the narrow brick patio and through the little white gate. She kicked off her shoes and trudged across the sand, finally settling down next to him. "You broke your promise."

"I know," he replied, but he seemed so sad and lost she didn't have it in her to beat him up over it.

"Dad, I talked to Dr. Shiller. He wants you there immediately."

"No he doesn't. He's washed his hands of me. Admit it."

"Dad, *please*."

"I'm right, aren't I?"

"He said he won't chase you around, and I don't blame him."

Herman nodded, then picked up his little laptop computer that was sitting open on the sand next to him and handed it to her. On the screen was Roland's e-mail.

She read it hurriedly, then looked up. "He got the corn file. They only did minimal testing. This would have been great if we hadn't been thrown out of court."

"Yep," Herman said, then pointed to one specific sentence in the e-mail. "He sent us an encrypted file from DARPA. I transferred it to a disk. It's inside."

"What is it?"

"Fifty or more pages of code. You read the e-mail. Roland wants us to take it to his friend, Zimmy. He told me about this guy. His name is Dr. Gino Zimbaldi, out at the Jet Propulsion Laboratory in Pasadena. He uses JPL's computers to break code. It's like a hobby with him, so he does it on the sly after hours."

She sat still for a long time not sure what to say. Then she handed the computer back. "Dad, you've got to go back to Cedars and get the operation."

"Honey, they won't release Roland's body. Worse still, the feds took his murder investigation away from the San Francisco police. They scooped up the whole case. They shipped what's left of Roland's corpse to Washington. I think it was feds who killed him, and now they're investigating a murder they committed themselves. Good luck solving that one, huh?"

"Dad, you have got to get this procedure done."

"Just give it a rest with the fucking doctors, okay? I'm trying to tell you something."

Susan was stunned. In thirty-plus years she only remembered one or two times that he had snapped at her like that.

"I've been sitting out here thinking about Roland. About him going up there trying to get this stuff for us and then getting murdered. Shredded. Pulled limb from limb."

"Dad, don't. Don't do this to yourself."

"I've been thinking about why. *Why* would they kill him like that? What did he get from Gen-A-Tec that was so dangerous he had to be murdered for it? And why so violently? I think the answer is sitting inside. I think it's in that fifty-page encryption. In fact, I know it is. That printout is waiting to tell us the secret that got Roland killed."

"Dad, you have to let go of this."

"I can't, sweetheart. I just can't."

"Are you afraid of the surgery? Is that it?"

He didn't answer. He was looking out at the late afternoon sun hanging in the L.A. smog, floating above the rolling Pacific like a big, orange Japanese lantern.

"Are you *afraid* to get the operation?" she asked again.

He seemed to think that over. "I confess

I'm not the bravest guy on the planet," he answered softly. "Y'know all those tubes and drip bags and the smells in there . . . I just . . . I . . . Yeah, kinda . . . I guess."

"But, Dad, it's only going to take a day, then a week or two of rest and its over."

"I know . . . I know. But . . . I just . . . I just can't."

Now she knew she was being conned. He was bullshitting her and she shook her head sadly. "You're a rat, you know that?"

"Why, because I'm scared of this operation? 'Cause I need a day or two to get myself up for it, get my mind in the right place?"

"You're not afraid of surgery. You just don't want to let go of this thing and take two weeks off. Not with Roland's e-mail in there, so you're trying to get me off your back."

"Honey, this could be much bigger than even I thought. DARPA . . . you saw that mentioned in his e-mail."

"Yes."

"I know about DARPA. A secret government think tank. They developed weapons and special projects. Very twenty-first century. I always suspected DARPA might be behind all of that stuff going on at Area Fifty-one."

"Dad, please don't start up with that. Not now."

"Honey, what do you suppose killed Roland?

'Cause, it was a *what,* not a *who.* A *what.* That's what Sergeant Cole said. A thousand pounds per square inch. Gimme a break, what could do that?"

"Some kind of monkey," she said. "A gorilla or a chimp."

"Not on your sweet life. Monkeys don't have the mental acuity to undertake a military mission . . . commit a complicated B and E, then a premeditated murder. They live in the here and now. They don't have memories, pasts, or futures. Trust me, they would make piss-poor assault weapons."

"What then?"

"Roland says that the fifty pages of code he sent us is something called the Ten-Eyck Chimera Project. Gen-A-Tec's research on it is being funded by DARPA. I couldn't find anything on a Ten-Eyck, but I looked up chimera in the dictionary, and you know what it says?"

"What?" She was beginning to get a feeling of hopelessness. She'd been on these scavenger hunts before.

"So, what is it?" she finally said dutifully, because he was waiting for her to ask.

"It's spelled C-H-I-M-E-R-A, but it's pronounced ki-mir-a. It's from the Greek: a fire-breathing she-monster having a lion's head, a goat's body, and a serpent's tail."

"That's ridiculous. You're saying DARPA's making one of those?"

"It's also an illusion of the mind."

"I like that better."

"Or," now he turned and looked right at her, "any life-form consisting of tissue of diverse genetic constitution." He was still staring at her after he finished the sentence, seeing her thoughts turn stormy, but still reading them like rain through a window. "Not corn or soybeans, not plants, but flesh and blood — *tissue*."

"Dad, just say it, will you?"

"They're making a hybrid animal. It's just the kind of thing those DARPA guys would try for."

"Why? Why would they? Why would anybody want to make a genetic monster? For what possible reason?"

He looked out to sea, reluctant to answer.

"I'm listening," she challenged.

"Honey, you know what's been happening in this country — you more than anyone. You've seen it. You've been with me fighting against the shallowing out of American values. In the new America the total doesn't have to equal the sum of its parts anymore. 'If it bleeds, it leads.' Don't debate, obfuscate. This country is suffering from the complete loss of a moral imperative in the face of profit and power."

"You're not answering my question. And stop with the rhyming polemics, Dad."

"The war in Kosovo is when it started.

That war changed everything."

"And don't shift to history. Get to the point."

"No, listen. This is the point, because it's the basis of my theory."

She nodded, so he went on. "Clinton had a huge problem in Kosovo, and it became real clear to Milosevic that, despite the ethnic cleansing and mass murders, the American public didn't really give a shit. They weren't willing to lose even one GI over it. The same problem existed in Afghanistan and Iraq. If thousands of U.S. soldiers start dying the American public will throw in the towel. The U.S. is the last remaining superpower, we have a responsibility to be world policemen, but as a nation we no longer have the stomach for it. It's okay to fight an air war, use smart weapons, push buttons where no one is hurt — everybody gets some popcorn and watches it on CNN. But what happens once our smart bombs have knocked out all the military targets?"

"I don't know." She was getting angry. "The war's over, I guess."

"No. You have to send in ground troops to mop up. You still have to put boots on the ground to wipe out pockets of resistance and hold the terrain. That's where the problem arises. This country won't sit still for losing any troops in a place like Kosovo or Iraq. We want our new fall fashions; we want to know who Britney Spears is dating. We've got appointment television and Tiger Woods. So, what do we do?"

"Dad . . ."

"We make disposable soldiers."

"We do?"

"Look, honey, the science already exists. Gene splitting began in the early 1980s. In the late nineties we were cloning sheep and pigs. Then we started splicing genes and crossbreeding animals like the beefalo. Four years ago a company named Celera made a DNA map of the entire human genome. Millions of genetic base pairs. Once you can isolate a gene, you can employ gene-splicing techniques to incorporate any genetic trait into any plant or animal on earth, just like they're doing with that damned genetically engineered corn. This is not far-fetched. It's not science fiction. It's today."

"And what do you suppose they're designing?"

"I think . . ." He stopped and looked out to sea, almost afraid to say it, so she said it for him.

"Aliens?" but she sort of hissed it, or sighed it.

"Honey, why not? What if Ten-Eyck stands for some kind of alien life form? You believe they have aliens on ice out at Area Fifty-one, don't you?"

"I'm not so sure about all that, Dad." She

said it because she'd never been able to get completely behind that one, but it made her feel like a traitor to put the thought into words.

"Not *sure?* We've filed two lawsuits over it." She finally just nodded.

But Herman was just getting started. "If there are dead aliens at Area Fifty-one, and if we harvested their DNA, what's to stop DARPA from doing some careful gene splicing, putting some of that alien DNA into the human zygote, upgrading the *Homo sapiens,* making a hybrid with selected alien powers mixed with our human dexterity and intelligence? The human-alien, this chimera, might have shadowy thoughts, or some genetic memory from outer space. It might have a strange appearance, but even that isn't necessary. The human zygote — the human egg — could be spliced to make the chimera look more physically acceptable to us. Then we raise it and train it to fight. Imagine disposable soldiers with ten times human strength. You could gene-splice them to be heat-resistant for desert warfare, or cold-resistant for places like Kosovo. Put 'em on the ground and let 'em do what we are no longer willing to have our own children do — fight and die. Chimeras have no parents. They are test-tube-grown and lab-incubated, so there is no one to grieve if they die in battle. They're the perfect conscription soldier. I'm telling you, honey, this is just the kind of shit those guys at DARPA come up with."

"Dad, I don't think . . ." She stopped, skeptical as she was, because her father was shaking his head sadly now. Then he slumped and looked down at the sand between his feet.

"I'm always alone," he said softly. "Always fighting everything by myself. I need someone to believe in me." He looked at her. "I need someone to be on my side."

"Daddy, I believe in you. God, how I believe in you. Don't you know that?"

"I can't let this go. I can't check into a hospital with this going on. Can't you see what's at stake here?"

It was then that she knew she had lost. "Yes, Daddy. I see." She was so afraid she was going to lose him, afraid that this fight would consume him.

They sat for a long time watching the waves blast the shore, then suck the whitewater back up to build a new wave that slammed onto the sand again a few seconds later. The rhythmic motion of the ages.

"Did you find us a detective?" he asked, his voice tired.

"Yes. His name is Jack Wirta. He has good contacts on the San Francisco PD. But the feds took the case away from the locals, so he probably can't help us anymore."

"The local cops may have lost the case, but

they have a duplicate file tucked away someplace. Cops are like that. Information is power. Believe me, there's a record of the investigation somewhere in their files. Mr. Wirta has to get them to show it to you."

"And what are you going to do?"

"I've gotta raise ten thousand dollars in three days."

"That's all?"

"This month's payment. She still wants the whole mil — ten a month for eight years."

"Oh, Daddy, I'm sorry."

"I'm also gonna go out to JPL — find out what's on those fifty pages of encryption," he said, changing the subject.

They sat quietly. After a while, she reached over and hugged him. He looked closer to defeat than she had ever seen him. "I'm on your side, Daddy."

"I know." But it broke her heart the way he said it.

Chapter fifteen

It was raining in the Bay Area, and the flight was bumpy. They careened off cumulonimbus clouds and bounced violently on pockets of hard air, dropping hundreds of feet without warning, then straining up again. The passengers all had the same tight, anxious smiles people get when they're trapped in an elevator. Jack and Susan both heaved a sigh of relief when the plane finally touched down.

Rental car — map of the city — heading toward town, windshield wipers clicking. They said almost nothing until they passed the old Candlestick Park, each lost in separate thoughts.

A lot of things were on Jack's mind. First and foremost, his back had been battered on the plane ride and he was miserable. His thoughts had already begun to circle the pill bottle in his faded briefcase.

He was wearing ironed jeans, a brown corduroy sport jacket, a yellow shirt, a blue necktie, and his best Cole Haan loafers. He was dressed for bullshit because he had promised to get Eleanor Drake of the SFPD to cooperate, but it was more likely she'd yank out that little nine millimeter Titan

Tiger she always carried and start blasting.

Jack had cheated on Eleanor. Not that they'd been exactly betrothed or anything, but they had been serious enough to be taking long weekends together, meeting up in Monterey, making love, walking on windblown beaches, holding hands. He should never have stepped out on her with Angela Macabe. Angela had a centerfold's body. He'd made a glandular mistake.

He was also thinking about how to get the Institute for Planetary Justice (an irredeemably corny name, he thought) to pay him something in advance. She was his first client, and he'd never done this before. He'd sort of been expecting Susan to write out a check, but all those natural opportunities had come and gone, and now he was just going to have to flat-out ask for it.

Susan sat in the passenger seat mulling over problems of her own. She was consumed by worry about her father. She had to get this job done fast and get back to L.A. so she could find a way to get him checked into the hospital. She was also praying that whatever was on those fifty pages would turn out to be nothing. A traitorous thought, but there it was. If that coded material was just more corn research, which they didn't need anymore, maybe she could get him back into Cedars-Sinai. Lastly, she was wondering how to avoid paying Jack Wirta anything in advance, because, quite frankly, they were selling the Washington, D.C., furniture and office equipment to pay for Melissa King's fine, so there sure as hell wasn't a thousand a day lying around for the Wirta Detective Agency.

"I usually get my money in advance . . . at least some portion of it," he said, startling her by reading her thoughts like John Edwards.

"Is that normal? I figured you'd just bill us and we'd handle it in the normal course of business."

"Some of the larger agencies do it that way, but us little guys go for cash up front. I'm already out my airline ticket, and expenses are supposed to be in advance."

She smiled at him and he melted like ice cream on a summer day.

"Well, that is . . . normally they are. Not always . . . sometimes, though," he stammered.

"Well, I suppose I could write you a check."

"Good! That works." *Problem solved,* he thought.

While they continued into the city she took out her checkbook, holding it up to her chest like a losing poker hand. Then she wrote him a thousand-dollar check, tore it off, and handed it to him. "There you go," she said brightly.

"Thanks."

The downtown San Francisco Police Department station house was a large brick job on Williams Street. By a stroke of good fortune

— or karma, or dumb luck — a branch of his bank, Wells Fargo, was conveniently located just across the street.

He parked in the pay lot, fed the meter (another buck twenty-five on the expense sheet), and they walked inside the cop shop.

Now that he'd been paid, the next big problem was to make sure he avoided Eleanor Drake at all costs. Jack was going to have to find another way to get what Susan wanted. Since Juvie wasn't officed here, but over on Mission Street, at least he was confident he was not going to run into Eleanor. He walked up to the desk sergeant and opened his P.I. identification, laying it on the counter.

"Wow," the sergeant said. "Like Magnum or something?"

"I'm looking for Eleanor Drake," he said.

"Sergeant Drake — third floor — Special Crimes. Check with the desk sergeant up there."

"I thought she was in Juvie," he said, surprised.

"You haven't been reading the department newsletter. She's in Special Crimes now. You want her, she's upstairs." Already bored with him.

Susan led the way toward the stairs. Jack hurried to stop her.

"Listen, Ms. Strockmire." Jack reached out and took her arm.

"You can call me Susan."

"Right. Okay . . . look, Susan, this is one of those deals where, because I'm going to be asking her to give us access to a sealed department record, it might be better if I do it without witnesses — kinda cop to cop."

"Okay. Yeah, that makes sense. I should get lost, then."

"Right." Uniformed police officers were streaming past them while they stood at the foot of the stairs. Jack was starting to feel very vulnerable and exposed. It was just noon, and any moment Eleanor Drake could come down on her way to lunch. Most cops were extremely punctual when it came to eating.

"Should I wait outside?" she asked.

"Yeah, maybe outside would be best." His plan was to go upstairs and hide in the men's room for a while, then come out, claiming she'd been sent to Oxnard on a case, something like that, and try to figure out an alternative plan.

"Wirta!" a woman's voice rang in the stairwell.

Jack spun around and there she was, standing on the landing not ten feet away with three uniformed cops. "What the fuck are you doing here?" Eleanor Drake demanded, glaring down at him. Like most female cops, Eleanor had a mouth on her.

Jack gave her his best smile. It had no effect.

177

Zero. "I came to talk to you. My god, Eleanor, you look marvelous." Now he sounded like Fernando Lamas.

"You prick," Eleanor said. "You've got your full ration of nerve coming here." She was wearing a tailored suit with a short skirt. It was her legs that had gotten him in trouble in the first place.

"Is that her?" Susan asked, almost whispering.

"Uh . . . uh . . . yeah. Gimme a minute, here."

"Get outta my sight, you asshole. I'm not kidding. You'd better get the fuck outta my precinct house."

"One doesn't have to use foul language to make one's point." Stealing Miro's lines.

"I'm not fooling, Jack."

"Right. Let's go." He turned and grabbed Susan's arm and led her out of the building. He could feel Eleanor's eyes tracking him like gunsights until he was out the door and on the street. It had stopped raining, but his lower back was still a fire zone, his emotions in turmoil, his honor in question.

"I thought she was supposed to be a close friend — that you had an outstanding working relationship," Susan said angrily. "What kinda liar are you? She looked like she wanted to kill you." His karma with women hovered near zero.

Time to come clean. "Look, Susan, you're right. I lied, okay? I wasn't planning on running

178

into her. She hates me. We used to date. I cheated on her and she damn near shot it out with me in a motel room in Monterey. It ended about as badly as possible and I . . ." He paused. "Look, I needed the work, so I fudged a little."

"*Fudged?*"

"Yeah, but I still have a way to get what we need. Actually, this new way is smarter than asking sworn personnel to steal confidential records. That probably would have backfired. This idea is much safer, okay?"

She was really pissed. "What kind of an asshole are you?"

Some questions are better left unanswered. "How much cash do you have in your wallet?"

"I don't carry cash. I told you, we're a nonprofit institute. I need checks as receipts for our tax-exempt status."

"A check won't do it. Okay, in the spirit of cooperation, and because I see how upset you are, I'll front the Institute a couple'a hundred dollars. Deal?" She was calming down, he thought . . . hoped.

"Why? What are we doing?"

"We're gonna find a Chinese lab attendant and bribe him. The Chinese are easy marks."

"I'm really not much on racial slurs," she said, looking daggers at him now.

"It's not a racial slur. It's a cultural reality. I happen to know that a lot of Chinese people end up working in the police lab up here. They're good technicians and they work at minimum wage. Most are immigrants with big debts to the triads for getting them or their families over here from mainland China. Two hundred bucks will buy a lot of cooperation if I can find the right guy. We go downstairs in the ME's building on Turpin Street. It's not a secure location. We go to the cafeteria, do a little eavesdropping, pick somebody with a thick accent. Believe me, it works. I've done this before."

It pissed her off that he'd lied to her. But then, she reasoned, she'd lied to him, too. He'd be in for a big surprise when he tried to cash her check, so she figured they were even . . . more or less.

Before they got back in the car she watched him with concern as he sprinted across the street to the Wells Fargo Bank to deposit her bad check in the ATM.

His name was Shing Nam Shan, but he went by "Danny." He was twenty years old and weighed only one hundred and fifteen pounds all in, canvas shoes included. He had short, bristly hair and eyeglasses thick enough to start a fire. Danny snatched the cash out of Jack's hand like a lizard snapping up a fruit fly. After Jack explained that they wanted a copy of Roland Minton's crime scene and ME reports, Danny smiled and said in broken English, struggling with each sentence: "I know where keep. Make some . . . same kind . . . copies. You rait here." He turned and left them standing in the maze of hallways in the basement of the Medical Examiner's building.

The smells were putrid. A mixture of odors so dense and complicated that it was hard to separate them — except to say that the brutal tinge of Lysol enveloped everything.

"You were right," she said, feeling slightly better about him.

He smiled, then added a few slices of baloney to the sandwich. "When you hire the Wirta Agency, you get all the Bs of police science: basic brilliance and boundless bullshit."

She cocked her head at him as if she didn't quite know what to make of that. So he added, "But I don't charge for the bullshit. It's an agency extra."

Twenty minutes later Danny returned and handed them a light Xerox still warm from the machine. "It faded. We outta toner," he said. "You not say Danny get, hokay?"

"Don't worry, we're leaving town in two hours. Now all I need to know is how do we get outta here? This is a maze down here." That brought Danny's worst sentence to date.

"Go light, den reft . . . den up stair to erevator."

"Why don't you go ahead and pay for lunch. You can just put it on your expense sheet," Susan suggested.

They were at Fisherman's Wharf sitting in Alioto's Fish House. The windows overlooked a picturesque little tuna fleet adorned with outriggers, high bows, and women's names. He counted four Marias, a few Magdalenas, and a Madonna (probably not the one in the leather concert bra). The food was great and the bill was reasonable. Jack peeled off some twenties thinking he hadn't been a private detective for that long but that he was pretty sure this wasn't the way it was supposed to work.

Before lunch they had gone over the crime scene and the ME's reports, and there was still no getting around the fact that the death of Roland Minton was very violent and damned strange. Sergeant Lester Cole's crime sheet was very specific — he had particularly noted that there was no *obvious* way anything or anybody could have gotten in or out of Roland's room. Cole had speculated that somehow someone must have hung outside the window thirty stories up, pried open the frame, which he noted would be a super-human feat, then had gained entrance to the hotel room. Sergeant Cole had no theory on how that could have been done or how the thick metal could have been bent.

The coroner's descriptions were unemotional but graphic: felonious homicide, extreme mutilation, blunt-force trauma, antimortem severance, multiple commuted fractures, decapitation, cutaneous subdural matter . . .

It went on like that, detailing shredded body parts and blood-splatter evidence. Jack read it but didn't comment, because Susan had become very quiet and seemed on the verge of tears. The coroner called the murder extreme homicidal mania. What it came down to was Roland Minton had been ripped apart while he was still alive.

The only other noteworthy thing was in the short paragraph listing stomach contents: a partially digested Big Mac approximately six hours old, Coca-Cola, minibar peanuts, and a note. According to the coroner, it had been swallowed seconds before Roland died but was still readable. Just one word:

OCTOPUS

Chapter Sixteen

The briefing was at 5:00 p.m. in the main conference room on the sixth floor of DARPA headquarters. The building was a nondescript, brick-faced affair located inside the Virginia Square Plaza in Arlington, Virginia.

In attendance were Deputy Director Vincent Valdez; his assistant, Paul Talbot, and his two assistant military attaches, Captain Norm Pettis, U.S.M.C., and Captain Stanley Greenberg, U.S.N. There were also two Acquisitions and Technology special assistants, an information special tech, a liaison officer, a defense science officer, and a captain from the Special Projects office. A naval lieutenant JG, Sally Watts, the youngest person in the room at only twenty-three, was also a top forensic computer specialist. Next to her was a program interrogation coordinator and a woman from the comptroller's office.

For such a large gathering the sixth-floor conference room was opened and they had put out coffee and donuts. A low murmur of voices filled the corridor, finally, two-star Air Force General William "Buzz" Turpin, director of DARPA, swept into the room and took his place at the head of the table.

Young at sixty-eight, Turpin's demeanor was hard and humorless. He began without preamble: "Did everybody get the oh-eight-hundred Re-Op?"

The room nodded. Re-Op stood for Report of Operations. This one was the detailed description of a breach of the secure computer at Gen-A-Tec.

The room was hushed. This was Turpin's meeting.

"Since the penetration at the New Fairview Hotel in San Francisco by our high-risk special response team at oh-five-hundred yesterday morning, and the subsequent collateralization of the computer hacker by our DU, we have, unfortunately, experienced further breakdowns," Buzz said softly. He always spoke in a very quiet voice — a trick he'd learned on the debate team at the Air Force Academy. Everybody in the room was leaning forward to catch every word.

"The DU recovered Roland Minton's computer. Minton attempted to erase his last e-mail after he sent it, but Lieutenant Watts managed to digitally reconstruct the message. We have copies for all of you."

Vincent Valdez stood and passed Roland's last e-mail around the table. Turpin paused while it was read. When all eyes were once again focused on him, he continued.

"This message was e-mailed to a portable

computer. We have the name of the owner but not his location."

Several ballpoint pens clicked and people began making notes.

"You'll note that the e-mail address is Strockmeister at earthlink-dot-net. That turns out to be somebody named Herman Strockmire Jr. I'm going to go over the pertinent facts in the e-mail, then you can address questions to your section leaders or to Mr. Valdez after the meeting.

"One: The dead hacker sent the fifty-page Chimera file to Herman Strockmire's computer. Location unknown. The only address we have is his office in D.C. He's not there. Apparently his secretary doesn't know where he is. More on that in a minute.

"Two: According to our cryptographer the encoded file is going to take around two days for Roland's 'bud' to decode, even with ten sun solar work stations. That means we have as little as two days to get it back before we end up in a public-relations disaster.

"Three: The forensic computer section under Lieutenant Watts is working up a list of companies in the Western U.S. that have ten sun solar work stations. It has to be a big lash-up. Once we have that list we cross check it against an employee named Zimmy. It's undoubtedly a nickname, so it could stand for anything from Zim to Zimmerman. And, Lieutenant, I need all of this yesterday."

Sally Watts nodded as she jotted notes furiously.

"Four: Herman Strockmire Jr. runs a legal firm called the Institute for Planetary Justice. To put it politely, he's a tree-and-bunny hugger who has sued just about every federal letter agency in the government. I'm evaluating the possibility of picking up his secretary and debriefing her, but these people are fanatics, and I'm not sure that's our most prudent course of action. Besides, if Strockmire's the delusional paranoid our profile makes him out to be, she may have been kept in the dark."

Buzz Turpin leaned back in his chair and paused for emphasis, then said, "Strockmire is in possession of devastating material that could create huge problems for us. Last week he was in L.A. suing a bunch of federal agencies and private labs over GMO food. He got Rule-Elevened in Judge Melissa King's court and fined a million dollars. I think a primary course of action might be to contact Judge King through a blind and see if she can lure him in again. Maybe, if she offers to cut his fine, he'll show up and we can grab him. We're running a logistics scan on that and one or two other potential operation plans. We'll have something in a few hours. As of now nobody seems to know where Strockmire is. We have to change that.

"Five: This person Susie who's mentioned

in the e-mail is undoubtedly Susan Strockmire, Herman's daughter. She is leverage, and I want her. Get a sniffer on her bank account and on Strockmire's. Five-hour updates."

Buzz Turpin cleared his throat and leaned forward. "Okay, people, one more thing — and this is important: I'm not looking to turn this into a major news story. One of the problems with this guy is that he has celebrity friends who are environmentalists and animal-rights fanatics. The last thing I need is for fucking Marlon Brando or Cher to jump on the *Today Show* and start screaming we murdered him. This means Strockmire needs to be neutralized but *not* necessarily collateralized — at least not yet. What we've got here is a big, sloshing bucket of shit, and I don't want to get any more of it on us than necessary. Any deviation from this op plan gets cleared by either Vincent, Paul Talbot, or me. Nobody moves on his own initiative. Are we all absolutely clear on this?"

Everyone in the room nodded.

"Okay. Get going. We're going to have twelve-hour debriefs in this room at oh-seven-hundred and fourteen-hundred hours. Everybody, except people assigned to location field ops, will be in attendance. No exceptions." General Buzz Turpin stood and exited the room with long strides and a face that looked like it had been hacked out of granite. Once he was gone Vincent Valdez turned to the room.

"Okay, organize into subgroups. Operations on the right side and Lo-Recon on the left."

Operations was headed by the two Marine and Navy captains. They were joined by the information officer, the defense weapons specialist, and the captain from the Special Projects office. Lo-Recon was Logistical Reconnaissance, and that was everybody else.

In his office at the end of the sixth-floor corridor, General Turpin slumped behind his desk and looked out through his large picture window at the mall parking lot. A light mist was falling. He glowered down at the slick pavement feeling a surge of impotent fury.

He had fought for DARPA, defended its projects on the Hill in front of the Armed Services Committee, fended off a liberal congress that questioned not only the military applications of their research, but even DARPA's very usefulness to the country's defense. He had artfully steered huge sums of money from Pentagon research accounts into DARPA's coffers. He found promising research at various aviation companies and science labs, then proceeded to funnel DARPA money into those private programs that he controlled. He hired leading scientists and formed think tanks to conceptualize the weapons of the future. The Stealth Bomber was the brainchild of a Northrop engineer, picked up by one of Turpin's science advisers. ₁The project, financed by DARPA, eventually produced a new generation of attack aircraft.

Now, the Chimera Project, his most innovative accomplishment, was in mortal jeopardy, and with it the entire agency. The concept and execution of the project was brilliant — a chance to create test-tube soldiers, better by far than their human counterparts, with abilities far superior to any grunt who ever wore the uniform or fought and died for his flag. Never again would General Turpin be forced to stand at a military funeral and engage the tearful eyes of a dead soldier's parent, wife, or child.

Buzz Turpin had found the ultimate solution to ground warfare. He was about to rewrite the book on military effectiveness. With these chimeras, never again would even one American GI be forced to go into battle or be sent home inside a flag-draped coffin.

But, because of Stockmire's silly lawsuit to protect a bunch of damn butterflies, this legal joke, this accident in a three-piece suit was threatening to destroy everything. The lawyer had compromised the security of the Gen-A-Tec computer system. With this security breach, General Turpin's crowning career achievement was in jeopardy of being exposed before he had his public-relations plan in order.

Turpin was well aware of how the liberal

media would portray this scientific adventure. They would see only the science-fiction horror movie aspects of the program: *"Genetic Monsters Created in Government Labs."*

They would attack the program as evil or perhaps even criminal. They would come after Turpin with a vengeance, forcing him to defend his program in a peacetime vacuum. From the beginning he had known that the only way to introduce disposable soldiers was in the field. If the Development Units had been ready during Kosovo he would have used them there. Then, after they had been victorious — after no American soldier had been lost on the ground — Turpin would reveal them to the world. Under that scenario he could verify their military superiority. He would have results to parade before the press, pictures of the DUs in action. He would be able to show their overpowering effectiveness, their courage and strength in battle.

But this — this discovery, these so-called dirty secrets stolen from a secure computer would make all his efforts appear nefarious, evil, and illegal.

Turpin sat in his office and studied the mist-wet tops of cars six stories below. He steepled his fingers under his chin and his mind went back to the snow-blown fields of North Korea — thousands of miles and fifty years behind him. He was nineteen, on the ground behind enemy lines, his jet shot down by ground fire. He wandered in desperation, cold and weak, until he finally hooked up with a forward-area communications battalion. It was the same day the Chinese under the command of General Chai Ung Jun attacked the DMZ, swarming down from the north under leaden skies filled with shrieking artillery.

He remembered the horde of screaming North Koreans, their heads and feet wrapped in rags for warmth, charging insanely while vicious artillery barrages exploded around him, the concussions rupturing his eardrums. He saw American GIs being blown to bits by incendiary grenades, some shredded above ground by Chinese Bouncing Bettys. He could smell brave American flesh burning, the odor choking him. Even now he could hear the GIs screaming, see their blood spurting from open wounds, splashing in ugly patterns on the frozen snow.

And then his mind bolted, and with a fast-beating heart and shortness of breath, he escaped this nightmare and was back in the safety of his office in the Virginia shopping mall. "He hasn't been there," he whispered, thinking of Herman Strockmire. "He hasn't heard the screaming. He doesn't know what he's trying to destroy."

Chapter Seventeen

The Jet Propulsion Laboratory was nestled in the foothills of Pasadena at the head of the Arroyo Canyon, near Devil's Gate Dam. The buildings were a mixture of styles, from Old California Mission architecture to a collection of two-story, no-frills additions that resembled giant air-conditioning units because of their boxy shapes and huge perpendicular louvered windows. The complex sat protected in the shade of a hundred oak trees, under the looming San Gabriel Mountains.

Herman thought Dr. Gino Zimbaldi was too lean, too intense, and, okay, too geeky. He stood in front of his tiny office in a white JPL lab coat, complete with plastic penholder. He was a "buzzword" specialist, and Herman had to constantly interrupt him to find out what the hell he was talking about. Example: "Sorry I kept you waiting, but the BDB working our APOGY program was bit-busting and came up with garden salad."

"Huh?" Herman said. Gino gave him a tight little grin before translating.

"The brain-dead bozo who wrote the program we're running on the satellite screwed up and wrote some bad code."

"Oh." Herman handed him a disk containing fifty pages of encryption. "Roland asked if you would decode this for him, Dr. Zimbaldi."

"Everybody calls me Zimmy," the nervous little man said, then smiled. "So how *is* that ol' placenta head?"

"Not very good," Herman said sadly. "He was murdered in San Francisco while he was retrieving this. I guess I should warn you — it may be dangerous for you to even work on it."

"Murdered?" Zimmy repeated. His expression caved in. His cheeks and eyes went hollow.

"It happened yesterday morning."

"How? How did he. . . ." Now blood drained. His face went as white as his lab coat.

"He was attacked in his hotel room and was sort of. . . ." *Shit,* Herman thought. He didn't want to tell him this, didn't want to scare him off. But he owed it to the doctor to at least give him the scope of the problem. "He was mutilated," Herman continued. "More or less shredded. The police up there don't know what could've done it. It was something with superhuman strength."

"*Shredded?*" The buzzwords were gone. Panic hovered. And then, while Herman watched, Dr. Zimbaldi visibly pulled himself back together. "Fucking unbelievable," he

194

wheezed, color slowly returning.

Then Zimmy surprised him. He squared his scrawny shoulders and said, "If Rollie died getting this, then we damn sure gotta find out what it means. I'll get rid of the NCG who's on the workstations right now and get going on it myself."

"The who?"

"New college grad. He's the one who snarled up the system by writing all those spaghetti codes." He flipped open the sheaf of paper, and began riffling through the fifty pages packed with encryptions. "It's a lot, but if I get lucky I'll have it done by to-morrow night."

"Here's my new number and a private e-mail address." Herman handed him one of his cheap Institute cards.

Zimmy shook Herman's hand. "You know what I always liked most about Roland?" he said unexpectedly.

Herman waited.

"Absolutely no phase-jitter, y'know? He was never afraid to throw it over the wall."

But that was Zimmy.

Chapter Eighteen

When Jack Wirta finally met Herman Strockmire Jr. he was disappointed.

After hearing Susan talk about her father he was expecting a cross between Clint Eastwood and Clarence Darrow. What he got was a short, squat man who looked like he was in his fourth week of chemo. The only encouraging thing was the pad he was living in. It was a beautiful guest house that fronted a French Provincial mansion, with an Olympic-size pool on one side, and the rolling blue Pacific on the other.

The pool house décor was modern — lots of beige leather and polished chrome furniture. Small, round glass-topped tables were sprinkled here and there like art-nouveau mushrooms. A billiard table with a red-felt playing surface dominated the main room, squatting amidst the chrome and glass like a carved oak mistake. There was also a state-of-the-art entertainment center that put most studios' screening rooms to shame. Susan had mentioned that Whoopi Goldberg and Steven Spielberg were Institute friends, and that this was Barbra Streisand and Jim Brolin's house — so, if it was true, it seemed

Herman Strockmire was in a high-celebrity orbit.

After the introductions they went out onto the back porch — or was it the front? Anyway, the one overlooking the ocean. They sat on Brown Jordan deck furniture watching the afternoon sun sparkle off the windblown surf. Jack took out the copy of the San Francisco ME's report and handed it to Susan's father, then watched his face while he read it. Herman didn't screw up his features or grimace like most civilians as he went through the gruesome passages detailing the mutilation of his friend.

When he got to the stomach contents and the note Jack could see a puzzled look cross Herman's face.

"You know what that could stand for?" Jack asked.

"Octopus," Herman said. Not a statement or a question, just a statement. Then he shook his head.

"It's probably some kinda acronym. The government loves acronyms," Jack theorized. "Operational Center to Protect the U.S. or something."

Herman leaned back and sipped on his Diet Coke. "What if it stands for exactly what it is?" he finally said. "Octopus: an eight-legged creature with tentacles."

"Why put that in code, Dad, if that's all it is?"

"Because it doesn't stand for a real octopus, but for something with the same properties: eight legs, tentacles, uses ink to camouflage itself — like a spy apparatus of some kind. Lemme get on my computer, maybe it's listed on one of my favorite conspiracy sites."

Jesus, Jack thought. *This guy has "favorite" conspiracy sites.*

"Those domains get lots of classified stuff. They have great antennae." Herman wandered into the house.

"Sounds like a great idea," Jack said to Strockmire's back as he left. Then Jack looked over and saw Susan glaring at him.

"Don't patronize him." There were sparks in her eyes.

Shit, Jack thought. *She's reading me. I used to be better than this.*

"Herman Strockmire Jr. is the most courageous, brave, dedicated person you will ever have the privilege of meeting." She was pissed.

"I'm already sensing that," he lied. "Really. I'm getting that loud and clear."

"And he is one of the few people you'll ever meet who has actually committed his life to making a difference. He's trying to stop the corruption of our national values."

"Right. Right. That's obvious to anybody who even looks at him." Jack was falling back, cursing his transparency.

He sensed that he was just seconds away from being fired. If he wanted to stay on the clock he needed to instantly find a way to make himself indispensable. He got up and went into the house before she could terminate him.

Once inside he saw Herman hunched over his portable computer. "Mr. Strockmire, I've got good federal contacts in L.A., and if this is a federal program, I think I can get a quick rundown on this Octopus thing for you. I have a buddy who's on the LAPD Anti-Terrorist task force. Guy's got top Pentagon and White House security clearance. Be no problem for him to punch it out for me. 'Course, it will mean you'll have to keep me on for at least another day. But I think it's probably a good investment, given what's happened."

Herman looked up at Jack and heaved a heavy, tired sigh. "I couldn't find anything about Octopus in here," he said.

"Whatta you think?" Jack prodded. "Should I stay on this one more day, see what I can turn up?"

Herman looked at Susan, who had just entered from the beach and was standing by the door frowning.

"If you have a good contact I guess we don't have much choice," Herman said. "Susan, write Mr. Wirta another check."

"Certainly, Dad." She turned to Jack. "I'll show you out."

She took Jack's arm and led him firmly through the guesthouse, out to the side of the pool.

Once there, she spun him around. It was surprising how strong she was. His back spasmed as she forced him to pivot.

"Stop trying to milk this," she said. "I'm trying to get him to go into the hospital. He's got a heart problem."

"Milk it? You kidding? You don't want me around, I'm gone. Just say the word."

They stood there glowering at each other. Actually Susan was the one glowering; Jack was just trying to look indignant. For some reason, his assortment of oft-used street expressions — so devastatingly effective on skid-row junkies — were useless with Susan Strockmire.

"One more day," she warned.

"In advance," he reminded her.

"One thousand dollars." She pulled out her checkbook and started writing him another rubber check.

"Uh — not to be troublesome, but how 'bout twelve hundred. Don't forget the two Benjies I advanced you."

"What a bargain," she growled as she ripped it off and thrust it at him. "Listen," she said as he put this check into his wallet, "this is important to him, okay? This is what his life is about and —"

"Don't rip him off. I know," Jack finished,

trying to end the conversation. His back felt more tender than pounded steak. He needed to get the hell away from here and take two more pills.

"If you take advantage, if you try and play him or con him, I swear I'll find a way to kick your ass." That unfriendly thought hung there until Jack turned and walked through the gate at the side of the house.

Chapter Nineteen

Once he was in the car, Jack called his friend Chick O'Brian at the LAPD Anti-Terrorist squad and asked him what he could find out about Octopus. "Will do," the big, bull-headed detective agreed. Jack gave him his new number and address, then rang off.

An hour later Jack parked in his office lot, locked his primered and patched Fairlane, then walked around the corner past the 4:00 p.m. fishing party. Ten guys sitting on the wall in front of the Hollywood Sports Connection casting their lines at the cruising whitefish.

"Hey!" a short blond man with a sculpted upper body and a mesh T yelled at him. "Don't I know you?"

"Don't think so," Jack said as he kept moving.

"Do you have a little Scandinavian in you?"

" 'Fraid not."

"Want one?"

It drew a laugh from the others.

Jack hurried on.

He climbed the staircase to the third floor because there was a new *Out of Order* sign on the elevator. Although he had taken two pills at the beach just an hour earlier, his back was again beginning to spasm.

He arrived at the third floor at the far end of the hall and froze. His office door was ajar. He knew he had locked it when he left. He reached around and unpacked his AMT Hardballer. It was a lightweight forty-five that had seven in the clip and a burnished 125-mm barrel. He slid it from his belt-mounted Yaqui slide holster, chambered it silently, and crept slowly down the hall toward his office. As he got closer he could see that the lock on his door had been shattered. Wood splinters decorated the yellow linoleum corridor.

He paused next to the door and listened . . . Someone inside was talking in a low voice:

"If you don't, I'll have to do it for you . . . that's no damn way to act," the voice whispered.

Jack took a deep breath, then kicked the door open. It slammed against the inside wall hard and he came in fast behind it. A man he had never seen before was sitting at his desk.

The guy yelled: "Yeeeeeekkkkk!", threw the telephone receiver over his head, and jumped to his feet. He was wearing iridescent plastic blue jeans and a silk pirate's shirt.

"Who the fuck are you?" Jack demanded, pushing the Hardballer into his face. Jack guessed he was about twenty, but his eyes were ageless.

"I'm Gary. Miro told me to sit in here and answer phones and shit," the boy shrieked.

Then Jack heard footsteps in the hall and Casimiro Roca came running — sliding actually — into the room. He had to grab the door frame to keep from falling. "What? What? What!" he squawked as he skidded to a stop in the threshold. He was wearing ballet slippers. "What is it? What's going on?" Miro demanded.

"Jesus, Miro, who the fuck is this?" Jack holstered his Hardballer and looked at these two guys who were dressed from the beach bonanza section of the *International Male* catalogue.

"When I came in about two this afternoon your little office had been broken into," Miro said. "I figured you'd want it, so I called a man to fix the lock, but he said the door hadda be replaced. So I asked Gary to sit in here to watch your stuff, 'cause those nasty people from the herbal place down the hall kept looking in. I thought they might steal what was left."

"That's really nice of you, Miro," Jack said, feeling bad that he'd pulled his gun. "Sorry I scared you." He looked at the narrow-shouldered, panicked boy in the iridescent jeans and billowing pirate shirt who, on second glance, looked more like an ice skater than a pirate.

"Jack Wirta, meet Jackson Mississippi," Miro intoned delicately.

"My God. My God," Jackson whined. "My heart is pitty-patting like a little bunny."

"I'm really sorry, guys . . . I'm having an off day." Then Jack sat in the guest chair and began looking around his office, taking inventory.

His clock radio was gone, along with his old desktop calculator. The calculator was a candidate for the Smithsonian anyway. His two police certificates were missing, along with his formal Academy graduation picture. He wondered why the picture was gone. "Not much of a heist," he muttered softly.

"Beg pardon?" Jackson Mississippi huffed, hands on his slender hips.

Miro glanced at Jackson. "It's okay, Honey, thanks. I'll take over now."

"I would say 'any time,' except I'm never coming in here again. Here's your only message." He handed Jack a slip of paper. "That lady from your bank called. I put her name and number down, but she said they close at five . . . so they're closed." He snapped this off savagely. Then he got up and flounced out of the office.

"I hope you didn't scare him back into the closet." Miro grinned, then sighed theatrically. "This neighborhood . . . there's a lot of drug use and break ins. Some of these boys have deep sexual anger and depression. They do all kinds of bad shit."

"Maybe it's only that, maybe it's something else."

"Something else?"

"Yeah. Look, thanks for keeping an eye on the place." Jack opened his bottom desk drawer and found a bottle of Blue Label scotch that, surprisingly, had not been lifted during the robbery. He pulled it out and showed it to Casimiro Roca. "Do you think a seasoned drug bandit would leave a good, fifty-year-old downer like this behind?"

Casimiro looked at the bottle and shrugged. Jack pulled two chipped jelly glasses out of the bottom drawer and set them on the desk, just like Sam Spade.

"Join me?"

"I never refuse a drink from a handsome, well-intentioned gentleman."

"Listen, Miro, if we're gonna be friends, we gotta get past the sexy repartee, okay? I'm not used to it from guys."

"I'll try, but in your case it's gonna be hard — no pun intended." He smiled and nodded at Jack, who poured him the drink and then handed it across the desk to him. They clinked glasses and sipped scotch, both thinking separate thoughts.

"Tell Jackson I'll pour him a shot if he needs something to calm his nerves."

Miro tossed off his drink like a Singapore sailor and went next door to fetch Jackson Mississippi and bring him to the party.

Chapter Twenty

When Chick O'Brian — the policeman's policeman and one-time LAPD heavyweight boxing
champ — entered Jack Wirta's office it was a
little past 6 p.m. He was surprised to find his
old bud with his shoes off, sitting behind the
desk, feet up, drinking scotch with two
nutsack chorus boys. Chick was massive and
kept things simple: guys were guys, girls were
pussy. Everything else was perverted. He had
shoulders like an American buffalo. His face
was pink and oily and he always looked like he
just finished running two miles — a condition
he blamed on acute dermatitis. Miro looked
up at the huge, glowering apparition in Jack's
doorway and set his jelly glass down quickly.
He knew homophobic intolerance when he
saw it.

"Well, it's been ever so . . ." he said, getting up from the chair where Jackson Mississippi was perched on the arm like a parlor
ornament. Then the two of them hit the
road, grinding their way out the door.

"Jesus," Chick said, watching them go.
"Whatta you doing hangin' with those two
sternwheelers?"

"In this neighborhood you have to adapt.

Come on over here, big guy, and give your little Jackie a sloppy, wet kiss."

Chick actually took a step backwards.

"That ain't funny. Don't even joke about that shit."

"You find out what I wanted?" Jack asked. "You coulda just called."

Chick moved over to the chair that Miro and Jackson had been using and looked at it cautiously, inspecting it for the AIDS virus. Then he sat down carefully, like an Episcopalian taking a dump in a public toilet.

"I ran what you wanted through my secure contact in D.C. He called back two hours ago and said Octopus is a black op computer lab."

"Really?"

"Yeah, he found only one mention of it, but it was in a secure Pentagon computer. This lab is located out at Pepperdine University, in room 212 of the Computer Science building, if you can believe that. It's being supervised by something called Echelon which my friend tells me is like a satellite spy network — real hush-hush."

"No kidding. That's what my client thought."

"Yeah. But that's all he could find on it. He said it was buried under a layer of UP codes. That's Ultimate Priority. It's supersecure. But here's where it gets interesting . . ."

"Good, 'cause so far that doesn't quite figure."

208

"An hour after my guy gives me this he calls back, and Jack, I never heard him in such a panic."

Chick squirmed slightly in the brown leather chair, screwing his ass in for better traction, then he leaned forward and said, "He tells me to forget everything he just told me. Says, whatever I do, don't tell a soul. He said his career is cooked if it gets back to anybody on his agency flow chart that he gave me this. Apparently he wasn't supposed to be able to access it, but because of his White House security number he leaked in. Big mistake! The systems administrator traced the breach to him. It's called a back-finger. Anyway, a team of federal hitters shows up in my friend's office twenty minutes later and they put him through a half hour of bullshit. He tells these two suits that he'd heard about Octopus, got curious, and was checking because he thought it might be part of one of his drug cases — that it was all just a dumb mistake. He doesn't think they bought it. They rattled him good, but he held up, didn't tell them he gave it to me, and I didn't tell him I was doing this for you. Whatever it is, Octopus is not supposed to see daylight."

After Chick finished Jack poured the big cop a scotch to calm him down. He slid it over, but Chick O'Brian just looked at the glass . . . stared at it as if Jack had just rolled a live grenade across the desk.

"What?" Jack asked, slightly perplexed. Then it hit him. It was Miro's glass and Chick was afraid it was crawling with herpes simplex 12, or dick fungus, or some other form of sexual leprosy. So Jack switched glasses, handing his to Chick and taking Miro's for himself. He began sipping, while Chick watched him with something between awe and disgust.

"You got guts, I'll say that."

"No, I'm just not a moron. You can't get a sexual disease from a glass."

"Your dick falls off, don't come crying to me."

"Right," Jack said. "You'd be my first stop if that happened."

They sat there for a long minute savoring their drinks.

"Computer lab, huh? Okay, look, is there any way to track this thing from another direction? Find out more about it?"

"Don't you listen? This guy freaked out on me, and he's no wuss. We did some doors together. He's solid, and he was scared pissless. I'm telling you Jack, don't mess with it. It's why I came over here in person to warn you. Whatever it is, leave this Octopus thing alone." Chick stood, put his empty glass back on the desk, then stopped and examined the shattered lock. "What happened here?"

"These guys around here all find me irresistible," Jack said, deadpan. "I'm thinking about not wearin' my Brute cologne anymore. Fucks 'em up."

"I'm worried about you, Wirta," the cop's cop said over his shoulder as he left.

"Me too," Jack said softly, wondering what the hell kind of nightmare Strockmire had stumbled into.

Chapter Twenty-One

Jack Wirta met Herman Strockmire in the paved lower parking lot off Seaver Drive at Pepperdine University.

It was strange, the way it happened. Jack arrived first, at 10:00 a.m., and waited. Twenty minutes later Herman pulled into the lot in a silver Mercedes SL500 with a license plate that read FUNY GRL.

Herman sat motionless in the car after he parked it, so Jack got out of his sagging Fairlane and waved.

No response.

He walked a bit closer and stared right through the windshield at the fat, unhealthy man sitting behind the wheel of Barbra Streisand's luxury Mercedes. He waved again.

Still nothing.

He thought maybe Herman was just gathering his thoughts in there.

When Herman didn't get out, Jack walked over and tapped on the window. Raccoon eyes turned to look at him, and only then did Herman Strockmire Jr. attempt to move. He grunted and strained as he dragged his huge bulk out of the car.

Finally, he heaved up, gulping mouthfuls of

morning air, grabbed his suit coat and shouldered into it, then slowly retrieved his briefcase.

"You okay?" Jack asked, concerned.

"Yep, tip-top. Piss and vinegar."

Herman certainly looked warm and yellow, but the vinegar was missing.

In the distance over Herman's shoulder was the Pendelton Computer Science Center, a large, multi-storied white stucco building with red tile patios, arched windows, and a dormered roof. Clustered around it were all the little Pendeltons: the Pendelton Learning Center, the Pendelton Foundation Building, Pendelton Hall. The Pendeltons had obviously dropped some big green on Pepperdine U.

The campus was spread across a rolling hillside, and they had to climb two levels of concrete steps to get from the parking lot up to the Computer Science Center. By the time they got halfway, Herman was leaking air like a buckshot dirigible, wheezing and gasping, holding onto the stair rail like somebody's ninety-year-old aunt.

Susan had been right. Jack was actually beginning to feel a little guilty. They should get this guy hooked up to an IV bag fast. Herman started up the last, steep flight of stairs.

"Don't you want to wait for your daughter?" Jack said, looking for any excuse to give the guy a little longer to rest.

"Susan isn't coming. She's at the Registrar's office at UCLA," he answered, turning to face the last flight. Jack thought the twenty-step climb would surely kill him.

He grabbed Herman's arm and stopped him. "How come? What's out at UCLA?"

"She's going to law school there."

"Wonderful," Jack said, thinking how much he hated lawyers.

"She's worked hard, took prelaw in night school. She went out there this morning to see if she could qualify for academic aid." Herman looked wistfully up the final flight of stairs like Sir Edmund Hillary at the last base camp on Everest. Then he grabbed the rail again and heaved himself up.

Jack moved along with him, trying to slow the pace. "Man, slow down. These stairs . . . I'm a little out of shape," Jack lied.

But Herman just lumbered along.

Room 212 was on the first floor, despite its two hundred number. They looked through the open door. It was a large computer lab. There were fifty or sixty work stations, but only ten or twelve of them were being used. College-aged boys and girls were dressed in baggy, saggy plumber jeans. As they peered into the computer room, a tall, rather good-looking blond man with a Vandyke beard and tweedy sport coat materialized behind them.

"Something we can do for you?" He used the pronoun "we" as if he took up more intellectual space than just one ordinary person. He was also one of those guys that Jack ran into occasionally who he hated on sight. His bullshit meter was instantly redlined.

Jack took a step back and studied the man while Herman reached into his wallet for his card. Jack intercepted the process before the card got into the man's possession.

"Uncle Charles," Jack said scolding. "I don't think the man wants to buy insurance." Then Jack looked at the blonde man and smiled. "My uncle has frontal-lobe dementia. He thinks he's still at Aetna." Jack looked at Herman to see if he was going to play along.

After a moment Herman smiled and said, "Sorry. Forgot."

Vandyke replied, "How can we help?"

"My kid sister, Paulette, is thinking of coming here next year," Jack said. "She's amazing with computers, and over at Administration they said we shouldn't leave without seeing the Pendelton Computer Science Center, so here we are."

"This is a closed lab." Then he actually reached past Jack and pulled the door shut. "I'm Dean Nichols, head of the computer center."

"Oh, just the man we should be talking to," Jack enthused.

"I'm afraid I can't talk right now. This is my class. Call my office for an appointment."

He re-opened the door and pushed past them into the room. Jack used the moment to again look inside and scope out the students furiously pounding keyboards and clicking mouses. Then he was looking at polished pine, as the door was slammed in his face.

"Frontal-lobe dementia?" Herman said, scowling.

"Listen, Herm, you don't go around passing out the little Institute cards. Don't forget what happened to Roland. Somewhere hiding in this cheese souffle is a madman with acute homicidal mania."

"Yeah . . . yeah. You're right. Thanks." He heaved a deep sigh. "I didn't think of that. What now?"

"We wait in the quad for class to be over. I spotted a few kids that looked worth talking to."

"You mean just then, while he was going in?" He seemed impressed.

"Yep. You've hired class-A help here."

A bell rang, doors opened, and it seemed as if two million teens wearing more or less identical outfits flowed into the plaza. All were carrying the same oversized, stuffed backpacks, the same CD headsets. They overran the Pendelton Center patio.

Jack caught a glimpse of one of the girls he had spotted in the lab: yellow CD player, backpack, plumber bib overalls, curly red hair, and thick glasses. Nerd.

Nerdy girls were good, because they don't get hit on too often, so they don't get pissy when you talk to them. Jack followed her and Herman caboosed along behind, wheezing and grunting.

"Excuse me," Jack called out. "Excuse me, Miss."

She looked back at him, a puzzled frown on her freckled face. "Huh?" She didn't remove her headset.

"Hi, I wonder if I could ask you a question?"

Nothing.

"My kid sister, Christine, wants to major in computer science at Pepperdine. She's a senior right now, over at Pali High. I was wondering if you could tell me if you're enjoying your courses here?"

"Huh?" She was proving to be a conversational treat.

"I was wondering if you get a lot of computer time in the labs, if the terminals were state of the art, that sort of thing . . . if you had good job opportunities upon graduation. Do companies come on campus and do job-placement interviews?"

"Oh."

"What I mean is, do you like it here?" Getting one simple sentence out of her was tough as animal dentistry.

"Huh?" She looked at him, then added,

"You mean do I like it here?"

We have ignition, Jack thought. "Yeah, that's what I was wondering."

"What's not to like?"

"Right," Jack said. "What's not to like? But could you be slightly more specific?"

"Well the labs are great . . ."

"Like the one you were just in?"

"Well, that's not so much a lab, really, it's — it's . . ." And she stopped and looked at him closer. "Do I, like, know you?"

"No." Jack wondered what was going through her fuzzy head besides Metallica music.

She finally said, "It's not a lab, it's paid work. We work like on a scholarship program. Some of us got recruited outta high school 'cause we scored high on computer aptitude, so Dean Nichols gave us these partial scholarships. He runs this special program at the lab three times a week. At least, I have it three times. I think there's also a Tuesday, Friday, and Sunday lab for some other kids."

"And you get paid," Jack smiled. "That's pretty cool."

"Half tuition and all our books."

"Really? And what do you have to do?"

"Like, we just monitor stuff. It's pretty complicated. You should ask Dean Nichols. It's supposed to be like a secret. We're not supposed to say. Gotta go. I hope your daughter comes here, it rocks." She turned and bebopped away, mixing with the others until he lost sight of her.

It took them as long going down the two flights as it had going up, Herman grabbing the rail and slowly lowering himself step by step. Jack had seen piano movers make better time. Herman finally folded himself into the silver Mercedes, dropping his ass in first, then backing in like the last clown in the Volkswagen. Jack got in beside him on the passenger's side.

"What do you think?" Herman wheezed softly, still out of breath from the walk.

"You heard her. She's, like, on a scholarship. She works in a lab, like, monitoring stuff."

"She said it was secret," Herman wheezed.

"Vandyke's an academic. These guys guard their research. He's probably writing a book." Jack was studying Herman, thinking the man really did need to get his ticker fixed, and he was just about to suggest that when the over-weight man turned and looked him right in the eye. Jack saw something in that raccoon glare that almost scared him — a latent intensity that didn't square up with his broken-down condition and schlubby build.

"I want you to follow Dean Nichols," Herman said. "See where he goes, who he talks to."

"You mean a stakeout? Goody, those are neato." Jack was trying to make it sound as stupid as he thought it was. He didn't want to run a stakeout on a tweedy asshole like Dean Nichols. "Look, Herman, I really don't think there's much here. That's my trained, law-enforcement opinion. Furthermore, I think you need to address your medical problems."

"But you said there was a homicidal maniac here."

"I didn't say that. I said don't hand your card around like you're Mike Ovitz until we know what we're dealing with. In police work you have to rate your possibilities — you have to figure where your best opportunities are. I'm telling you, in my professional opinion, this is a dead end."

"But it's a secret lab," Herman challenged.

"Yeah, and my guess is that the Pentagon and DARPA aren't using teenagers to work top-security programs with sexy names like Octopus. We went off the track somewhere. I think we need to back up because we missed something."

"I want you to follow Dean Nichols. I have a hunch."

"That's not a hunch, that's a chemical reaction. I had it too. He's an arrogant shit with oh-so-slick hair, but that doesn't make him a government spook."

"I think it's worth pursuing. Since I'm paying you a thousand a day, you should do what I say. If that doesn't work for you, I'll get someone else."

Jack got out of the car. "I'll call you if I get anything."

Herman nodded and drove away.

"Bitchin'. A stakeout," Jack said to himself. "And he's *payin'* me."

Of course, Jack didn't know that both checks had already bounced, and by the time he found out, it would already be too late.

Chapter Twenty-Two

After Herman left, Jack tried to call Wells Fargo, but his cell battery was fried. So he walked to the Administration building and used their pay phone. After laboring through the bank's computerized help menu, a recorded voice informed him that Mrs. Donovan wasn't available — please leave a message. He left his name, then picked up a two-hundred-page academic catalogue, sat in the air-conditioned waiting room, and looked up Dr. Nichols, dean of the Pepperdine Computer Science School, who was listed as a "distinguished professor." A string of letters hung off the end of his name like knots in a kite's tail: A.B.M.A., M.A., Ph.D.

Jack already knew he was distinguished, because he'd seen the neatly trimmed Vandyke. But it was his pedigree paragraph that caught Jack's interest. Dr. Paul Nichols had done his graduate work at Georgetown University in Washington, D.C., right down the road from CIA headquarters in Langley, Virginia. It wasn't exactly a big "wow," but further complicating the dean's curriculum vitae was his doctorate degree. His Ph.D. was in political science, not computer science — which begged the question: What was he doing running the computer science school at Pepperdine?

He read on. Dr. Paul Nichols had been a dean since 2001 — a short-timer. Strangely, he also coached women's volleyball. An interesting sideline. But then, everybody loves tall, muscular girls in sports bras.

He found a listing for the campus police office and used the guest phone to make a call, pretending to be one of the names he picked at random off the faculty listing page.

"Hello, University Police Department," a man's voice answered.

"This is Dean Harry Gransky, Communications and Journalism," Jack said, pinching his nose for acoustical effect. "That damn Dean Nichols is in my parking space again. I can't park anywhere, 'cause the lot's full."

"Are you sure it was Dean Nichols's car?" the man asked.

"Think I don't know his damn car by now? This is the fifth time he's done it. The brown Chevy Nova with the purple antenna feather?" Just fucking around a little, trying to shake a case of boredom.

"Just a minute." And he was on hold, listening to a strange rendition of "Eleanor Rigby" done on the bagpipes.

The man came back. "I just punched out Dean Nichols's parking pass. He's not driving a brown Nova. He drives a blue Chevelle."

A *Chevelle?* Jack thought. *Who, except postal*

223

inspectors, drive Chevelles? "Are you sure? Gimme his plate number."

"EWU 357," the man said. "Listen, Dean Gransky, maybe just for today you could find an empty spot in the Baxter Drive lot."

"I'll try, but this always makes me late for class."

Jack hung up and walked back across campus to his Ford Fairlane, vehicle of champions. He backed out and drove around looking for Dean Nichols's blue Chevelle. He found it in a freshly paved upper lot off Tower Road. Jack waited until a woman in a red Volkswagen nearby pulled out, then he stole her space, turned off his engine, and adjusted his side mirror so he could watch the dean's old Chevelle drip axle grease on the fresh, new pavement. He spent the afternoon watching his minute hand make three painfully slow laps around the dial, gobbled some Percs, washed them down with bottled water, then belched loudly. Whatta life.

At 4:30 Dean Paul Nichols wandered out to his Chevelle, unlocked the trunk, and put his briefcase and stack of papers inside. No volleyballs.

Damn. Jack had been looking forward to volleyball practice.

Dean Nichols got behind the wheel and tooled the little blue Chevelle out of the parking lot. Jack backed up and followed.

The next few stops were studies in

adrenalized exhilaration. Paul Nichols went to the supermarket, pulled into the lot, then added to the day's excitement by committing a parking lot felony and stealing a handicapped stall.

Jack wished he'd never heard of Herman Strockmire Jr. or the Institute for Planetary Justice. Susan was still on his wait-and-see list.

He sat in his car, yawning occasionally, until Dr. Nichols finally pushed his shopping cart out of the market and loaded his groceries in the trunk.

Then it was off to the laundry and a heart-pounding trip to the drugstore. Breathtaking. This stakeout was definitely going in the book.

Next, Paul headed up the Coast Highway, turned right, and snaked over Malibu Canyon road to the Ventura Freeway, drove east toward Studio City, got off on Coldwater, drove back over the hill, and finally dropped down into Boy's Town. Then Paul veered right and drove toward Beverly Hills.

Jack wondered where the hell Paul Nichols was going. And then he found out.

He was going home.

The house was amazing. It was in the middle of the block on the very expensive part of North Canon Drive. Jack parked a couple hundred yards down the street. The houses were huge, and the one Paul Nichols turned his blue Chevelle into was among the biggest. It had a kind of nouveau-Ali-Baba motif. The architects in L.A. were doing way too much coke in the '80s.

Jack watched as Paul Nichols took out his house keys, unlocked the massive oak front door, then made three trips back and forth, carrying the contents of his trunk into the house and disappeared inside.

Jack flipped on his cell phone to see if it might have regenerated after a few hours of inactivity. He was in luck and getting a little power residue. He disconnected the battery and rubbed it vigorously on his pants, feeling it warm with the friction. He hoped he'd added to the charge as he put it back in, turned on the phone, dialed Wells Fargo Bank, and navigated the computerized customer-service system again.

It was almost five and he had a sinking feeling there was trouble with one of Susan's checks.

"Yes, this is Mrs. Donovan," a brittle voice said.

"Jack Wirta, returning your call," talking fast, trying to beat a battery flameout.

"Mr. Wirta . . . good. Yesterday you deposited two checks totaling twenty-two fifty-one, twenty-five, both of which have . . ." and the phone went dead.

"Which? What!?" he shouted into the dead receiver, but she was gone. The phone was beeping and the display flashed LOW BAT. He had to restrain himself from throwing the damn thing at the dash — but he knew there was only one way her sentence probably ended — with the words "insufficient funds."

The Strockmires had stiffed him.

First he had to find a pay phone to finish the conversation with Mrs. Donovan, then he was going to head out to the beach house and start collecting wallets and watches. Just as these ignoble thoughts overtook him the front door to the house opened again and Paul Nichols came out.

He'd changed. No longer a tweedy academic, he was now decked out in cat-burglar black.

As Jack watched, he backed the blue Chevelle out of the drive and headed toward Sunset.

Decision time.

Why should I continue to tail this guy? I'm not being paid, but my instinct says go for it. But why? Why should I stay on the job when both checks undoubtedly have bounced?

Let's cut to the bottom line then. What do you really want, Jack?

I guess what I really want is to get laid.

There it was: as cheap and transparent as a political promise.

At its heart, the most appealing thing about this case was its beautiful check-bouncer, Susan Strockmire.

He put the Fairlane in gear and rolled out after Paul Nichols. Paul took Sunset west to the 405 Freeway, drove south to the Santa

Monica Freeway, headed out to the Coast Highway, then took the PCH north to Malibu. Just after sunset he arrived back at Malibu Beach and parked half a block down from Barbra Streisand's house.

Then Professor Doofus actually took out a pair of binoculars and started scoping the front of Barbra's, looking a lot like Kurt Jurgens in *The Enemy Below.*

Jack parked a block up the street and tried to figure out what to do. The guy he was staking out was staking out the guy who hired him to stake out the guy he was staking out. A perfect circle.

Jack got out of the Fairlane and dashed across the street to the large mansion next door. He paused, recited the Big Dog Prayer, then jumped the gate, trotted down the side-walk between two huge houses to the beach, and trudged up the sand until he stood opposite the guest house. He looked through the window and saw Herman and Susan working at a table in the main room. He walked through the low gate, crossed the patio, and knocked on the glass door.

Susan saw him and opened the slider, looking at him skeptically before asking: "Why didn't you just ring the buzzer and use the front door?"

"Since you're such a stickler for protocol, why don't you cover your damned checks?"

"Huh?"

"You heard me, both of the checks you wrote yesterday came straight from Goodyear rubber."

"Dad, did you remember to make the deposit on . . ."

"Cut the b.s., lady. I'm at least ten percent smarter than I look." He pushed past her, entering the house.

Herman was on his feet, but with one hand still on the game table for support. "Aren't you supposed to be following Professor Nichols?"

"I am following him. I'm on my break."

"I don't see how you can be here and following him at the same time," Herman wondered aloud.

"It's complicated, but I'm gifted." Jack walked over, picked an apple out of a fruit bowl, then took a big bite. He needed to get some nourishment into his system, some natural sugar, because his brain was stalling out on him.

"How can you be following him and be here at the same time?" Susan demanded.

"Because he's parked on the street outside scoping out this house with binoculars. I followed him over here. My cell battery is fried, so I couldn't call and announce myself — which, let me hasten to add, is my normal business practice." Pissy now, dripping sarcasm. "But, before we go any further, I must warn you that the Wirta Agency Business Affairs

Office is instructing me to withhold further service until the matter of your two NSF checks can be dealt with. Failing that, my Legal Affairs Department is suggesting court remedies."

"Mr. Wirta, I'm sorry, but at this particular moment we don't have the money to pay you," Herman said. "I thought I would have it when we hired you, but conditions have changed, due to a courtroom setback. A very steep fine. I may still be able to get your money, but right now we are a little strapped."

"I see." Jack thought, *It shouldn't be this hard for a P.I. to make a living. Maybe I should open a dating and escort service. Take Miro's overflow. Call it Deflections.*

"Please, Jack," Susan said earnestly. "We really need your help. Dad told me about the secret lab — those kids are working for the government. I changed my mind. If Professor Nichols came out here that means something is definitely wrong. You've got to help us."

Jack could feel himself falling for it but he said, "I'm gonna need more than that."

"Here." She took off some rings and her watch.

"Honey, that's your graduation watch," Herman said sadly.

Jack thought, *This can't be happening.* "I don't take used jewelry," he said, retreating deeper into the guest house.

"Will you help us? Please? We'll figure something out about the money," Susan said.

"Do you have a cell phone?"

She nodded and handed him one. "But I don't think it's worth much."

"No — not for payment. For communication. Look, I'm gonna go back outside. Herm, I need you to go with me. We'll be back in about an hour. Take your cell phone, get in Barbra's car and pull out."

"Why?" he asked.

"I want you to lead Paul Nichols up into the hills. There's a road off Malibu Canyon I know about. We did a crystal drug bust up there when I was a cop. Buncha bikers. It's nice and empty. There's a clearing with a baseball diamond. I'll give you directions, talk you in using the cell. You drive up there. Paul follows you, I follow Paul."

"What am I supposed to do?" Susan said.

"Call downtown and get us a parade permit."

"Funny," she snapped.

"What's your plan?" Herm persisted.

"Once we get him up there I'm gonna pull his scrawny ass out of that blue Chevelle and beat some answers outta him. Like Susan said, something is definitely wrong here."

231

Chapter Twenty-Three

Jack slid back into his Fairlane, then used Susan's phone to call Herman inside the house. "Okay, I'm set. He's still parked out here. Get in the Mercedes and head up to Malibu Canyon Road."

"Okay," Herman replied. "But Susan just decided she wants to go."

"You tell Susan if I see her in that car I'm turning around and going home."

He heard a muffled conversation as Herman and Susan argued about it, then Susan was in his ear, buzzing like an angry hornet: "I'm not going to be left behind like somebody's little sister."

"I know you have an extensive background in law enforcement, Ms. Strockmire, but let me stress this, and I'll say it slowly, so even you can understand . . ."

Why was he being such an asshole? Was it because he couldn't control her? Was this why he had had such a string of uninspiring relationships?

"Ms. Strockmire," he continued with exaggerated politeness. "It is always a bad idea to have all your assets stacked up in one place. You're rear guard — a position usually assigned to the most dangerous motherfucker in the outfit, which, without a doubt, is you."

"Now you're really going over the top."

"Do I have your word on this? Otherwise, I'm going home."

"Dad's coming out," she hissed. "But Wirta . . . if anything happens to him, I'm coming after you."

"Your challenge. So, I get to pick time and choice of weapons. How 'bout midnight, with thongs and nipple clips."

"What an asshole!" she said, but he heard her laugh as she hung up.

Ten minutes later Herman lumbered out, climbed into the silver Mercedes, and backed out of the driveway. Jack watched in amazement as Paul Nichols actually turned on his headlights, hung a U-turn and followed.

Jack dialed Herman's cell phone. When he picked up: "Herm, he's behind you."

"How could I miss him?" Herman wheezed sarcastically. "He's got his high beams on."

"Okay, listen: Take Malibu Canyon Road up about two miles. Just before the tunnel there's a dirt road on the left with a wooden gate. It's always unlocked. You don't have to get out, you can butt it with your bumper and it'll swing open. Drive up the road and take the first fork. You getting this?"

"Yeah, take the first fork. Then what?"

"Keep going until you get to a meadow. It's up on top of the hill. There's a sports field up there. A little baseball diamond, a track, some volleyball nets. Pull across and park by the dugout, then wait."

"Okay."

Jack hung up and dialed Shane Scully, his ex-partner.

"Hello," the dark-haired cop answered.

"Shane, it's me."

"Me? Would that be L.A.'s newest gumshoe? How's the office? You set up yet?"

"We've already had our first robbery, our first client, and I'm on our first stakeout . . . just like Magnum, only without the Ferrari."

"Whatta you need?" Shane asked.

"Can you find out who owns the residence at 2352 North Canon Drive in Beverly Hills? A guy named Paul Nichols lives there, but I want to know if he owns the place, is a guest, or what?"

"Any reason to think he doesn't own it?"

"It's big, maybe worth four or five mil, but Paul drives a cheesebox with wheels so I have my doubts. Run the address through county records for me. There's a cold beer in it for you."

"Done."

Herman turned left off Malibu Canyon Road and followed a small dirt drive to the wood fence. He nudged the gate open with his bumper as Jack had instructed. It swung wide. He saw the blue Chevelle pulling in behind him.

Herman was feeling very alive. His heart rate was steady, and when he checked his pulse it was up around 92 — not arrhythmia — excitement. It made him feel more energized than he had in weeks. But he was glad he had Jack Wirta back there for protection.

The baseball diamond came up on the right. He pulled across the outfield, then parked near the batting cage and turned off the headlights. In his rearview mirror he watched the blue Chevelle pull up onto the field and stop thirty or forty yards behind him with the headlights off. His cell phone rang again and he picked it up. "Yeah?"

"He up there?" Wirta asked.

"Yep. Parked in the outfield."

"Okay. Get out and walk slowly toward him."

"Do what?"

"Don't worry, I just need you for a diversion. I'm twenty yards down the road. I'm gonna move in on foot. I'll take him before you get to him."

"Okay."

Herman hoped his heart didn't spin out on him. He took his pulse again: 98 — still in the high-normal range. He got out of the car and began to walk slowly toward the blue Chevelle. It was strange how exhilarated he felt. He was actually enjoying this.

When he was about fifty feet from the car, he heard somebody yell: "Hey! Hey, whatta you doing? Stop it!" And he knew Jack had made his move.

Herman lumbered up as fast as he could without running, and when he arrived at the Chevelle he found that Jack Wirta had Professor Nichols face down on the ground, handcuffing him.

"You'd better unhook these if you know what's good for you," Nichols demanded.

"If I knew what was good for me I wouldn't be driving a Fairlane and working these hours. Why don't you tell me why you're following Herman Strockmire?" Jack pulled him into a sitting position.

"None of your fucking business!" Nichols's forehead was wet and he had a little damp grass stuck to his bullshit Vandyke.

Then all hell broke loose.

It started with a whispering sound that brought a wind with it, bending the long grass around the baseball diamond. Herman looked up and saw a huge helicopter, unlike anything he'd ever seen before. It had a sort of stealth configuration and was extremely quiet as it hovered over them. He glimpsed the underbelly and part of the nose for only a second before a huge xenon light snapped on, blinding him.

"Stand where you are! Put your hands in the air!" a bullhorn blared down at them.

In that split second before the light went on Herman saw what he thought were noise-cloaking panels on the belly. These "whisper panels" had been described to him when he'd filed a class action against the government on behalf of Tom Lawson and Gil Grant, two Marines who had gotten horribly sick from something they'd contracted at Area 51, the supersecret government airbase at Groom Lake, Nevada. It was Tom and Gil who had originally gotten him interested in Area 51. He had hoped his lawsuit would force the government to reveal what testing was really going on out there.

The helicopter hovered, blowing sand and dirt as it whispered silently above the field. Suddenly, men appeared on the ground all around them. They had either jumped from the low hovering helicopter or had been up here already waiting. They converged from all sides. Herman felt hands grabbing him as ten or twelve soldiers swarmed them. They were all dressed in camouflage jumpsuits with a strange, red Delta insignia sewn over the uniform's left breast pocket.

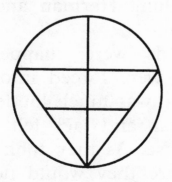

I was right! Herman thought, recognizing

the Dulce Base insignia that had been drawn for him once by Tom Lawson.

Herman and Jack were quickly frisked. Jack's AMT Hardballer was yanked out of his holster. They were both cuffed while Paul Nichols was uncuffed, then they were hustled to a spot at the side of the field as the strangely-shaped black helicopter landed, throwing dirt and stones everywhere, stinging their skin and eyes.

Ten commandos dragged Herman and Jack toward the helicopter, but Paul Nichols yelled something at the soliders who had a hold of Jack.

"Huh?" one of the commandos yelled back, over the windstorm coming from the idling futuristic chopper.

"Turn him around," Nichols demanded, pointing at Jack. They did as he instructed, then Paul stepped up and fired a right cross.

Jack's lip split and blood flowed. "That all you got?" Jack yelled at Nichols.

The commandos yanked Jack around, then continued pushing Herman and Jack toward the helicopter.

Canvas hoods were snapped over their heads as they were forced into the chopper. The roar inside was much louder than on the outside. Herman and Jack felt the helicopter shudder and rise. As they took off they were both pretty sure they would never be heard from again.

Chapter Twenty-four

While he breathed his own hot breath inside the blackout hood Herman felt the annoying tickle in his throat. He felt sluggish and without energy and knew his heart had gone into another arrhythmia.

As he and Jack Wirta were whisked away into the night, Herman cursed his heart. He was almost certain the strange, futuristic helicopter taking them to God-knows-where was one of the new Aurora Hyper-aircraft that Tom and Gil had told him about.

An hour later the helicopter began to slow. Herman felt the vibration increasing as the pilot added power and pulled up on the collective, making the chopper hover.

"Dreamland Control, this is Psych Twenty-seven. We are downrange and entering the box," the pilot reported.

Herman knew all about Dreamland.

It was the secret testing site at Groom Lake, Nevada. He also knew that "Psych" was the call sign for all experimental aircraft being tested at both Groom Lake and Papoose Lake, which was located ten miles to the north. It was hard for Herman to believe, but it now seemed that he and Jack were actually being taken to The Ranch, the nickname given to the ultrasecret test facility encompassing the two five-mile-long runways on the two dry lakebeds.

If that was true, they were about to land at the secret facility known as Area 51. Only people with top Pentagon security could work there.

Herman had spent two months out there in the late eighties, staying in a motel named the Little A-Lee-Inn. He had been taking sworn statements from government radiologists and toxic waste people at Area 51. He'd been refused entry to the base and was forced to take his depositions off-site. His sinuses were always plugged while there, because he was allergic to something that seemed to be perpetually blooming in the central Nevada desert. It was the only place he'd ever had sinus trouble.

Once, when he was still working the case full-time, he'd taken a rented, four-wheel-drive Jeep up to Bald Mountain, the highest peak in the Groom Mountain range. He'd squatted in the old, deserted silver mine with his tripod and long-lens camera pointed at the secret base almost four miles away. All the while he was afraid that he was being observed by the telescopes mounted on the top of the east-end Area 51 support buildings. Those roof scopes were always pointed toward the mountains, surveying the growing crowds of conspiracy addicts who were convinced that alien research was taking place on The Ranch. In the nineties the government had finally taken over the Groom Mountains, making them a part of Area 51. He'd heard stories about the CDF troops that sometimes raided these hills to keep snoopers out. Luckily, he'd gotten his photos before that had happened, snapping almost twenty rolls.

He blew them up and showed them to Tom Lawson and Gil Grant, who, at the time, were sick and dying from some strange toxic waste or radio-electric illness. They claimed they had gotten sick from working in S-4, a secure area with test beds for the antigravity propulsion systems. These systems were later called pulse-detonation wave engines, or hydrogen-powered scramjets. When Herman had shown Gil and Tom the pictures he intended to use in court the two men identified much of what he had caught on film.

They pointed out a restricted block of military airspace located in the center of Groom Lake. It was marked on all military and civilian air charts, as R-4808-E, but it was known as "The Box." The two men explained that a military Code 61 restricted all flights over The Box, from the ground to deep space. Even most military pilots stationed at Area 51 were forbidden to overfly this zone. At the center of this flight-restricted area was a small, insignificant building that looked to be only one story high, but according to Gil and Tom had six levels underground. This huge, subterranean facility housed the legendary Level Four, known as Nightmare Hall, where bizarre genetic experiments were supposedly taking place.

Nightmare Hall was officially labeled the Secure Dulce Biogenetics Lab. Tom said that he had worked there in the late eighties and had seen grotesque, bat-like creatures that were seven feet tall. He described lizard-like humans, gargoyles with scaly skin that he called drago-reptoids.

To be honest, Herman hadn't believed much of it because Gil and Tom were both very sick and toward the end had been hallucinating. Back then it was hard to believe that any of this was really going on. But Herman knew without a doubt that both men had contracted their strange illnesses at Area 51 — sicknesses that none of their civilian doctors had ever seen before.

Herman attempted to compel the Air Force to identify the project the men had been working on so a cure might be devised. His secondary goal was the total exposure of the illegal science he suspected was taking place out there. He'd failed to even get his case to trial.

Through it all Herman learned that published reports of scientific discoveries often lagged many generations behind what was really going on, especially if the experiments were supersecret "black projects." As more and more reports surfaced on gene splicing and hybrid animal experimentation, along with the spectacular arrival of Dolly, the cloned sheep, Herman began to suspect that unimaginable horrors might really be lurking in Nightmare Hall.

Tom and Gil died of their illnesses in 1997, but Herman, working pro bono, was still trying to get a lawsuit for damages into court on behalf of their children. In the process he'd seen more redacted material than was in the Warren Report. Ultimately, the government did what it always did — claimed national security and withheld all of his subpoenaed information.

Since the men's deaths Herman often studied his blowups of Area 51 — particularly the secure Dulce buildings that were circled in ballpoint. He pondered Tom and Gil's stories about the "igloos" — dirt-covered hangars that hid the Psych Experimental Aircraft from the Russian satellites that passed overhead twice a day. He wondered about their tales of the antigravity flying machines that were supposedly reverse-engineered from a flying saucer that had crashed on the Foster Ranch in New Mexico in July 1947. He looked at his photos longingly, like a father studying shots of his dead children. His sense of loss was profound, the dream of what his lawsuit might have discovered running wild.

In the end it was hard to know what to think, hard to believe that such grotesque experiments were taking place under our own government's supervision.

Or was it?

One fact was certainly clear and rose above all others. Whatever was happening at Area 51, the U.S. government was determined to keep it a secret from its citizens. That fact alone fueled his suspicions.

Herman was jolted back to the present when the helicopter touched down. The whining engine finally silenced and he heard people talking softly outside. He became aware of Jack Wirta breathing next to him. The smell of fear was sharp inside his hood. His eyes stared into the black cloth as he imagined everything but saw nothing.

Suddenly, strong hands pulled Herman out of the helicopter and he was led to a vehicle. A door was opened and he was pushed roughly inside.

"Where am I?" he said, to find out if they would respond.

"Shut up," a voice growled. Then two doors were slammed and the car accelerated. Then he heard someone say "Dulce Lab."

The car stopped and he was taken out of the back seat and led across poured concrete. He felt no seams or irregularities in the pavement as he walked, deciding it might be some sort of runway. An electronic beep sounded. A door hissed open. He was led inside.

Cool air-conditioning. Even at night, this building was temperature-controlled. Another airlock hissed, then he was in an elevator descending fast, his stomach pressed up against his diaphragm as they went down. Soon the elevator door opened and there was another long walk down an airconditioned corridor. Two security locks chirped. He was pushed into a chair and finally the hood was snapped off. Herman blinked his eyes in the harsh neon light.

He was looking at a man with a shaved head and thick glasses wearing a white lab coat with a stethoscope around his neck. The lab coat had an insignia on it similar to the one the Rangers wore, but slightly more complicated:

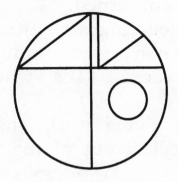

Tom and Gil had drawn a bunch of different insignias for him, but never one that looked like this.

"Take off your clothes."

"I beg your pardon?"

"We're giving you a physical exam."

"The hell you are!"

"Mr. Strockmire, you are going to have an examination whether we give it to you in your present state or do it under anesthesia."

"You kidnapped me."

"I wouldn't know about that. I only have your name, medical records, and instructions to verify your health. That's it. You want to know more, ask the colonel. But either you take your clothes off or I'll get someone in here from CDF."

Herman knew from his now-deceased clients that CDF stood for Central Defense Forces. The secret police for Area 51. He began to unbutton his shirt, then took off his pants. The doctor went over him quickly: blood pressure — high, lungs — clear, heart . . .

"What's wrong with your heart?" the doctor asked, concerned.

"I have a recurring arrhythmia. It started up again when they kidnapped me," Herman answered. "It's why my blood pressure is —"

"That's not gonna work. Just a minute." The doctor walked out of the room, leaving Herman alone.

The examination area had security cameras pointing down from two corners. He could smell the air coming through the vents. It had some kind of pleasant odor, faint, sweet, and medicinal.

After a minute the doctor returned with two CDF men wearing camouflage. "Lie down. Take off your underwear and spread your legs."

"Ain't gonna happen," Herman said.

"I'll give it to him," the doctor ordered. Immediately the two CDF commandos jumped Herman and held him while the doctor gave him a shot. In seconds he was asleep.

Herman didn't often dream, or at least he didn't remember much if he did. But now he dreamed a strange, terrifying tale. The nightmare was populated with half-reptile, half-human monsters and large bat-like creatures.

He also dreamed of Gino Zimbaldi — relived his trip to JPL, talked with Zimmy about the Ten-Eyck Chimera file, explaining Roland's death and his desperate need to get the fifty pages decoded. As he was talking to Zimmy the huge monster bats hovered over him.

Herman woke up.

He was back inside Barbra's car with a terrible headache.

He squinted out the window at the little baseball diamond. The sun was already up. He looked at his digital watch. The battery was dead. *Strange,* he thought. *The watch is only six months old.* His groin was killing him so he unbuttoned his pants and looked down at his abdomen.

He had a bandage there. Herman slowly peeled it off. Underneath were four sutures closing a tiny incision.

They'd done some kind of operation on him!

Shaken, he opened the car door and stumbled out, leaning against the silver Mercedes, fumbling with his pants while he tried to remember what had happened. The dreamlike nightmare was receding quickly, but he tried hard to recall it so it would stay in his conscious. Everything up to when the doctor gave him the shot was clear. After that only the hateful dream. When he got to the part about Zimmy it seemed less like a dream and more like a memory.

Herman took his pulse.

His heart was normal, beating a steady seventy-eight beats per minute. He'd had the arrhythmia when he went to the base and now it was gone. From everything he'd learned from his doctors, once an arrhythmia started it had to be converted in order to reverse the condition. But this one had gone away on its own. Herm wondered how that could be.

He was pretty sure he had been on the fourth level of Dreamland, somewhere near Nightmare Hall. Gil and Tom had said that the experimentation unit was on the same level as the medical facility. Of course, he had no physical evidence, and he couldn't prove any of it. Except for one thing.

His sinuses.

Whatever was blooming in the central Nevada desert always got him. Every time he was there his sinuses ended up packed tighter than a Midas muffler, and right now they were completely plugged.

Herman pushed away from the Mercedes and walked across the baseball diamond looking for Jack Wirta's Fairlane. He found it parked a short distance down the dirt road. Wirta was sleeping in the back seat.

Herman reached in and shook his shoulder. "Jack . . . hey, Jack. Wake up!"

The P.I. opened his eyes and looked up at Herman. "Shit," he said and sat up. "What happened? Where am I? What time is it?"

"I'm not sure what happened. We're back at that little baseball diamond in the Malibu Mountains. My watch is fried, so I don't know what time it is."

Jack looked at his watch. "Mine's dead, too." He shook his head. "One minute I'm pissing in a cup and getting a shot, next thing I'm back here and I got some fucked-up dreams."

"I think I know — at least, I have an idea. But we gotta make sure Susan's okay first."

"Susan?"

"If they took us, I'm worried they mighta snatched her, too."

249

Herman ran back to the Mercedes. It was strange, but he ran as he hadn't been able to run in years.

He climbed in the car, started it, then drove past Jack, who made a k-turn and followed.

Herman sped down the small road heading toward the beach and Susan, dreading what he might find there.

Chapter Twenty-five

What they found was Susan sitting in the guest house with a strained, worried expression. She had been half-heartedly working on a UCLA application for student aid, and sprang to her feet as they came through the door.

"Thank God you're all right," Herman said.

"Where the hell have you two been? I called the cops, but they said they don't investigate missing persons cases for forty-eight hours."

"Honey, you remember Gil and Tom?"

"Of course I remember. How could I forget them?" But she was furrowing her brow.

"Honey, you won't believe it. You won't, but you have to."

"What?" She was getting impatient now.

"We . . . Jack and I were kidnapped by CDF troops. We were taken away in an Aurora Hyper Whispership — a prototype, I think."

"A what?" Jack mumbled. His split lip where Paul hit him was sore and causing a lisp.

"It's a prototype aircraft. An Aurora Whispership."

"You sure it wasn't a Klingon Star Fighter?" Jack blurted.

"I heard the pilot calling Dreamland Control. He said, 'We're entering The Box.' He said, 'this is Psych Twenty-seven.' Tom and Gil told me that Psych series aircraft were Aurora prototypes being tested at Area Fifty-one. They said the government was working on noise-cloaking devices for aircraft called 'Whisperships.' "

"Wait. Hold on a minute. *Who* went to Area Fifty-one?" Jack asked.

" *We* did."

"We did?"

"You bet we did. What kinda detective are you? We were out there inside the secure Dulce Genetics Lab on Level Four." He turned to Susan. "You remember what's done down there, honey?"

"Nightmare Hall," she said. But the way she said it was disbelieving and incredulous.

"It's where the government is doing research on aliens," Herm said. "At least, that's what Tom and Gil thought."

"Whoa! Hold it! I'm not doing any *X-Files* shit."

"Look, Jack, that's where we were."

"That's where *you* were. I was at a plain old military base in the desert with guys wearing standard GI camouflage. There were no Star Fleet salutes and no aliens. Trust me, I saw everything."

"We had on hoods. How could you see it?"

"My hood was leaking. They got a moth problem they need to address."

"You're kidding? You saw what was out there?"

"Kinda." Now Jack was taking a step backward because Herman was moving in on him, that intense look back on his raccoon face.

"Like what?" Herman challenged. "What did you see?"

"Like what? Like miles of runways. Looked like they went all the way to the horizon."

"The long strip on Papoose Lake! What else?"

"I don't know . . . little dirt-covered hangars. Calm down, will ya?"

"The igloos!" Herman shouted and spun triumphantly toward Susan. "He saw the igloos!"

"No igloos. No Alaskans, no polar bears, no ice. Just little hangars built into mounds of dirt."

"They're called igloos. They drag the prototype aircraft off the runways and hide 'em in there when the Russian satellites go over." Herman was really getting excited. "This proves what Tom and Gil were saying."

"Really?" Susan seemed less sure.

"We were *there*, honey. I *know* it! My sinuses . . . my sinuses were plugged when I got back. You know that's the only place I get sinus allergies."

"You use your sinuses for global positioning?" Jack sneered.

"Dad, slow down a minute."

"We were there. Right inside Dreamland, right where Gil said they were doing tests on the aliens."

"Herm, you've gotta stop with this alien stuff," Jack pleaded. "You sound like some lunatic who just took a ride in a spaceship. Keep it up and you're gonna start getting your meals delivered under the door."

"Roland was killed by something that went right up the side of a glass tower, hung there, and pried open a window. A feat requiring superhuman strength. Then whatever it was ripped Roland apart. Shredded him."

Jack turned to Susan. "Make him stop."

"I think a hybrid, a Ten-Eyck chimera did it. Yes — some half-man, half-space-alien, gene-spliced by using DNA from a dead intergalactic traveler."

"From the planet Ten-Eyck?" Jack said sarcastically.

"Maybe. Yeah . . . why not? A hybrid made at Dreamland in Nightmare Hall."

"Excuse me. I gotta go outside and cough up a furball." Jack turned and walked out of the room onto the porch.

He sat in one of the Brown Jordan deck chairs, his ass right there, pressed against the same white plastic that Barbra Streisand and Jim Brolin pressed their asses against. Not much of a thought, admittedly, but he was trying for some earthly reality. He decided that regardless of his attraction to Susan, he had to dump this gig.

His memory of the trip was nothing like Herm's. Okay, the helicopter *had* been strange. He'd seen something with angled sides and all kinds of panels hanging off it. And, yes, it *had* been incredibly quiet, and he'd heard the Dreamland Control radio transmission, same as Herm. But that was a long way from hybrid aliens.

What Jack remembered about their kidnapping was a little out there, but certainly not from some George Lucas epic. He remembered seeing the guys in camouflage with little round patches on their pockets. He remembered being put in a car and driven across the base, seeing the whatevers — the igloos, and the little one-story building with all the security. He had caught a glimpse of that door lock, squinting through the pinhole in his hood. There was a unique procedure for getting into the place: Everybody was dressed the same and each had an ID card that, he guessed, must have been reissued every morning, because it confirmed the individual's *exact weight*. The soldiers stepped on a scale and were weighed along with their weapons, then they inserted the card into a slot to verify the scale weight. Jack guessed nobody got to take a piss or sweat on duty. Next there was some kind of eye scan where a laser went into the left eye and read capillaries or indecent thoughts — something. After which the door slid open.

Jack remembered the ride down in the elevator, going to the little medical room, and the doctor with the bushy brown hair. Then Jack Wirta, private eye, was pissing into a cup like an NFL wide receiver. *DNA?*

Then came the shot and the strange dream. The dream was sort of a replay of the trip he and Susan took to San Fran. He never remembered having a dream that seemed like a memory before. He and Susan were back in Alioto's Restaurant. He'd been telling her what the coroner's report said. . . . He'd also dreamed about several of the conversations he'd had with Herman.

He stood up and walked over to the patio wall, propped his foot up, and wished he hadn't stopped smoking. While he was having these thoughts he looked down and saw it.

The sand was still wet from the rainstorm that had passed through after making its way south from San Francisco. The midnight downpour had darkened the sand and hardened it. Just outside the low brick wall there were a bunch of footprints. He leaned over and studied them. They all had the same sole markings, but appeared to be three different sizes. That meant three men.

This is good detecting, Jack. Too bad you're not being paid.

He walked around the wall to get a closer look, knelt down, and examined the footprints. The treads on the boot soles were identical. Crepe soles in a zigzag pattern. Uniform boots — military issue, like the ones the soldiers who had put him in the car were wearing. It was then that he noticed the three holes punched into the damp sand. They were about two and a half feet apart, at the angle of an isosceles triangle.

A tripod!

Somebody stood out here after the rain and took pictures.

Still shots?

A video transmission uplink?

So, what were CDF commandos doing out here taking pictures of Susan?

He already knew the answer: They were doing surveillance, ready to kidnap her if they thought it was going to be necessary. He was now pretty certain the dreams he'd had were not dreams. He and Herman had been debriefed — quizzed under drugs while a commando team waited here to be told whether or not to seize Susan.

Had he and Herm "passed" the test? Is that why she had been left alone? Is that why they had been released?

Herman saw hybrid aliens, but Jack was trained to see evidence, and these footprints under the wall were definitely evidence.

He turned and walked back inside. He sat

down on the sofa and listened to Herman's rant.

Herman was jazzed, talking about Area 51, Dreamland, The Ranch, Aurora Whisperships, and a bunch of other Roswell nonsense. Jack listened, but his mind drifted. Suddenly, Herman unbuttoned his pants and pulled them down.

Okay, Jack thought. *I'm outta here.*

Herman was showing Susan an abdominal surgical wound with four stitches.

"What is it?" Susan asked.

"Somebody did some kinda operation on me."

Jack didn't like this. In fact, he hated it.

"I had an arrhythmia in the helicopter," Herman was saying. "It was gone when I woke up."

"Dad, you've got to go get checked out."

"I will. But, honey, I've never felt better. I feel reborn, like I'm ten years younger. Like this heart problem somehow got fixed."

Herman and Susan sat transfixed, but Jack needed air again, so he told them what he had found under the wall. They all trooped outside and looked at the footprints. Herman took photos.

Jack had another thought. "Herm, did you have any dreams while you were asleep out there?"

"Yeah, I dreamed about some huge, winged bat-humanoids, and some reptile men that my old clients, who once worked there —"

"Forget the Japanese animation," Jack interrupted. "Was there anything else, more like memories of what you did over the last few days?"

"Yeah. I had a strange kinda dream that was exactly like my trip out to JPL. My talk with Dr. Zimbaldi."

"I think before we take you to the hospital we need to go check on Zimbaldi."

"Why?"

"I don't think you were dreaming, Herm. I think we were both spilling our guts. I think Zimmy is about to eat it."

Chapter Twenty-Six

Zimmy wasn't at JPL, but Jack got his home address from the Security Office by flashing his fancy new imitation ostrich P.I. license holder and saying: "Police." The girl handed him a slip of paper and said, "Zimmy told me yesterday they're painting his apartment. I think he's staying at his ex-wife's place."

"Could I have her address, please?" Jack smiled, giving her his best ten-megawatt meltdown.

"Montrose Apartments, 2300 Montrose Boulevard in Montrose. Apartment ten."

He ran back to Barbra's Mercedes, where Herman and Susan were waiting. He jumped in the car and headed west on the Foothill Freeway, hoping Montrose was in that direction. He was lucky. Montrose Boulevard was a freeway exit.

The apartment house was a two-story, six-ties-type building: a gray stucco box with white trim. He pulled past and parked across the street in somebody's driveway.

Jack had grabbed his backup gun from the trunk of the Fairlane before they left Malibu. It was an S&W Model 60, lightweight, three-inch barrel, burnished finish, and it was under his coat, jammed in his belt Billy-the-Kid style. "Okay . . . whatever you do, don't leave the car until I get back."

Herman and Susan nodded grimly.

He walked to the corner and bought the *Los Angeles Times* from a newspaper box, transferred the revolver from his belt to the inside of the folded newspaper, tucked it under his arm and crossed the street.

He entered the building courtyard, spotted apartment ten on the second floor at the end of the corridor, then climbed the interior stairwell and banged on the door. "Dr. Zimbaldi?"

Nothing.

He knocked again and tried the door. Locked. When he rattled the knob, it felt like there was no deadbolt, just a button lock. Another job for Wells Fargo Bank. Jack took out his credit card, slipped it into the space between the door lock and the jamb, then pushed.

Credit approved.

It was a very ordinary, sparsely furnished apartment. He moved quickly through the neat two-bedroom, one-bath layout, then ended up in the small kitchen. There was no sign of Zimmy or his ex-wife.

He walked out onto the balcony, which offered a quasi-view of the Valley. Jammed into that small space were a wooden chair, an orange Webber barbecue, and a chest-style

Amana freezer from the horse and buggy era. Jack opened the freezer, praying that Zimmy wouldn't be inside curled up next to the flank steak. The Amana was filled with ice cream. He snagged a container of Rocky Road, pried it open, then went back inside to borrow a spoon from the kitchen.

The P.I. takes an ice cream break.

Two blocks away a windowless, brown Econoline van pulled up and parked off Foothill Boulevard. Inside Vincent Valdez watched a GPS monitor with a small locator light flashing on the LED map screen, then said: "He's around the corner on Montrose."

Marine Captain Norm Pettis, who had flown in from D.C. with Valdez on a private jet that morning, was seated next to the assistant director in a little command chair bolted to the floor of the van.

"Strockmire should lead us to Zimbaldi," Valdez continued. "We move in fast and take everybody. But, whatever you do, make sure you get that encrypted file." It was hot in the van and moisture was collecting under his armpits. He didn't want to stain his Armani jacket, so he took it off. "Turn on the engine and get the air going," he ordered the driver.

"Whatta you wanna do?" Captain Pettis asked. "Looks like he's just parked over there."

"Take a walk down the street and hang an

eyeball on them. Lemme know what you see."

Pettis pushed a computerized receiver chip into his ear, fixed a pin mike to his lapel, then opened the van doors. He was dressed in chinos and a sport jacket. The only uniform issue he wore were his J-6 laced leather jump boots. He liked them because they gave him good ankle support and had reinforced metal toes. He jumped out of the van, then sauntered casually down the block, turning the corner on Montrose Boulevard.

Almost immediately, he saw Herman Strockmire and his daughter, Susan, sitting in a silver Mercedes.

"I have our people in sight," Pettis said into his lapel mike. "Whatta you want me to do? They're just sitting in a Mercedes looking across the street at the apartment house."

"Go check the mailboxes, see if anything over there lights up."

Captain Pettis entered the Montrose Apartment courtyard and began to quickly scan the mailboxes. On the second row, two from the end, a typed face card read: DONNA ZIMBALDI.

"Looks like a sister, or an ex-wife or somethin' lives here. Donna Zimbaldi, apartment ten," he said into the pin mike.

"Go sell her some mags," Valdez instructed.

"Roger."

The mailboxes were locked, but bulk mail was in open trays under each box. So Captain Pettis went magazine shopping. He picked out a *Vogue*, a *Redbook*, and a few other women's magazines, then went upstairs and knocked on the door of Donna Zimbaldi's apartment.

Jack heard the knock, set down the ice cream, and crossed to the door, snapping up the newspaper off the kitchen counter as he passed. Holding his gun in his left hand, he folded the paper over it, then opened the door with his right.

"Hi," Norm Pettis said. "I'm with Helping Hands and we're selling magazine subscriptions to benefit the Children's Cancer Center. Is Mrs. Zimbaldi at home?" Pettis thought the guy in the apartment looked familiar — like the P.I. in the briefing photos they'd taken at Area 51, but he wasn't absolutely sure.

"There's no Zimbaldis live here. Just me and my brother, Lonnie, but he ain't home." Jack smiled, then glanced down at the magazine salesman's feet. Crepe soles on black leather jump boots.

"Maybe you should write your number on this newspaper, I could have him call you. He's always giving to charities."

Jack pressed the paper at him until the man finally took it. Once he did he was looking at the revolver.

"This is a big mistake," Pettis said.

"Why don't you come on in? We're having ice cream." Jack yanked him through the door, then closed and bolted it. "You wired?"

Pettis didn't respond, but Jack spotted the pin mike on his lapel, ripped it off, and stomped on it. Then he saw the earplug. "Get the receiver out." Pettis dug it out with his thumb and index finger. It was a microchip about the size of an eraser with no wire. "Nice," Jack observed, dropping it into his pocket.

Just then he heard someone coming up the stairs, whistling. He spun Pettis around and frisked him quickly, pulling a Glock 9 out of a waist holster, a SIG P-232 off his leg, and a stun gun with two batteries out of his coat. "You really came to party," Jack quipped as he pulled the clips and both slides, then threw the guns across the room.

"You're just making things worse for yourself."

"You, too," Jack said, and clocked him hard on the head, banging the side of the Smith and Wesson against the man's transverse occipital bone — police academy combat tactics. Guaranteed to produce a snooze.

Pettis went down in a clutter of stolen magazines.

A key scraped in the lock.

Jack aimed his gun and waited.

When the door opened he was looking at a very intense, wirey man wearing Bermuda shorts, grimy tennies with no socks, and a threadbare red-checkered shirt, complete with pocket protector.

"Dr. Zimbaldi?"

"What are you doing in my wife's apartment?"

"Trying to save your life. I'm with Herman Strockmire. We've gotta get you out of here."

"You're what?" Zimbaldi said.

Jack heard a car squeal to a halt in the parking lot below followed by four doors slamming. "Listen, Doctor, we need to leave right now. Your life is in danger. It's about that stuff Herman gave you — the fifty-page encryption."

"That's silly."

Jack didn't have time to discuss it, so he turned and pulled the confused Dr. Zimbaldi out of the apartment and into the corridor.

"Where's the service elevator?"

"There isn't one."

Just then the doorway to the staircase flew open and two men in jeans, combat boots, and windbreakers appeared. Both were holding guns that were unlike anything Jack had ever seen — long elliptical shapes with narrow frames and breeches, laser sights, and banana grips — deadly looking two-handed ordnance.

Jack jumped back inside the apartment,

pulling Zimmy with him just as the men fired. Two laser beams of light zapped ominously, ripping holes into the door frame.

He slammed the door shut. "Is there a back way outta here?"

"This way." The doctor led Jack into the bedroom. Zimmy dug under the bed and came out with a rope ladder. "Fire ladder," he explained.

They opened a window, hooking the rope ladder to the sill, then throwing it down. Jack helped Dr. Zimbaldi out, then climbed after him. In seconds they were standing in the carport.

"You got a car?" Jack asked urgently.

"Yeah, the white Nissan." Zimmy pointed to it.

A Nissan Sentra. *Shit,* Jack thought. *A roller skate with seat belts.*

"Okay, I'm going across the street," Jack told him. "Hopefully, Herman and his daughter are in a silver Mercedes over there. After I leave, count to ten and get moving. We're using your wheels. Pick us up. You with me?"

"Yeah."

Jack ran to the corner and looked across the street. He could see Herman and Susan, but they had ignored his instructions and gotten out of the car. They stood looking right at the apartment building across the street, like gawkers in Times Square. They might as well have been holding a neon sign over their heads with an arrow pointing down.

Jack crossed Montrose Boulevard, threading his way through traffic, and as soon as he got to the car he grabbed Susan's arm.

"You're both leaving in a white Nissan. Here it comes now. Leave the rear, right side door open for me. Go."

A gray sedan Jack had never seen before skidded around the corner at the other end of the street. There were four men inside.

Jack pushed Herman and Susan toward the Nissan, shouting at them to get in. Then he jumped behind the wheel of Barbra's Mercedes, gunned it, and shot backwards out of the driveway, right into the path of the fast-approaching government sedan.

A symphony of tortured rubber, crashing metal, and broken glass filled his ears as the sedan plowed right into the driver's side, knocking Barbra's little silver jewel halfway up the block and Jack halfway down into the knee well. He didn't have time to worry about whiplash.

Jack rolled out of the passenger side and started sprinting. He ran straight at the Sentra, then dove headfirst through the open rear door into the backseat, landing right in Susan's lap. "Go, go, go, go!" he yelled.

Zimmy floored it, but not much happened. The car choked and wheezed, whirred, and woofed, and then, as fast as you could say, "This car really sucks," they were slowly moving up the street.

"Can't it go any faster?" Susan yelled in dismay. And then it finally picked up speed. Jack sat up and looked out the back window. Montrose Boulevard was a mess. The government sedan and the silver Mercedes were crumpled up in the middle of the street, twisted together and blocking both lanes. Traffic art. Other cars had skidded to a halt behind, completing the ugly sculpture.

"My God, what the hell will I tell Barbra?" Herman said, looking back at the wrecked Mercedes as the Nissan rounded a corner and took the horrible vision away.

"Tell her the airbags didn't deploy," Jack answered.

Chapter Twenty-Seven

When Jack called Miro, Jackson Mississippi answered: "Reflections. We mirror your fantasies."

So *that's* what it meant. "It's Jack."

"Jack with the nipple pierce, or Jack with the fox terriers?"

"Jack with the gun."

"Oh. Hi." Not too enthusiastic about it either.

"Is Miro around?" Jack said.

"Uh . . . yes."

"Could I speak to him?"

"Uh . . . I guess." Then Jack was put on hold.

Barry Manilow was halfway through "I Write the Songs" before Miro picked up. "Hi, big guy. How's my trifle who's an eyeful?"

Jack let it go. "Miro, look, I got a little problem and I need a quiet place to hang for a while. I pissed some guys off and I can't go home, can't go to my office. I was wondering if we could use the little side office you rent, the one next door to mine."

"The Lipstick Lounge?" Miro said.

"The what?"

"We have a few cross-dressers."

"Great," Jack sighed. "Can I borrow it for an hour?"

"Bring it on, sugar."

"And Miro? Don't send anybody down to answer my phone. My office isn't safe."

"Don't worry. You cured us of that. Come ahead."

Jack had Zimmy drop him on the corner, then jogged past another fishing party while he scoped out the building. He was looking for a gray sedan with four guys with muscles and crewcuts. Of course, everybody looked like that in Boys' Town, but there were always the telltale jump boots.

The building lobby looked clean so he went upstairs and checked his office. He hoped nobody had kicked the door this time, but the lock was still busted, so it was moot. If these guys from Montrose were the same ones who broke in earlier, they'd be showing up soon. By using the office next door Jack hoped he could get a visual ID when they rolled in. It's always nice to be able to recognize the assholes who are trying to kill you.

He went back downstairs and waited while Zimmy parked the Sentra, then led the three of them up the stairs toward Reflections. He heard some male giggling in the escort service waiting room. As soon as Jack opened the door the laughing stopped.

Sprawled on a couch across from a desk were four young men. "Meet Chip and Jeff,

Steven and Mark," Miro announced to Jack, pointing a ringed index finger at each one as he ticked off their names. The escorts all smiled and gave Jack a quick visual frisk.

"Come on." Miro picked up a ring of keys and led the fugitives up the hall and opened the door to the office that adjoined Jack's. It was empty, but there was a wall-to-ceiling mirror, a sofa, a folding clothes rack with gowns, Spandex dresses, and hats. A shelf on one wall contained boxes for wigs and a huge shoe rack filled with stiletto heels and clear plastic mules in large sizes.

Miro didn't seem to want to leave, so Jack did the introductions: "Casimiro Roca, this is Herman Strockmire. You met Susan, I think, and this is Dr. Gino Zimbaldi."

Miro lowered his eyes demurely and extended his hand palm down to each of them.

Jack said, "We're being chased by thugs and I don't want something ugly to happen. You'd be much safer in your office down the hall."

"Don't worry about Miro. Miro has his green belt in tae kwan do and a certificate from the Royal Academy of Dance. The boy can kick ass," he replied. "And after all, this *is* Miro's office and Miro's dying to know what private eyes do when they're not drinking coffee and taking infrared pictures." Jack looked at the others for approval. They all shrugged.

"Okay, but it's gotta stay between us."

"Stop teasing," Miro gushed.

Jack smiled in spite of himself, then turned to the Strockmires. "Herm, we've gotta go over some things. We need to figure this out fast, because I think we have some big gaps in logic that need to be discussed before we make a mistake that kills us."

"I agree," Herman said as Miro sat.

"How did these guys know we were following Paul Nichols in Malibu? We weren't on that baseball diamond three minutes and in comes the . . . whatever."

"The Whispership."

Miro said, "Sounds naughty."

Jack turned to Miro. "You can listen, but be a bud and stay out of this, okay?"

"Okay."

"I don't know how they knew we were there," Herman said. "You're right, it's pretty damn strange. The helicopter . . . the ground troops. They got there seconds after we did."

"As far as I can see, only one or two things could be responsible for that, and both of them are bad."

"Like what?" Susan asked.

"They could have had some way of picking off my cell phone transmission when I was giving Herman directions, which means they know a lot more about what we're up to than we thought, because we've been discussing everything on the phone. Or somebody could

273

have hung a bug on Herman's car, which makes me wonder how long they've been tracking us."

"The government has a spy network that reads computer or cell transmissions from outer space," Herman said. "It's a computer lab called Echelon. Maybe that's what Octopus is, a new, more accurate version of Echelon."

"I have a stupendous idea," Miro interjected.

They all looked over at him. "Go ahead," Jack said. "We can use the help."

"We have finger foods next door. If anybody is hungry, Miro could go get them."

Stunned silence, then: "Great. Good idea," Jack said. Miro jumped up and hurried out of the room.

"But we didn't use the cell phone before we went to Gino's wife's apartment in Montrose," Susan said after he left. "So how did they know to go there? How did they find that apartment seconds after we did?"

"The Mercedes has to be bugged," Herman pondered aloud.

"I don't like this, Dad." Susan took her father's hand.

"I don't like it either," Jack acknowledged. "I don't like that computer lab at Pepperdine, and I don't like guys shooting at us with weapons that look like they belong on the set of *Star Trek*."

"Those guns sound like PB ordnance," Herman said. "That's a particle beam weapon. Gil and Tom told me they were developing something like that at Area Fifty-one."

"Great," Zimmy groused.

Jack turned to Herman. "I know what happened to me, but explain again what happened to you while we were out there at the military base. Give it to us point by point."

"Not much, other than what I already told you." Herman took them through it again, up to where the doctor discovered his arrhythmia and said, "That won't work," and left. Then he got the injection and had the dream.

"The doc said what?" Jack interrupted.

The door opened and Miro returned with some finger sandwiches on a tray. He passed them around.

"He said, 'that won't work,'" Herman repeated.

"What won't work?"

"My heart being in arrhythmia, I guess."

"Okay, so then they fixed it, right?" Jack said.

"Well, it feels like they did."

"But that doesn't make sense, Dad. They follow you, kidnap you, debrief you under drugs, then fix your heart condition? Why would they do that?"

Zimmy cleared his throat. "I may have the answer to that."

They turned in unison to look at him. "I know when the CIA debriefs they often use a lie detector to determine the veracity of the answers. I don't think you can administer a polygraph to someone who has a heart condition. The lie detector uses heart rate and skin electrical conductivity to measure a response. If Herm's heart was out of rhythm I don't think they could have gotten an accurate result."

Herman leaned forward. "Maybe my heart had to be fixed so they could find out if I was telling the truth."

"We need to get to a hospital and see what they really did." Susan sounded worried.

Miro pointed to the sandwich tray. "Try the little deviled ham ones — they have caviar."

"Thanks," Jack said as he took one, then continued. "Next are the fifty pages of encryption Zimmy decoded."

All eyes turned to Dr. Zimbaldi. "It was just a bunch of genetic base pairs. A slice of a gene map of some kind. I checked it against the Celera map of the human body that I keep in my research computer. But it wasn't human, wasn't anything I could determine, so I e-mailed a copy to your computer, Herm, and then I ran my copy over to a friend in Santa Monica, Dr. Carolyn Adjemenian. Her field is genetics."

"Can you get her on the phone?" Herman asked.

"We can't use our cell if it's being tracked by satellite," Susan reminded them.

"You can use the phone in here," Miro offered. He handed the phone to Zimmy. "But what on earth is going on? This sounds juicy."

"Herm thinks we may have been invaded by aliens," Jack offered glumly.

Miro nodded. "We don't have many down here, but I know a lot of illegal aliens have been moving into Pico Rivera."

Nobody cleared up the misunderstanding. Zimmy got Dr. Adjemenian on the office phone, then explained who Herman was and handed over the receiver.

Herman spoke quietly, cupping the receiver so that Miro couldn't hear. Finally, he hung up and looked over at them. "She wants to see us. She won't tell me what it is over the phone, except to say it's like nothing she's ever seen." Herman seemed jazzed.

Jack was just about to open the door when he heard something next door.

"Shhh." He put his ear to the wall. Somebody was moving around his office. He heard drawers opening and whispered: "Somebody's in there again."

"It's that bunch of drug addicts from down the hall," Miro said angrily, then started to storm out to protect Jack's stuff. Jack made a grab for him and stopped him just in time.

"Wait a minute. Hold it," Jack whispered urgently.

They waited for almost ten minutes until they heard the office door close and footsteps retreating down the hall.

Jack slipped outside and silently followed two men who were just disappearing down the stairs. He went to the end of the corridor and looked out the window. From that spot he could see the street below. After a few seconds, he saw the two men walk out of the building, climb into the back of a brown Econoline van and pull the door closed. They were both in their mid-twenties, with crew cuts, jump boots, jeans, and windbreakers.

The van didn't leave. While Jack watched, the door opened again and the two men got back out. They looked up at the building and scratched their heads. One of them gave the other a *beats me* shrug, then they headed back inside the building.

Jack returned to the Lipstick Lounge and waited until the door to his office opened and the men were again walking around inside. He put his ear to the wall and faintly heard the two men arguing. The sentences sounded garbled, like cartoon fish talking, but Jack could make out what was being said.

"He ain't here," one of the voices insisted.

"He's gotta be," the other answered.

"Go tell that to Valdez, why don't ya?"

"You're right . . . this is stupid. The equipment must be screwed up. Let's go."

And they left for the second time.

Jack followed them out as they headed back into the stairwell, then watched from the window until they appeared on the street. Then they both climbed back into the van and closed the door.

Jack returned to the Lipstick Lounge and reported. "They're parked out there waiting. We gotta find a way to sneak out of here and slide past 'em."

"You could wear some of these," Miro said, pulling some dresses off the rolling rack. "We've got wigs in those boxes, some triple-wide pumps."

"Not even during Gay Pride Week," Jack said. He was trying to be enlightened, but he wasn't going out on the street wearing plastic pumps and a ball gown.

"The wigs are a good idea," Susan said, and began opening boxes, pulling out a few. She chose a long black one for herself, then gave Herman a blond bob. Zimmy tried on a gray shag. Jack got the strawberry pageboy.

"Oh, Jack, that's *so you*," Miro gushed.

When Jack looked in the mirror he saw Wynonna Judd on steroids.

They took off their jackets to further change their appearance, and Susan borrowed a blue plastic raincoat.

Jack led them down the staircase and out the front, hugging the building, using a crowd of laughing men coming out of The

Sports Connection as a screen. Miraculously, they made it to the Nissan Sentra.

Jack snatched off his wig. "Let's get the hell out of here."

They pulled past the Econoline van, and as Jack was looking out the back window one of the CDF troopers got out and looked up the street after them. It was almost as if he knew they had just driven away.

Chapter Twenty-Eight

Dr. Carolyn Adjemenian was a tall woman in her mid-thirties with a pockmarked, narrow face and a spectacular body. Her muscles were etched on tight skin like lines on an anatomy chart. She had blondish hair, grayish eyes, and wore her reading glasses up on her head like a geek tiara.

"Come in," she said after Zimmy did the introductions. The house was a two-bedroom duplex in Santa Monica. Neat lawn, white shutters, a carport.

She led the three of them to her computer room in the guest bedroom. As they were walking down the hall, Herman caught a glimpse of the master. She had turned it into a full gym: free weights, a pull-down lat bar, stacks of heavy plates and pulleys. He wondered where she slept — maybe on the flat bench.

"Sit down," she said as if she were ordering sprinters onto their marks. She sat in front of her computer, booted up, and found a Web site called basic alignment search tool:

BLAST

"We use this Web site in genetics research

to identify any unknown DNA sequence," she said. "It has the gene maps for all plant and animal species that scientists have catalogued to date."

While she waited for it to load she turned toward Herman. "Zimmy gave me your decoded encryption. As you may or may not know, DNA is made up of thousands of base-pair genes. There are only four different kinds of proteins that make up a gene. Each protein has its own designated letter: A, C, G, or T. The combination and sequence of these base pairs determine our genetic makeup." She reached behind her and grabbed the printout of what Roland had died for. It contained pages and pages of the same four letters in varying chains and sequences.

ACACACACCAG TGTACCACA TTGATCAG TTCAAGTA CCAAGGTAT GGATTCAGTCC ACCATGGATTA TTAGAACCTA CCTTAGC ACCAACCAAG ACACACAGTATA TATCCG

"When I first saw it I knew it had to be a DNA sequence for some animal or plant, so I fed it into the BLAST program to compare this sequence of yours with all the gene maps of species already stored in its databank. It gives you a percentage of homology."

"It does what?" Herman asked.

"It takes your DNA sample and matches it to all others, then tells you what percentage one is to the other." She turned back to her computer and clicked on two icons. "For example, if you put in a chimp and ask BLAST to match its DNA to the gene map of *Homo sapiens,* this is what you'll get." The BLAST program displayed a percentage: 98.4 PERCENT HOMOLOGY. She pointed to the percentage printed on the screen. "That's how close human DNA is to a chimpanzee's. A chimp is closer to a human genetically than the African elephant is to the Indian elephant. It's hard to believe, but chimps are closer to humans than they are to their ape cousins, like bonobos, or gorillas, or orangutans. So, despite outward appearances, the chimpanzee's closest relative is *not* any ape species, but us. Some geneticists believe humans are nothing more than a third more developed species of chimpanzee. You with me?"

"Yes," all four of them said at once.

"What comes up on a typical BLAST search is a list from the most homolistic to the least," Dr. Adjemenian continued. "Then if you want to narrow it you can set your search to focus on particular irregularities between species. Those irregularities can also be determined by percentile. A single gene can be a gene-to-gene perfect match between two species, or it can differ by a percentage. Okay?"

"Okay." This time only Herman answered.

"We are usually trying to determine the identity of the animal in question," Carolyn went on. "If we recover a DNA sample and we want to know what animal left it, we might run a BLAST search comparing it to a human. If we find that it is 98.4 percent human we know it's a chimp. If it's only 96.4 percent we know it's an orangutan. Still with me?"

"Yeah, I guess," Herman said.

"So . . . once I got my basic DNA comparison, I set BLAST to asterisk any gene in this map that doesn't match on the over forty thousand genes in this particular base-pair string. I ran a BLAST search on your sample, but it doesn't correspond to *any* exact species we have here on earth . . . at least not as far as I can determine."

She looked at them and let this sink in. "It's close, very close. But this genome does not represent any species now in existence."

Jack rubbed his eyes. He hated this more than he hated gang violence or checks bouncing. More than just hating it, he was also terrified of it. Jack didn't mind facing off some murderous asshole like Matasareanu outside a bank in North Hollywood, because at least Emil wore pants and pissed standing up. But aliens? Space monsters? No way. That was not in his emotional zip code.

"Are you saying that this animal, whatever it is, is from somewhere else?" Herman said,

284

creeping up on his next thought like an Apache in the dark. "Are you saying that it's perhaps from some other world . . . like . . . well . . . like from outer space?" He'd finally said it.

Jack shuddered, but Carolyn Adjemenian shook her head, sending her geek tiara flying. She got up and retrieved her glasses. "For God's sake, no!" she laughed.

Herman actually slumped, but Jack was sure as hell relieved.

"No, no," she went on. "It's definitely from this planet, but it's not a pure breed. It's some kind of mixture of species, and since separate species can't interbreed, that means this animal has more than likely been engineered."

That remark hung over them like ripe fruit.

"Basically, it is very close to a chimpanzee, but with some interesting upgrades."

"Upgrades?" Herman leaned in, looking at the gene map on her computer screen, studying it intently.

"To answer the question of *what* it is exactly I had to try and isolate the asterisked base pairs . . . the genes that were different from normal chimp DNA. Then I tried to determine how those genes differed from a chimpanzee's normal DNA and what parts of its body were affected by the change.

"As I said, a chimpanzee is our closest living relative . . . 98.4 percent of human

DNA. We know now that chimps and *Homo sapiens* basically split into two separate species only about four million years ago. Gorillas, for example, split from us nine million years ago, orangutans split fifteen million years ago. Since the chimpanzee's split with *Homo sapiens* is so recent, you can see why chimps and humans are almost identical on the DNA scale. In some sequences they are perfectly parallel, in others they differ only slightly."

"Which ones differ?" Herman seemed energized by this new idea.

"Well, chimps don't have the same communication abilities as humans. They have less-developed fine-motor dexterity. They have an opposing thumb like us, but their fingers are longer, designed to walk on their knuckles, so they're less adept with tools. However, chimps are the only animals besides humans who use tools. For instance, a chimp will use a pole to knock down a banana."

"But he can't change the transmission on a Chevy," Jack countered. Susan turned and glared at him, so he decided he'd better keep quiet.

Dr. Adjemenian continued. "Chimps have a different intelligence. They score about like a three-year-old human child on a standard IQ test. But that doesn't mean they're less intelligent than us. It's just that their intelligence is different. If you took the smartest human — Einstein, let's say — and you dropped him in a chimpanzee's natural habitat deep in the Congo, poor old Albert would last about two days." She paused. "So, intelligence is a relative concept. Chimps are stronger than humans and can run much faster over short distances. They have a better sense of smell, but, beyond these, and a few other minor discrepancies, they are far more similar to us than different, with a variation of only one-point-six percent on the entire gene map."

Herman pointed at the computer screen. "This animal we have mapped here is different from a chimp in what way?"

"One difference I found was for neurotransmitters. They signal impulses between neutrons in the brain, which means this animal thinks more like a human than a standard chimp would."

"Fascinating," Herman said, studying the screen.

"That neurotransmitter gene had to have been spliced into the chimp zygote," Dr. Adjemenian went on. "It would improve rapidity of brain processing, facilitate nerve growth, as well as dexterity. The genetic engineering would also change various muscle proteins." She paused and looked at them.

Susan picked up the fifty-page gene map. Zimmy went to a chair across the room and sat. Like Jack, he didn't want to hear any of this. He and Jack liked chimps just the way they were.

"Next, I looked at the second asterisked gene, called the Troponin Myglobin gene, which deals with communication. This animal, while it still may not be able to talk, will understand much more than a normal chimp when it comes to human language. Next is the Conexin gene. It's involved with processing sounds, so it's also part of what I see as a communications upgrade. Put it all together and, in essence, the animal we have here has been upgraded from 98.4 percent *Homo sapiens* to about 99.1."

"What does it look like?"

"Beats me," she said, then she looked at Jack and smiled. "But it's probably not going to buy its clothes at the Gap." Jack smiled back.

"It has fur, probably for warmth, but its face might be more human than chimp-like — maybe a slightly larger head because it has more developed areas in the brain. Its fingers are probably shorter, and it doesn't walk on its knuckles. It might prefer walking upright, yet could still run on all fours. But these are only guesses."

Now they all sat in silence trying to conjure up this beast.

"I have a question, Doctor," Susan said.

"Sure."

"Does this animal really exist, or could this just be some gene map that somebody put together, a hypothetical or virtual animal?"

"Good question," Jack blurted.

"It *is* a good question," Carolyn Adjemenian agreed. "There is no way anybody could do this without taking a DNA sample from the animal and scanning it. It would be virtually impossible to come up with this by reverse-engineering it. There are things in the genome that would be impossible to make up — like the structure of the coding regions and their connections to one another. Is that clear?"

"No," all of them said at once.

"The answer to your question is: This is legit. Somebody has actually upgraded a chimpanzee and fed the hybrid animal's DNA into the computer to construct this map. But I haven't a clue as to why."

Zimmy didn't have a clue either, but Jack and the Strockmires had been over it all before when this thing was an imaginary, hybrid space alien. Now they were back to Herman's theory of a genetically engineered monkey-human. A chimera with the strength of ten. A disposable soldier.

Suddenly, Jack heard the same noise he'd heard outside Donna Zimbaldi's apartment — four car doors slamming. Then he caught a glimpse of someone running past the window in a low crouch.

Chapter Twenty-Nine

Herman was holding the printout of the chimera gene map, thinking he had to find a way to get this into court. DARPA was doing illegal science on chimpanzees, so he could file under the federal rules of civil procedure, section 65. It was during this thought that Jack interrupted him.

"I think the CDF is outside."

"What?" Carolyn Adjemenian asked as Zimmy jumped to his feet and began looking frantically for some place to hide.

Herman glanced around, his eyes wild like a drunk caught in a hotel fire. Susan grabbed his arm.

Carolyn demanded: "What the hell is CDF?"

"The guys who designed this damn animal want the plans back," Herman said, clutching the encryption.

"Leave it," Jack ordered. "It's what they're after. Let 'em take it. Zimmy e-mailed a copy to your computer anyway."

"Good idea. If they think they've got it, maybe they'll stop chasing us," Susan agreed.

"They're outside now?" Carolyn blurted as she shut down the computer and retrieved the disk.

"Somebody just ran past the window," Jack replied. He dug the receiver chip he'd taken from the phony magazine salesman out of his coat pocket and jammed it into his ear.

"Angel Two, we're covered. Set up your entry," he heard someone announce. "Get ready to kick the door."

"Hold positions until we're all in place," came the reply.

"They're getting ready to kick the door," Jack said.

"Let's go out the back," Zimmy urged, then bolted. Jack grabbed him and yanked him back. "It's covered. These guys are noisy getting out of vehicles, but their special entry tactics aren't bad."

"How'd they find us? We ditched them at your office." Gino was looking to Jack for an answer.

"They still have a bug planted on us."

"Where could they hide it?" Susan said.

"Inside Herm," Jack said. "Planted during the operation at Groom Lake. They couldn't believe we weren't in my office. The GPS said we were, but we were two feet away, hiding next door."

"Okay, we're good to go," the chip in Jack's ear announced.

"They're coming in," Jack stressed.

"We could go next door," Carol suggested.

"We can't go outside," Jack repeated.

"We don't need to, it's a duplex. My boyfriend's a doctor. We sleep on that side. There's a door between the units."

As they ran down the hall, Herman saw Jack duck into the master bedroom, remove one of the weights from Carolyn's lat machine, and take it with him. They went through a door in the back that led to a laundry porch shared by both units, and slipped into the apartment next door.

Carolyn's boyfriend turned out to be huge. A bodybuilder. He got up from his office computer and wide-armed his way into the hall.

"What's going on, Carolyn?" he said, his voice an octave too high for a guy that big.

"Tim, somebody's trying to take the gene map I've been working on."

"We gotta split before they decide to look over here."

While Tim was talking, Jack heard the order to go in. Both doors were kicked, followed by the sound of running footsteps in the hall next door. They could hear them shouting through the shared wall.

"Living room clear!"

"Bedroom clear!"

Carolyn opened the side door to the carport, and sitting there under a light was a red Chevy Suburban. Jack immediately reached up and knocked the light out with his gun barrel.

"You're coming with us," Jack told them.

Carolyn and Tim nodded and headed for the front seat of the Suburban. But Jack held Tim's muscle-bound arm, pulling him back. "I'm driving."

Jack grabbed the keys out of his hand and piled everyone into the SUV. He dug the chip out of his ear, started the engine, and handed Herman the ten-pound lead weight. "Put this over your heart."

"Why?"

"It's lead. It'll mask the transmission."

"But, we don't know for sure I . . ."

"Lawyers — always an argument!" Jack snapped.

Herman clutched the weight to his chest as Jack started the engine. "Everybody down."

They ducked below the windows while he backed out, making a slow, three-point turn, doing it like he had all the time in the world. He switched on the headlights and began cruising up the street at about ten miles an hour. Herman popped up and peeked out the rear window. The brown Econoline van was still at the curb in front of the duplex. Then Jack rounded the corner and they were out of sight.

"The bug quit," Valdez said. He was inside the van looking at the GPS monitor. "They musta found it."

"How could they find it? It's *inside* the fucking guy," Pettis answered.

"I'm just telling you, there's no signal." Valdez was uncharacteristically pissed. His dry-biscuit calm had evaporated in a surge of genuine panic. He waited as the four plain-clothes CDF troops rushed out the front door of the duplex and motioned that everything inside was clear.

"This can't be happening." Valdez glared at Pettis, who was still buckled into the command chair next to him.

"What about the SUV that pulled out a minute ago?"

"Maybe you're right and the bug did quit," Valdez said. "Let's go." He waved his men back to the van. The CDF troopers piled in. One handed the fifty-page encryption to Valdez. "They left this."

The driver punched it, speeding after the SUV. When they reached the end of the block they turned left, then right, then left, trying to get to the freeway on-ramp, but in their hurry they had misread the GPS map and taken a wrong turn. They wound up at the end of a cul-de-sac, half a block from the 405.

"Fuck!" Valdez raged, the recovered gene map forgotten in his hand.

It was the first time Captain Pettis ever saw the assistant director lose it.

Chapter Thirty

"Whatta you think you're doing with that thing?" Dr. Shiller asked, looking at the ten-pound weight that Herman was cradling against his chest like a lead blankie.

Herman was back in the cardio unit at Cedars wearing one of their fashion-ugly, balloon-decorated backless nightgowns. Susan was standing next to his bed. Jack was out of sight behind the open door.

Shiller glowered. He'd definitely had enough of the Strockmires. He took the lead weight off Herman's chest. "This is for a weight machine."

"Doctor, I'm ready for the procedure now," Herman said.

Doctor Shiller looked down at him as if he were deciding whether to hit him with the weight in his right hand or the metal clipboard in his left. "The nurse said your heart was fine when she took your vitals. She saw the sutures above your groin, so it looks as if you've already had the procedure. This is a busy hospital, Mr. Strockmire. Believe it or not, there are people in this cardio unit who are in actual medical danger."

Herman looked at Susan. "You tell him.

He won't listen to me."

"Okay, Doctor, you're right, we think an operation was performed," she admitted. "Dad was kidnapped yesterday, and he was taken to . . ." she stopped. "He went out to . . ."

She couldn't say Area 51. He'd throw them out.

"Yes?" Shiller was seconds away from calling security.

Herman took over. "Somebody did an operation on me. They may have implanted a radio transmitter inside me. A bug. Now they're following us, tracking me via satellite."

"You people are wonderful," Shiller said, shaking his head. "From outer space is it? Nice twist."

"Okay, you don't believe me? Take an X ray."

"I'm not wasting any more time on you." Shiller started to leave, but Susan jumped up and blocked his exit.

"Doctor, listen, please! My father has been involved in a very treacherous lawsuit. I told you about it before, remember?"

Nothing from Shiller. No reaction at all.

"Yesterday Dad came into possession of some very sensitive material that in the wrong hands could embarrass some very high-ranking Pentagon officials, maybe even the President. Because they wanted the material returned, my father was drugged and kidnapped. But Dad didn't have it on him. He'd given it to an expert to decode. They knew Dad would lead them to the material, so they planted a bug inside him to follow him until they got their hands on it. After the operation they let him go. Now they've got the material back. But they're still chasing us, because they want to kill us. The lead weight was to mask the bug and keep it from transmitting . . ." She stopped because Shiller's look had shifted from anger to one of psychiatric concern.

"If you will just open the incision and put a scope up there you'll find the transmitter, then you'll know we're telling the truth," she finished softly.

"Please leave the hospital immediately," he finally said. "Otherwise, I'll call security and have you removed."

Jack had been sitting quietly, unobserved in a folding chair behind the heavy door. As Susan explained her ridiculous story, he was trying to decide just how much deeper into this gunnysack he was prepared to go for no money — and then as soon as he asked that question, he knew he was in all the way. He also knew he was in love with Susan Strockmire.

"Hey, Doc," Jack whispered from behind the door.

"What?" Shiller spun around, surprised to find him there. "Who are you?"

"I'm Dr. Wirta, with the Wirta Eye Clinic."

"An eye doctor?"

He nodded. "A private eye institute. I've been consulting on this case, and I'll have to insist that you do exactly as the lady just instructed."

"Oh, really?" Shiller was giving him an angry little smile that barely turned the corners of his mouth up. "Well, Doctor, unless you're a cardiologist or have some pretty good juice with the Physicians Review Board at this hospital, it's not going to happen."

Jack pulled out his revolver and pointed it at Shiller. "Dr. Smith and Dr. Wesson are also consulting. You don't want to argue with these guys unless you're wearing Kevlar."

"You can't be serious."

"I'm dead serious — excuse the pun — and unless you want to decorate that wall you're standing next to, you better get this man into preop."

"I'm not gonna perform surgery at gunpoint."

"Yeah? Why not?" Jack asked.

"Well . . . well, just because . . ."

Jack brought the S&W up chest high. " 'Just because' only works in third grade. I'll need something a little more substantial."

"I . . . I don't have an operating theater. I don't have an anesthesiologist."

"They got all that stuff in the ER. Do it down there."

"You know all about it, huh? You know what it takes to do one of these?"

"It's an outpatient procedure. How tough can it be?"

"This is outrageous."

Jack thought that was a bit of an overstatement. It wasn't outrageous, at least not compared to the North Hollywood Bank shootout. Next to that, this was only highly unusual.

The procedure took about forty minutes.

On Jack's instructions, Shiller only gave Herman a local anesthetic, because Jack wanted to leave with him immediately after surgery.

A probe and chip camera were fed into Herman's upper thigh, then threaded up through the vein to his heart. After a few minutes of searching, Shiller said, "There's where they fixed the arrhythmia. See on the scope . . . the little burn mark?"

Jack couldn't see it; the video screen looked like a plate of spaghetti to him, so he took Shiller's word.

Another minute or two of searching and they found the bug.

"I got something," Dr. Shiller said through his surgical mask.

After carefully unhooking one small suture, he grasped the tiny computer chip with the microscopic pincers on the surgical probe and withdrew it. They all watched on the TV monitor as it made a fascinating journey from Herman's sternal region, down the subscapular vein, through the thoracoepigastric vein, to the umbilical region, then into the great saphenous vein and out.

Shiller dropped the tiny chip on a metal tray. The bug was about one-quarter of the size of an aspirin tablet. Jack had never seen a satellite transmitter that small.

"What is it?" Shiller asked.

"Transmitter," Jack said, then reached over and smacked it with his gun butt, turning it to powder.

"You mean all that stuff was true?" Shiller seemed amazed.

But Jack was a student of human nature, and he could still read anger and defiance in the doctor's eyes. Shiller was just the type of guy who would try to get Jack to put the gun down and then either jump him or call security.

"How long until he can be moved?" Jack asked.

"That's up to him. Depends on how he feels."

"Herm?"

"I'm a little woozy, but I can make it."

"Okay, then we'll get you a wheelchair and leave." He opened the OR door and looked out at Susan, who couldn't bear to watch and was waiting in the hall. "Get a chair."

"How's Dad?"

"He's fine. We got it out," Jack said.

A few minutes later she rolled the wheelchair into the OR. Jack instructed Shiller to lift Herman off the table and settle him into the wheelchair. All five of them trooped out of the hospital. Susan led the way, carrying Herman's clothes. Jack brought up the rear, strolling casually behind the doctor with his S&W in his sport coat pocket, feeling like a character in a Scorsese movie.

Zimmy, Carolyn, and her muscle-bound boyfriend had picked up a car for them at Rent-a-Wreck and left the keys on the top of the right front tire. Then they all decided to get lost, promising not to return to their homes.

Jack retrieved the keys and loaded Herman into the backseat of an old Chrysler Imperial. Then Dr. Shiller, Susan, and Jack stood awkwardly next to the passenger door and searched for a way to say good-bye.

"I'm sorry it had to happen this way, but thank you, Doctor," Susan said earnestly. Jack thought Dr. Shiller thawed about two degrees, but he didn't choose to say anything, so Jack got behind the wheel. Susan sat beside him, and with Herman sprawled in the back, they pulled away from Cedars-Sinai Hospital, fairly confident that nothing was beeping or flashing on a screen anywhere. No satellite tracks or Octopus tails, just three frightened people on the run in a beat-up car that barely ran.

Chapter Thirty-One

They stopped at a gas station, and while Jack filled the tank Herman changed out of the hospital gown and placed a call from the pay phone to Ted Danson and Mary Steenburgen's Hollywood office. They had donated money to the Institute in the past and were fierce environmentalists who worried about the destruction of the ozone layer, global warming, and the pollution of the oceans.

He didn't expect to actually get them on the phone, because when they weren't in production they were at their home on Martha's Vineyard. Their secretary, Louise, answered.

"It's Herman. How ya doing?" he said as soon as she picked up.

"Jeez, Strock, we were just talking about you. Mary wanted to invite you to a Memorial Day party on the Vineyard, but we didn't know where to reach you."

"Send the invite to the office in D.C. I'll be sure to make it if I can," he said. Then he told her that he wanted to borrow Ted's fishing boat for a few days because he needed a quiet place to work. Louise put him on hold while she got her bosses on the phone.

She came back a few minutes later. "Ted says okay. Just be sure to lock up when you leave, and reset the alarm." She told him where the Hide-a-Key was and gave him the alarm code.

Minutes later they were back in the rented Chrysler heading to Lido Island in Newport Beach.

As he rested in the backseat new strategies and plans were forming in Herman's head. He was considering filing a temporary restraining order against the Defense Advanced Research Projects Agency. A TRO was only good for ten days, renewable for an additional ten. Twenty days just might be enough time to do what he needed to do. There were federal laws already on the books prohibiting genetic cloning, and, although those laws were rarely enforced, Herman could still file under them.

He made a mental list of things to do. He needed to retrieve his computer that was still at the beach house and download the gene map that Zimmy had e-mailed. He also had to contact Sandy Toshiabi, his animal-rights expert. He would need to talk to his secretary, Leona Mae, get her to pull together all the background material, legal precedents, and any other laws restricting genetic research or genetic engineering. There was a helluva lot to do and almost no time to do it.

Also hovering in the back of his mind was what Dr. Adjemenian had said. This new animal, this chimera, was 99.1 percent human — only nine tenths of one percent different from *Homo sapiens.*

His preliminary strategy was simple yet compelling. Animal-rights activists had been trying to achieve legal standing in the courts for gorillas, chimps, and other primates for a long time. Legal "standing" currently only applied to *Homo sapiens* under the U.S. Constitution.

Because no other species on the planet enjoyed legal standing, they had to seek injunctive or compensatory relief through an organization that would sue for redress on behalf of the animal. It was this very fact that had compelled Herman to create the Danaus Plexippus Foundation.

The legal history on standing was fascinating and taught to every first-year law student.

At one time even slaves could not avail themselves of the benefits of the United States Constitution. In 1857, a slave named Dred Scott attempted to go into court to sue for his freedom. The Supremes ruled that he was property and, as such, had no rights under the law.

Later the Dred Scott ruling was reversed.

Using that as the historical reference to show the fallibility of the Supreme Court on the issue of standing, animal-rights activists like his friend Sandy Toshiabi had been trying unsuccessfully for years to obtain legal standing for primates. But the courts were constantly shifting the boundaries that defined humanity. At one point the federal courts said that humanity was simply the ability to walk upright. But then when chimps were taught to do that, they said that *speech* was the threshold. With Lucy, the "talking" gorilla who used American Sign Language to communicate, a new threshold was found. A species had to be capable of believing in God to claim standing. Sandy Toshiabi fought that one and had managed to prevail. "What is God?" she had argued. "When your dog looks up at you does he see God?" Currently there was no standard . . . but for one: beings must be classified as *Homo sapiens* to have legal standing. But what, Herman wondered, constituted *Homo sapiens?*

He had one other thorny problem to overcome. He had no attorney-client relationship with the chimera. His lawsuit could be voided on that fact alone. In order to represent these chimeras, one of them had to ask him to represent it. He needed a creative loophole.

The boat was at a yacht anchorage on the eastern tip of Lido Island, in Newport Beach. There were several hundred slips just across a parking lot from a high-end trailer park. It

305

was 7:00 p.m. when they found Ted's fifty-five-foot Bertram Sportfisher stern-tied to the dock. When they parked behind it they saw the name printed in foot-high, gold-leaf letters: *The Other Woman.*

Jack walked down the ramp to the dock, listening to the halyards on the surrounding sailboats rattling against their metal masts in the sharp evening breeze. He went aboard and found the keys hidden where Louise said they would be. After Susan turned off the alarm, Jack opened the rear doors and they entered, flipping on lights.

The main salon was beautiful: dark mahogany cabinets filled with cut-crystal glasses backed a mahogany bar, beige carpets, an antique table with chairs, and a beautiful, off-white silk sofa completed the decor. It seemed more like a stylish New York condo than a fishing boat.

Susan went below and forward where she found the master suite. A brass plaque on the door read: *Ink* — an homage to the show Ted and Mary costarred in together. The suite had a queen-size bed and a large bathroom featuring a shower complete with steam heads. There were two guest staterooms aft.

They went back outside to help Herman onto the boat, then settled him in the master suite, where he flopped back on the quilted bedspread, still exhausted from the surgery.

"I'm starved," Susan complained, looking

at them. "How about you, Dad?"

"There's nothing in the fridge," Jack said. "I already looked. We could go out and get something."

"Why don't you two get dinner?" Herman suggested. "Get me something to go. Bring it back after you've eaten. I saw a fish restaurant on the way in just a block from here. You could walk it." He wanted to get them out of there so he could work.

"What do you want?" she asked.

"Surprise me, honey," he answered, then closed his eyes, put his hands across his chest, and feigned sleep.

Susan stood there for a long moment, then hesitantly turned to go. "Okay, if you think it's all right."

"I'll be fine," he said. "Just turn off the light."

As soon as he heard them leave the boat, Herm pulled himself upright, turned on the bedside lamp, opened his Palm Pilot, and began scrolling for Sandy Toshiabi's number.

Chapter Thirty-Two

"I think I owe you an apology," Susan began as the drinks arrived, "an apology and some money." She took out her checkbook and a fountain pen, then wrote him a check for thirty-one hundred and eighty-one dollars. She blew on her signature to dry the ink then handed it to Jack. "For three days work, your airline tickets, lunch, and an hour of parking."

"I'm getting a nice little collection of these," he said suspiciously.

It was 6:00 p.m. and they were seated on the patio of a Newport Beach fish restaraunt named The Cannery. Small boats were tied to the wharf below the sprawling deck.

"That one will clear."

Jack studied the check skeptically. "How? I thought Herm said you guys were out of money."

"We're liquidating some things."

Earlier he had noticed that her rings and the gold graduation watch were gone. "You sold your watch?"

"We've sold a lot of stuff," she said. "None of it important."

"I can't take your graduation watch."

"Listen, Jack, this money didn't come from my watch, okay? If it's easier for you, pretend it's from Dad's old clunker station wagon that we also sold. Besides, what does it matter? We've got bills, obligations, and we're meeting them.

"If it hadn't been for you, Dad and I would probably be dead. In the face of that, I think your thousand-dollar-a-day fee is a re- markable bargain."

"Viewed in that context, you're right. Maybe I'm not charging enough," he smiled down at the check in his hand. "I'll use you as a reference."

"Any time."

The waitress returned and Susan ordered swordfish and a shrimp cocktail. Jack had a steak and mixed green salad. They ordered two more drinks.

Jack's cell phone rang. He looked at it, hes- itating. "I'm beginning to hate this thing. It feels more like a locator device than a phone."

"It might be Dad. What if he needs us?"

"Yeah." So he opened it. "Hello."

"Jack, where the hell you been? I've been trying to reach you for three or four hours." It was his ex-partner, Shane Scully. "You were right. Paul Nichols doesn't own that spread in Beverly Hills."

"Not surprising. Who does?"

"The house is owned by an Indian tribe."

"You're kidding. Which one?"

"They're called Ten-Eycks."

"Thank God they're just Indians," Jack said softly.

"They have a reservation out by Palm Springs. I punched 'em out on the Internet. They've got a Web page: Ten-Eyck-dot-com. You'd love this site . . . got an Indian sitting on a blanket smoking a peace pipe, Indian prayers, medicine-man poetry. All that's missing is the price sheet for peyote. It's a small tribe. Only thirty people in the entire Ten-Eyck nation. The administrator's a guy named Scott Nichols."

"Not Paul?"

"It's Scott. He was voted in as Tribal Administrator a few years back. He took over for the chief, some guy named Russell Ibanazi. There's a picture of Chief Ibanazi on the site. He's about thirty and looks like a Calvin Klein model. Since they own that one house on North Cannon Drive, I ran the tribe through the Real Estate Tax Board and found out they own a few other houses in Beverly Hills. Got a pencil?"

Jack pulled one out of his pocket and grabbed a paper cocktail coaster. "Gimme the other address."

"Aside from the one you gave me at 2352 North Canon, there's another one at 2443 and a house at 160 Charing Cross Road. Then, there's a big, three-acre spread at 264

Chalon Road. Altogether, this tribe owns over thirty million worth of prime dirt."

"Those Palm Springs reservations got valuable," Jack said. "The property out there's probably worth a fortune."

"Only, the Ten-Eycks got boned on that score. I checked around, and their reservation is located way out in the desert, past Indio, near the Mexican border. The property out there isn't worth much, unless you're breeding jackrabbits. So, your question is, how do they get to own all of this expensive housing in West L.A.?"

"Thanks, Shane, I owe you, man." He said good-bye and closed the phone.

"What is it?" Susan asked.

Jack told her what he'd just learned.

After he finished she sat quietly thinking, then asked, "You think they're using Indian DNA for the gene splicing, using it for the chimp upgrades?"

"I don't know, but that's as good a guess as any."

"Ten-Eyck chimeras. It fits."

The food came and they ate in silence. After he finished the main course, to get his mind off genetic nightmares, Jack decided to find out more about the beautiful woman sitting opposite him. "Tell me more about the Institute."

"It's dedicated to fighting for justice. Everywhere you look you see abuse of power or the ecology. This country fosters the triumph of the almighty dollar over common sense. Dad has dedicated himself to fixing that — to leveling the odds."

Jack already knew that Herman was more than just a conspiracy nut. He was an advocate for lost causes, and, although some of those causes seemed foolish and otherworldly, the longer Jack stayed on the case the more he felt Herman might actually be right this time.

Susan sighed, but then a smile followed and lit the edges of her mouth. "You know, Jack, when I'm not frustrated out of my gourd with Dad's tactics, I'm so proud to be part of it, I could dance on the table. I feel like there are actually times when Dad, and to a much lesser degree, yours truly, are really making a difference." She whispered this thought like a treasured secret, then leaned forward and added: "The game is rigged. We've faced more government audits than Martha Stewart. But Dad says cowardice can't be the reason to give up. You can't let people win by default when they put selfish interests above the greater good. So we just do the best we can. Dad gets up very early every morning, straps on his armor, and grabs his weapon of choice." She smiled. "Not thongs or nipple clips, but the federal criminal and civil statutes of justice. Then he goes out hunting polluters, constitutional violators, and moral criminals. And, you know what's amazing? Every so often we win."

She reached over and took his hand. "I just want you to know how much I appreciate what you've done, not quitting when my check bounced — not just turning around and leaving us."

His reasons hadn't been that noble. He started blushing.

"You're not very good at accepting compliments, are you?"

"Probably because I don't get that many."

All of her life Susan had devoted herself to details, had followed her father around, tying up loose ends, trying to make everything come out right. She had learned during her fifteen years as a soldier in Herman Strockmire's underfinanced Army Against Injustice that, although he was brilliant, dedicated, and heroic, he wasn't very organized or specific.

He was always about a hundred yards out in front of himself — leaving mistakes, unanswered questions, and knotty legal problems in his wake; often going into court unprepared, because there was always too much to do and never enough time. This had produced a string of angry judges and a spate of malpractice suits filed against the Institute by disgruntled former clients who had initially hired Herman because of his passion, but

313

then sued him because of his sloppy tactics. The malpractice suits always followed the same inevitable course: First, clients became frustrated over missed opportunities; then they become angry over courtroom blunders; and, finally, they got enraged as Herman lost and was disciplined by angry jurists. Although they occasionally won — striking important blows against their enemies — Herman and Susan often fell short. When this happened, Susan was left to pick up the pieces and placate angry clients, trying to head off the malpractice suits with all the beauty and charm she could muster.

Jack was right; she had been Herman's rear guard and tail gunner for the Institute since graduating from high school. But now Susan was scared. This time Herman had hooked too big a fish. DARPA was the government Great White, and they were all in a leaking boat, hanging on for dear life, being dragged through heavy seas. The angry shark had just spit the hook and was coming back at them.

As she sat in the restaurant she felt such a sense of gratitude toward the good-looking blonde detective sitting across from her that she reached out and touched his hand. She had written a check that they couldn't afford, but she reasoned she would much rather pay Jack Wirta than Judge King. For the first time in days she felt the knot in her stomach ease slightly; felt the warmth from the two drinks loosening her up.

She also began to evaluate Jack Wirta as a man.

There was no doubt he was attractive. But as she looked at Jack, she wondered at his awkward embarrassment and self-deprecating humor. It was a quality she loved in a man yet rarely found.

"You said you got shot in the North Hollywood Bank thing?" she said, trying to find out more.

"Yeah. It was spectacular. Charged in . . . ate the first Parabellum. Didn't realize those two assholes were already out front in that white Ford. The other guy, Phillips, damn near ran me over. Whatta mess. I really screwed up."

"You risked your life."

"The idea in police work is the bad guy is supposed to be risking *his* life; the police are supposed to make *him* bleed. Anyway, after I got shot that was it for me and police work. Now, five years later, I'm finally outta court with the department. Settled for a partial disability pension. My back got redesigned by a Winchester bullet, and here I am, at your service."

"And you're addicted to those little pills you take," she said, surprising him, but before he could say anything, she continued. "I've seen my share of addictions. I've watched you try to take them when I'm not looking. You're on about a four-hour cycle."

"Jesus Christ," he said, shaking his head in disgust.

"It's okay, Jack, I understand. You got hooked on pain killers — it happens. There's nothing to be ashamed of, but you need to deal with it."

"You and Herm got your own little twelve-step program, am I right?" he said, anger replacing embarrassment.

"When you and Dad were taken out to that base at Groom Lake I had lots of time on my hands. I researched the North Hollywood Bank shooting on the Internet. There were news stories about your injury and your lawsuit. I read your doctor's courtroom statement."

He looked across the table at her, not sure what to say.

"I don't fault you for it." She was still touching his hand. "But don't you think you should do something about it?"

Jack hated being hooked on the pain pills. He was furious that he had been reduced to buying them from a street dealer, shamed by the fact that he was committing a felony. But some part of him relaxed when she busted him. He felt a flood of relief that somebody else finally knew — that she understood and didn't hate him for it.

"I understand human weakness, Jack. It's been a big part of my life. I'm scared to death that I'm not up to the tasks Dad and I have chosen. But Dad says weakness is only a problem if you give in to it. My God, look at him . . . Daddy sure has his share of weaknesses. I've struggled to hide them, struggled to put his mistakes right. But I love him *because* he struggles on despite his defects and defeats. I see those same qualities in you."

"If you start pitching a bunch of new-age bullshit at me I'm gonna go into the men's room and blow my head off." He smiled ruefully. When he looked across the table at her she had real concern in her eyes.

"I think you're a very special person, Jack, and worth getting to know better. Sound okay?"

"Sure," he whispered. "Great."

They walked back toward the boat holding hands. Neither of them wanted this time to end, so instead of going aboard, they went over to the little beach at one end of the trailer park and sat on the sand. As they listened to the sound of the water lapping on the shore the bay was tipped with silver light from a three-quarter moon. Across the harbor, a mile away, old wooden car ferries, with their festive red-and-white hulls and Christmas-tree rail lights, chugged back and forth from Balboa Island to the big up-lit pavilion on the Newport Peninsula. Sailboat stays slapped in the breeze. Hundreds of crickets serenaded them.

Then Jack kissed her.

He didn't know if she would respond, but he had to find out. She did, putting her arms around his neck and pulling him down onto the sand with her.

They were soon caressing each other — Jack determined not to mess this up with some adolescent hormonal overload. He stopped, pulled back, and looked carefully at her.

"Are you sure?"

"Yes," she said softly, then pulled him down again, and they slowly began peeling off each other's clothes.

He kissed and caressed her, and their passion grew. Jack wanted her more than anything on earth. But, more than the sex, he wanted a woman with whom he could have an honest relationship and a friendship — somebody who understood his weaknesses and wasn't dismayed by them; somebody who saw events for what they were and didn't try to arrange them to fit some narrow, self-involved definition.

Susan Strockmire was more of a hero than he had ever been . . . much braver and stronger. She had dedicated her life to supporting her wheezing, lumbering father. She had followed Herman, serving his needs, loving him without question, fixing his mistakes —

standing in front of him, shielding him, often taking his punishment. For the first time in Jack's life he needed to give that kind of passionate dedication to someone.

Almost magically, they were entwined and he entered her. They held off for as long as they could, each giving pleasure to the other, exploring their newness. She held him tightly, kissing him, caressing him, taking him deeply inside her, until they both released, lying in the dew-damp sand, reveling in ecstasy.

Afterwards, he felt her hot breath on his ear, felt her tender hands stroking his wounded back, gently touching the welts and scars left by the North Hollywood shootout.

"Don't worry," she whispered softly. "We'll do this together."

A little later they collected their clothes, dressed, and walked back to *The Other Woman* holding hands as their shadows danced beneath them in the moonlight.

It wasn't until they turned to go down the gangplank onto the deck that Jack realized something was wrong. At first it was just a tickle in his head.

What is it? What's wrong with this picture?

Then it hit him.

The Rent-A-Wreck Chrysler was gone.

They ran aboard the boat looking for Herman, throwing open doors, but Herman Strockmire Jr. was nowhere to be found.

Chapter Thirty-Three

The DARPA van was parked almost a block away from the Malibu beach house. Captain Silver was asleep on an air mattress next to Pan's cage while a video operator watched a bank of monitors. Captain Pettis was seated in the command chair looking at an infrared shot that focused on the street leading up to the house. They could both smell Pan's dank odor, hear his steady breathing.

Suddenly, Pettis saw a Chrysler drive up the street and pull into Barbra Streisand's driveway, parking in front of the closed garage door. He turned in the command swivel and tapped Captain Silver on the shoulder. "Got something here."

Captain Silver woke up from a sound sleep looking fresh and rested. They squinted at the glowing, green infrared image on the monitor.

Less than a minute later a yellow Toyota Corolla pulled up and parked next to the Chrysler. As a slender Asian woman exited the Toyota, Herman Strockmire heaved his big, wide body out of his car. He lumbered toward the woman, then the two of them appeared to be having some kind of an argument.

"Gimme her plate," Pettis ordered. The video operator pushed in on the back of the Toyota using his twenty-to-one lens, finally getting it full screen: EKI 154.

Pettis picked up the phone, dialed DARPA headquarters in Virginia, asked for wants and warrants on California plate EKI 154, and waited.

Moments later, a man in Virginia was back on the line. "Sandra Toshiabi, 1656 Huntington Avenue, Santa Monica, California. No wants or warrants."

"Fax me her DL picture," Pettis said as he hung up. He was already entering Sandy Toshiabi's name into the satellite uplink that connected him to the DARPA mainframe databank in Virginia. Herman and Sandy were just deactivating the alarm on the side gate. The video operator chased after them with his zoom lens, moving in tight on the alarm. But Herman's squat frame blocked a clear view of the keypad.

"Couldn't get the number," the video man said.

Herman and Sandy went through the gate and closed it. The red light went back on as the alarm reset.

"Here she comes." Pettis watched as Sandra Toshiabi's DARPA file came up on the screen. "One of our old flames: Doctor of Veterinary Medicine, Committee to Protect Animal Rights, SPCA, Save the Whales,

Green Peace, Coalition of Conservationists . . . animal-rights activist." Then her picture came through and showed a pretty Asian woman with black hair and brown eyes.

"Whatta we do?" Captain Silver asked.

Pettis responded, "We got the gene map, so I think we should put your DU over the wall and jerk this problem out by the roots. But we first need to get Valdez to sign off."

"What if Strockmire made a copy of the map?" Silver wondered aloud.

"If he has one, we'll deal with it later. We've got to contain these people now."

"You shouldn't have come here," Herman said, still arguing with Sandy as they moved past the Olympic-size pool. "I told you I'd meet you at your place. Why won't you or Susan ever do what I ask?"

"Because we love you," Sandy grinned. "Besides, what are they gonna do, kill us?"

"Yeah. That's exactly what they're gonna do." Herman led Sandy into the pool house, turned, and locked the door.

Sandy watched as he punched numbers on the keypad, then waited for the alarm to beep, indicating it had rearmed itself. "You're really scared, aren't you?"

"You didn't read the coroner's report on Roland."

"On the phone, you said it's some kind of hybrid, a chimera?" she said.

He turned on his computer, found Zimmy's decoded e-mail, then brought it up. "Here's the gene map." He handed her the laptop, and while she scanned the pages of decoded base pairs he gathered up his extra batteries and cords, then stuffed them into his carry case.

"This is what they're trying to get their hands on?" she said, frowning at the pages.

"We left a copy of that for them at Carolyn's house. They don't know Zimmy sent this one to my computer."

"You say this hybrid is 99.1 percent of a human?"

"That's what the BLAST search indicated."

"That still doesn't make it human, Herman. To achieve standing in federal court, plaintiffs have to be pure *Homo sapiens*. Add to that the problem of representation and you're out of luck."

"Okay, I'll admit I'm not sure about the attorney-client thing yet, but I've got a great theory on how we can bust the shit out of that *Homo sapiens* restriction. If I'm right, I think I can get legal standing for this chimera. Once we break that barrier, all the others should crumble right behind it. But we can't stand around here and discuss it. They must have this address, so we need to keep moving. I'm gonna file a TRO against DARPA, but I need to collect my casebooks. I still have some legal precedents to research."

They went into a small bedroom that Herman had been using as an office, then began packing his *Shilling Lawyer's Guide* and several thick volumes of landmark federal precedents. After he retrieved his black suit, Herman grabbed his toilet kit, and they hurried back into the main room.

"Once an alarm blows in Malibu, the cops have a four-minute response time," Captain Pettis said over the secure sat-phone. "If Dave and I try to do this with just the two of us we might lose containment."

Vincent Valdez was on the line from DARPA's L.A. office with General "Buzz" Turpin conferenced in from D.C. When nobody spoke, Pettis continued:

"This is the same DU that took out the computer thief in San Francisco. He's right here in the van with us. Captain Silver says he's good to go."

"If you use a Development Unit, make sure he has on the abort-destruct vest," General Turpin said. "If it goes wrong I don't want anything left. And Vince . . ."

"Yes, sir."

"If you use the DU, make sure it doesn't go nuts and start shredding corpses again. Be sure you two sanitize the crime scene before clearing out this time."

"Roger that." Pettis clicked off the transmission. "Okay. Just Strockmire and Toshiabi are in there — maid's day off. No fuck ups."

Captain Silver opened the cage, then led the chimera to the front of the van. Pan jumped up on the seat and sat looking out of the windshield. Seeing his intelligent gray eyes, Pettis thought Pan's face and ears were uncannily human, but the rest of him seemed more like a standard chimpanzee. Except for the hands. He had hands exactly like a grown man. On his forehead was a new satellite-transmitter camera unit the size of a quarter, mounted on a white tennis headband.

"Two people this time," Captain Silver instructed as he picked up the file photo of Herman Strockmire and showed it to the Chimera. Pan reached out, took the photo, then held it up and studied it. Pettis watched, thinking how strange Pan was. Half man, half beast.

Captain Silver grabbed Sandy Toshiabi's DL picture that had just come off the sat-link, then handed it to Pan. The chimera looked at it and cocked his head.

"No shredding and no urinating," Silver said. "We've practiced this stuff. You know how to do it, right?"

Pan reached down onto his arm and typed on the small computer strapped there.

"Pan understands," the mechanical voice responded from his vest speakers.

"Good."

"Get him in the other vest," Pettis said.

325

"Is that really necessary?" Captain Silver protested.

"Direct order from the general. You heard."

Norman Pettis grabbed the abort-destruct vest and handed it to Pan's trainer, glad that Captain Silver was in the van, because he hated to touch these strange animals. He watched as Dave Silver unbuckled the normal computer clothing, removed it, then put on the slightly bulkier abort vest.

"Pan, I'm going to give you the knife," Captain Silver said. "You kill these people with the knife. I will also give you a Particle Beam-99. Do not use the PB-99 unless you must. It is only to help you get away if you are trapped."

Pan fingered his armband, hitting several keys. *"Pan understands."*

Silver then handed one of the particle-beam weapons to Pan, who dropped it into a webbed holster on his vest. Silver put leather gloves on Pan's hands so he could run on all fours, and handed him a knife. Pettis had once witnessed Pan kill a vicious, attacking Doberman in less than three seconds with the combat knife. He opened the door and let the chimera out of the van.

The men watched as Pan ran on all fours, streaking across the street, easily vaulting over the alarmed wall and disappearing onto Barbra Streisand's property.

Chapter Thirty-four

"Where could he have gone?" Susan was standing in the main salon of the boat, panic washing over her.

"If I know Herm, he's not going to quit on this," Jack said. "So where'd he go?"

"Zimmy sent that gene map to Dad's computer, and the computer is at the beach house."

"Nah . . . come on, he wouldn't go over there. Your dad's smarter than that."

"He's . . ." she stopped. "He's . . . well I think . . ."

"Streisand's house? You can't be serious. We used her car in Montrose. They'll run the plate and have the beach house completely staked out. Herman might be a tad mistake-prone, but is he a complete bonehead?"

She glowered at him. "Damn it, Jack, if he needs that gene map to file his lawsuit then he'll go and get it. That's the way he is."

"How can he file a lawsuit?"

"Knowing him, he'll come up with something. A temporary restraining order . . . use the gene map as proof of the chimera's existence. That's probably gonna be hard to get in as evidence, but Dad is resourceful, and the evidentiary rules are more lax for a TRO. He'll charge that these chimps are having their DNA illegally messed with, then try and get a restraining order to prevent it."

"What's his cell number?" Jack asked. "I hate calling it, but we gotta stop him from going there."

"Won't help. I've got his phone." She pulled it out of her purse and showed it to him.

Jack went to the phone in the salon, picked it up, and pulled out the business card Susan had given him two days ago. He dialed Streisand's number, but got Herman's answering machine in the guest house. "You've reached the temporary L.A. office of the Institute for Planetary Justice," Herman's tired voice announced. "We are off creating havoc for world polluters and environmental criminals, so leave a message and we'll take it from there." *BEEP.*

"Herman, it's Jack. Pick up that chimera file and get the hell out of that house. It's not safe. Don't stop to call me until you're out of Malibu. I'm at 949-555-1242." He hung up and looked into Susan's worried expression. "He's out creating havoc for world polluters."

She nodded. Both of them sat there brooding, trying to figure out what to do next.

"I think we should try to head him off,"

she finally said, her face a mask of apprehension.

"If he left right after we went to dinner we'll never make it in time."

Paul Nichols was doing a line of kickass Poluo Blanco when his computer's incoming mail feature beeped. He wiped the residue off his nose, went to the screen, and read the transcription of Jack Wirta's phone message. Octopus had picked up the keyword, *Chimera,* and located the point of origin in area code 949. He punched out a code on his keyboard, accessing a GPS map and a stored record of the call to Streisand's house along with the precise longitude and latitude of the caller, which was displayed on the electronic map. The call had originated from the third-to-last boat slip at the end of Lido Island. He tried to still his cocaine rush as he dialed the command room at DARPA headquarters in L.A.

Jack felt a slight sway from the stern of the boat. He reached over, flipped off the lights, and whispered, "Somebody just came aboard."

"Dad?"

He felt the boat rock again as two more people came aboard. " 'Fraid not," he whispered.

Earlier Jack had seen a spear fishing locker

located in the forward bulkhead across from where they were now standing. He opened it, grabbed three spear guns along with a handful of shafts, then led Susan into the master stateroom, closed the door, and locked it. Then he'd guided her into the master bath where he remembered seeing an overhead fire hatch in the shower.

He heard footsteps outside in the companionway.

Jack pushed open the fire hatch, then helped Susan scale the ladder. Once she was out on the foredeck he handed up the three spearguns and spears. She looked puzzled and started to say something, but Jack put a finger to his lips, then followed her through the hatch and closed it.

They knelt on the wide teak bow of the Bertram Sportfisher while Jack loaded and cocked all of the guns one at a time, pulling the spear shafts back, straining the rubber tubing until the triggers clicked and they locked in place.

"Why those?" she whispered.

"No noise. Pick 'em off one at a time," he whispered.

"Kill them?" She was appalled.

"Susan, we're down to basics here. We can do the dying, or they can. How do you want it?"

Someone was coming forward. Jack pushed Susan behind a mahogany locker then crouched down beside her. A figure appeared silhouetted against the moon dressed in SWAT gear. The man must have sensed him, because the commando spun suddenly, holding one of the strange laser weapons. He was pointing it right at them. Jack fired the first spear. *Fong. Thump!*

The shaft buried itself deep in the man's chest. He groaned, toppled over the rail, and fell loudly into the water.

As soon as the splash sounded, they heard a shout below and feet running.

Jack grabbed Susan's hand. "Come on, we're goin' swimming." They jumped off the bow into the bay, with Jack clutching two un- fired spear guns. Once they hit the cold water, and fought their way back up to the surface they started stroking away from the boat. In soaked clothing, they were making way too much noise. Jack stopped swimming and pulled up the second spear gun. He treaded water, holding the weapon at the ready, kicking his feet hard to stay afloat.

Susan kept going toward a line of sailboats moored halfway across the channel. The moonlight made them easy targets.

A second man ran to the bow of the boat, knelt down, and aimed his weapon.

Jack fired.

The spear flew high and wide, hitting the wheelhouse just above the window. It thunked and quivered, embedding itself deep into the wood next to the man's head. He scrambled back off the bow.

Sorry about that, Ted.

Jack dove, and made his way underwater, after Susan. With each lunging stroke, his back knifed with pain.

Finally, he caught up to her. She had stopped and was treading water, waiting for him.

"Keep going, around that boat. Get underwater," he gasped, swallowing a mouthful of water.

They both dove just as two laser weapons zapped. A horrible tingling sensation electrified the water all around them. But the laser weapon's particle beam was quickly dissipated by the water.

Underwater, Jack saw the dim outline of the moored sailboat, now only three yards away tied to two cans in the center of the channel. They frog-kicked toward it and somehow reached the far side before they surfaced, totally winded.

"Let's go. Keep the boat between us and them." he instructed. "We gotta get to that beach." Jack pointed to an expensive residential island that was another fifty yards beyond. As they reached the shore, they heard the CDF troops swimming after them.

"Let's get out of here!" Jack grabbed Susan's arm and they sprinted up the small beach between two bay-front houses, then onto the residential street beyond, where a few cars were parked. Jack ran to a classic Jag XKG convertible.

He broke out the window with a Rockette-worthy kick. Then he reached through, unlocked the door, got in, and found the ignition wires. He pulled them out, twisted them, and almost immediately the Jag purred to life.

Susan ran to the passenger side and jumped in as Jack put the Jag in gear, powering away from the curb. He roared down the narrow street, then he turned right onto the Coast Highway.

Chapter Thirty-five

Pan is outside the pool house. He sees the Geegas. They are in the lighted room behind the sheet of hard air.

He leaps, hitting it, putting his head through, but feeling no pain as pieces crash onto the floor around him. Green, savage memories overtake him — shadow thoughts he can never identify. Violence! Rage! Killing for his tribe! Now Pan is inside the room and the Geegas are standing still, frightened, so easy to slaughter.

The male Geega, standing next to the light pad on the wall, does something Pan doesn't understand . . . he turns and pushes a button. "Run!" he yells at the female Geega, who lunges toward the door. But Pan blocks her path. He knows to kill the male Geega first. This is the rule.

Pan charges.

The male Geega swings a heavy canvas bag, hitting him in the chest, catching Pan by surprise. Pan falls backward, squealing.

"The pool!" the female yells. Pan knows he can't rip them apart. He must use the knife. He knows that disobeying a direct order from the Alpha is worse than death.

Pan brings his gloved hand up, flashing the

knife. Pan spends hours practicing with the killing knives. He prefers to use his hands — the glorious shredding ripping, but the Alpha Geega has said no. So, Pan now approaches slowly, just as he is taught. Creeping toward the male Geega on three extenders, his gloved hand in front of him, the five-inch blade flashing. He can hear his breath coming in rasps, snarling in the back of his throat.

Pan is happy.

Herman saw the beast seconds after it crashed through the window. It was far more terrifying than he had imagined . . . an almost-human face twisted in animal rage, a body covered completely with brown fur. He hit the emergency panic button sending a silent alarm directly to the Malibu Sheriff's substation a few miles away, then turned to face the beast. The animal reeked like an unwashed hound. It wore a white headband, soaked red with blood from glass cuts.

"My God," Herman said, as the chimera brandished a vicious-looking, five-inch blade in its gloved hand. The beast was wearing a vest that contained some kind of complicated computer. The stench coming off the animal was growing worse by the second, clogging Herman's nostrils.

Then the chimera charged.

Herman swung his heavy canvas bag full of law books, catching the beast in the chest and rolling it backward onto the floor. He grabbed Sandy's hand and started for the back door.

"No!" Sandy yelled. "The pool!"

She ran right through the broken sliding glass door, pulling Herman after her, as the chimera rolled to its feet and with amazing speed leaped forward, running on all fours, quickly closing the distance between them.

Herman could hear the strange sound of the leather gloves scraping against the concrete pavement behind them. Sandy yanked him hard and suddenly they were both in the pool. As they landed in the deep end the chimera skidded to a halt inches from the water. It screamed, then ran around the edge, jumping and grunting, looking for a way to get at them.

"My God, what is it?" Herman said.

"I think it's one of your new clients," Sandy gasped as they treaded water. "A chimera. They can't swim."

"How do you know?" Herman yelled as he watched the frightening animal growling at them, its eyes filled with murderous rage.

"It looks mostly chimp. They're too heavy to swim. Too much muscle. No body fat. Chimps are afraid of the water," Sandy treaded water and stared at the angry beast. She obviously knew what she was talking about, because it was now clear that this thing had no intention of going in after them.

As the hybrid ran back and forth around the pool it finally noticed the steps in the shallow end. Screeching angrily, it waded in up to its waist — but now the electronic vest was getting wet. Herman could hear circuits popping. After a moment of indecision, the chimera waded out of the pool, then scurried around to the diving board. It ran out to the end and clung to the edge, reaching toward Herman and making a loud, plaintive scream.

"It wants us to help him." Herman started to swim toward it.

"Get back . . . are you nuts?" Sandy yelled, then grabbed him, pulling him further out of range.

The chimera jumped up and down on the diving board, regret on its hairless face.

Suddenly they heard police sirens winding down outside the house. A pair of car doors slammed and a moment later the first of the Malibu sheriffs jumped up to look over the wall into the pool area.

"Help!" Sandy called. "We need help!"

The deputy climbed to the top of the wall, then jumped down, landing twenty feet from the enraged chimera.

"What the *fuck?*" the deputy sheriff said when he saw the beast.

Pan sees the Geega female turn and drag the male out through the broken place. Out to the wet place where water shimmers.

Pan knows he must stop the Geegas before they get there. If Geegas get to the wet place he will not be able to follow. He will fail.

Pan is almost on them, reaching out with the knife, slashing, but getting nothing but Geega clothing. Pan screams in fear and anger, almost falls, teetering on the edge of the wet, but finally regains his balance. The Alpha Geega Dave is yelling in Pan's earpiece.

"Kill them! Get them!" Pan wants to do what Dave commands. He can imagine the Geega bodies in his grip, ripping, shredding. Pan wants to use the PB-99, but the Alpha Geega says no, not unless he is being captured.

Pan runs around the pool, stopping at some steps where the water looks shallow. He runs down, feeling the warm wet against his fur. He goes deeper, almost to his waist.

"Pan! No! Don't get the vest wet!" Dave is yelling at him. "You'll short it out."

Pan hears the vest popping, but he ignores it. He is a warrior. He has come from a faraway place to shred and kill. He will not fail.

Pan backs out of the water and runs to the wood plank hanging out over the other side. He creeps out to the end and can now almost reach the male Geega. He grabs the underside of the wood that is hanging over the water and stretches out as far as he can, reaching for the big Geega, but he is still too far away. The Geega begins moving toward him . . . maybe close enough to grab.

338

Pan hears something behind him, turns, and sees another Geega jumping up on the wall. This Geega wears a cap and has silver on his shirt. The Geega jumps down off the wall.

"What the fuck?" the Geega says.

Pan screams his warrior scream. He runs at the new Geega standing by the gate. He grabs him and jerks him forward. Using the knife, Pan rips him open. Blood spews. Pan keeps jabbing and cutting. The Geega's screams are gurgles now as he chokes on his own blood. Pan has no mercy.

The Geega falls forward. Blood spills from the huge wound in his neck. Pan jumps up and down on the ground, then snarls at his dead enemy.

Maybe this will make Dave happy. Pan knows he must go. He turns and easily leaps over the wall, landing on the other side, then runs toward the van. But as he does he hears two loud bangs. He knows that these are from a Geega fire-stick. Then a third bang. Something hits him hard in the back. Pan flies forward, feeling nothing but the impact that turns him in the air as he falls. Pan lands on his back and sees a second Geega wearing the same uniform with silver pinned on his shirt. He is standing off the walkway pointing his fire-stick.

The man shoots again.

"No!" Dave Silver said, watching on the monitor as his chimera lay bleeding in the street.

339

"Abort destruct," Norm Pettis ordered, but Silver's face was twisted with indecision. Pettis reached out and pushed a radio detonator. The vest Pan was wearing would react to the radio command by injecting the chimera with an explosive chemical that would travel quickly to five areas in Pan's body, drawn by electromagnets located in the vest. Pettis pushed a second button, which sent a radio wave to the DARPA satellite in space, then bounced it back to the detonator on Pan's body computer.

Nothing happened. The vest had shorted out.

Dave Silver knew Pan was mortally wounded. Pettis grabbed the mike. "Pan! You must go. You must hide!"

They watched on the monitor as the deputy approached Pan, gazing down in wonder.

"Pan, run! Run!" Pettis ordered angrily.

Surprisingly, Pan rolled to his feet and shoved the deputy aside.

"Son of a bitch," Pettis said softly. "These little fuckers are tough."

As Dave Silver watched in awe, Pan started to run. Leaking blood, the chimera limped up the beach road, crossed into the brush by the hillside, then disappeared.

Chapter Thirty-Six

Jack and Susan were halfway to Malibu in the stolen XKE when Herman's cell phone rang. Susan dug it out of her purse and answered.

"It's me." Herman's tired voice seemed to come from far away. "We gotta meet, but I'm pretty sure these calls are being intercepted."

"Hang on a minute, Dad," she said and turned to Jack. "He wants to meet."

"Pick some place you both know, but don't mention the name."

"Dad, without saying it, remember where you took me for my birthday?"

"Yeah."

"Meet us there. It'll take us less than an hour."

"Right." Herman hung up.

The separate structures that made up the Malibu Beach Inn clung to the rocky crevices like brightly painted barnacles. Some units were wedged into the hillside, others perched on granite pads high above the ocean, with views that looked down on spectacular rock formations. The entire ocean side of the inn was wrapped by a meandering patio that contained six tables for the tiny gourmet restaurant.

Susan and Jack walked into the lobby and stopped at the front desk. Herman had registered, taking two rooms under his own name.

Great, Herm . . . why don't you just take out an ad? Jack thought.

Herman had left a note for Susan that read: *We're on the veranda.*

They made their way out onto the rambling, narrow cliff-side patio and found Herman and Sandy seated at a table overlooking the ocean. The crashing waves spewed foam that glistened in half a dozen powerful Xenon spotlights.

Herman was in his lawyer mode, half-glasses perched on the end of his nose and yellow pad open, scribbling hieroglyphic notes as they approached.

When Susan hugged her father he felt her damp clothing. "You're wet," he said, looking at her with concern.

"So are you," Susan said. Jack turned to the Asian woman seated with him. "You must be Sandy."

Herman introduced them. After Jack and Susan were seated, it took about fifteen minutes for them to bring each other up to date.

Herman listened to the account of Jack's speargunning of the DARPA commando on Lido Island and their close escape. His basset jowls were pulled tight, and he frowned when

Jack told him about the stolen Jaguar. "Where's the car now?"

"In the parking lot, but I switched the plate with another car parked there." Jack smiled. "That oughta keep the ride cool for a few hours."

"Maybe you should ditch it and get a rental."

"Except the Wirta Agency is ever vigilant as it watches over your expense sheet." If Jack was expecting some kind of praise for his courage and frugality, he was disappointed. What he got were strained looks all around. It seemed the spear gun caper and car theft had turned his karma brown.

Sandy and Herman recounted their ordeal with the chimera in Streisand's guesthouse. Jack thought it was by far the better story.

"You actually *saw* one?" Susan asked, amazed.

"Honey, not only did I see it, but it wanted us to help it."

Susan frowned. "I thought you said it tried to kill you."

"The more I think back . . . I'm not sure. Sandy doesn't agree, but I think it was reaching out to us, with a pleading look all over its face . . . in its eyes."

Sandy looked over at Jack. "Herm wants to believe it was pleading for help, but I can tell you the only way we got away was by jumping into the pool. They can't swim."

They all sat awkwardly at the small table searching for something to say. Finally it was Herman who continued. "We grabbed my things, then went out through the side gate and escaped up the beach. We had to leave the cars. Since the chimera killed the deputy, there're enough cops standing around at Barbra's to open a donut franchise. We walked the two miles to get here." Then Herman announced his legal strategy. He was going to file a TRO against DARPA on behalf of "Charles Chimera, a being." He was going to use this case to change the rules on standing. Then, as they sat in stunned silence, he detailed the rest of his plan.

"I hope it works," Sandy said softly. "If it doesn't, you'll be on CNN, eating crow."

Herman and Sandy ordered food while Jack and Susan had coffee. Sandy Toshiabi started sketching on her paper place mat while waiting for the food to arrive. By the time they had finished dinner she had completed the drawing. She turned it around for all of them to see. It was a remarkably good sketch of the thing that had chased them into the pool.

"It really looks like that?" Jack asked, thinking it resembled a prehistoric man, but with a more intelligent face.

"That's exactly what it looks like," Herman confirmed.

After paying the bill they walked back to

344

the lobby. Herman said he and Jack could share one room, Susan and Sandy the other. At Jack's suggestion, they stopped at the front desk to change the registration into Sandy's name.

Jack said, "I wanna check on this address in Bel Air that Shane gave me. See who lives at 264 Chalon Road. I'll be back in two or three hours."

"I'm coming with you," Susan said. Jack started to refuse, but, the truth was, he was really enjoying her company, so he ended up agreeing.

They left Sandy and Herman plotting the lawsuit and got back into the Jag and drove south on PCH, then followed Sunset toward Beverly Hills.

What they were about to find wasn't as strange as Herman's chimera, but it sure as hell would change the events that followed.

Chapter Thirty-Seven

Halfway to Bel Air, Susan opened the glove box and started searching around inside.

"Whatta y'doing?" Jack asked.

"I want to see who, exactly, is gonna be charging you with grand theft auto." She pulled out the registration and read it. " 'Baxton Hammond Jr.' " She looked at Jack. "I think I've heard of him."

"You're kidding, right?" Jack said. "And the hits just keep on coming."

"Who is he?"

"Bax Hammond. The Orange County D.A."

Suddenly, Susan started laughing. Whether it was just a release of tension or she thought it was really funny, Jack couldn't tell, but her laughter was infectious, and soon he was roaring as well. He had tears in his eyes. Hopefully they'd still see the humor after completing their two-and-a-half-year GTA sentences in Soledad.

Jack continued down Sunset. "That's it up ahead."

They were both still smiling as he turned into the Bel Air entrance. After driving for about six blocks up into the foothills they found 264 Chalon Road.

It was an impressive Spanish mansion, and there was some kind of a high-profile party going on. Black-suited security was checking every invitation at the foot of the pillared driveway. Valets in red coats scurried back and forth, jumping into arriving cars, pulling away fast, and racing them up the hill to park. A truck from Along Came Mary Catering was parked across the street.

Jack pulled up to the nearest attendant. "Is this the Goldberg's party?" he asked a teenage boy, who looked like he had probably just started driving about a week ago.

"No sir, this is the Ibanazi house. Invitation only." The valet wrinkled his nose in distaste. Jack's wardrobe was finally dry, but it must have fallen well below the guest profile.

"Wrong blast. I'm going to Whoopi's. Sorry!" Trying for some payback.

Jack put the Jag in gear and pulled up a side street away from all the valet madness. As he looked for a place to pull over, he handed Susan the car phone. "Call 411 and see if he's listed."

She dialed Information and asked for Russell Ibanazi's phone number on Chalon Road. She scribbled it down and hung up.

Jack mulled options. Then he picked up her cell phone.

"What're you gonna do?" she asked.

"Gonna get us invited to this party." He dialed the number.

"Ibanazi residence," a pleasant-sounding woman said.

"Good evening, this is Mr. Wirta. Project supervisor for Along Came Mary? To whom is it that I might be speaking?" Saying it like he had a broom handle up his ass.

"This is Mrs. Dorsett. I'm Chief Ibanazi's record company vice president."

"Good. Right-o. I was in the neighborhood, just wanted to make sure all of your catering choices were delivered exactly as planned." Adding a tinge of Limey accent now for flavor.

"Yes, I guess. But I'm not the one who made the catering arrangements."

"Did the smoked-duck empanadas with caviar centers arrive?" Jack breezed on.

"Uh . . . I don't . . . did we order those?"

"Three trays. I specifically told John to have those over by five."

"Uh . . . John?" She seemed confused.

"How 'bout the Roma tomato bruschettas, and the brie en croute with raspberry walnut sauce?"

"Uh . . . well . . . I think I saw some shrimp scampi and some spinach quiche."

"Can't be. The quiche was for Warren and Annette's pool party. Don't tell me the cold octopus pie didn't make it?" Just sort of screwing with her now.

348

"Uh . . . cold octopus?"

"It seems there's been a horrible flummox. To begin with, please tell that wonderful Chief Ibanazi that we are absolutely not charging him for any of the things that he didn't order, and I will personally deduct twenty percent from the invoice for this horrible mistake. I'm going to dash right over to check into this personally. I'd appreciate it if you might notify your security people at the gate, that Mr. Jackson Wirta and Ms. Susan Strockmire from Along Came Mary will be along directly. In the meantime, could you be a dear and make an inventory sheet of what's already out so we can get this mess unscrambled."

"But the catering was handled by Louis. I didn't arrange for any of this." Ass-covering, pure and simple.

"Not your fault, Mrs. Dorsett and it's not Louis's either — it's ours. And we can thank the Queen's butler, you and I caught it in lickety-split time." Jack almost said "Tallyho," but thought he was already over the top, so he just hung up.

"That Brit accent really stunk," Susan grinned.

"It got us into the party."

They waited a few minutes for Mrs. Dorsett to make the call, then pulled down within sight of the security/valet station. Jack waited until the first valet he'd spoken to whizzed off to park a Porsche Targa. Then

349

he put the Jag in gear and pulled up.

"I'm Jackson Wirta," he said to another teenager as they both got out. "This is Ms. Strockmire. I think Mrs. Dorsett rang you up." Still using the phony accent.

"Right," the security goon said. "With the caterers. She just called. Go on up."

Jack took a valet ticket and then headed up the long, winding brick driveway toward a sprawling Spanish mansion with a red-tiled roof. There were at least four acres of manicured lawns with an Olympic-size pool and seventy-foot palm trees that swayed overhead, waving their giant fronds like skinny, fan-wielding eunuchs. Fountains gushed and spurted. Young Beverly Hills trophy wives clutched their geriatric keepers and mingled competitively.

Jack and Susan skirted the growing crowd of about a hundred and fifty guests. Across the pool, holding court under the cabana, sat the Indian chief.

Russell Ibanazi was a remarkably handsome man who, as Shane had mentioned, was only thirty years old. His dark good looks and Hollywood dress gave him a definite nouveau tilt. He laughed at something one of the women near him said, and when he did his smile sparkled like bone china. He was wearing an Armani suit with Gucci sunglasses hanging off his top shirt button. An Amstel Light was clutched casually in his right hand.

"Groovy-type Indian," Jack said.

"What were you expecting, a loin cloth?" Susan frowned.

"No, but I was hoping for a couple of hair feathers."

Jack began circling Chief Ibanazi like a reef shark scoping prey.

"He's so young," Susan said.

"He's also listed. In Beverly Hills, you're only in the book if you're still hoping people will call you. Sure sign of social insecurity. Could be a sucker for my *Daily Planet* thing."

"Your what?"

"Just play along," Jack said, and strolled toward Russell, pulling a pen out of his pocket along with his small spiral detective notebook. He waited for a hole in both the conversation and the swirling entourage, then stepped neatly through both.

"Mr. Ibanazi? Clark Lane, with *213 Magazine*. This is one of the nicest events we've been to in months." *213* was the first area code assigned to Beverly Hills and was also the name of a slick magazine that featured its rich and famous.

Russell Ibanazi's head snapped up like he'd just been hooked with a twenty-pound test line.

"*213?*" the Chief grinned. "You guys thinkin' about doing a story on me?"

"Maybe . . . maybe . . . could be . . .

could be," Jack mused. "This is our society editor, Lois Kent."

"Hi," Susan smiled, seductively.

From that point Russ Ibanazi was hooked like a Baja game fish. He shook Jack's hand energetically. He smiled at Susan longingly.

"I just started my own record label. That's why we're having the party. To promote Miracle Records." He exuded charm.

"Watch out for the critics on that one," Jack warned. "They're sarcastic bastards. You don't wanta give them an easy shot."

Russell's face scrunched up into a confused frown.

Jack spread his hands. " 'If it's a good song, it's a miracle.' Easy slam. See the problem?"

Ibanazi's face fell. "I never thought of that. I see your point. We just went in business. Maybe I should come up with something else?"

"I love this record angle, Clark," Susan enthused. "I think we could be talking cover."

"Maybe . . . maybe . . . could be . . . could be. If you can get Mimi to go for it."

Russell smiled broadly, trying to close them. "We just finished our first week in the studio. Next week we do slap backs. My songs mostly. I compose my own stuff."

"This record producer thing is definitely our angle," Susan gushed.

They had him. *Just reel the boy in,* Jack

thought. So he looked skeptical and sang the chorus. "Maybe . . . maybe . . . could be . . . could be."

Russell steered them away from the cabana and his guests, heading toward his house. Jack guessed he wanted privacy so he could nail down the cover without interruptions.

Chief Ibanazi led them through a patio door into his study, then locked it behind him.

"When my songs come — my inspiration — I always work in here. Once I'm in the zone my shit slams." He opened a wall cabinet and produced a sound system and a keyboard.

"I see some wide shots in here, Clark," Susan enthused, framing the room with her hands. "All this equipment . . . Russell at the piano." She was really getting into it.

"It's not a piano, Lois, it's a Yamaha Sound Machine," Russell corrected her. "I design sounds by sampling everything from automobile horns to bagpipes."

"Mimi's gonna flip, Clark. This could be perfect for the cover story on the 'L.A. Sounds' edition," Susan said.

"Maybe . . . maybe . . . could be . . . could be."

Russell was drooling. The cover of the "L.A. Sounds" edition. Does it get any better than that?

"Look, Russell . . ." Jack started.

"I go by Izzy." Off their puzzled looks, "Short for Ibanazi."

"Right. Very cool," Jack continued. "So Izzy, if we're going for the 'Sounds' cover, Mimi is gonna demand all her usual cover profile and background stuff. She's a stickler for facts. If we bring this to Mimi we gotta really sell it. A take-no-prisoners approach always works best with her. You with me?"

"Right. Of course."

"So I'm gonna need the whole soufflé — why you're living in Beverly Hills and not out on the res. I need the old mystic music from the native soul rap. See where I'm heading, Lois?"

"It's fantastic," Susan said.

Izzy's face actually fell. "Do we really need all that? The reservation stuff, I mean. It's so . . . *Dances with Wolves*."

"Oh no, Izzy, you misunderstand," Susan jumped in. "It's not for the magazine. We don't want the reservation material in the body of the story. *213*, as you know, is very high-profile. A Beverly Hills society magazine. But Mimi absolutely demands full backgrounds on all cover subjects."

They watched his handsome face scrunch up again, like a squirrel trying to crack a walnut. The last thing Izzy wanted was a *213* cover shot of him with a peace pipe sitting in front of a rusting trailer on an Indian blanket. He saw himself in an Armani jacket

354

and Gucci shoes, maybe some cool leather pants.

" 'Course, if you'd rather not . . ." Jack stood and put his pen away.

Izzy actually lunged across the desk and caught Jack's arm. "No, no. It's okay. No problem. If it's just for Mimi, what's it gonna hurt?"

"Exactly," Jack nodded. He had his spiral pad and pen back out in a flash, and licked the end of the ball point for effect, leaving a little streak of ink on his tongue. "You're the current chief of the Ten-Eyck tribe?" Jack asked.

"Yes. Ibanazis have been chiefs going back two hundred years."

"Mimi'll probably want to know exactly where the reservation is located," Susan prompted.

"It's way out past Indio," Russell said, and now he was wrinkling his nose, as if he could almost smell it all the way from Bel Air. "But it's nothing," he added quickly, "just seventeen hundred acres of old truck tires, cactus, and jackrabbits. It's worthless land."

"I see. Okay," Jack looked at Susan, then back at Izzy. "If it's so poor, how do you afford all this?"

"Oh . . . now I see where you're heading."

Jack was glad Izzy got it, because he wasn't sure he did.

"I lease the reservation out," Izzy continued. "I mean, the tribe leases it to the federal government."

"You do?" Jack looked at Susan, who smiled.

"Yeah. It's a great deal, too," Izzy went on. "Each month the government pays us about two thousand dollars an acre on seventeen hundred acres. There're only thirty-two members in our tribe, so once we cut it up the annual take comes to over a million dollars apiece. My end, for instance, covers the payments on this place, living expenses, and my monthly recording studio fees. In return, we had to vote in a non-Indian administrator that the government chose for us. He just deals with the day-to-day running of the reservation. We moved out. Now most of us live around here or on the far West Side."

"Who's the administrator?" Jack asked, guessing it was Paul Nichols's brother or cousin.

"Scott Nichols," Izzy replied, confirming Jack's suspicion. "But, like I told you, it's just a pile of rocks and gopher holes. Seventeen hundred acres of nothing. Your magazine wouldn't care about it. Dingy, y'know . . . few old buildings an' shit."

"Right . . . right." Jack sounded disappointed. He made a few notes and furrowed his brow theatrically, like this story was about to get up off his notebook, stagger around the room, then fall over dead with a spike through its heart.

"Something wrong?" Izzy leaned forward anxiously.

"Well . . . I just . . ." He let it hang there.

"What? You just what?" Izzy was actually wringing his hands now.

"Well, I was wondering why the federal government would pay the Ten-Eyck tribe almost forty million a year for seventeen hundred acres of cactus and gopher holes. Doesn't seem to make sense."

"Oh," Izzy actually sighed in relief. "I can tell you that. That's easy: EPA standards."

"EPA standards?" Susan and Jack did that one together. Pretty good harmony, too. Maybe Izzy would give them a recording contract.

"Yeah. See, Indian land isn't subject to the same state and federal laws that the rest of the country is. Each tribe in the U.S. is like an independent nation, and we can make our own laws. The federal government has big toxic waste dumping problems for both nuclear and chemical gook. They don't have enough EPA-sanctioned sites to handle it all, so they started renting a few remote reservations where they could dump it cheap, without all the EPA hassles. It's a good deal for them *and* for us. Right after we signed the lease they started to dig a huge waste pit. Started even before we left. A hole to pump all that toxic shit into. On the res there's no EPA inspection, so the feds don't have to

357

worry about tests to check for pollution of the groundwater. Nothing. As long as the Tribal Council votes an okay, then it's done."

"Which you obviously did," Jack said.

"You bet."

"So that's how you end up living like this," Jack motioned toward the garden and smiled. "Pretty cool."

"Right." Then Izzy wrinkled his handsome brow as it finally occurred to him that maybe he was telling too much. "But please keep this confidential. I mean, all the EPA stuff and everything. That gets out, it's really gonna cause problems. This has to be just between us."

"Right, us and Mimi," Jack nodded.

"For background," Izzy repeated.

"Don't worry," Susan chipped in. "*213* does stories about celebrities, Marvin and Barbara Davis fundraisers, stuff like that. Nobody on our staff wants to write about a dumb old toxic hole in the ground."

Izzy looked relieved. "Thank God." Then his smile lit him up. He really was a great-looking guy. "You guys wanna hear some of my new sides?"

"God, wouldn't that be a gas," Susan said, shooting a do-we-have-to look at Jack.

They had to.

Izzy's music was hard to describe. He had the Yamaha Sound Machine on gargle mode, or maybe it was on cats fighting. It lingered between muffled screeches and something that resembled a four-car traffic accident. The rhythm section sounded like drunks pounding ash can lids with hammers.

People outside were banging on the door, adding to the racket, but Izzy was in the zone, lost in his tunes. Somebody out there was shouting about there being some kind of problem with the catering, but Izzy didn't care. He was slamming.

An hour later Jack and Susan managed to shake away, but before they left Izzy gave them both business cards.

Sure enough — Miracle Records.

Jack shook his head and frowned as he looked at the card. "How 'bout Orgasm Music? If it's good music, it's an orgasm."

Izzy smiled. "God . . . I *love* it. If you don't mind, maybe I'll use it."

"My gift."

As Jack and Susan headed toward the front door, she smiled at him. "Clark Lane and Lois Kent?"

"Just trying to keep things interesting," Jack said. Then they turned a corner and ran into two uniformed cops who had just arrived and were asking who owned the green XKE parked up the street. Jack grabbed Susan's arm and diverted her up the hall. "Shit. When I was on the job a car theft hardly ever got solved."

"Maybe it's because they weren't out

looking for a pissed-off D.A.'s classic Jag," Susan observed.

When they reached the end of the hall, Jack smiled at the coat-check girl. "She had the red fox with the snakeskin collar and cuffs," Jack said, adding, "I lost her ticket."

"The what?" the coat-check person said, wrinkling her nose at the description.

Susan smiled and nodded. She didn't know what the hell he was doing, but she was playing along as instructed.

"I don't think I saw anything like that," the girl hedged.

"Can I look?" Jack asked. "It's got her initials in it."

"I guess."

She led Jack into the coatroom and watched him like a prison guard while he went through half a dozen coats. He found what he was looking for in the side pocket of a nicely tailored gray gabardine.

A blue valet parking stub.

He deftly switched tickets.

"I don't see it . . . maybe it's in the hall closet," he hedged, then pulled Susan out of there.

They sauntered past the cops, down to the driveway. Jack handed the new blue claim check to one of the snooty red-jacketed valets, who sprinted off to get the car.

"I can hardly wait to see what we'll get this time," Jack said.

"If it wasn't a class-A felony, it would be more fun," Susan complained.

A beautiful, royal blue Rolls Royce Corniche convertible with a champagne interior rolled down the hill and stopped. The valet opened the door and looked at them with appreciation. Jack got behind the wheel, handing the guy a folded-up one-dollar bill, then pulled away fast before he could unroll the bill and throw an orange or something.

Susan began digging in the glove box for the registration. "Ever heard of anybody named James K. Hahn?" she asked.

"You're shitting me? Our luck can't be that bad. This is Mayor Hahn's car?"

"Just kidding," she smiled. "It belongs to Carlos Ibanazi."

"See. Not even stolen. Purchased with our very own tax dollars," Jack said, already feeling better about the theft. "We're gonna have to ditch it, though. Too obvious. We better get a rental, like your dad suggested." Then, to get her off the theft, he changed the subject. "I can hardly wait to see your dad in court. All dressed up, leaning on the rail, representing a chimp."

Chapter Thirty-Eight

Herman's phone rang, blasting him out of a deep, dreamless sleep. He rolled over and snatched it up. After listening to the recorded wakeup message, he called the federal court clerk's office, and confirmed that his TRO had arrived. He had been assigned a hearing for 10:30 that morning in Courtroom Sixteen.

Looking at Jack Wirta's rumpled, empty bed, he rolled to a sitting position feeling surprisingly good. He showered his big, ugly body, soaping and lathering, being careful not to get the stitches too wet on his lower abdomen. Then he toweled down and shaved with extra care, dressed in his number 4s, using a Wellington knot on his black-and-white-striped tie. His last grooming touch was to plaster his unruly hair down with water.

Herm surveyed his sagging, basset hound reflection and said, "You are one goddamn beautiful son of a bitch."

He woke Susan and Sandy by knocking on their door, then found Jack having breakfast out on the patio overlooking the ocean. Herman heard him come in around three, and rolled over and snarled at him to be quiet, before going right back to sleep.

"Our TRO goes before a judge at ten thirty, Federal Court Sixteen," Herman said as he sat at the table. "A very lucky number, if you believe in numerology."

Jack looked puzzled.

"Sixteen. One and six equals seven."

"Shit, I always miss that one," Jack said sourly.

"How'd you and Susan do?"

"Depends on the category."

Herman looked troubled. "It isn't that I don't want you to take her out, Jack. Hey, she makes her own decisions on who she dates. It's just now may not be the most appropriate time."

"I'm known for my bad timing. Celebrated for it, in fact."

They sat in silence for a moment. Then Herman reached over and snagged a slice of Jack's rye toast, buttered it, ladled on some strawberry jam, and started eating.

"Chief Ibanazi lives at 264 Chalon Road in Bel Air," Jack said. "It's a three-acre Spanish mansion. He's a record producer just setting up a new company. So far, I think he's still just working on getting cool stationery. The real news is why he's not living on the reservation." Then Jack proceeded to explain the federal government lease and the seventeen hundred acres rented by the feds to beat the EPA restrictions. Herm listened while he finished the first slice of toast, then helped himself to another.

"I can get you some of your own," Jack offered.

"Always tastes better off someone else's plate."

"Perfect sentiment from a lawyer."

"I think we need to find out what's out there on that reservation," Herman said.

"I just told you — a pit full of toxic or nuclear waste. No EPA leakproof containers, no EPA standards, no ground-pool testing — so everybody drinking the water out in Indio will probably glow in the dark ten years from now."

"How do we know it's really toxic waste?" Herm was skeptical.

"Ahh . . . you mean a CIA cover story? Conspiracy, right?"

"Right." Herman took another piece of toast.

"Steal another slice and you're gonna wear this fork as a tie pin."

"Jesus, you're touchy." Herman grinned; he was really enjoying the morning . . . the crashing waves and cool ocean mist. He was looking forward to the legal jousting that would take place in a couple of hours.

"I think you should go out to Van Nuys airport, rent a plane, head to Indio, find the reservation, and do a fly-over," Herman suggested.

"Maybe I'll do that first thing this afternoon."

"I wouldn't wait for the afternoon."

"Herman, if you think I'm gonna miss seeing you in court with a monkey as a client, then you've got better drugs than me."

"Except he's not gonna be there. His DNA chart is gonna be there. It's gonna be very dull."

"You may be a lot of things, Herman, but dull ain't one of them."

The good news was that the surprise TRO made DARPA scramble. Their lawyers arrived in the second floor corridor outside of Federal District Courtroom Sixteen obviously unprepared. They sat on wooden benches, riffling through law books propped on their knees. Some were rereading the rules governing TROs, others were studying Herman's show-cause order. There were six of them, and they all looked and dressed identically. If the feds ever started cloning attorneys as well as chimps, Jack thought these guys could be Exhibit One.

The bad news was, Herman had been notified about ten minutes after he arrived that the judge assigned to the case was none other than his old nemesis, Melissa King. Since that devastating revelation, Herman, Susan, and Sandy had been off in a corner, whispering and gesticulating. Herman's entire strategy had been to get a liberal judge, then squeeze through a legal loophole. Now he was forced to argue his TRO on behalf of Charles the Chimera in front of Melissa the Merciless. Impossible.

Jack was left standing alone with Dr. Adjemenian. She was in tailored brown, and her long hawk face and sculpted body looked dangerous and ready to rumble.

"How's Tim?" he said, trying to be friendly and release some tension.

"We haven't been able to get back to our place for two days," she said angrily. "The landlord said somebody broke in and searched it."

"Really? Well, my gosh." So much for small talk.

The bailiff opened the door and stepped into the hall. "Everybody for Judge King's Federal Court hearing on the temporary re-straining order against DARPA, we're getting ready to start," he announced.

The cloned attorneys all spun around and looked over their shoulders like guys caught jerking off.

Nobody seemed ready — not Herman, or any of DARPA's gunslingers.

Jack found a seat in the back next to an old woman dressed in a forty-year-old run-ning suit with "L.A. Thunderbirds" printed on it. She smelled a little like wine and moldy newspapers. Next to him on the other side was a thirty-year-old, stringy-haired man who had cleverly released the pressure on his swollen feet by cutting the toes out of his shoes.

Good spot. I fit right in, Jack mused.

After the "oyez" the door opened and Melissa King waddled into her courtroom.

Herman had moved behind the plaintiff's table with Susan and Sandy. Everyone stood as Melissa hoisted herself up the four steps using the rail, pulling on it like a stevedore dragging a line ashore. She made it to the landing then into her chair.

The baby had dropped since Herman had last seen her, she was now carrying it low in front of her like a basket of laundry. She banged her gavel just as Joseph Amato, the government's lead attorney, swept into the courtroom dressed to kill. He was late and still reading the TRO as he came through the door.

"All here, Mr. Amato?" Melissa said.

"Seems so, Your Honor," he replied, still scanning the document.

"Okay, so what's the deal on this one, Herman?" Starting right in on him.

"Your Honor, I've filed all of the paperwork with your office and —"

"I've read it. Seems pretty flaky, if you ask me."

"Flaky, Your Honor? Well, uh . . . we'll

have to trust you to see the merits once we've argued them."

"Right. So who is this Charles Chimera? Where is he?"

"Your Honor, he's not able to be here. I will shortly enter evidence of his existence. However, if I might have permission to do this in the way I have planned . . ."

"How's that, Herman? With balloons and a dancing bear?"

Herman heaved a deep sigh. He wasn't going to get into it with her this time . . . at least, not if he could help it. Fortunately there was no jury.

"I see in this TRO, words like, 'being,' and 'end-product.' I hope Mr. Chimera isn't some kinda animal, Herman, 'cause if he is, you're outta here feet first."

"Your Honor, you ask a very good question, and that leads me to my first request."

"Oh, for the love of God, who's your client? We did butterflies last week. What is it now?"

"Your Honor, are you familiar with DNA and its use in regard to the identification of a specific species?"

"Of course, Herman. I'm a federal judge. We deal with DNA constantly."

"Since Your Honor is familiar with DNA identification techniques, then you must agree that DNA is an infallible tool for classifying species. If, for instance, a tiny speck of DNA is left behind at a crime scene, we know we can determine exactly what species left it. We can run a DNA scan on that tissue, and, for example, if it was left by a dog, we can determine that it is a dog's DNA beyond a scintilla of a doubt. But more than just any dog, we can determine its exact breed. We can even determine between close breeds such as an Alaskan Husky and a Siberian Husky. We can similarly determine if the blood or tissue was left by a *Homo sapiens* — a human being. It is very exact.

"Your Honor, we will stipulate that DNA is a perfect yardstick for species identification," Amato said, putting a tinge of both frustration and boredom into his voice — a thing that Jack knew, from hours in court as a cop, was very hard to do. Only a guy billing out at over a thousand dollars an hour would even attempt it.

"Good. Counsel stipulates," Herman smiled. "But I would also like Your Honor's ruling."

"Okay, Herman, I accept the stipulation of the parties that DNA provides exact identification of a species. For the record, that fact will be deemed established for all purposes in this case. Now what or who is Charles Chimera? Stop messing around here."

"Charles Chimera and the five John Doe chimeras I represent are all human-chimp genetic hybrids," Herman said softly.

"I beg your pardon?" Judge King leaned forward.

"Charles Chimera is a genetically designed being. He is a chimpanzee who has illegally had his DNA altered and upgraded, making him much closer to *Homo sapiens* than a normal chimpanzee."

"Objection, Your Honor," Amato chimed in, coming to his feet this time. "If this TRO is being sought on behalf of an animal, that strikes to 'standing.' As Your Honor knows, animals don't have rights under the United States Constitution. Furthermore, we demand that this TRO be voided on the grounds that animals can't hire attorneys, so therefore Mr. Strockmire has no authority to represent this so-called being."

"Herman?" Judge King said, scowling at him while at the same time trying to find a position that was more comfortable. Her huge stomach had somehow gotten wedged below the desk. She pushed her swivel chair back to make room for the baby, who Herman thought would probably be born wearing a black cape.

"Your Honor," Herman continued, "Charles Chimera, in fact, did hire me. Last night, out at Barbra Streisand's pool. There is a witness." Herman glanced at Sandy. "He reached out his hand and beseeched me to help him. If Mr. Amato disagrees, let him bring Charles Chimera into court to testify

370

that he didn't hire me."

"How about you bring him in to say he did," Amato responded.

"Your Honor, in due time, when he is able, that will happen. As to standing, Charles Chimera and his John Doe brothers are, in fact, chimpanzees who have been made almost human with DNA upgrades."

"That's it! I've heard enough. We're done." Melissa started to rise, but it was an awkward procedure that took her a moment, so Herman rushed on.

"Your Honor, I need only a few more minutes. I beg you to listen. If you will not, then I will be forced to take this problem elsewhere."

"Yeah, like where's that, Herman? The Zoo Association?"

"No, Your Honor, to a full judicial review."

"You're really asking for it." She glowered, but sat back down.

"I intend to put a doctor of genetics under oath who will explain to you that a normal chimpanzee's homology is 98.4 percent of human DNA."

"Right," she shot back. "But it's not a human, so it *has no legal standing,*" Melissa growled. "I'm so sick of your sloppy, unorthodox behavior. When will you start practicing the law like the rest of us?"

"It's a hybrid," Herman persisted. "But if, as has been established, we're using DNA to

371

determine the boundary line for humanity, then at least we can probably all agree that chimpanzee DNA is extremely close."

"But it's not human. So, that's it." She rose again.

"Your Honor, would you accept a case on behalf of a Down's syndrome child? Can anyone seriously posit that such a child is not human for purposes of legal standing?"

"Of course — there's standing there. But a Down's syndrome child *is* a human being."

"That's right, Your Honor. It's human, but with DNA that is only 99.1 percent of normal human DNA. That extra chromosome alters the DNA by nine tenths of one percent. But Charles Chimera actually has DNA that is *closer* to a normal human being than a Down's syndrome child. This being's human-enhanced DNA is ninety-nine point *three* percent of a normal *Homo sapiens*. It has just been established by this court that DNA is the proper measurement for determining humanity. Since you just agreed you would accept a Down's syndrome child with only 99.1 percent homology, it is the plaintiff's position that this court cannot refuse standing to one Charles Chimera, whose DNA is two tenths of a point closer to human homology than that of a Down's syndrome child."

Melissa King was on her feet looking down at Herman with her mouth open.

"You can't be serious."

"You accepted the stipulation, Your Honor."

"You son of a bitch. When is the Lawyer Review Board gonna just be done with it and jerk your license?"

"With all due respect, Your Honor, the court must rule. Will you hear this case on behalf of Charles Chimera, whose DNA is closer to normal human DNA than that of a Down's syndrome child? Or will you refuse him his rightful access to due process provided under the Constitution of the United States of America?"

She was trapped. Herman had tricked her into an impossible situation.

Melissa King was furious at him and at herself, but she was dammed if she was going to hear a case with a chimpanzee as the plaintiff. She'd be an even bigger laughingstock in the legal community than Herman Strockmire Jr.

So Melissa King did the only thing she could do to avoid handing down a ruling . . . her water broke and she went into labor.

Chapter Thirty-Nine

Jack accessed the Ten-Eyck Indian reservation Web site. The cartoon Indian with the peace pipe on the welcome screen was probably designed before Izzy's Bel Air record career blossomed.

A map of the reservation indicated it was, as Izzy said, way out past Indio. The exact location was in the Joshua Tree National Forest, which sounded shady and restful, unless you realized that Joshua trees were actually misnamed cactus plants with no leaves and covered with thorns.

After he located the seventeen-hundred-acre plot on a California road map, Jack bought the cheapest digital camera he could find at The Good Guys, then drove out to Van Nuys Airport and cruised around until he found a small, oddly named charter service called Air Jordan.

It was run by an overweight gray-haired woman wearing Ray-Bans, named Jordan Phoenix, which sounded to Jack like a misplaced desert monument. Jordan — who liked to be called "Jordy" — had small planes for rent. A few were in Jack's limited budget range. He picked a fifteen-year-old

Cessna 185 at one-fifty an hour. After being assured that the plane was "top-notch," he watched with concern as Jordy, who it now appeared was also going to be his pilot, walked around and did a preflight check, which consisted of rattling control surfaces, then banging her fist a few times on the engine cowling. When she saw the look on his face she quipped, "Wakes up the birds that nest in the carburetor." Then she got in and motioned to the seat next to her.

"Okay, honey, fly your ass right on up here and drop anchor." No doubt about it, Jordy was a pip.

"Contact," she bellowed in a voice that would blow the fur off a cat. Then the Cessna burped to life.

Jack decided to try to break the ice. "Must be pretty exciting, being a pilot."

"Not if I do it right," she deadpanned.

They taxied out toward the runway. Jordan keyed her mike, identified herself as November-eight-six-eight-Charlie-Bravo, and started talking to the Van Nuys tower. They were cleared for takeoff, and in a few minutes they were streaking down the runway and lifting off into the Southern California smog. The wings immediately started jitterbugging in unstable, choppy air.

"I'm gonna get up over this chop at ten thousand," Jordy shouted at him. "Air's a little thin, but I hate flying through Indian country at standard altitudes."

"Indian country?" Jack yelled back, wondering if she was talking about the Ten-Eyck reservation.

"Yeah, it's what we call all this airspace between here and San Bernardino." She smiled, "Buncha dentists out here flying around in Cherokees and Apaches. Most docs can't fly for shit. I hate it when they park their birds in my front seat."

"In that case, don't worry about oxygen. Go as high as you want, I'll hold my breath."

She nodded, keeping the 185 in a steep climb.

She was right. There were a lot of little planes. Some were flying in circles, practicing maneuvers, others were just sightseeing.

Once Jordy was at altitude, the San Bernardino Flight Center routed them in tight behind an American Eagle twin prop shuttle. After fighting his slipstream for a few miles, Jordan keyed her mike and asked San Bernardino Flight Control for more separation.

A frustrated and overworked air traffic controller came back at her immediately: "If you want more room, Captain, push your seat back."

"Asshole," she muttered.

There were enough comics up here to book an open-mike night at the Comedy Store. Soon they were out over the desert past Indio and turning southeast. Jordy called air traffic control to discontinue her flight plan. She notified them she was going to visual flight rules and dropping to two thousand feet.

"Roger, eight-six-eight-Charlie-Bravo," the traffic controller said. "But, if you stay on that heading, in twenty miles you'll be over a Code Sixty-one."

"San Bernardino Center, that's not on my map."

"Roger, Charlie-Bravo, this is a new directive. One month old. Turn right at Longitude one-one-six point seven and notify Palm Desert Flight Control. Good day."

She looked over at Jack.

"Trouble?" Jack asked, reading her look.

"Yeah. That place you wanna go look at is in restricted airspace. Code Sixty-one is a military no-fly zone."

"How close can you get?" Jack asked.

"Not very."

They flew out toward the reservation, but before they could see much of it Jordan banked right and flew along the perimeter of the restricted area.

"This is my hold point," she said.

"What happens if you just do it anyway?"

"I'd have to trade in this Cessna for a taxicab."

"They'll take your license?"

"And feed it to me."

While they were flying along the perimeter

a Blackhawk helicopter suddenly appeared on their starboard side. In the open bay door of the huge military chopper were several men dressed in black helmets and SWAT gear. In a side door, behind a fifty-caliber machine gun, sat a waist gunner. The pilot waved Jordan off. The two aircraft flew on the same heading only about thirty feet apart.

Jack took out his digital camera and photographed the Blackhawk. As soon as he did one of the SWAT soldiers flipped him off. Then Jack aimed the camera at the terrain to the east. Somewhere out there in the desert beyond their hold point was the Ten-Eyck Indian reservation. He took a few more shots, hoping he could blow them up or digitally enhance them and maybe discover something.

Suddenly the door gunner let loose a short burst of tracers that didn't hit the Cessna, but streaked past the nose about forty or fifty feet in front.

"That's it. I'm gone." Jordan made a circle motion with her hand, and the pilot of the Blackhawk waved back and nodded. Then she banked the Cessna and headed back to L.A.

"Sorry," Jordy said. "But I ain't looking for no fifty-caliber renovations. Not much else I can do."

Jack was shaken by the incident.

When they landed at Van Nuys there was a

windowless van parked out on the tarmac. Jordan Phoenix shut down the Cessna, and as they climbed out the doors of the van opened, revealing four men in plainclothes and blue windbreakers. They jumped onto the tarmac and headed toward the plane. Jack recognized one of the men from the stairwell at Mrs. Zimbaldi's apartment. He turned, looking for an escape, but two other men were already walking toward the plane from the hangar on the right, two more appeared from behind a fuel truck.

The plainclothes feds pulled out Berettas. No lasers this time — just good, old-fashioned, Italian hardware.

One of the men, who was tall and lean with a dark Hispanic complexion, spoke: "Get down on your face, please."

Jack assumed the position. They frisked him, but he wasn't packing. His hands were cuffed and he was yanked quickly back up to his feet.

"Federal arrest," the Hispanic man said, showing a badge to Jordan, who was standing there looking at them through her Ray-Bans, her sun-dried complexion as expressionless as theirs.

"You boys can have him, but he still owes me for two hours of flight time." Jordy was a good pilot, but pretty much worthless when it came to backup. "Two hundred an hour for two hours, fifteen minutes," she calculated,

379

adding fifty bucks to their hourly agreement.

Somebody reached into Jack's back pocket, pulled out his wallet, and extracted cash. "You oughtta have a discount when your clients end up in handcuffs," Jack groused at her as they pulled a hood over his head and pushed him toward their van.

"Renting airplanes is like renting sex," Jordy said, counting her money. "It's expensive, and someone is always keeping track of time."

The case was really starting to piss him off.

Chapter Forty

After Melissa King went into labor, the Federal Court Clerk's office notified Joseph Amato and Herman Strockmire that the TRO was being assigned to a new jurist and they would be notified of his identity in less than an hour.

Herman packed up his files and, along with Sandy and Susan, returned to his borrowed office at Lipman, Castle & Stein to wait.

The secretaries were thrilled to see him. They checked three times to make sure it was still okay for him to use the office.

At four that afternoon, Herman, Susan, and Sandy were still waiting, trying not to become overly concerned about the prolonged delay for judicial notification, or about Jack Wirta's unexplained disappearance.

He was way overdue.

Herman's anxiety finally redlined. "Honey, get on the phone and call around. See if you can find out what air charter service Jack used."

Susan left the office and returned with the three-inch-thick L.A. Yellow Pages. She cracked it open to "Air Charters" and started making calls, speaking urgently and softly into the phone, trying to find out if one of them had chartered a plane to Jack Wirta.

While she was working her way through the list, Sandy and Herman were going over their legal notes and strategies.

"On the plus side, I'm certainly glad to be rid of Melissa," Herman conceded. "But unfortunately I revealed my DNA strategy. I'm afraid whoever they assign next is going to be ready to block us on that."

"Herman, it was always a long shot," Sandy argued. "And what was all that about the chimera hiring you? Where the hell did *that* come from?"

"He reached out to us when we were in the pool and he was on the diving board. You saw him pleading with his eyes." Sandy cocked an eyebrow at Herman. "Hey, let Amato prove otherwise."

"Herm, you've got a huge attorney-client problem. Why can't we just refile using the SPCA on behalf of the chimeras?"

"Two reasons. First, if we refile it's gonna take another two days, and with Jack missing, that takes the pressure off, gives DARPA a chance to plan their next move, or maybe even kill him. Second, with a new judge, maybe I can get this in. If I can, it will change the way all animals are treated under the law from this point forward. That's the whole reason I did it this way."

"Except this may not be the way to do it, Herm," Sandy frowned.

"If I can get legal standing for any species other than pure *Homo sapiens,* then I've changed the law. My God, Sandy, you above all people should . . ."

"I know, I know. Don't preach at me using my own sermons. It's just, even though these chimeras are being illegally experimented on and need injunctive relief, I'm afraid this strategy is gonna backfire."

"We *know* they exist, Sandy. We saw one with our own eyes. They're being illegally designed and cloned."

"Then file your TRO with the SPCA as a client," Sandy argued. "This other thing about legal standing is more of a conceptual issue."

"Democracy is conceptual," Herman said hotly. "The death penalty is conceptual. Everything important worth fighting for is conceptual!"

After that outburst they sat in silence while Susan continued calling charter services.

The intercom buzzed. "Federal Court Clerk on line two," one of the LC&S ice goddesses chirped.

Herman lunged at the phone. "Herman Strockmire," he said into the receiver while Sandy and Susan watched intently. Then he said, "Thanks," and hung up. "Look up Warren Krookshank, with a *K.* I've never heard of him."

Susan put her phone on speaker, went to the bookshelf, and retrieved the federal judges directory. It was a loose-leaf binder that Lipman, Castle & Stein provided for each office. She flipped it open, found his page, and laid the binder on Herman's desk. In the upper right hand corner was a picture of a middle-aged African-American man.

"Harvard Law," Herman read aloud, as he scanned the page. "Maybe we can sing the fight song together." Then he grinned. "Been on the bench for ten years. This guy seems perfect. Look at this! Pro-civil rights, pro-gun control . . . liberal record. He's one of us."

"Then why would he get this case?" Susan asked, immediately suspicious. "You know DARPA had a hand in getting Melissa assigned. If Warren Krookshank is a friendly ear, why would they let that happen?"

"Because they didn't expect Melissa King to go into labor. Somebody took their eye off the ball, or they didn't have enough time to rerig it. So we simply got the next available guy — Krookshank." He looked up and smiled. "We're back in court, nine a.m. tomorrow. It's still fast-tracked."

"You really think it's gonna be that simple?" Susan wondered. She walked over and took the phone back off speaker, cradling the receiver under her ear.

"Yeah, it could be just that simple," Herman replied. "We're due for a break."

Suddenly, Susan snapped her head back toward the receiver. "You did?!" she asked. "When? How long ago? Who is this?" She listened, then turned to her father, "I found the service — Air Jordan. This is the pilot who flew him, Jordan Phoenix." She put the phone back on speaker as Herman hustled across the room to get closer.

"Yes. Say that again," he demanded.

"Just like I told her." A rough female voice came over the phone. "We got chased out of the desert by a military chopper. Once we landed, a buncha federal cops swarmed the plane with guns. They arrested Wirta and took him off in a van."

"How long ago?" Herman asked.

"Must've been a little past three. By the way, he left his camera if you wanta come pick it up. But, except for a shot or two of the helicopter that chased us, he didn't take many pictures."

Herman thanked her and said they'd get it. Then Susan disconnected the call.

"What do you think they're gonna do to him?" Susan asked with concern.

"I don't know," Herman answered. "But we've gotta do something to turn the heat up on those guys. We need to get some headlines fast . . . something to keep them from killing Jack and dropping him in a hole somewhere."

Susan's beautiful face was distorted with

worry. "How . . . how do we do that, Dad?"

"Get my phone directory," he said.

Susan reached into her briefcase and pulled out a leather book full of his important numbers.

"Call Barbra's PR guy . . . Swifty something. Little guy. We met him last year at her Christmas party."

"Swifty Sutherland?" Susan said, finding it in the book.

"Right, that's the guy. And while I talk to him, try to reach Donald Trump in New York."

Chapter Forty-One

T. Jerome Sutherland had more catchy nick-names than a minor league baseball team. During his forty-plus years in PR, he was "The Flack in a Hat," because in the fifties he favored snap brims. In the seventies, he'd been called "Deadline," and for two years during the eighties, when some of his clients were Wall Street crooks, he was "Junk Bond Jerry." But the name that fit him best and lasted the longest was Swifty. He was a hundred and twenty pounds of kinetic energy packed in a diminutive, fast-moving body. His bald head was shaved and his eyebrows loomed like tangled brush, dominating a face that never stopped smiling.

Swifty had played high-stakes celebrity roulette for almost half a century, scraping up more nasty messes than a waste-removal contractor. He got fluff printed and bad news buried while cornering the market on insincerity.

One of Swifty's patented tactics was to dig up and archive scandalous, unpublished stories on stars he didn't represent. When one of his own clients checked into Betty Ford, or was on the verge of being outed by *The*

Advocate, he would call up the reporter who was about to print the career disaster and offer up somebody else's horror story in return for keeping his star's indiscretions secret. This practice had earned him the nickname "Liar for Hire." He definitely knew how to walk the edge of a troublesome press release.

Swifty suggested that Herman meet him for dinner at the trendy Bistro Garden in the Valley where the flack had a reserved nightly "gunfighter table" that commanded a good view of the high-ceilinged, attractive room. The happy little man who never seemed to stop smiling sat with his back to the wall and gazed over Herman's shoulder at restaurant traffic while Herman filled him in. Swifty nodded as if the unusual nature of the tale was not in the least bit troublesome.

"Babs says this is on her account. She's the best, so you got the best," the little man said after Herman finished. For a behind-the-scenes employee, the statement showed a surprising lack of modesty. During all of this Swifty almost never looked at Herman, preferring to watch the busy room instead. "Dick Zanuck with Richard Cook. Wonder what those two guys are up to?" he said unexpectedly.

"Huh?" Herman was getting irritated.

"Nothing. So, what's the drill? You want me to get this trial you're doing into the press?" he said, shooting his gaze to the right as two new groups of patrons came through the door. They must've been nobodies, because he discarded them immediately, finding something else that interested him to Herman's right, slowly leaning around Herman's bulk.

"Am I in the way?"

"Nope, just workin' the hall," Swifty smiled. "So tell me how soon you need this published and what you're looking to accomplish."

Herman explained some more about DARPA and their mission to develop advanced weaponry. He explained about the TRO. When he got into more detail about the chimeras, Swifty flicked his gaze back to Herman. But instead of commenting on the strange nature of hybrid soldiers he commented on the story's newsworthiness. "Sounds more like an *Enquirer* lead." He spread his hands and contributed a headline: "New World Police . . . Government Breeds Genetic Monsters."

"Our story's gotta go in the *Wall Street Journal* or the *L.A. Times,*" Herman insisted. "My investigator is missing and I need this played up big and legit so they won't do something stupid, like kill him. If I shine enough light on the case maybe they won't commit a high-profile murder."

Swifty buttered his bread, took a bite, then

shot his cuffs. His links would have paid Herman's office rent for a month — rubies the size of a robin's eggs.

"Okay, hitting the high points then." Swifty recapped: "We wanna make it look like he was snatched because of this restraining order against DARPA. That somebody bagged this Jack Wirta character because he got wind of something big. We wanna make it look like maybe these DARPA cats are the ones who have the most to gain by grabbing your boy, but we can't prove it, so we can't exactly say they did it, but we imply it. Probably try and get that in the lead if we can." He took another bite. "And it has to go in a rag like the *Journal* or the *L.A. Times*?"

"Exactly."

"And you need this when?"

"The morning paper. Time is everything here."

"Jesus. Aside from the fact that the chimpanzee-clone thing sounds like silly putty, they put the *Times* to bed in an hour. They usually keep some holes open in Sports and Metro for late scores and hot breaking stuff, but, shit."

"That's why I came to the best."

"Never ass-kiss an ass-kisser," Swifty admonished sternly, then pulled out his cell phone and dialed a number from memory. "Go ahead and order. They know what I want."

He asked for somebody named Leon at the *Times* Metro section. "I need something planted, Bubee," he cooed once he got him on the phone. "Above the fold . . . with a picture." While he talked he glanced at Herman and motioned to the menu. Herman picked it up and tried to read, but he wasn't hungry — he was too worried to eat.

"You bet," Swifty said, then dropped his voice to a confidential whisper and went into his pitch. "Since I owe you one, you get this first. My gift. When you accept the Peabody just remember to mention me at the ceremony." He turned his twinkling eyes back to Herman and shrugged impishly. Then he continued: "It's a fantastic legal action taking place in Federal Courtroom Sixteen downtown. It involves top government security, DARPA commandos, missing government secrets, the disappearance and probable kidnapping of a private investigator, illegal genetic engineering, a secret government weapons team . . . and, get this, bubala: the movie rights are still available. You write it, Leon, you're in first position." He listened, wrinkled up his nose, and then shook his head. "Why give those pricks the Pulitzer? This is my gift to *you*, boychick . . . and I swear it's righteous. I can back up every word, every scintilla. Every participle and modifier is *emes*." A moment of listening, then, "Credibility is my middle name, babe. This is public record.

The TRO is in federal court. Go down there tomorrow and see for yourself. I never lie." Another pause while Swifty pulled his happy countenance into a frown. "Come on . . . no fair. He thought his ex-wife was balling his trainer." He listened to Leon for at least a minute more before the smile returned. "Okay, I'll scribble up the release and get it over to you with the artwork in . . ." He looked at Herman, then pointed at his twenty-thousand-dollar Cartier watch.

"An hour," Herman said. "My daughter's picking up Wirta's picture now."

"In an hour you'll have the scoop of a lifetime. And, Leon? If you can get it on the *Times*' wire and leak it to the AP for the next news cycle, I'll owe you my firstborn. If I'm lyin', I'm dyin'." A moment more of eyebrow calisthenics, then Swifty nodded. "You're a mensch. Be back atcha." He closed the phone, sighed theatrically, then looked at Herman. "He's down. Now let's see if I can write this up the way you want and still not come off like a complete asshole when Leon reads it."

At 8 p.m. Susan stood in the corridor outside of Jack Wirta's office in Boy's Town and waited. The office door had been replaced and was bolted. She didn't have a key, but she had called Jack's ex-partner, Shane Scully, whose son's estate owned the

392

building. After she'd filled him in on the phone, Shane said he'd stop by the realtor's for a key and come right over.

Ten minutes after she arrived, a good-looking, dark-haired man came up the stairs and into the hall. He was dressed in blue jeans, an LAPD windbreaker, and tennis shoes. He smiled as he approached.

"Ms. Strockmire?"

"Shane Scully?"

"Yep." After they shook hands Shane put a key into the lock. "You said on the phone you think Jack's been kidnapped by the feds. You real sure about that? Jack would be a hard guy to snatch. Maybe he's just working your case and hasn't had a chance to phone in yet."

"He was arrested by federal police at the airport, then disappeared. There's been no sign of him since. Besides that, we've been under surveillance by some kind of urban commando unit since the day before yesterday."

"That sounds ugly." He pulled the key out of the lock, looked at it, then tried again. "This isn't working."

When Scully looked directly at her she saw that he had beautiful aqua-blue eyes and was attractive in a rough-and-tumble kind of way. His vibe was all male.

"It's a new door, maybe the lock was changed when they replaced it," she said.

Shane smiled then reached into his pocket, withdrew a little leather case full of long-handled picks, and started to feed them one at a time into the lock. First he pushed in a slender, flat one, then slipped in several tiny picks with hooked ends behind it.

"You pick locks, too?"

"We're a full-service police department," he quipped, carefully turning the four picks in his hand. In a second she heard the lock spring. He opened the door, checked inside to make sure it was safe, then stepped back and said, "Your party."

Susan walked into the office. The place had been thoroughly tossed and whoever had done it had made no effort to hide the search. The file cabinets were open, the dividers strewn all over the floor. The desk had also been ransacked. The closet door was ajar and the boxes Jack had stacked in there had been ripped open, their contents — mostly law enforcement reference books and manuals — strewn everywhere.

"Not very neat, were they?" Shane commented.

"Dad and I were hiding next door when it happened. That was yesterday."

She moved to the east wall and looked at the pictures hanging there, finally taking down one of Jack and Shane. "This is you?"

"Yeah. Police barbecue, the first year we partnered in Southwest. My third year on the job. Jack and I rode together in a Plain-Jane for almost eighteen months."

"Was he a good cop?"

That brought Scully around fast. "He was a *great* cop, okay?" he growled at her. "He took chances out there, for all the good it did him. He probably didn't tell you this, but during that bank shoot-out in North Hollywood, even after he stopped the Parabellum and couldn't walk, he was crawling around under cars, exposing himself to fire, cranking off rounds while those two assholes emptied armor-piercing ordnance at him. Guy is a hero, but all he got for it was a buncha shit and a disability check that he had to sue the department to collect."

"Don't snap my head off," she said.

"Pisses me off, is all."

"If I need your help down the road on this can you give it?"

"If you need me to help pull Jack Wirta out of a hole, I'm here. I can also line up some guys to join us if you want. Jack still has a lot of friends on the job."

"Thanks." She looked down at the picture again. They appeared young in the shot . . . young and eager. Untouched by the cop cynicism that she sensed had finally scarred them both. In the picture they looked boyish and heroic, full of idealism, comfortable inside their skins.

"I need a picture of Jack, so I'm going to cut you out of this," she said, holding up the picture.

"Why should you be any different?" he quipped, confirming her suspicions about his now-dark view of law enforcement.

Then Susan noticed something on the floor under the desk. She leaned down . . . it looked like dried blood.

Shane crossed to where she was standing.

"That wasn't there when I was here the first time," she said. "I hope Miro didn't try to . . ."

"Who's Miro?" Shane interrupted.

"The guy who runs the escort service next door."

Shane followed as she hurried out of Jack's little office and down the hall. The door to Reflections was locked. "That's strange, it's a dating service. They should be open. They operate at night."

"Dating service, as in young men for rent?"

"I try not to be judgmental."

"And you're to be heartily congratulated for that," he said sarcastically, but she let it slide.

While they were standing there a man wearing a ripped T-shirt came up the stairs at the end of the hall. "They're closed," he called out.

"Why?" she asked.

"The guy who owns it got the shit kicked out of him. He's in Cedars. They took him outta here in an ambulance about four hours ago."

Chapter forty-Two

He was in a private room in the trauma ward conscious but hooked to a drip trolley, his face swollen and already turning purple. Two of his front teeth were missing.

"I didn't tell anything," Miro slurred proudly, looking up at Susan through puffy eye sockets. She was holding his hand trying not to wince as she took in the damage. The doctors would only allow one visitor, so Shane was waiting downstairs in the coffee shop.

"Miro, Jack told you not to go to his office," she scolded.

"But I had to get the door fixed. We couldn't leave Jack's office open." His voice small, "I was just locking up when they came."

"But why would they beat you?"

"They wanted to find all of you. I told 'em to stop threatening, that it was against the law. But that just made them angry. They said if I'd tell them they'd let me go. But I didn't tell."

"Jesus, Miro . . ."

"Make sure Jack knows I didn't say anything . . . not about the DNA or the Octopus thing, or Dr. Adjemenian. Nothing."

"Even after they beat you?"

"When they thought I was unconscious they left me on the floor under the desk. But I wasn't unconscious. I just kept my eyes closed." Proud of himself now. "They called a man named Mr. Valdez from Jack's phone. Told him what happened. Promised Valdez they would find all of you and take you to some place called Black Star in Cleveland."

"Miro, I'm so sorry. Nobody meant for anything to happen to you."

"Tell Jack I didn't say anything. Tell him Miro's one gay man who knows how to keep secrets."

"I'll tell him." But she seemed hesitant, and Casimiro Roca, expert on human dishonesty, picked up on it immediately.

"Is Jack okay?" he asked, frowning.

"He's missing. They got him, Miro. But maybe with what you just told me we can figure out where he is in Cleveland," she said, wondering how they would ever find Jack in a city of several million.

"Black Star," Miro said. "Don't forget, Black Star."

"I won't," she said, and squeezed his hand.

"If anybody hurts Jack I'm going to the police," he said defiantly.

She leaned down and kissed his forehead. "I hope Jack knows what a great friend you are," she said as he smiled at her through cracked lips.

When Susan arrived at the cafeteria Shane Scully was sitting in a booth one over from where Dr. Lance Shiller had drawn his crude oval heart on the place mat and explained to her about Herman's arrhythmia. It seemed as if that had happened years ago.

Susan got some coffee and then slipped into the booth across the table from him.

"He okay?" Shane asked.

"Yeah, I think so, but, my God, his face is a mess. He lost some teeth . . . he took that beating but refused to talk." She paused to sip her coffee as she thought about it, then added, "Sometimes people surprise you, what they do, how strong they are, underneath." She told him what Miro had overheard while under the desk, about the call to Mr. Valdez, and the plan to take them to a place called Black Star in Cleveland. After she finished, they sat there looking at one another, each lost in thought.

"He's not in Cleveland. That doesn't make any sense at all," Shane finally said.

"But that's where Miro said . . ."

"I don't care. He must have misunderstood, or they said that because they knew he was listening. Why take Jack two thousand miles away? DARPA is a federal agency with access to offices everywhere. What's in Cleveland that they can't get here? It's nuts."

"I don't know, maybe that's where Valdez is."

Shane pulled out his cell phone and dialed a number.

"Who're you calling?"

"My wife, Alexa. She's the exec at Detective Services Group downtown and twice the cop I am. Let's get her take." After he got her on the phone and told her what Miro had overheard, he listened.

Susan watched and waited.

"Where is that?" he finally asked. "Okay, I'll get a map and look. Thanks, babe." Another pause, then, "Okay, I'll call and let you know." He folded the phone and put it back in his coat pocket.

"Alexa says she thinks there's a wilderness area east of here, between Orange County and San Bernardino County, called the Cleveland National Forest."

"A national forest. That would be federal land," Susan said.

"Makes slightly more sense than Cleveland, Ohio."

They left the cafeteria and went upstairs to the hospital gift shop where they bought a travel book that included a map of Southern California. They found the Cleveland National Forest and huddled together, staring at it.

"Some cop I am. It's less than sixty miles away and I never even heard of it," Shane muttered.

Susan borrowed a pair of magnified

reading glasses from a display rack and squinted closely at the page. Little fire roads and trails crisscrossed the wilderness area. She could just barely read the tiny print on the map. She saw areas marked as Blue Jay Camp Ground and Trabuco Canyon Trail on the southern section of the Cleveland forest, then continued searching the tiny roads to the west. Finally, on the northeast section of the map, up around Lake Elsinore, near Riverside County, she found it — a little trail that splintered off something called Santiago Road and lead to Black Star Canyon.

Chapter Forty-Three

The room was small, locked, and windowless. The air-conditioner cranked freon-cooled air down on him through two large ceiling vents.

He'd been taken there in the van from the airport in Van Nuys — no stops — his head sacked up again like a bag of vegetables. Toward the end of the two-hour drive he'd felt the tires bouncing on what seemed like a badly paved road. He thought he smelled pine needles, but that could have been his imagination.

The van stopped, the door was thrown open, and he was dragged out and roughly pushed across some open ground by commandos who kept the conversation simple and guttural, sticking to phrases like "Shut the fuck up" and "No talking, asshole." Mind-expanding discourse.

He was shoved into a room where the temperature was around fifty. Only two places Jack knew of kept the thermostat that cold: the Polar Bear exhibit at the Los Angeles zoo and the LAPD Computer Center. Crude as his captors were, he didn't think he was about to be fed to a bear — so maybe he was in some kind of computer lab.

Detective reasoning at its tip-top best.

Taking it a step further, if this was a computer lab, maybe it was part of Octopus or Echelon.

After they pushed him into the cold room they uncuffed him and left. A few minutes later he decided, *What the hell, go for it,* and removed his canvas bag.

The room was concrete block — no windows, no chairs. Minimalist digs.

The hours ticked by while he grew goose bumps. He paced the room. He put his ear next to the concrete wall and listened. Something was humming faintly in two separate octaves behind the thick concrete. Water pipes? Power lines? Motown singers?

"Well, Jack, you've really fucked up big this time," he said to the humming wall.

Later, the same, dark-skinned, snake-cold Hispanic man he'd seen at the airport entered the room and closed the door behind him. "I'm Vincent Valdez."

Jack thought it probably wasn't a good sign that the man told him his name. Valdez stood close, not ten feet away, as if Jack posed absolutely no physical threat to him.

Jack stood and growled: "Before ripping your geek head off and shoving it up your ass, I'm required to inform you that I'm a black belt in four martial arts disciplines." Tired old bullshit, but there it was. The guy was pissing him off.

"Let's see what you got then."

Jack shrugged and gave him his best police academy hand-to-hand move, the old feint-to-the-left and pivot kick to the right. Before he got halfway through it he was flying backward, spinning wildly in flight, yelping something Three-Stoogish, like *woo-woo-woop!* He flew against the wall, landing with a thunk like a load of wet laundry, then slid down to the floor. Immediately, his worthless back went into a full spazoid convulsion. He was jerking around on the floor like a power company lineman with a handful of hot ends.

"I'm a fifth-degree black belt." Valdez was looking down at Jack who was now desperately trying to get his lower lumbar region under control. "This might be a good time for you to tell me what you think you know," he instructed.

Jack finally stopped spasming and cleared his throat. "Okay . . . here's one thing I heard."

"I'm listening."

"Ashly Lynn may be getting out of porno."

Valdez didn't answer. He just glared and walked out of the room, relocking the door. No "Nice knowing ya," no "Have a nice day." He just froze Jack's balls with a look and left.

Incompetence pissed off Vincent Valdez more than anything else he encountered in life . . .

more than stupidity, more than insanity or moral corruption. Incompetence was usually bred from a combination of careless thinking and bad tactics, both elements within the sphere of control. Failure indicated that you had not adequately foreseen problems inside your command venue. That reflected directly back on Valdez and made him angry with everybody around him, but mostly at himself.

This whole leak on the Ten-Eyck Chimera Project was totally unacceptable and had been getting worse with each passing hour. General Buzz Turpin had actually yelled at Vincent over the phone yesterday — something the whispering general had never done before. God only knew how many people now had information about the existence of the supersecret project, and all because of a silly lawsuit to protect a butterfly. The whole tangled mess had started there and had somehow gotten completely away from him.

He had no choice but to collateralize Wirta. They were in the middle of the Cleveland National Forest, at the Black Star Octopus Lab, and had good containment of the area. He would just march this wisecracking bozo out to the woods, crank a round into his fuzzy head, and bury him in a sack of lye. End of story.

He was getting set to give that order when the phone rang in the secure HQ. He snatched it up. It was the DARPA routing officer in D.C.

"Mr. Valdez?" she asked.

"Yes."

"I have a call for you. It came into our L.A. office ten minutes ago. I had to find you through Mr. Talbot in D.C."

"I don't want any calls."

"Mr. Talbot said you might want this one. It's from somebody named Herman Strockmire Jr."

"Yes. I do want to talk to him. Have you got an STL?" Referring to the Octopus designation for Satellite Trace and Location.

"Apparently he's calling from a cell phone and he's on the move right now. Octopus has him on the Hollywood Freeway just passing Sunset."

"Okay. Vector some units in on that location and put him through."

"I already have a team rolling on Mr. Talbot's instructions."

Then Vincent heard some clicks and the hiss of a cell phone.

"This is Valdez," he said sharply.

"Mr. Valdez," Herman said. "Are you the one quarterbacking this disaster?" Herman was in the passenger seat of another rental car looking at Susan, who was driving. They had just left Shane Scully at the Hollywood station where he had volunteered to scare up some friends to go out to the Cleveland National Forest and help look for Jack. The lights from the freeway signs strobed across the windshield. Herman pressed the phone tightly to his ear.

"Let me make you aware of something, Mr. Strockmire," Valdez said softly. "You are committing federal crimes and disrupting your country's national security."

"You're the one breaking laws and committing crimes," Herman snapped. "Kidnapping happens to be a crime; so is murder. I know you're holding Jack Wirta. I know you're evaluating your options. Before you commit to something you can't undo, I just wanted to tell you to be sure and read the Metro section in the *L.A. Times* tomorrow morning. There's going to be an article about my restraining order against DARPA and the hybrid chimeras, including a great drawing my friend made of the one who attacked us. It's going to be about Jack Wirta and how he mysteriously disappeared after a federal arrest orchestrated under your command. Jordan Phoenix, a witness to the bust, has already given her sworn affidavit. In view of all this, I know you're going to want to keep Mr. Wirta in good condition."

"Is that it?" Valdez's voice was cold and menacing.

"That's it," Herman said. "Hurt him and you're going to have a lot of 'splaining to do, Lucy."

Valdez hung up without responding.

"Dad, I think somebody is following us

". . . a gray sedan." Susan had been watching it suspiciously in her rear view mirror while listening to Herman's side of the conversation.

"Get off on Melrose and head back to the Hollywood Division," Herman instructed.

It took five minutes before they finally pulled into the Hollywood station on Wilcox Avenue. Herman asked the lot guard for Shane Scully and gave their names. After the officer made a call inside they were allowed to park behind the chain-link security fence. As they got out the gray sedan cruised past.

"You know what pisses me off most?" Herman said as the sedan turned the corner at the end of the block and disappeared. "Those fucking guys are doing all this with *my* tax dollars."

"Dad, stop it. You're beginning to sound like a Republican."

They hurried past the parking guard and into the brightly lit lobby.

Valdez stood in the Black Star HQ with the phone still in his hand, listening to an update from his L.A. field unit. They had followed Herman and his daughter to the Hollywood police station and had just told Valdez that the Strockmires were inside.

"Okay, wait there," he ordered. "Call me when they move."

Valdez hung up the phone thinking he had to get rid of Jack Wirta, regardless. The man knew too much. He was troubled by Strockmire's threat of press coverage, so he would have to alter his plan — do it in a way that wouldn't produce too many questions. Wirta's medical file was in front of him. It included the blood work they had done on him out at Groom Lake. The file indicated that Wirta had a high level of some kind of powerful painkiller in his blood stream. Apparently the ex-cop was taking a triple-hit narcotic. Percodan or Percocet. If that was the case, there would also be a medical record of the doctors who prescribed it. If he had run out of doctors who would write him, which was often the case with pain-pill addicts, then maybe there was even a trail of street dealers who could be found and convinced to make statements. If he couldn't find one of those, he'd get a volunteer of his own to make the allegation. People with drug histories made believable traffic fatalities.

He picked up the phone. "Get me Captain Pettis. He's in the lobby, out front."

"Yes sir," Pettis's voice came over the phone a moment later.

Valdez told the commando what he wanted: "We'll need to give Wirta a few tabs of Special K. Use the new designer stuff, the Ketamine-twelve, and round up a few unimpeachable witnesses. Get this done quickly. I need it set up in less than an hour."

"Yes sir."

Valdez hung up the phone. Anger swirled inside of him, filling him with poison. Valdez, a man who exhibited no emotion, was now seething. He knew that uncontrolled anger was dangerous . . . angry people made mistakes.

But no matter how hard he tried he was furious. For the first time in his life Vincent Valdez was dangerously out of control.

Chapter forty-four

Shane Scully made five calls and got five volunteers, all cops who had worked with Jack Wirta. They started streaming into the Hollywood station an hour later. Most were carrying ordnance-laden gym bags that tented suspiciously. Even Jack's old boss, Lieutenant Matthews, showed up. Shane's wife, Alexa, had arranged for them to use the department's large Bell Jet Air Unit.

At a little past ten, the gray and black six-passenger chopper landed on the roof of the station house, settling down on the helipad like a giant, nesting insect. The squad of volunteers who were waiting with Shane climbed aboard, leaving Herm and Susan standing on the roof.

"I'll call once I get my hands on him," Shane yelled from the helicopter over the rotor noise. "Alexa's on her way over to give you a lift."

"Thank you," Susan shouted back.

Shane nodded and waved, then the helicopter engine roared as the blades picked up rpms. The big chopper lifted off and flew into the night sky.

Alexa Scully arrived ten minutes later. She

pulled up to where Herman and Susan were now waiting by the back station entrance, reached over and unlocked the rear door of her black-and-white D-car, then shoved it open.

"I'm Alexa. You guys look like you need a ride," the surprisingly beautiful black-haired woman announced.

Herman and Susan introduced themselves, then got in the back seat of the car. They ducked down out of sight as Shane's wife pulled out of the Hollywood station parking lot and drove past the unmarked government sedan.

"Four guys in a gray Lexus," Alexa reported as she left the DARPA vehicle behind. "They're doing lot of hand-wringing. Got some confusion going on there."

After they were a mile away Susan and Herman sat up.

"You and Shane have been unbelievable," Susan said. "Without you, I don't know what we would have done."

"Jack's our friend. Of course we'd help."

Alexa drove them to the Van Nuys Airport and dropped them at the Peterson Executive Jet Terminal. After saying good-bye she waved and drove off.

Susan sat in the Jet Terminal thinking about Jack, who had somehow managed to slip by her emotional defenses and had been silently rearranging the furniture in the private, ruminative part of her head. Worse still, he was nothing like what she had been looking for. His list of superficial negatives seemed mind-boggling. He was a broken warrior who ignored, or seemed to laugh at, most of her important beliefs. He didn't belong in her temple of dreams, yet there he was dripping sarcasm and disrespect all over her carefully constructed value system. To her amazement, he seemed a perfect fit. Now he had been kidnapped, possibly was in mortal danger, and she couldn't get her mind to stop spinning or her heart to stop pounding. Her father had once told her that when you worry, you define your weakness, and when you dream you define your goals. She wondered how these feelings defined her.

Susan had a strange sense of impending disaster. She had been pushed into an unfamiliar role, not knowing if she would be able to hold up her end. She felt tiny and overwhelmed.

At a little past 10:30 a private jet landed; a green-and-white, forty-million-dollar Global Explorer. The main door hissed down and Donald Trump was standing in the threshold dressed in a perfect New York ensemble — a black three-piece suit, yellow silk tie and matching pocket square. His blonde combover flapped slightly in the light L.A. breeze. He came down the steps and across the tarmac toward them, smiling as he approached.

"Herman! You've gained weight since you stopped suing me. You need better adversaries." Trump was referring to a suit Herman filed against his casino division a year earlier, when they had tried to build a hotel in Tahoe, cutting down trees and adversely impacting the environmental resources of that small community. In the end Herman and Donald had compromised and found to their amazement that they liked one another.

Herman smiled. "Thanks for coming, Donald. I'm kind of in a crack here. You're the only person I know who can dig me out."

"Hey, this could be great for me. Are these guys ready to meet?"

Herman said. "They're gathered and waiting."

"Then let's go," The Donald said, smiling while his blue eyes danced with excitement.

When Susan and Herman escorted Donald Trump into Chief Ibanazi's den, the room was at standing-room-only. Thirty members of the tribe were present. It may have been billed as a tribal lodge meeting, but Chief Ibanazi was looking very record-industry chic in Gucci and Rive Gauche. He couldn't believe that Donald Trump was standing in his temple of creativity — the very room where he laid down his grooves and slammed on the Yamaha Sound Machine.

"My God, it's you," he started off, shaking Trump's hand. "It's really you."

"Yep. Me," Donald said.

"I mean, you're Donald Trump."

"Yep, sure am. No doubt in my mind," he chuckled.

"I mean, 'The Donald' is in my house. Amazing . . . I can't believe you're really here."

"Yep . . . in the flesh. It's me."

It went on like that for two or three more rounds, until Herman stepped in and broke it up.

"I'm Herman Strockmire," he said to Russell Ibanazi and the rest of the people in the room. "I'm the one who called you six hours ago. I think you know my daughter Susan."

"You mean, Lois," Russell corrected, smiling at her. "How's Clark? Did Mimi like the background stuff we did?"

"Uh . . ." She shot a look at Herman, whose eyebrows had climbed up somewhere in the middle of his forehead.

Susan stammered: "Uh, Izzy, I'm afraid that wasn't exactly all true, what we told you about *213 Magazine* . . ."

"What part of it wasn't true?" His handsome face wrinkled in distress.

"Well, more or less . . . all of it."

"Clark doesn't want to do the 'L.A. Sound' cover story?"

"Well, he would if he could, but since there *is* no Clark Lane, and no 'L.A. Sound' cover, and since we're not with the magazine at all . . . I don't think you should count on it."

"Not with the magazine?" Distress morphed into depression.

"No. We were just trying to find out more about the reservation and what was going on out there. It's why Mr. Trump is here now."

Russell Ibanazi looked at Donald, then at Herman.

"Okay," he said. "Then what's going on?"

Donald stepped forward, dropping his cashmere overcoat over the back of a large club chair. He looked at the faces of the rest of the Ten-Eyck tribe that included men and women of all ages, as well as half a dozen teenagers and a few children. They were handsome, black-eyed people, all dressed in the best Rodeo Drive had to offer.

"As you undoubtedly know," Donald began, "I'm involved in some big casino developments in Atlantic City and elsewhere . . ."

"Yes, of course we've heard," Russell Ibanazi said, leaning forward respectfully.

"I understand from Herman that you've voted in a government administrator to run your reservation and that he now has total control," Trump went on. "Is that pretty much the gist?"

"Yes, sir, that's exactly the situation. Correct." Russell was measured and precise —

no more show-biz buzzwords. He was back to being tribal chief.

"I also understand that the government pays you around forty million a year for the use of your seventeen-hundred acre reservation east of Indio."

Russell Ibanazi looked at Susan, then nodded. "It nets out at a little over two thousand dollars an acre a month."

"I hate to be blunt," Donald said. "But you're being screwed. Who negotiated that deal?"

"We . . . well, I set it up, and the entire tribe approved it at council." Concern shadowed his features.

"Since California passed the Native American Casino Gaming Bill, I'm sure you're aware that your reservation can now host a full-service gambling casino. That reservation is a tremendously valuable asset. Seventeen hundred acres could be worth a fortune if developed correctly. However, it can't be done if the government is fouling the land, dumping toxic waste into illegal ground fills." Trump had them all listening intently.

"There can't be much waste yet, Donald, it's only been eighteen months," Herman said quickly.

"Look, I can most likely deal with the toxic waste issues. I can probably force the government to clean it up at their expense or face a shit-storm of negative publicity. What I can't deal with is this non-Indian administrator hired by the Defense Advanced Research Projects Agency," Donald said. "He will block any attempt of mine to redefine land usage."

"Don't worry about him. We can vote him out anytime we want," Izzy said. "We could even have an election tonight and reinstate me as administrator. It's in the Tribal Charter."

The rest of the men and women in the room nodded and mumbled their assent.

"But the res is way the hell and gone, out in the desert twenty miles east of Indio, almost at the Mexican border. The choice reservation properties for casinos are the ones in and around Palm Springs. Why would you want to build a casino way out there?" Izzy said, trying not to look stupid for recommending the DARPA deal in the first place.

Trump didn't seem worried. "I'm not concerned about its remote location. That's one of the reasons I'm gonna get it for a good price, but I'll offer you a great percentage of my back-end profits in return. Even at my up-front lease rate, you're going to do three times better than the government is paying now."

The room murmured with excitement.

"The second reason it doesn't matter," Donald continued, "is that we will make this casino absolutely magnificent. There will be pools and fountains, solariums and traveling walkways, trams and amusement parks. Seventeen hundred acres of holiday fun with an airport to service it. It doesn't matter if it's twenty miles east of Indio on the Mexican border or twenty miles east of Egypt." Then he smiled, his white teeth and blue eyes glistened. "Because, in the words of my favorite actor, Kevin Costner: 'If we build it, they will come.' "

Chapter forty-five

Now this is more like it. Jack was grinning. He felt better than a troop of traveling clowns, more lit up than a Macy's Christmas window.

Okay, so maybe this little room is colder than a pimp's heart, but does that make it a bad place?

There were no windows and no furniture, and Jack Wirta, America's most engaging private dick, was forced to sit on the floor, contemplating concrete. Does that make this a bad experience? Fuck no. Concrete can be beautiful. Behold, its rough-hewn perfection. Study the poured-block worlds below. There are shapes lurking behind this gray molecular mass . . . little mountains and valleys, tiny fields of creation . . . microscopic and pure. A complete gnat-size world full of itty-bitty bumps and crevices that make up a carnival of untold beauty. Or an untold carnival of beautiful bumps and crevices . . . or a concrete carnival of untold bumpy canyons. Anyway, all kinds'a good shit.

Better still, Jack Wirta, heavy thinker, is having some world class thoughts. Even Emil Matasareanu and his dimwitted buddy Gene Philips couldn't fuck up this shoot-out. Jack was grinning, but suddenly, he felt sick. *Time out . . . need to vomit. Auggh . . . auggh . . . ahhh . . . wooph, splash. Oh-oh . . . Jack did a boo-boo.*

But, hold on . . . let's take a closer look. Even vomit can be morphed into something beautiful. What used to be a Big Mac is now a pool of regurgitated floor art.

He put his fingers in it and began to draw designs.

Sure it smells a little funky, but Jack Wirta, grinning artist, can work past that. Picasso had his oils. Wirta has his vomit.

The door swung open, crudely breaking his creative flow. Jack saw two of the neatest-looking commandos coming toward him dressed in cammies, with their heads in shiny metal pots.

"It's kicking in," one of them said to the other. "He's stoned outta his mind."

"Let's get this fucking asshole outta here."

"Jack Wirta, fucking asshole, is ready to go, *sir!*"

They yanked him up to his full forty-foot height. It was awesome up there, his feet dragging a perfect line of vomit across the floor. Toe art. Would the wonders ever cease? "I gotta go. Yes, yes. Here we go," he caroled as they pulled him out the door.

They muscled him down the corridor. A beautiful concrete corridor full of abstract microscopic crevices. How could he have missed all this before? Oh yeah, he remembered now. He'd had his head in a canvas sack.

And then he was outside. "This is so fucking great," he told the man on his left. "I've got to do this more often — get out in the forest with all the little creatures." He smiled at the man on his right, who didn't answer but shoved him into the back seat of a car.

"Shut your piehole, you moron."

"Moron Jack, shutting his piehole as instructed, sir," Jack giggled.

Valdez came out of the concrete block building.

"Hey Vinnie," Jack waved at him. "We're going for a ride."

"Take him down the mountain, then put him behind the wheel. Head him onto the 134," Valdez said.

"Hey, good idea," Jack grinned. "Bye, Vinnie." He waved at Valdez.

The car started moving. Jack was having a ball. "We're going on the freeway, we're going on the freeway," he chanted.

The two men in the car with him didn't seem to find him amusing. "Hey Wirta, for the last time, shut up!" one of them growled.

Jack put his finger to his lips and turned an imaginary key. "Birds . . . I see birds," he shouted, and pointed out the window at some hawks sailing above.

The man in the back seat with him hit Jack hard in the stomach. He doubled over, gasping for breath. "No fair," Jack whined.

After a moment he struggled upright and looked over at the glowering man who had just punched him. Something wasn't right. He felt strange. *What was it? Oh yeah, I know.* "Gotta puke." And he let fly, hitting the commando in the chest and lap with projectile vomit.

"Goddamn!" the man said.

They were down by the gate that went across Santiago Road, leading them out of the Cleveland National Forest. A ranger opened the gate and waved the car past.

"Hi," Jack grinned. "We're going to go on the freeway."

The man didn't hear him. They continued on, heading down toward the 134 Freeway that was coming into view a short distance in front of them.

Jack heard a helicopter overhead. "Hey!" he cried out happily. "Helicopter!"

"Shut the fuck up," the man with the vomit on his uniform growled.

"But, it's a *helicopter*," Jack persisted.

The roar became deafening, then for a second Jack could see the chopper was hovering in front of them, cutting them off. The car swerved, and in that instant Jack thought he saw someone he knew hanging out of the helicopter door. "Hey . . . it's Shane!" He called out.

The car skidded sideways attempting to manuever around the chopper, then careened off the road, down a dirt trail, and into the trees. The helicopter was forced to pull up to avoid hitting the tall pines. Jack felt the car come to a stop, then the two commandos were pulling him out of the back seat.

"Are we here?" he grinned, as they shoved him into the front seat and buckled him in behind the steering wheel. The man without the vomit got in beside Jack, butting him over slightly so he could also squeeze behind the wheel. Then the car started rolling again; the man wedged in next to Jack was driving awkwardly, negotiating a narrow track through the overgrowth. The helicopter sounds faded.

"Wheee!" Jack grabbed for the steering wheel, but the man knocked his hand away.

"Not yet, asshole."

"Okay," Jack grinned stupidly.

A half mile further, the car emerged from the trees and came to a stop at the base of a freeway ramp. The man jumped out. "Now. Get it on up there."

"Yes sir. On the case, sir."

The man slammed the door shut and Jack hit the gas. He was shooting up onto the freeway. "Here I come!" he shouted at the windshield.

Damndest thing, though. Cars were honking at him and the drivers all seemed angry. "What'd I do?" Jack whined. *Something is definitely wrong. What the heck is it? What is pissing these other drivers off? Is it . . . yes, yes*

424

. . . maybe this is it: The cars are coming at me. "Hey, everybody! I'm going the wrong way!" he shouted.

Suddenly, the helicopter was in front of him again, flying sideways along the freeway, trying to warn oncoming traffic, rising occasionally to pop over an overpass then dropping down again. It was trying to block him.

Traffic was pinwheeling everywhere, tortured rubber burning and squealing. Jack was aiming the car more than driving it. He spun the wheel to the right as a horn blared and a big rig started jackknifing, all eighteen tires smoking. "Good one," Jack shouted.

His car began pinwheeling as well — round and round, trees and signs and off-ramps whirling by in a confusing array of colors and shapes. Then it shuddered to a stop.

The helicopter hovered in front of him, and landed on the freeway. Men were running around waving their arms and stopping traffic. Jack was still sitting behind the wheel smiling when the door was yanked open. Shane Scully unbuckled him and pulled him out.

"Shane, we're taking a trip. We went up the freeway off-ramp," Jack grinned.

"What the fuck's wrong with you?" Shane asked, looking into Jack's eyes, staring at blown-out pupils.

"Nothing, Shane. Nothing," Jack said. "I'm having great thoughts. Oops, Gotta vomit."

And he threw up on his ex-partner's shoes.

Chapter Forty-Six

Jack's head was throbbing. It felt thick as oatmeal, heavy as a fifty-pound medicine ball. He was in the back row of Federal District Courtroom Sixteen, wedged between two more unlikely characters. On his right was a skinny old man with a string bean. On Jack's other side, snoring like Bluto's wife after a hard night of drinking, was the fattest woman he had ever seen. She was slumped over sleeping, and kept oozing toward him.

The TRO against DARPA was back in court and Herman was droning on. Susan was sitting next to him at the plaintiff's table, making notes. Warren Krookshank was up on the bench. He was a handsome African-American judge with silver-gray hair, rimless glasses, and a quiet, no-nonsense demeanor. The defense counsel, all ten of them, were gathered around their rectangular mahogany table in a pregame huddle.

Jack tried to focus on Herman's argument and ignore the old geezer muttering on the wooden bench next to him.

". . . reviewed the whole question of Charles Chimera's DNA," Herman was saying as Jack's attention returned.

"Objection, Your Honor," shouted Joe Amato. He was on his feet, his white cuffs and porcelain caps glittering. "The law clearly dictates denial of this TRO solely on the issue of standing. Counsel is attempting to sue my clients using an animal as his plaintiff. So before we get into the merits of the TRO, or whether this beast even exists, I want to get a ruling with regards to whether counsel can stand over there and represent a chimpanzee."

Herman was also on his feet.

"Not a chimpanzee, Your Honor, a being who has DNA closer to human homology than that of a Down's syndrome child. Judge King has already accepted the stipulation of the parties, that DNA is the yardstick for measuring humanity. That fact has already been established in this case."

"I know what Judge King ruled regarding stipulation, Mr. Strockmire. I've read the court transcript." Krookshank removed his glasses and looked down at Herman sternly. "Before I rule on that objection, is there anything else you want to submit, counsel?"

Herman moved out from behind the plaintiff's table. "Yes, Your Honor." He cleared his throat, then took a breath to center his thoughts. "Inequalities have existed for as long as people have been on this earth. We are a species that seems to treasure our ability to defend and fight for our inequalities, and there are many. We have religious, racial, and gender inequalities. We have inequalities of social status and of wealth. There are even commercial inequalities like those afforded to people flying first class as opposed to those flying coach. As a society, in order to grow we have to learn to embrace the natural inequalities that exist between us and reject the artificial ones. I'm not in favor of banishing all inequalities, Your Honor. Perhaps some of these differences exist between us for a reason, and perhaps some of them aren't bad — at least the nondiscriminatory ones. Perhaps by seeing certain people differently, others will strive to be better.

"But what happens, Your Honor, when a person, no matter how hard he or she tries, cannot redefine their station in life, and for that reason they are discriminated against? For instance, no matter how hard each of us tries, we will always be our same race, we will always have our same genetic or gender differences. Therefore we must accept that there are some things that simply cannot be changed. For instance, the makeup of our own DNA. Our DNA is a map of our personal genetic history, and up till now it was unchangeable no matter what we did.

"But my client's DNA has been changed to within a few tenths of a percentage point of human DNA. This, I will remind you, was done without his permission. Should the fact that Charles Chimera's DNA does not now exactly match the rest of us be enough to deny him Constitutional rights? Should that fact cause him to have to suffer further torture and inhumane testing? Because, Your Honor, this is what is happening here. Charles Chimera and his John Doe chimera coplaintiffs have had their DNA altered, causing them grave bodily harm. Only this court stands between them and any future irreparable experimentation."

"Objection," Amato said.

He sounded bored. He sounded amused. He sounded frustrated, Jack marveled. *All of that in one nine-letter word. The guy was simply magnificent.*

"What does any of this have to do with the fact that Mr. Strockmire is representing an animal in this court and doesn't have a shred of standing for his plaintiff," Amato challenged.

Warren Krookshank seemed to ponder that, and looked down at Herman. "This court concedes that inequalities exist, Counselor. However, this court is also bound by legal precedent. The defense raises a good point. Historically, only *Homo sapiens* have been allowed access to our judicial system."

"Your Honor, need I remind you of Dred Scott — a slave who was told that because he was a slave, and therefore was defined as property, he could not sue for his own freedom in a court of law? That decision was eventually overturned by the Supreme Court.

But before that it was the law. He was denied court standing, just as Charles Chimera is being denied his legal access. Even though he is closer to a human, by virtue of his DNA chart, than a Down's syndrome child or a genetically damaged fetus — many of whom have availed themselves of their legal rights in federal court.

"I have here a table of federal cases in which the court has heard lawsuits on behalf of beings with DNA further from the human norm than Charles Chimera's, together with a description of their DNA status. I would like to submit this as Exhibit B." He rummaged in his folder and withdrew a stack of pages, then handed his list of cases to the clerk, who marked them. Herman handed out copies to the defense, then reached up and ceremoniously laid one on Judge Krookshank's bench.

"I have to admit, there is something in this argument that is intriguing," Krookshank said. "The law must be prepared to change with the times. However, I'm still not convinced. I'm going to let you continue on the assumption that as we proceed you will establish facts to bring this more clearly into focus. I will rule on the issue of Charles Chimera's standing at some point down the road."

"Objection, Your Honor," Amato roared.

"Overruled."

"Exception."

"Noted."

A break in the action. They all sat around looking at one another wondering what to do next.

"Your Honor," Mr. Amato finally argued. "We don't accept the existence of any such thing as a chimera."

"I have submitted to this court a chart of Charles Chimera's DNA base pairs. It proves without a doubt that he exists, even though his presence in court is not possible today. However, we will have testimony from witnesses who have seen Charles Chimera. I heard him speak, and will offer my own declarations as to those facts."

"It's not possible, because there isn't anything or anyone called Charles Chimera. This hybrid animal doesn't exist and Mr. Strockmire has no proof that it does," Amato said.

"Your Honor, I'm prepared to put on a genetic expert, Dr. Carolyn Adjemenian, who will testify that this gene map could not be reverse-engineered."

"And we will put on ten experts who will explain how it can be reverse-engineered," Amato shot back. "This map of base pairs is nothing but a puzzle designed in a computer. There is no chimera, or whatever. Counsel can't prove there is! If he could, you'd see it sitting there."

Herman stood and handed up a discovery motion. "Your Honor, the gene map speaks for itself, but if Mr. Amato wants the real thing, the chimeras are currently being held and experimented on at the Ten-Eyck reservation out by Indio. They're being trained out there to be soldiers by an agency of the federal government. I want this court to grant this discovery motion to allow us to go out there and see for ourselves."

"A fishing expedition? Is that what this has finally turned into?" Amato said. "Perhaps we should also go looking for Bigfoot."

"No," Herman shot back. "It's not a fishing expedition, it's a discovery motion, a document whereby you, sir, are ordered to produce the hybrid animals in question."

"Your Honor, I resent that and object. Moreover, if counsel is making a discovery motion, the defense has not been given proper notice."

Warren Krookshank had his glasses back on and was looking at the motion, flipping pages. Then the judge looked up from the document. "As to the lack of notice, in the interest of time I'll consider this motion now and give Mr. Amato a chance to submit opposition in a minute, if I think it warranted."

The drones on the defense team were huddled over the motion, reading fast.

"This discovery motion seems in order, Mr. Amato. I don't think I'll need anything further from you," Krookshank announced.

"Except for one thing, Your Honor."

Amato wasn't out of it yet.

"And what's that?" Krookshank said, looking up.

"It's an Indian reservation, and as such is not covered by the discovery requests of this court. As you know, tribal lands are sovereign territories much like foreign embassies, and therefore are not subject to U.S. federal laws or rules of evidence. Anticipating this move by Mr. Strockmire, I have already talked to the Ten-Eyck Tribal Administrator, who has informed me that it is their long-standing policy to deny legal summonses and motions with regard to the reservation. With that in mind, we are objecting to this discovery motion under *Apache Nation v. the Office of Indian Affairs, U.S.A. v. the Chippewah Nation, U.S.A. v. the Seminole Nation, et al.* The list is extensive, Your Honor. Lengthy precedent exists here. This is an old burial ground of legal arguments — excuse the pun."

"Your Honor, I would like to call a witness who I think can clarify this matter for all of us," Herman said.

"And who is that?" Judge Krookshank asked.

"Russell Ibanazi, chief of the Ten-Eyck tribe. He has pertinent testimony regarding the issue counsel raises."

"Your Honor, Chief Ibanazi has no position with regard to this land. He doesn't even live on the reservation. The Tribal Administrator

433

is a man named Scott Nichols. He and he alone is in charge of Ten-Eyck tribal affairs on the reservation. I have his prepared affidavit here denying access."

"Your Honor, Scott Nichols is no longer —"

"Just a minute. Let me review this affidavit first," Krookshank said as Amato handed up his paperwork. Judge Krookshank readjusted his glasses and began to read. Herman didn't bother to read it because he already knew it was irrelevant. "Counsel seems to have a point," Krookshank said after shooting through the document. He removed his glasses and looked at Herman.

"Your Honor, may I please call Russell Ibanazi? I promise he can clarify all of this for you."

"All right, call your witness," Krookshank said.

"Objection."

"Overruled."

"The plaintiff calls Russell Ibanazi," Herman announced.

The bailiff opened the door and Izzy strode into court. He was dressed in a charcoal suit, starched white shirt, with a black-and-red tie and matching pocket square. His black hair glistened. Jack thought he looked better than Wayne Newton on *Hollywood Squares*. Izzy took the stand and was sworn in.

Herman moved toward him. "Mr. Ibanazi, could you tell us your position with respect to the Ten-Eyck tribe?"

"I am the chief. My male ancestors have held that position for almost two hundred years."

"I see. And who is currently in charge of tribal affairs at the Ten-Eyck reservation?" Herman asked.

"I am."

"Objection, Your Honor," Amato said. "This statement is clearly in conflict with the affidavit I just submitted, which confirms that Scott Nichols is the Tribal Administrator."

"Was the Tribal Administrator," Herman said. "He was voted out of his job last night by the entire Ten-Eyck tribe."

Herman stepped forward. "I have here a copy of the Ten-Eyck tribal laws, which provide that the Tribal Administrator may be replaced at any time by a majority vote of the Tribal Council. I also have a notarized record of that vote, which was taken at ten thirty-five last night." Herman opened a folder and removed the notarized records, then dealt out copies like a blackjack dealer.

"Your Honor, the Ten-Eyck tribe has entered into a binding contract with the U.S. government to lease that land," Amato persisted. "This vote is in violation of the government's lease agreement." He was scanning the document.

"Counsel?" Krookshank said looking over at Herman.

"Didn't Mr. Amato just say that reservation land was sovereign and not subject to the jurisdiction of the American courts? Didn't we just hear that?" Herman crowed.

"I believe we did," Krookshank was smiling slightly.

"Then I think if he wants to argue that one he needs to file a breach-of-contract suit and see if he can get some civil court to overrule the long-standing list of decisions he just provided us with."

Herman held up Amato's list of *V*s.

"I agree," Krookshank said. "Proceed, counselor."

"Chief Ibanazi, I'm going to show you a discovery motion and ask if you have any objections to the court making a trip out to your reservation to see if Charles Chimera and these five John Doe chimeras can be located?" Herman said.

"Absolutely no problem," Izzy responded. "You're all invited."

Judge Krookshank looked at his watch. "In the interest of preserving the evidence, how 'bout three this afternoon? I'll have the marshal arrange for some vans." He banged his gavel. "This court stands in recess."

Chapter Forty-Seven

While everybody else waited for three o'clock and the vans, Jack Wirta took a taxi over to Cedars-Sinai to see Casimiro Roca. As the cab driver bounced through a construction zone south of Pico, Jack's head felt like sun-rotted fruit about to explode. He silently cursed everybody, especially his driver, who was a Greek. The name on the hack license looked like it belonged on the Rosetta Stone.

"Slow down," he growled to the man who replied "Hokay," but didn't.

When they arrived at the main entrance of Cedars, Jack felt like he'd gone ten rounds with Lennox Lewis.

After a few minutes of wandering the polished, antiseptic halls of the hospital he finally found himself outside of Miro's door. He pushed it open and discovered the little ex-dancer reading *The Advocate*. When he looked up, Jack winced . . . Miro's face had gone half purple with bruises. His swollen eyes were greased with some kind of ointment and, as Susan had said, he'd lost several teeth.

Jack moved into the room and sat next to the bed on an institutional metal chair that sagged in the middle. He tried to ignore his own symphony of aches and pains as he focussed on Miro's damaged face.

"Are you using too much Maybelline blush, or is that actually a bruise?" he said, trying to keep it light.

"I guess I got myself kinda stomped," Miro said. "Those men . . . they came back."

"Yeah, I got it all from Susan. What you did for me . . . that was something pretty special. I just wanted you to know if you hadn't gotten that info about Black Star in Cleveland I'd be opening at Forest Lawn this weekend."

"That's what neighbors do for one another."

"Listen, Miro, neighbors just call the cops when the music is too loud. What you did was heroic, man. We're buds for life. I owe you."

"You do?" he smiled suggestively. "How were you thinking of paying Miro back?"

"Don't start with that," Jack smiled. "But you saved my life. I just want you to know I'll never forget it."

"Now you're making Miro blush."

"How can you tell?" Jack quipped.

"Take my word . . ." Miro smiled, then winced. "Oooh . . . sorry . . . hurts."

"So, what can I get you? Anything. Just name it."

"Jack, would you go to my office, make sure the Reflections answering machine isn't maxed? Pick up the messages and call the boys in the book to give them their appointments?"

"Uh . . . sure," Jack said. "You mean set up some, uh . . . whattayacallit . . . dates?"

"Yes . . . dates." He didn't smile because it hurt, but his eyes were twinkling as he gave Jack the key.

"I have to be back in court at three this afternoon, but I guess I could do that," Jack agreed hesitantly.

So Jack Wirta, ex-LAPD sergeant and one-time kick-ass homicide dick, cabbed across town to Reflections where he opened the door with Miro's key, entered, and hit the playback button on the answering machine.

"This is Leon," a voice said. *"I'm calling for Marlon. I'm ready to party. Call me at 555-3478."*

Jack wrote it down: Marlon — Leon's ready to party. He found a book of names, flipped it open, then had to scan the whole book because he didn't have a last name. There was only one Marlon, so Jack phoned and left a message on his machine with Leon's number. So far so good. Forgetting that prostitution was a crime, he thought this was pretty easy.

The next message was from somebody named Carl, for somebody named Jack, but Wirta didn't know if that was Jack with the nipple pierce or Jack with the fox terriers.

Jack Wirta, temporary escort service intern,

439

worked on the Reflections weekend business for almost an hour. He had done some strange things in his life, but this was number one on his list of all-time favorites.

The van ride to Indio was long and nobody had much to say. Jack thought the driver, an overweight deputy marshal in a too-tight uniform, might have been snoozing between Banning and San Bernardino, but that was just an impression and he hoped he was wrong. Jack rolled down a window to perk himself up some. He'd had enough freeway madness for awhile.

On the highway to Indio the terrain became decidedly less interesting. Shopping malls and gas stations thinned down to roadside jewelry stands and faded real estate signs.

There were two Indio Sheriff's cars parked at the side of the road as the Econoline vans turned onto the dirt lane leading to the Ten-Eyck reservation. The deputy had cut the old padlocks off the gate and it was now standing open.

"This the whole shebang?" an Indio deputy sheriff drawled as he stood in the desert heat with his stomach and gunbelt sagging.

Judge Krookshank got out of the lead van and stood at the side of the road while Joseph Amato gathered up his collection of identical cocounsels. Most of the attorneys looked slightly more human to Jack with sweat on their faces and their ties rolled up in their pockets.

"Okay," Krookshank said to Herman. "This is your discovery, so you do it."

They all squeezed into the front van and rumbled past the main gate led by the Sheriff's department escort car, jouncing along on the dirt road, all of them cheek to jowl, scowling like prisoners who didn't make bail. Herman was looking out the window trying to spot the chimera lab, which he was pretty sure would be a big brick or concrete block science pod. What they saw was considerably less noteworthy. There was certainly no shortage of cactus, broken trucks, and old tires. It was an impressive collection of rubble, but there wasn't one chimera to be seen. There were a few trailers rusting away in the dusty sunshine, but no huge concrete research facility. No little furry soldiers with human faces and talking computers. No spirited games of Capture the Flag taking place in the desert heat with DARPA coaches holding clipboards, scoring, and shouting instructions . . . just seventeen hundred acres of arid desert.

"Let's look in that one," Herman said with a sigh, pointing at a rusting, silver Airstream trailer. They climbed out of the van and Herman knocked on the door. Russell Ibanazi had some keys and opened up. It was empty.

441

"This was Bob Horsekiller's place," Izzy said. "He's got a big Spanish Tudor on Charing Cross Road now."

Good for Bob Horsekiller, Jack thought, as he looked inside the threadbare trailer. *I'd rather live in a mansion on Charing Cross, too.*

There was nothing inside the Airstream but broken furniture.

Back in the van, they headed off again. Herman was getting frustrated. "It has to be a large facility," he said, then pointed at a dirt road. "Try that one — there."

The van swung right and headed in that direction. More tires, more trailers, some stables, and an occasional dilapidated wood barn.

Herman got out and checked everything, walking into empty living rooms, kicking old rugs, unlocking the empty barns and leading them inside where there was nothing but empty stalls and piles of petrified horse shit. Through it all they were getting strafed by horseflies large enough to carry passengers.

Up until now Amato had remained silent, but he had started smiling. "Seen enough?" he quipped, managing to sound bored and ballsy, prickish and disgusted. Ten letters, two words and it was all *Brilliant,* Jack thought.

Then the tour was over. Izzy seemed glad to be heading out of there. His dark childhood memories of the place reconfirmed. He was a resident of Bel Air now and his Michelins were where they belonged — under his Porsche, not his porch.

They stopped at the gate. The sheriff waited as Russell Ibanazi locked up tight, putting on new padlocks he had brought with him. What he was protecting seemed a mystery.

"Anything else before we go home?" Krookshank asked.

"No . . . no . . . I guess not," Herman replied. He looked over at Susan, who shrugged.

Jack watched Herman carefully. He looked very old in that moment, older than his fifty-five years, heavier than his two hundred and forty pounds, more worn and tired than his shiny black suit.

"Oh well," Herman said. Two words, and they conveyed nothing but fatigue. Herman seemed outgunned and out of luck.

Jack felt sorry for him. It must be hard to believe in something so passionately and be completely wrong.

Chapter Forty-Eight

"I'm worried about Dad," she said. "I've never seen him this way before."

They were sitting in La Dome, a very trendy Hollywood restaurant. Jack had made the reservation. He couldn't afford the place. Jack usually tried to avoid restaurants where the price of a dinner for two was higher than his golf score and where the waiters were better looking than he was. La Dome definitely fit that classification, but women liked this place. Stars dined there. What a thrill to look over and see Jim Carrey comically spitting his water out onto the floor while your date is nibbling a seventy-dollar plate of Duck ala Bordelaise. The cheapest thing on the menu was a monkfish cooked whole. Jack ordered that. Susan had the lobster. After the waiter left she said, "I'm worried about what will happen in court tomorrow. We only have Carolyn Adjemenian to verify that this gene map is legit and proves the existence of the chimeras. Amato will have a parade of lying experts, all guys from government labs, paid through secret government contracts, who will bullshit like car salesmen to prove his point. I can't let Dad fail. I can't let them

444

destroy him, steal his soul."

"Yeah," Jack said. Strange way to put it, but he knew she was right. As he was looking at her in the dim light of the restaurant he was thinking that she had to be one of the most remarkable women he had ever encountered. It wasn't just her physical beauty, it was the way she kept standing in there, fighting for her poor, wheezing father right to the end, never once doubting him, even in the face of total defeat. Their trip to the desert had revealed tumbleweeds and dust devils, but not one furry hybrid monster. But she had never lost faith. Even now she was still trying to salvage the mission, still trying to bail Herman out.

"Dad and Sandy saw a chimera," she said suddenly. "You saw Sandy's drawing. We need to find out where the government took them . . . where they are. We need to catch one."

"Right. Good idea," Jack replied somewhat less than honestly, as his plate of monkfish arrived. The head was attached and his meal was staring at him, giving him the fish eye.

Susan was saying, "He just never looks crushed like that. Even after the MK Ultra case he got angry and rededicated himself. He's just sort of sluggish now, going through the motions with Sandy, like his spirit is gone — like he doesn't care anymore."

All afternoon Jack had been plagued by a

thought, but he'd been trying to ignore it. Part of him wanted to just bag this whole case, shake hands with Herman, kiss and make love with Susan, and hope the business with the chimeras would all fade away. But another part of him, the heroic, rarely seen part, wanted to help pull lumbering Herman Strockmire Jr. out of his funk and save the day for the corny but valiant Institute for Planetary Justice. This thought he'd been having — this epiphany — had been rattling around in his empty head like a marble in a metal bucket for about three hours. He had desperately tried to push it away. It was a question really, and maybe there was no answer. But maybe there was; and if the answer was what he thought it was, it threatened to not only ruin this romantic evening with Susan, but to take them down a road that Jack was pretty sure he didn't want to travel.

All of this must have been playing across his big movie screen of a face, colorful and obvious as a Steven Seagal flick, because suddenly Susan asked, "What is it? What are you thinking?"

"Huh?"

"You look like you just had an idea."

"I don't get many ideas. It musta been gas."

"What were you thinking, Jack? I want to know," she demanded.

"Well, if you must know, I was thinking

you are one of the most beautiful people I've ever had the pleasure to know, and I think I'm falling in love with you."

"Jack, that wasn't it."

"But it oughta earn me some points, though." He smiled. "It was sweet and endearing and . . ."

"Jack!"

"Okay, okay, what I was thinking was . . ." He took a deep breath. "Everything that happened today makes no sense at all when viewed against what happened yesterday. That's it. That's the whole idea. Let's go to the next subject. Hey, this is a great-looking fish, isn't it? I love it when you can have eye contact with a meal."

"Whatta you mean?" she said. "Explain that. And I'm not talking about the food. The thing about what happened yesterday not being in sync with today."

Jack put down his fork and sighed. "We go out to that reservation and it's nothing but a used-tire exhibit . . . some old trailers, a few run-down barns. Nothing."

"So?"

"So, why is . . ." he stopped.

"Yes?"

"Why is there a Code Sixty-one on that place?"

"A what?"

"It's a federal no-fly zone restricting all flights over that reservation from the ground all the way to outer space. They only have Code Sixty-ones over top-secret military installations. If there's nothing out there to hide, why the FAA restriction, and why did a Blackhawk helicopter chase me off when I tried to fly over it? Why did they arrest and try to kill me if there's really nothing out there?"

She sat in silence pondering it. "You're right. It makes no sense."

"Right, none at all. So that means something *is* out there — something they don't want anybody to see."

"But there was nothing there. You saw. The place was deserted. There was no lab. They couldn't move a whole science facility in a day."

"It's not the missing lab. It's the other thing that's missing that's got me puzzled."

"What other thing?"

"The toxic waste pit. Where the hell was that?"

"Huh?"

"Izzy told us they were digging it even before the tribe left, that it was a huge hole in the ground. But we didn't see a toxic waste site . . . no dumping platforms or flow tanks, no sealed concrete hatches, nothing. So where the hell is the toxic waste station?"

"My God, you're *right*."

"Yeah. That happens with me about once every ten years or so."

"What're you thinking?"

"I'm thinking maybe that hole they were digging wasn't for a waste pit," Herman said. "These DARPA spooks love their underground facilities. The Dulce Lab at Area Fifty-one was underground. What if this chimera testing lab was built underground and the no-fly zone is because they don't want pictures from the air of the chimeras playing war games and doing training exercises out in the desert? What if the research lab is in that hole? After Herman filed his discovery motion this morning they just went underground, pulled the dirt up over their heads and disappeared."

There it was — his big ugly idea. Now it was out in the open, sitting between them, ruining his Monkfish with Champagne Sauce and her Lobster Florentine. The idea leaked intellectual pollution onto their expensive feast . . . because, if they accepted this as truth there was really no turning back for either of them.

"You're right. You're right, Jack. Izzy said they were digging it even before the tribe left; so, at the very least — even if they changed their minds about dumping — there would still be a huge hole in the ground — and there isn't."

"Right. I think Amato knew what was out there and when Krookshank allowed Herm's motion he called 'em. By the time we got there everything was safely underground.

That means somewhere in this big complicated mess we've got lawyers lying. Unique concept, huh?"

"What do we do?"

"I think we need to go back and see Izzy. Get him to draw us a map of exactly where that pit was."

All of a sudden they weren't hungry, so they had the waiter bag up their food.

"Was everything to your liking?" the handsome maitre d' asked skeptically as he handed them two tinfoil containers twisted into the shape of ducks.

Hard question, Jack thought. Everything most certainly *wasn't* to his liking. In fact, he was scared to death. The last thing he wanted was to sneak back out to Indio and crawl under a barbed-wire fence with a knife between his teeth. But the guy looked so sad that they hadn't eaten that Jack assured him. "Everything was tremendous." He held up the two containers of artistically packaged food. "Just ducky," he added softly.

Chapter forty-nine

It was eight at night and the temperature in the desert near Indio was dropping faster than Jack's meager stock portfolio.

He and Susan were kneeling in a sand culvert with Chief Ibanazi and three other members of the Ten-Eyck tribe.

A war party.

Everyone was dressed in jeans and tennies, except for Izzy, who had added a chic leather vest from Brioni and a headband from Costume National. He looked like a painting of Cochise as they knelt in the moonlight. Jack had his trusty hunting knife in a leather scabbard on his belt, determined to put it between his teeth at some point during the raid. They were all packing handguns, nine millimeters mostly. But Russell's cousin, Carlos Ibanazi, had a scoped 30.06.

"It's down here about another quarter mile," Izzy informed them in a stage whisper worthy of any of the great Warner Bros. Indians.

"Okay," Jack nodded. "Susan, you're rear guard. You have the cell phone. If we need help you know what to do."

"I'm through being rear guard. *You* be rear guard."

"You can't go with us," he argued. "Too dangerous."

"Then, I hope you brought your hand-cuffs," she shot back. Her eyes were flashing angrily and he could see there would be no stopping her. "Either that, or we can do what I suggested before — call the cops and let *them* sneak in here," she added.

"No cops," he said.

"I still don't see why not," Susan argued.

"Because as an ex-cop I can tell you we're shitty at covert ops. We always start by announcing stuff over bullhorns. We need to catch one of these chimera things out in the open *before* we add all the police confusion."

It was good logic, but she still seemed worried about their safety; that was okay, because Jack was worried about their safety, too.

"Okay, show time. Let's do it," Jack said, borrowing that tired line from just about every corny action film he'd ever seen.

They stood to the side and let Russell Ibanazi take the point.

Izzy headed down the culvert, his three-hundred-dollar tennies making squeaking sounds in the fine sand.

Jack Wirta, renegade commando and complete medical mess, took the second position. Behind Jack was Carlos, who on the ride out from L.A. never stopped complaining about the assholes who stole his Rolls. As he

452

gripped his long scoped rifle he asked Jack over and over if, as an ex-cop, he knew how to catch car thieves.

"Gee, Carlos," Jack had finally said, trying to calm him down, "that's a tough one. But, since you got it back, if it was me, I'd just forget about it."

"Can't forget about it," Carlos said. "Nobody steals my car. Gonna get the fuckers." He wouldn't shut up about it. It was making Jack wish he'd never stolen the damned thing.

Behind Carlos Ibanazi was Bobby Horsekiller, who looked like he really could kill horses: six feet of gristle and bone stacked under mean eyes and a cruel mouth. Jack was glad he hadn't stolen Mr. Horsekiller's Rolls.

Susan was behind Horsekiller, and bringing up the rear was somebody named Digby. Jack hadn't caught the last name, but he sure didn't look like a Digby. He looked like an Indian version of Andre the Giant, all three hundred fifty-plus pounds of him. His tennis shoes looked like tuna boats. The guy was immense.

So, off they went Indian file . . . apparently no lack of political correctness there either, because that's what Izzy called it.

When they finally reached a large, metal drainage pipe Izzy stopped. Jack pumped his fist up and down, like John Wayne in *The Green Berets*, to announce that the column was coming to a halt. It was a cool-looking signal, and when you did it, everybody was supposed to put on the brakes. Trouble was, Carlos wasn't watching and climbed right up Jack's already tortured back. Then they all ran into each other. In a remarkable demonstration of human kinetic energy the entire column went down.

"Shhh," Russell said as he regained his balance and stood. "Okay, this drainage pipe goes under the perimeter fence. When I was a kid, this was my way off the reservation to score girls after my folks were asleep. On the other side is an open field, and we'll have to stay very low. In this full moon we can be seen over a long distance in the desert, unless we get on our bellies." He looked at Jack and the others, who all nodded.

"Okay, show time. Let's do it," Izzy said, sounding even sillier than Jack had.

They crouched down and duck-walked through the four-foot-high metal drainage pipe that was full of rust and unimaginable stuff that slithered away in the dark. Jack could hear Digby grunting somewhere back there as he lumbered along.

Soon they emerged on the other side and came up behind Russell who had proned out on the sand. Everybody stretched out next to him.

Jack had a pair of old Bushnell binoculars around his neck, but he was lying on them and they were now punching a hole in his already injured chest. After he dug them out he could feel the hunting knife poking him as well. Maybe now would be a good time to slip it neatly between his teeth. White Eyes prepares for battle . . .

Instead he focused the binoculars and began scanning the open terrain between where they were and the reservation beyond. Some pretty good tires out there — looked like they still had lots of tread on them. He panned left and brought the old stables into view.

"We got some choices to make here," Izzy was saying. "Those are the stables off to the left about a quarter mile . . . you can just see them in the moonlight. That's where the open pit was dug."

Jack kept his Bushnells on the stables and sharpened the focus. They looked deserted.

"Or, like I said in war council, we could try the old tribal long house and sweat lodge over there couple a hundred yards to the north toward the mountains," Izzy whispered.

The war council had taken place two hours earlier at a Denny's restaurant off the Indio Highway. Jack had a cheeseburger with fries, Susan had the California salad, Russell, Carlos, and Bobby all ordered tuna melts. Jack thought it was unusual food for a war council. Indians preparing for battle should fast and ask the Great Spirit for courage. Digby made it worse by ordering everything else on the Denny's menu.

Izzy had showed Jack a map of the reservation he'd drawn and pointed out where the two pits that the government dug were located. "Over by the old stables and near the sweat lodge," Izzy said. It was the first time Jack had heard there were *two* pits.

Now, hours later, they were on their stomachs while Jack looked across the desert at the stables through his Bushnells, trying to make a decision: stables or sweat lodge?

"Let's stick with the stables," Jack finally said, partly because he always tried to stay out of buildings where naked men sat in circles sweating, and partly because it was two hundred yards closer, and he still remembered the elbow crawls he'd been forced to do at the Police Academy.

So they were off crawling across the desert on their stomachs. Halfway there Izzy stopped to catch his breath. "See anything?" Izzy said.

Jack's back was killing him so he dug into his pocket for his last two Percocets. He slipped the pills into his mouth, then brought the binoculars up and scanned the stables.

Jack shook his head. "Seems deserted."

Izzy was looking at the stables with a puzzled frown. "Y'know, I thought that stable was in the wrong place this afternoon when we were out here. It used to be about forty yards to the east, I'm almost sure."

"How?" Jack said, thinking he was sounding more and more like a real Indian.

"This was my old trail. I used it all the time when I was a kid. I'm sure the stables used to be further east. Don't you remember, Carlos? They were over by that big Joshua tree."

"I never went to the stables much," Carlos answered. "I had my brother's Jeep after he went into the Marines."

"Why move the stables?" Digby asked. It was his first sentence since he'd said "Pass the ketchup" two hours ago.

"I don't know," Izzy said. "But I've taken this route a hundred times and I'm telling you they moved 'em."

"Maybe to dig the pit . . . then they put the stables back for camouflage, but not in the same exact spot," Susan volunteered.

Just then the stable doors opened and five low shapes scampered out of the building followed by a man in cammies who turned and closed the door, locking up behind him.

Jack focussed the lenses on the five shapes. They were slightly smaller than an average man — maybe five-feet-four or -five and they kept low. They were dressed in metal that reflected the moonlight. Through the binoculars they looked like they had furry bodies and human faces.

Chimeras.

They were carrying long, two-handled

weapons that resembled the *Star Wars* ordnance the commandos had used at Zimmy's wife's apartment and onboard *The Other Woman.*

"Damn," Jack said aloud as the animals fanned out and started looking around in the moonlight. Their faces through the lens, even at this distance, looked amazingly human.

Izzy snatched the binoculars away and trained them on the distant shapes. "What the fuck are those things?"

"You don't wanna know," Jack said.

Susan took the binoculars and looked. "It's them," she said. "Chimeras!"

The hybrid soldiers turned, then headed in five separate directions across the desert, staying low in the natural crevices until Jack couldn't keep them all in the wide-angle lenses. He was panning frantically back and forth, but they had scampered away. They looked like they were fanning out and getting ready to attack.

"I hate this," Jack was saying. "I'm not sure what weapons they're packing, but they look like those rayguns."

"Rayguns?" Izzy turned and was looking at them, his Costume National headband resting slightly askew over an expression of grave concern.

"If these chimeras are the troops that I think they are, and they're armed with particle-beam weapons, we're fucked. Gimme the cell phone," Jack ordered. "Time to call in the badges and bullhorns."

Susan dug in her pocket and handed over her phone. Jack had memorized the number of the Indio Fire Department. He dialed. Long experience had told him that firefighters had the best response time and always brought the cops with them anyway. He pressed the SEND button.

"Indio Fire Department," a female voice said.

"This is Bob Bailey. I'm driving by the Ten-Eyck reservation and there's a huge brush fire blazing out here!"

"Where are you exactly, sir?"

"I'm at the old reservation road. This desert is doing a major flambé. Better hurry." Then he hung up. "Let's move. Forget staying down. I don't know how they did it, but I think they've already seen us," he said, deciding if they changed positions they might just avoid a pincer movement.

They took off running across the desert staying behind Jack who had now taken the lead and was running as fast as he could despite his impressive array of injuries. Izzy was right behind Jack. Susan was faster than Horsekiller, who lumbered. Carlos was keeping pace, but Digby was falling way back, grunting and woofing along behind them.

The first two chimeras suddenly appeared off to the right. One of them stopped and pointed a weapon, then fired. The gun made a buzzing sound and a red light arced at them.

"Down!" Jack shouted and dove to the right. The laser beam hit a granite boulder to his left. It instantly exploded.

"Holy shit!" Izzy shrieked in panic, sounding nothing like a Warner Bros. Indian now.

Susan was running in a zigzag until she caught up to Jack, who rolled onto his stomach with his Beretta out and chambered. She threw herself down next to him just as he fired at one of the chimeras. The animal was moving fast across the desert running toward them on all fours, its laser weapon slung over its back. Jack's wild shot missed badly. The bullet whined away in the dark, but the animal veered off.

"On the right!" Horsekiller yelled. Jack spun in time to see two other chimeras loping across the high ground. They stopped, sighted their laser weapons down on the war party, then fired as Carlos's 30.06 barked simultaneously. The laser guns sent arcs of red light streaking across the desert. The first hit Horsekiller, frying him on the spot, setting his whole body on fire. He fell screaming and smoking onto the sand next to Susan and died before he landed. The second laser shot went wide, cutting a fiery line into the brush.

As Susan looked up she saw that Carlos's shot had hit one of the chimeras. He was squealing in pain and rolling backwards on the sand. Seconds later, for no apparent reason the wounded chimera exploded and burned in a raging fire.

Adrenalized with fear, the war party was off and running, leaving Horsekiller and the lone dead chimera smoldering in the sand.

Izzy was now out front. "This way!" he screamed — panic taking over.

Susan didn't know where Izzy was taking them, but she ran for all she was worth. Jack ran beside her. She turned and saw that Digby was way too far behind. As she looked back, she saw a fast-closing chimera jump on Digby from behind. The big Indian and the hybrid beast rolled in the desert sand locked in a deadly struggle. The monstrously huge Digby screamed as his arm was yanked out of its socket. It wasn't completely ripped loose, but hung uselessly by his side. Susan saw that Jack had spun and was running back to help Digby, who seemed to be no match for the much smaller chimera. Although the hybrid warrior was only a third of Digby's body mass, the animal was easily winning the fight. In a last-ditch effort Digby finally slugged the beast with his good arm, knocking the chimera back slightly.

Jack was now only five feet away. He

461

steadied his Beretta in both hands and squeezed off a round. The weapon roared. The chimera was hit in the chest and blown backwards as Jack's Beretta tore a deadly hole in the animal; but despite the mortal wound the chimera wasn't finished. It regained its footing then launched itself again at Digby, grabbing the big man's head in both of its human-like hands. Digby had no strength to resist. His useless left arm hung limply at his side. Jack pulled the trigger again, but this time the Beretta jammed, so he yanked his hunting knife out and charged at the chimera in a desperate attempt to save Digby from a horrible beheading. He dove at the two of them, sinking the knife into the chimera's back. It let out a tortured yell sounding more animal than human. Then it turned in his grasp and Jack found himself staring into its human face and pain-filled eyes. While Susan watched helplessly, Jack and the beast rolled in the sand. The animal was quickly losing strength, whimpering. It let go of Jack and flopped onto its back. Jack struggled to his feet and looked down. There was agony and intelligence in its face as it stared back at him. Then the chimera cocked its head, whined once, closed its gray eyes, and died.

As Jack staggered backward the animal exploded with such a violent force that it almost blew his head off.

★ ★ ★

It had never really occurred to Captain Silver
that any of his chimeras would die in battle.
He had loved them and fed them, cared for
them, and fought for their well-being. Now
as he watched two of them first get hit and
then explode, he realized that Valdez was de-
stroying them from the command room. He
was suddenly struck by parental rage.

"No!" he shouted impotently. It was so different during war games when they had occasionally been hit by the rubber bullets fired
by DARPA commandos. They had squealed
in pain but none had died. Somehow Dave
Silver had come to believe in their invinci-
bility. Now two more were gone, and without
any thought he gave the order to return.

The three remaining chimeras fell back and
he opened the barn door for them. They
raced across the sandy terrain on all fours,
not in retreat, but in response to his command. Silver knew they would fight to the
last animal if ordered, but he was not prepared to lose anymore. He had made a
human mistake . . . Silver had begun to
value them as individuals instead of military
assets.

When the survivors were all inside the stables he saw that Gree, the lead chimera, was
still alive and looking up at him. Dave Silver
ordered them to take up positions at the
front windows. "Fire at will," he said, and

they began unloading the particle-beam weapons at moving shapes out in the desert.

Suddenly the hydraulic hatch opened, rising from the hay-strewn floor of the barn. Vincent Valdez emerged from the stairs and stepped into the darkened stables. "What the fuck are you doing?" he demanded.

"We were losing troops. I gave the order to pull back," Silver said.

"These aren't troops, you asshole. They're things . . . animals!" he raged. "Get them back out there! Destroy those people!"

"No, sir," Captain Silver said. "I can't . . . I won't."

Valdez's eyes burned with rage. He pointed his revolver at Captain Silver and pulled the hammer back. Dave Silver had seen this look in battle before. It was homicidal rage and he knew he was about to die.

"Gree," Captain Silver commanded. "Attack."

The chimera sprang across the floor just as Valdez fired. The bullet hit Silver in the chest sending him backwards to the ground. A split second later Gree hit Valdez, and in an instant had ripped his arm from his body and thrown it across the room.

Valdez screamed as he stared down at his shoulder and the bloody hole where seconds before his arm had been. Arterial blood spurted out of him as he staggered across the stables lit from below by the harsh light shining from the hydraulic staircase. Then he fell backwards and tumbled down the stairs into the command center.

"Gree. No more," Captain Silver said, his hand over the bullet wound in his chest. He could feel his heart still beating, but he could also feel blood leaking inside him. His lungs were filling and he started to cough. Foamy red saliva came out of his mouth and dribbled down his chin.

The three chimeras stood watching him with blank expressions, waiting patiently for their next command.

"Go. Hide inside the lab," Captain Silver finally managed to whisper. They quickly turned and ran below without ever bothering to look back at him.

Dave Silver crawled to the Navaho blanket hanging on the wall and pulled himself onto his knees. He was dizzy and could barely see. He knew his life was pumping out with each heartbeat. He was drowning from the inside, drowning in his own blood. He could feel his breath become shorter as his lungs filled. He reached out and managed to push the button. As he fell forward the last sound he heard was the hydraulic door in the floor humming closed.

Chapter fifty

Jack Wirta was running as fast as he could, his tortured back sending shots of electric pain up his spinal column and down his leg. He still had the smell of Robert Horsekiller's burning flesh in his nose.

They were all following Izzy, who was running across the desert in a wide right turn. Carlos had dropped the 30.06 somewhere and Digby was galloping in the rear, favoring his strong leg and grimacing as his dislocated arm flapped uselessly at his side.

Jack didn't know if Izzy had any specific destination or was just running in a huge semicircle, but followed him anyway. After all, he used to sneak off the res to get laid, so he had to know where he was going, didn't he?

He didn't.

They stopped in front of the old Airstream trailer that had belonged to the late Robert Horsekiller. Izzy had his hands on his knees and was sucking in great gasps of air as Jack and Susan pulled up.

"What's here?" Jack managed between gulps of air.

"Nothing," Izzy wheezed back.

"Then why did you lead us here?" Jack asked.

"Dunno," Izzy said.

"You're relieved. Some fucking chief."

Digby finally arrived at the trailer groaning and holding his limp arm, looking like a coronary case. Three-hundred-fifty-pound guys weren't designed to run in the sand.

"I don't see any more of them," Susan said.

Jack didn't either. "I counted five. We got two. That means the first squad is down to three. We're down to four, if you're still with us, Digby."

"I'll try," the big Indian groaned.

Jack paused. "I'm really sorry about Horsekiller. That wasn't supposed to happen." They all nodded and Izzy crossed himself.

"So let's go get some payback," Jack said. "Let's try to take the stables. Keep your weapons cocked and try not to shoot the guy out front . . . who's gonna be me." Jack crept around the Airstream in the general direction of the barn, then took off running, staying low, hugging the terrain.

As they approached the stables he dropped on his stomach, and led the others toward the structure executing the painful Academy elbow crawl. In the moonlight he felt open and exposed. Slowly, they all worked their way up next to the structure. Miraculously, nobody fired a raygun at them.

They stood and flattened out against the wood walls of the weathered stable. Jack reached around and tried the door. Unlocked. He pushed it open a crack, took a deep breath, and ducked quickly inside.

At first the barn appeared empty. They quickly fanned out inside checking for Chimeras or DARPA commandos. Then Susan tripped over something, looked down and shrieked. "Oh my God!"

At her feet was a human arm ripped from its socket and still encased in a black suit sleeve. The hay near where it lay was sticky with blood.

"Son of a bitch," Izzy said softly.

"Look for the body," Jack instructed.

They found the corpse of Dave Silver in one of the stalls. He had bled to death but still had both his arms.

"Nobody else," Izzy said, looking around. "Except for the arm and this one dead guy, it's empty."

"Can't be empty," Susan countered.

"But it is," Izzy argued, sounding like he wanted to get back to Bel Air.

Susan persisted. "We saw them all come out of here. There's gotta be a way down to the lab from inside this barn."

"She's right," Jack agreed. He looked at the front windows facing west. "Digby, can you keep a lookout? Cover us?"

"Left-handed . . . can't shoot," the huge man said.

"You could prop your pistol on that windowsill, and if any of those furry bastards come back this way light 'em up," Jack suggested.

"I'll try," Digby said, but he didn't look too sure of himself.

Susan was prowling around the stable checking the floor and the walls, but she couldn't find a hidden opening.

"What's that doing here?" Izzy asked, pointing at an Indian blanket hanging on the stable wall.

"It's a horse blanket, you moron," his cousin Carlos sneered.

"It's a Navaho blanket. We're Ten-Eyck," Izzy said, moving closer.

"It is?" Jack said. "How can you tell?" They all stood looking at the blanket until Susan finally took the initiative and removed it from the wall. Underneath was a large electrical box and a big, red button.

"Don't touch it," Jack said quickly. "What if it's an alarm or an entrance bell?"

"It's not an alarm or a bell," Susan said and pushed it.

Immediately they heard solenoids clicking, then a hydraulic engine whirred and the floor they were standing on started to rise. They yelped and jumped aside as five square feet of floorboards, hay, and horseshit rose up revealing a lighted staircase and a ten-foot-wide conveyor belt. They were looking down into harsh xenon lights.

"I think I saw this movie," Izzy said.

"Let's go down," Susan ordered, proving, Jack thought, that she had the most guts.

They followed a blood trail down the staircase until they reached the bottom of the first flight where a door stood slightly ajar. Jack decided that as a certified alpha-male and former Playboy Club member he should probably suck it up and go in first. Reluctantly, he stepped around Susan and pushed the door open.

They entered a large room dominated by ten television monitors, a sophisticated audio mixing panel, and the dead, bloodless, one-armed body of Vincent Valdez.

"Vinnie. You came apart on me," Jack said softly.

The monitor screens showed surveillance views of the reservation barely visible in the moonlight. They could also see the drainage pipe and two intense orange dots. None of them understood that the larger glowing dot was the heat-resonance image of the burning pile of ashes that had once been Robert Horsekiller.

Susan pulled a small digital camera out of her bag and photographed the room along with Vincent Valdez's corpse before they moved on.

The top floor was labeled B-1 and contained the command center and a garage with three vehicles — two Jeeps and a small truck that apparently could be driven onto the conveyor belt and up into the barn. Jack located the elevator and brought it up.

"Carlos, stay here. Cover this exit," Jack said.

"Good deal," Carlos said, glad to stay behind.

They found the sleeping quarters on B-2. The bedding on the cots was dime-tight. Personal equipment was packed in spotless foot lockers — but no soldiers and no chimeras. The floor was deserted.

B-3 was also empty and housed some storage rooms and the mess hall.

They found the empty chimera nests on B-4. It was a little less pristine down here. Jack saw some animal dung on the floor.

Since B-4 was also empty, they got back on the elevator and continued down.

All hell broke loose on B-5.

Chapter Fifty-One

General Buzz Turpin was watching them on the monitor at DARPA headquarters in Virginia. The security cameras on each floor of the Ten-Eyck lab were fed to Arlington via a phone hookup that displayed the video lead in his command center. Now that the Ten-Eyck facility had been breached it had to be destroyed. He watched as three men and a woman moved down the stairs from the barn into the lab.

"Where are our people?" Turpin snarled at Paul Talbot who was seated in the command chair next to him watching the screen.

"I don't know. Down on five, I think, but I can't pick 'em up on the corner cameras."

Turpin had already notified DARPA Control Center to arm the small nuclear devices located under the lab. The arming procedure, with its secure locking codes, took almost five minutes to accomplish. Time ticked by ominously. Turpin watched the intruders as they descended further. Anger flashed inside him. This project had been designed to free American children from the horrors of war. The DARPA chimera program could have guaranteed that not one more American soldier would ever have to die in a ground war. Now it was ruined. He watched as the intruders got into the elevator and took it down to the basement floor, B-5.

He could see that five DARPA commandos, three remaining chimeras, and several frightened genetic scientists had taken up new positions and were now visible on the B-5-level cameras.

Suddenly the elevator door opened. Two men and a woman stepped out into the laboratory.

Two DARPA soldiers opened fire immediately in violation of their orders, using the high-powered particle-beam weapons that had been designed for outdoor use only. In the steel-walled enclosure of the genetics lab, the beams broke up and ricocheted around the room uncontrollably.

"No, you assholes!" Turpin shouted into his communications console.

Streams of particle-beam laser light streaked across the lab like *Star Wars* special effects, hitting steel walls and lighting up everything they hit with high-energy voltage. After bouncing off metal walls they kept going, arcing back and forth, breaking up into energy particles and flying all around the lab like deadly fireflies.

Jack screamed out in fear and threw himself behind a metal cabinet.

Not exactly ideal alpha-male behavior, but it took him by surprise.

He finally pulled it together and tried without success to return fire, pulling the trigger on his already-jammed Beretta. Jack watched in horror as a second DARPA commando swung his particle-beam weapon toward him.

Izzy came to his rescue, firing twice with his square-barreled Glock 9, hitting both DARPA commandos and blowing them backward.

Izzy bought them ten precious seconds. Jack jumped up and ran on stringy legs across the lab, dove under a table then grabbed up one of the fallen laser weapons.

Payback.

Another commando fired . . . more red death arced around the lab ricocheting and filling the air with deadly particles. Computers exploded behind Jack. The room was filling with smoke and charged air. Everyone's hair was standing up from static electricity.

Jack turned the complicated laser gun over and studied it, then flipped a switch, hoping to turn it on.

He rolled right, put the weapon to his shoulder, and pulled the trigger. Nothing.

The chimeras were just standing there watching the fight. One was jumping up and down, but made no move to enter the fray. They had been trained to act only on command, and nobody had given an attack order.

While Jack tried a few more buttons on the laser gun, Izzy and Susan dove for cover behind a metal counter. Izzy was holding his Glock sideways, blasting away like a rock-video gangster. Jack rolled, punched some more buttons and tried the laser gun again. Still nothing. "How d'ya turn this damned thing on?" he shouted. Nobody seemed inclined to help.

The panicked DARPA commandos finally realized their mistake shooting the laser guns in a metal-walled room and pulled out pistols. They were now chopping up the lab with conventional ordnance.

Jack made a run for the cover of a metal counter. Suddenly he felt searing pain in his shoulder and went down.

Alarms started ringing.

While Jack didn't like the sound of the whooping alarms, on the plus side he, Susan, and Izzy somehow gained the tactically superior position close to the elevators.

"Let's go . . . pull out," Jack shouted, and they all started running like hookers in a vice raid. Jack sprinted to the nearest elevator and pushed Izzy inside. The DARPA commandos broke cover and swarmed the room. Susan unexpectedly looped back and was gathering something up off the counter. "Let's go!" Jack screamed while Izzy fired four more shots pinning down the swarming DARPA soldiers.

One of them finally shouted an order: "Gree! Attack!" Instantly, three chimeras leaped toward the elevator exposing themselves to Izzy's fire. Two of them went down. Susan was running toward the elevator carrying half a dozen glass vials in a holder. She slipped inside just before the last chimera reached her. Jack kicked the animal back with a karate move that shot a jolt of pain up his tortured spine to his wounded shoulder. The door closed before the chimera could regain its balance. Seconds later they were humming up amidst a horrible symphony of braying floor alarms.

The door opened on B-1 and they ran out of the elevator.

"What's with the siren?" Carlos asked.

"I think this place is about to blow," Jack said as he started flipping more switches on the laser weapon . . . a weapon so simple that even a monkey could operate it; but Jack Wirta, academy-trained firearms expert, was totally baffled. In frustration, he banged it against his palm, and must have accidentally hit something, because suddenly it started humming. Jack turned and fired a streak of red-hot particles into the elevator. They arced around like electricity in Frankenstein's lab, then the elevator whined, growled, and went dark. "Finally," he grunted.

The war party ran up the stairs. Jack felt wetness on his back where his blood-wet shirt was sticking to him. He lost his balance and accidentally dropped the laser gun. It rattled back down the stairs. "Shit." Jack started back down for it, but Susan stopped him.

"Leave it," she instructed as they heard heavy footsteps pounding up the enclosed staircase.

They picked up Digby in the barn and ran outside. Now the whooping alarm was joined by the distant sound of arriving fire trucks and squad cars. "Here come my guys," Jack said. "City services to the rescue." In seconds, the red lights from two fire units were ping-ponging on the stable walls. Four sheriff's squad cars boiled in behind.

"It's gonna blow!" Jack yelled as the firefighters got out of the trucks dressed in their red helmets and yellow slickers and started toward him.

"Get back! It's gonna blow!" he yelled again. Jack literally pushed one of the firefighters back into the truck.

Izzy was doing more or less the same at the second truck as Jack jumped onto the engine nearest him then pulled Susan aboard.

"Get it outta here!" Jack yelled. "Go! Go! Go! This place is gonna explode!" In all truth, he wasn't absolutely sure it was going to explode, but the alarms had him in an adrenaline panic.

The cops and the firefighters finally got the idea and backed the vehicles out fast. They were about two hundred yards away when the driver of Jack and Susan's truck stopped and set the brake.

"No! Get back further!" Jack yelled as the second truck with Izzy, Carlos, and Digby aboard pulled up beside them.

"There's supposed to be a fire out here. Where's the fuckin' fire?" the truck captain yelled at them.

Just then they felt the earth tremble. The ground around the barn began to explode upwards into the air. It blew mighty chunks of dirt and sand hundreds of feet into the night sky, one huge eruption after another. Boulders, rocks, and jagged pieces of the underground lab swirled around, then began raining down on them. The last charge erupted somewhere near the middle of the barn, blowing the walls and roof apart. More huge pieces of the metal-walled lab shot up into the sky, whirling around like deadly confetti then spiraled dangerously down to earth.

Jack dove under the truck, pulling Susan with him. Several firefighters followed.

Somebody's footlocker landed ten feet from the truck, blazing merrily.

Finally the explosions stopped and what was left of the lab was either flying around in the air or burning in little piles all over the desert.

"Fire's right there," Jack said to the cowering fire captain who moments before had been wondering where it was.

"Thanks. I see it now," the man replied sarcastically.

After the rest of the fiery debris landed, they crawled out from under the truck and watched it all burn. Jack and Susan hugged each other, just glad to be alive.

Izzy was standing next to them, his handsome features scrunched up into a frown. "I told you it was no fun out here," he finally said. "This place always sucked."

Chapter Fifty-Two

"I want to get out of here," Jack whined, looking up at Susan. His shoulder was stitched up and he was rigged with more plastic plumbing than a high school science fair. Some clear stuff was leaking into him and some evil-looking brown shit was leaking out. Pain radiated from his shoulder to his spinal column down his back and into his balls. From there it went into his toes. He reasoned that when you got shot in the shoulder your toes shouldn't ache, but they were killing him.

"What's this?" Susan said, picking up the clipboard hanging on the end of the bed.

"My meds."

"Percocets?" she cocked a suspicious eyebrow at him.

"Little Jack has a big boo-boo. He needs his pain meds."

"Jack . . ."

"I'm not hooked on this shit, okay?"

"You say."

"I'm not. If I was hooked I'd know it. I'm an experienced police specialist. I used to bust guys for drug abuse. Give it a rest, okay?"

"I think you should get checked into a clinic."

"Is that any way to talk to the guy you've been screwing?" He was dodging madly as she scoped him with a critical stare.

"Jack, if I'm going to have a meaningful relationship with you we have to be honest with one another."

"Susan, honesty is my middle name. Well . . . maybe not exactly honesty, but certainly expediency is. Or Wendell. And, hey . . . if there aren't a few tiny deceptions in a relationship it can get pretty damn boring."

She didn't smile.

"I'm serious," she said, then turned and walked to the door. "I've got to get to the courthouse. We're back in front of Krookshank at two."

"Susan . . . y'know, it's hard for me to . . . to . . . to come to grips with this."

"I know."

"I don't think you do. And it's not denial or anything, y'know. It's . . . well, it's just . . . I hurt a lot."

"I know."

"And I hope this isn't going to be a problem for us."

"If you don't get it taken care of, Jack, there is no us." Standing in the doorway, frowning, she looked at him for a long moment. "You can deny this, Jack, but then I'm gone. If you go to the clinic I'll be there. I'll help you through it. It's your choice." Then she walked out.

In that moment his life was as confusing as the tangle of tubes running in and out of him. He was wondering what to do when his chronic back suddenly went into spasms, making the decision for him. He buzzed for the nurse and she came in ten minutes later.

"I think I need my pain medicine," he said to her in a low whisper. He was sad, and lost, and consumed with self-hatred.

In Federal Courtroom Sixteen, Herman was submitting the rest of his evidence in support of the TRO.

He entered the vials of chimera DNA that Susan had taken from the lab. Izzy had already testified to the fact that they had found them five stories below ground on reservation land he had leased to DARPA. The Indio fire captain testified that the lab had been detonated and that there were trace elements of radioactivity, indicating the explosives had been low-yield nuclear charges.

Dr. Adjemenian and her two genetics experts explained the genome map and how it matched the DNA in the lab, proving beyond any doubt the existence of the chimeras. It was an awesome presentation. Now Herman was doing his closing argument, and he was in rare form.

"Your Honor, our expert scientific witnesses have testified that the DNA in this vial is in fact 99.3 percent human homology. We have here in court an actual DNA sample taken from the secret government lab. We also have irrefutable evidence that the government built this underground facility at the Ten-Eyck reservation. A lab, I might add, that they chose to destroy with a low-yield nuclear device to cover up the existence of their dangerous experiments. Mr. Amato challenged the existence of the chimeras, and it appears that now there are none left alive to bring before you as I had promised. It also appears that Charles Chimera and his five John Doe brothers perished in that nuclear explosion. However, if need be I could take the very material in this vial before you and hire my own genetics lab to harvest a chimpanzee egg, fertilize it with this genetically engineered DNA, and create a chimera zygote. I could then grow the very same hybrid being myself and bring it into this courtroom six months hence. My question is, Your Honor, is all of that really necessary?"

"Are you asking for a ruling on that now?" Judge Krookshank asked from the bench, looking at the government lawyers.

Amato had chosen not to be in court this afternoon, leaving the retreat and final surrender in the less-than-capable hands of a skinny government lawyer named Chris Webb. He was a lean, intense, boringly nondescript man who could not convey six conflicting emotions in one ten-dollar word, but was pretty good at his one expression, which was forlorn humiliation. It wrapped his features in a tight frown.

"Your Honor," Chris Webb said. "Before you rule on that I would like to put on my closing argument. That is, if counsel is finished with his."

"I'm not quite finished yet," Herman said.

"Go ahead then," Krookshank said.

"I think it is important to note here that, as a society, we give up certain powers and freedoms to our government . . . powers that we entrust to them by virtue of the fact that we, as individuals, cannot undertake ourselves. It is therefore incumbent upon our government when it accepts this gift of power not to abuse it.

"I think we have ample evidence of abuse of power here. Genetic engineering for the sole purpose of creating subhuman warriors is way beyond the scope of this society's gift of power. Here today we have seen not only ample evidence of this abuse of power, but also a staggering lack of good sense and scientific morality. Therefore I implore the court to grant my TRO and then injunctive relief on behalf of the DNA life-forms I have brought into court today. This court — your court, Your Honor — must make sure that these abuses will never occur again."

Susan entered the crowded room full of reporters and onlookers and took a seat at the back. Herman saw her but didn't wave. He had one more thing to say.

Sandy Toshiabi at the plaintiff's table turned to give Susan a smile and a thumbs-up.

"Life is precious, Your Honor," Herman went on. "Precious in all forms wherever it exists. But it is important that we don't try to redirect or redesign the course of natural evolution. The results can become ungodly nightmares, but they won't all stay in our dreams. Some are bound to get away from us and, like these chimeras, chase us into the streets. One day they may even overthrow us, become our masters and enslave *us*. It is with these frightening scenarios in mind that I beg the court to rule for the plaintiff."

He sat down.

Chris Webb didn't have much to offer. He wandered around trying to attack standing and Herman's lack of a fiduciary obligation. "Mr. Strockmire doesn't have an attorney-client relationship," he argued. "Earlier he claimed that this animal, Charles Chimera, reached out to him. But now he says the animals are all dead. He cannot produce his client or any evidence that he was ever retained. This alone is enough to disallow the TRO. Further, Mr. Strockmire doesn't have the legal right to represent vials of liquid." Chris Webb also argued that science had to be allowed to flourish if we were going to have a brave new world.

Herman smiled. This dipshit didn't even know that *Brave New World* was the title of a novel about science and government gone mad.

So there it was, lawyers dressed in black, bullshitting just as always. And once again only Herman seemed to be standing alone between the forces of tyranny and sanity. Only Herman the German seemed to give a damn.

Judge Krookshank called a recess and went into chambers to deliberate or maybe, Herman thought, he just went in there to take a whiz, because he was back in less than ten minutes.

They were all hustled out of the hall and reseated in the big, gothic courtroom looking up at the judge while he polished his glasses.

"On the issue of standing, which I said I would rule on at a later date . . . it is the decision of this court that these chimeras, this DNA, is not essentially human DNA, despite the fact that it is closer than the DNA of some humans who have been granted standing in court before. These animals, while close, are still not essentially *Homo sapiens,* so this court rules that they cannot be plaintiffs in a court of law."

Chris Webb slammed his palm down on the table in victory.

"However," Judge Krookshank said. "There are signs that grave criminal wrongdoing has been committed, and this court agrees with counsel for the plaintiff that these human-chimp hybrids might well present a serious threat to human beings if this experimentation is allowed to continue. This court will therefore hear a case for injunctive relief to prevent DARPA, or any other agency of the United States, from further engaging in this kind of reckless experimental activity on these chimpanzees or any other life-forms that have had their DNA unalterably changed. Mr. Strockmire, if you can find a human client and get that action filed, I will personally hear it at the earliest possible date."

"Thank you, Your Honor. I have contacted the SPCA and will file on behalf of that organization this afternoon."

Judge Krookshank looked down at his calendar and marked a date. "Is June fifth too soon for the hearing?"

"Works for me," Herman said, grinning.

"I'm afraid June is going to be impossible," Chris Webb said standing. "We have a lot of pretrial work to do on this."

"There are enough of you, so you'll just have to work quickly. Let's say June fifth then." Judge Krookshank banged his gavel. "Court is in recess." But before he stood he looked down at Herman and smiled. "Good try, Mr. Strockmire. I almost went for your argument on standing. Pretty convincing. Maybe next time."

"Thank you, Your Honor."

Herman turned and exchanged smiles with Sandy. Then he looked for Susan, but she had already slipped away.

Chapter Fifty-Three

While Jack lay in the hospital bed waiting to be released from Cedars he read the story in the *L.A. Times*. There was a small picture of him next to Sandy's drawing of the chimera — a toss-up which one of them looked better. Russell Ibanazi made a statement about how his beloved reservation had been exploited by the federal government and that he was personally offended by the horrible research that had taken place out there without the tribe's knowledge.

Way to go, Izzy.

Donald Trump was interviewed about his plans to build a new, luxurious casino on the Ten-Eyck land. He was calling it Indian Lakes Resort. That meant there was going to be a lot of concrete pipe going in out there because Jack couldn't recall seeing one drop of water on the reservation.

The paper confirmed that the nuclear devices used had been low-yield "clean" weapons detonated from a satellite in space. A sidebar story on the second page detailed computer-cracker Roland Minton's death. His body had finally been returned to his mother for burial.

At the bottom of the story was a picture of

General Turpin. Jack had never seen him before. It said that he ran DARPA but had resigned two days ago. His expression was as hard as Vince Valdez's. Both guys looked cold enough to freeze mercury. There wasn't much info about General Turpin, just a brief mention of a Senate inquest initiated by animal-rights activists who were going to march on Washington.

There was a long story in the Metro section written by the Liar for Hire. The diminutive PR man had profiled Herman and the Institute for Planetary Justice and provided his picture.

Jack had been left in the wake of the story, which was probably not great for the Wirta Detective Agency, but frankly he hated dealing with the press so it was more or less okay by him. He'd been safely tucked away in Cedars-Sinai and, except for a few phone interviews with a reporter at the *Times*, he had been left out of it. *Really* out of it . . . Susan hadn't been back to see him.

Now, three days later, he was getting ready to leave the hospital. His doctor had released him. Jack really liked his new doctor. When he'd asked how often he could refill his prescription for Percocets, the doc said, "Until the pain goes away."

Adios, Carbon Paper . . . at least for a while, anyway.

Things were definitely looking up. Except

that Susan hadn't come to see him.

It was ten in the morning and ten was when the docs at Cedars made their final rounds. Jack's guy came in and wrote him a nice painkiller prescription: forty Percocets.

"You can get this filled in the pharmacy downstairs," he said. "If I were you I'd try and back off a little each day. Percocets can become very addictive if you're not careful."

"Y'know, I've heard that can happen. I'll be sure and be careful."

Then came the ten o'clock parade of wheelchairs — patients being pushed into elevators carrying floral arrangements and get-well teddy bears.

Jack was wheeled out of his room by a nurse and found Miro waiting for him. His face had lost its puffiness but the ugly bruises were still there. He had a temporary bridge where his front teeth had been knocked out.

"Look who's going home today," Miro gushed.

"Thanks for coming," Jack smiled.

"Hey, it's the least Miro can do for his best bud."

They stood at the payment counter downstairs and Jack handled the bill with his Blue Cross card. "Hope I'm covered for gunshot wounds, since I'm America's favorite standing target." He smiled at the girl behind the desk.

"Oh, was this a gunshot wound? Let me see if your HMO reimburses for that." She started flipping pages on his form, then turned to her computer.

"I wouldn't talk too much," Miro whispered in his ear and Jack nodded solemnly.

But Jack was covered, so he signed the release document, then told Miro he needed to stop by the hospital pharmacy to get his pain prescription filled.

"We can do that later. I need to drop you at your apartment so I can get back to the office by noon." Something about the way he said it shot a warning up into Jack's fuzzy brain. Cops had world-class bullshit detectors. Miro wheeled the chair out of the hospital into the parking lot, then helped Jack into his yellow Ford Escort.

"Wait till you see all the flowers at your place. Smells so sweet Miro couldn't believe how gorgeous." He had slipped behind the wheel and back into third person as he started the engine.

"Yeah, flowers are always nice," Jack managed.

Jack's apartment was off Sepulveda in the Valley — a duplex that had seen better times. The apartment was in the back. Miro pulled into the drive and parked, then ran around to help the patient out of the front seat. Jack's arm was in a sling and his back was killing him. He needed more painkillers and he needed them now. He had the prescription slip in his pocket, but Miro had pushed the wheelchair right past the hospital pharmacy, then had driven past the corner drugstore. For a best bud this was not good behavior.

"Hey, Miro, you gotta take me to the pharmacy down the street."

"In a minute Miro will get that done. In an itsy-bitsy minute. Soon as Miro gets you settled."

"Okay, but my shoulder is killing me. So's my back."

"Stop being a noodge."

They were standing at Jack's busted screen door. Miro took the key out of the flowerpot. "Bad hiding place, honey. A cop should know better." He opened up and let them in. The house was full of flowers and people.

Susan was there with Herman, Shane, Alexa, Lieutenant Matthews, Chick, even some guy Jack didn't know who smiled way too much. Izzy was also there, this time looking a lot like Wayne Newton in tennis togs.

"Hi," Susan said as she stood to meet him, then came across the room and took his hand.

"What is this?" Jack asked. He could smell trouble. Trouble and carnations.

"We need to talk to you," Susan said. "Sit down."

"I don't wanna sit down," Jack grumbled.

Susan turned and motioned to the smiling man. "This is Dr. Marion Trent."

"I don't need a doctor."

"Dr. Trent is a drug-intervention counselor."

Jack looked over at Dr. Trent the way you look at a big black spider hanging in the corner of your garage.

Dr. Trent kept the old grin pasted up there, smiling like a Halloween pumpkin. As an intervention counselor he was undoubtedly used to silent disapproval. Jack's didn't bother him at all.

"Okay, so what's the deal here?" Jack said.

"Jack, we're worried about you," Susan said. "And we all care desperately about you. We're your friends."

"It's true," Miro said from behind him. "Your buds."

"Okay . . . you're my friends. Okay, good." Jack knew what was coming next and it pissed him off. After all, he needed to be in charge of his own life . . . *didn't he? Wasn't he?*

"Okay," Jack said. "But this still doesn't tell me what's going on." Although he knew.

"Jack, I think you have a serious addiction to pain killers," Dr. Trent said.

"You do? How can you tell? I never met you before."

"We do, too," Alexa Scully said. "Jack, sit down and listen to us, okay? We have your best interests at heart."

So Jack sat. Alexa was a police lieutenant and the cop in him always obeyed a ranking officer.

Miro perched on the arm of a chair, but

he got up quickly because there wasn't much upholstery there and it was like sitting on a split-rail fence.

"Okay, gimme the pitch," Jack said sullenly.

"You're angry," Susan said.

"Hey, you people don't know my problems. Are you forgetting I stopped a Parabellum with my spine a little while ago?"

"Hey, Jack, that was almost seven years ago . . . *seven years*," Shane said.

"Six," Jack corrected. But fuck it, even *he* knew he was quibbling.

"Six then," Shane said. "Hey, pal, six years of popping 'cets and you don't think you've got a problem?"

"No, I don't think I have a problem," Jack said. He was feeling ganged up on and outnumbered. Jack looked at those furrowed brows and said nothing.

"I think you do have a problem," Miro said from a spot behind him.

"I'm not talking to you, Miro. You led me into this ambush."

"Jack," Miro said, "I took a terrible beating to protect you, so if I don't have a right to be concerned about your health after that, who does?"

"Don't pull that old Japanese spiritual ownership crap on me. You know how I feel about what you did, but it has nothing to do with this."

"Yes it does," Miro persisted. "Because

now I care what happens to you, honey, and I'm not going to let you throw your life away on some stupid pain pills."

"Listen to him," Chick said. "He's talking sense."

This from the guy who was afraid to drink out of Miro's glass.

What the hell is going on here?

Susan came across the room and knelt in front of Jack. She took his hand in both of hers. "Jack, you've got to do this."

"Do what?"

"We've arranged for you to be admitted to the Betty Ford Clinic this afternoon. Dad and I are going to drive you there."

"I don't have an addiction. This is crazy."

"You *do* have an addiction," Herman said. "Listen, Jack, I owe you a lot more than I can tell you. Without you I would have lost everything. Now I'm on the cover of *Lawyer Magazine*. I'm so hot now I'm on fire. Judge King is even going to rehear my motion to reduce the fine. Childbirth may have mellowed her. I'm going to see to it that before I leave town your problem is taken care of."

"Don't do me any favors, Herman," Jack growled.

"Honey . . ." Susan this time, not Miro. He looked over at her. "I love you. In front of everybody I'm telling you I want us to be together . . . always. But not unless you get this problem taken care of. If you want us to be together you're gonna have to take it from here."

Miro slapped his hands together. "Miro loves it! A proposal."

Jack looked around the room. Shane and Alexa nodded. Chick was staring at his shoes, but as Jack's gaze fell on him he looked up, his ham-red complexion shiny in the hot room. The two of them locked gazes. "Do it, man."

"It's the right thing," Izzy said. "You do it and I'll write a song about it."

Cats gargling his name on the Sound Machine. How could he say no?

Then Lieutenant Matthews stood. He'd said nothing thus far, so when he spoke everybody turned to look at him. "Jack, listen. You get straight and I'll work on something downtown. Maybe we can get you assigned to work for us as a special consultant."

"Or you can come to work for the Institute," Herman suggested. "We've got an opening for a new detective. We'll never do better than Jack Wirta."

Two job offers and a marriage proposal and all he had to do was go see the former First Lady for a couple of weeks. It hadn't been a grand slam because Miro hadn't offered him a partnership in Reflections.

Jack *did* want to ditch this problem. He *did* want to get off the 'cets, but there was something very humiliating about all of this.

As Chick once told him when they were in Homicide, "If ten people tell you you're drunk, don't drive."

Cop logic.

So there you have it. Jack Wirta, America's foremost chimpanzee detective in a twelve-step program. Somebody call Swifty. Get this to the AP.

They parked at the Betty Ford Clinic in Palm Springs, and Herman got out and retrieved Jack's overnight bag from the trunk. Jack's back and shoulder were killing him but he was starting to feel slightly better about all this. *Maybe he could finally get this problem under control.*

"Jack," Herman said. "I was serious about wanting you to join the Institute for Planetary Justice."

"Really?" Jack didn't think he wanted to join the Institute unless they could rename it.

"I'm serious," Herman said. "Right now I'm working on a new class action suit against the Department of Energy and six oil companies. I could use some help."

"Gee, Herm, I don't know. My car uses lots of oil. I count on those guys."

"This is big," the heavy attorney said waving his hands around like he was cleaning a plateglass window. "Get this, Jack, I think the government conspired with the oil companies to steal the patent rights from the estate of a man who designed a paint that acts as a solar panel. I don't have to tell you what would happen if they used solar-energy-generating paint on cars."

"They'll get hot and explode?" Jack said, trying to look unsophisticated and dumb, something he could usually accomplish without effect.

"No, no. They'd run forever — without fuel. Think what that would do for the economy, for the environment . . . for the planet."

"Right . . . right, for the planet. Yeah, I can see that."

"You and Susan and I could make a difference here. You could be a part of this. We could reverse global warming."

"I'll give it some thought," Jack said.

Then Susan took his hand and led him up to the front door of the clinic where a tall, thin woman named Elizabeth Donovan was waiting for him. Jack had been expecting the other Betty.

"I'll be right in," Jack assured her. Elizabeth left and he turned to Susan.

"I'm so proud of you," she said. "And Dad is serious, you know. He really wants you with us."

"Is he always like that? I mean, does he always look like he's selling used cars?"

"Yeah, even though his ticker got fixed he still has a runaway heart."

"Right," Jack said. "I can see that."

"So gimme a kiss and call me every day."

Jack did as he was instructed: he took Susan Strockmire in his arms and kissed her. His love for her poured over his tortured body, soothing everything, making him whole again.

"I want to do it," he said.

"Do what?" she looked puzzled.

"Marry you." He was still holding her. "I want you to be my wife. I want us to grow old together. I want Izzy to sing at our wedding."

"I accept, but wouldn't Barbra be a better choice?" Then she smiled and kissed him again. This one lasted a long time. She pulled back and studied him. "You're my hero," she said softly. "Now, get in there and kick some ass."

So Jack Wirta, newly engaged hero, turned, but instead of riding into the sunset he walked into the Betty Ford Clinic. The door closed and Elizabeth Donovan took his arm.

"Mrs. Ford is in her office and wants to meet you. You'll really like it here. This month will just fly by."

Month? Nobody said anything about a month! But she had a death grip on Jack's arm and was leading him down the hall. There was no turning back. He had a job to do.

He'd ride off into that damn sunset later.

About the Author

STEPHEN J. CANNELL enjoys one of the most phenomenally successful careers in today's entertainment industry. After struggling for recognition as a television writer, Cannell's career took off in 1966 when he became head writer for the series *Adam-12*. Thirteen years later, he'd form his own production company; today his studio's annual production outlays amount to more than a billion dollars. In his thirty-five-year career, the Emmy Award–winning writer has created more than forty TV series, including such hits as *The Rockford Files*, *The Greatest American Hero*, *The A-Team*, *21 Jump Street*, *Wiseguy*, and *The Commish*. He also has penned the bestsellers *The Plan*, *Final Victim*, *King Con*, *Riding the Snake*, *Devil's Workshop*, *The Tin Collectors*, *The Viking Funeral*, and *Hollywood Tough*. A spokesperson on dyslexia, Stephen J. Cannell lives in Los Angeles with his wife and their children.

Check out his Web site at www.cannell.com and www.cannellbooks.com.